D0552572

JOHN SANDFORD
STORM PREY

**SIMON &
SCHUSTER**

London · New York · Sydney · Toronto · New Delhi

A CBS COMPANY

First published in the US by G. P. Putnam's Sons, 2010
A division of the Penguin Group (USA) Inc.
First published in Great Britain by Simon & Schuster UK Ltd, 2010
A CBS COMPANY

This paperback edition first published, 2011

1 3 5 7 9 10 8 6 4 2

Simon & Schuster UK Ltd
1st Floor
222 Gray's Inn Road
London WC1X 8HB

www.simonandschuster.co.uk

Simon & Schuster Australia, Sydney
Simon & Schuster India, New Delhi

A CIP catalogue record for this book is available from the British Library

ISBN 978-1-84983-932-7

Book design by Nicole Laroche

Printed and bound by CPI Group (UK) Ltd, Croydon, CR0 4YY

1

THREE OF THEM, hard men carrying nylon bags, wearing work jackets, Carhartts and Levi's, all of them with facial hair. They walked across the parking structure to the steel security door, heads swiveling, checking the corners and the overheads, steam flowing from their mouths, into the icy air, one of the men on a cell phone.

As they got to the door, it popped open, and a fourth man, who'd been on the other end of the cell-phone call, let them through. The fourth man was tall and thin, dark-complected, with a black brush mustache. He wore a knee-length black raincoat that he'd bought at a Goodwill store two days earlier, and black pants. He scanned the parking structure, saw nothing moving, pulled the door shut, made sure of the lock.

"This way," he snapped.

Inside, they moved fast, reducing their exposure, should someone unexpectedly come along. No one should, at the ass-end of the hospital, at fifteen minutes after five o'clock on a bitterly cold winter morning. They threaded through a maze of service corridors until the tall man said, "Here."

Here was a storage closet. He opened it with a key. Inside, a pile of blue, double-extra-large orderly uniforms sat on a medical cart.

The hard men dumped their coats on the floor and pulled the uniforms over their street clothes. Not a big disguise, but they weren't meant to be seen close-up—just enough to slip past a video camera. One of them, the biggest one, hopped up on the cart, lay down and said, "Look, I'm dead," and laughed at his joke. The tall man could smell the bourbon on the joker's breath.

"Shut the fuck up," said one of the others, but not in an unkindly way.

The tall man said, "Don't be stupid," and there was nothing kind in his voice. When they were ready, they looked at each other and the tall

1

man pulled a white cotton blanket over the man on the cart, and one of the men said, "Let's do it."

"Check yourself . . ."

"We don't hurt anyone," the tall man said. The sentiment reflected not compassion, but calculation: robbery got X amount of attention, injuries got X-cubed.

"Yeah, yeah . . ." One of the men pulled a semiautomatic pistol from his belt, a heavy, blued, no-bullshit Beretta, stolen from the Army National Guard in Milwaukee, checked it, stuck it back in his belt. He said, "Okay? Everybody got his mask? Okay. Let's go."

They stuffed the ski masks into their belts and two hard men pushed the cart into the corridor. The tall man led them farther through the narrow, tiled hallways, then said, "Here's the camera."

The two men pushing the cart turned sideways, as the tall man told them to, and went through a cross-corridor. A security camera peered down the hall at them. If a guard happened to be looking at the monitor at that moment, he would have seen only the backs of two orderlies, and a lump on the cart. The tall man in the raincoat scrambled along, on his hands and knees, on the far side of the cart.

The big man on the cart, looking at the ceiling tiles go by, giggled, "It's like ridin' the Tilt-A-Whirl."

When they were out of the camera's sight line, the tall man stood up and led them deeper into the hospital—the three outsiders would never have found the way by themselves. After two minutes, the tall man handed one of the outsiders a key, indicated a yellow steel door, with no identification.

"This is it?" The leader of the three was skeptical—the door looked like nothing.

"Yes," said the tall man. "This is the side door. When you go in, you'll be right among them. One or two. The front door and service window is closed until six. I'll be around the corner until you call, watching."

He'd be around the corner where he could slip out of sight, if something went wrong.

The other man nodded, asked, "Everybody ready?" The other two muttered, "Yeah," tense now, pulled on the masks, took their pistols out. The leader put the key in the lock and yanked open the door.

WEATHER KARKINNEN had taken a half-pill at nine o'clock, knowing that she wouldn't sleep without it. Too much to do, too much to think about. The procedure had been researched, rehearsed, debated, and undoubtedly prayed over. Now the time had come.

Sleep came hard. She kept imagining that first moment, the first cut, the commitment, the parting of the flesh beneath the edge of her scalpel, on a nearly circular path between the skulls of the two babies— but sometime before nine-thirty, she slipped away.

She didn't feel her husband come to bed at one o'clock in the morning. He took care not to disturb her, undressing in the dark, lying as unmoving as he could, listening to her breathing, until he, too, slipped away.

AND THEN her eyes opened.

Pop.

Dark, not quite silent—the furnace running in the winter night. She lifted her head to the clock. Four-thirty. She'd been asleep for seven hours. Eight would have been the theoretical ideal, but she never slept eight. She closed her eyes again, organizing herself, stepping through the upcoming day. At twenty minutes to five, she got out of bed, stretched, and headed to the en suite bathroom, checking herself: she felt sharp. Excellent. She brushed her teeth, showered, washed and dried her short-cut blond hair.

She'd laid out her clothes the night before. She walked across the bedroom barefoot, in the light of the two digital clocks, picked them up: a thick black-silk jersey and gray wool slacks, and dressy, black-leather square-toed shoes. She would have preferred to wear soft-soled cross-training shoes, like the nurses did, but surgeons didn't dress like nurses. She'd never even told anyone about the gel innersoles.

She carried her clothes back to the bathroom, shut the door, turned on the light again, and dressed. When she was ready, she looked at herself in the mirror. Not bad.

Weather might have wished to have been a little taller, for the authority given by height; she might have wished for a chiseled nose.

But her husband pointed out that she'd never had a problem giving orders, or having them followed; and that he thought her nose, which she saw as lumpy, was devastatingly attractive, and that any number of men had chased after her, nose and all.

So, not bad.

She grinned at herself, turned to make sure the slacks didn't make her ass look fat—they didn't—switched off the light, opened the bathroom door and tiptoed across the bedroom. Her husband said, in the dark, "Good luck, babe."

"I didn't know you were awake."

"I'm probably more nervous than you are," he said.

She went back to the bed and kissed him on the forehead. "Go back to sleep."

Downstairs in the kitchen, she had two pieces of toast, a cup of instant coffee, and a yogurt, got her bag, went out to the car, backed out of the garage, and headed downtown, on the snowy streets, across the river to the Minnesota Medical Research Center. She might be first in, she thought, but maybe not: there were forty people on the surgical team. *Somebody* had to be more nervous than she was.

AT THE HOSPITAL, the yellow door popped open and the three big men swarmed through.

Two people were working in the pharmacy—a short, slender, older man, who might once in the sixties have been a dancer, but no longer had the muscle tone. He wore a scuzzy beard on his cheeks, a soul patch under his lower lip. First thing, when he came to work, he tied a paper surgeon's cap on his head, for the rush he got when people looked at him in the cafeteria. The other person was a busy, intent, heavyset woman in a nurse's uniform, who did the end-of-shift inventory, making sure it was all there, the stacks and rows and lockers full of drugs.

Some of it, put on the street, was worthless. Nobody pays street prices to cure the heartbreak of psoriasis.

Most of it, put on the street—on more than one street, actually; there was the old-age street, the uninsured street, the junkie street— was worth a lot. Half-million dollars? A million? Maybe.

4

The three hard men burst through the door and were on top of the two pharmacy workers in a half-second. The woman had enough time to whimper, "Don't," before one of the men pushed her to the floor, gun in her face, so close she could smell the oil on it, and said, "Shutta fuck up. Shut up." Soul-patch huddled into a corner with his hands up, then sank to his butt.

The leader of the three waved a pistol at the two on the floor and said, "Flat on the floor. Roll over, put your hands behind your back. We don't want to hurt you."

The two did, and another of the men hurriedly taped their hands behind them with gray duct tape, and then bound their feet together. That done, he tore off short strips of tape and pasted them over the victims' eyes, and then their mouths.

He stood up: "Okay."

The leader pushed the door open again and signaled with a finger-tip. The tall man stepped in from the hallway, said, "These," and pointed at a series of locked, glass-doored cupboards. And, "Over here . . ."

A row of metal-covered lockers. The leader of the big men went to the man on the floor, who looked more ineffectual than the woman, and ripped the tape from his mouth.

"Where are the keys?" For one second, the man on the floor seemed inclined to prevaricate, so the big man dropped to his knees and said, "If you don't tell me this minute, I will break your fuckin' skull as an example. Then you will be dead, and I will ask the fat chick."

"In the drawer under the telephone," Soul-patch said.

"Good answer."

As the big man retaped Soul-patch's mouth, the tall man got the keys and began popping open the lockers. All kinds of good stuff here, every opiate and man-made opiate except heroin; lots of hot-rock stimulants, worth a fortune with the big-name labels.

"Got enough Viagra to stock a whorehouse," one of the men grunted.

Another one: "Take this Tamiflu shit?"

"Fifty bucks a box in California . . . Take it."

Five minutes of fast work, the tall man pointing them at the good stuff, sorting out the bad.

THEN THE OLD GUY on the floor made a peculiar wiggle.

One of the holdup men happened to see it, frowned, then went over, half-rolled him. The old guy's hands were loose—he'd pulled one out of the tape, had had a cell phone in a belt clip under his sweater, had worked it loose, and had been trying to make a call. The big man grunted and looked at the face of the phone. One number had been pressed successfully: a nine.

"Sonofabitch was trying to call nine-one-one," he said, holding up the phone to the others. The old man tried to roll away, but the man who'd taken the phone punted him in the back once, twice, three times, kicking hard with steel-toed work boots.

"Sonofabitch . . . sonofabitch." The boot hit with the sound of a meat hammer striking a steak.

"Let him be," the leader said after the third kick.

But the old man had rolled back toward his tormentor and grasped him by the ankle, and the guy tried to shake him loose and the old man moaned something against the tape and held on, his fingernails raking the big guy's calf.

"Let go of me, you old fuck." The guy shook him off his leg and kicked him again, hard, in the chest.

The leader said, "Quit screwing around. Tape him up again and let's get this stuff out of here."

THE OLD MAN, his hands taped again, was still groaning as they loaded the bags. That done, they went to the door, glanced down the hallway. All clear. The bags went under the blanket on the cart, and the three big men pushed the cart past the security-camera intersection, back through the rabbit warren to the utility closet, replaced the orderly uniforms with their winter coats, picked up the bags.

The leader said, "Gotta move, now. Gotta move. Don't know how much time we got."

Another of the men said, "Shooter—dropped your glove."

"Ah, man, don't need that." He picked it up, and the tall man led them out, his heart thumping against his rib cage. Almost out. When they could see the security door, he stopped, and they went on and out. The tall man watched until the door re-latched, turned, and headed back into the complex.

There were no cameras looking at the security door, or between the door and their van. The hard men hustled through the cold, threw the nylon bags in the back, and one of them climbed in with them, behind tinted windows, while the leader took the wheel and the big man climbed in the passenger seat.

"Goddamn, we did it," said the passenger. He felt under his seat, found a paper bag with a bottle of bourbon in it. He was unscrewing the top as they rolled down the ramp; an Audi A5 convertible, moving too fast, swept across the front of the van and caught the passenger, mouth open, who squinted against the light. For just a moment, he was face-to-face with a blond woman, who then swung past them into the garage.

"Goddamnit!"

The leader braked and looked back, but the A5 had already turned up the next level on the ramp. He thought they might turn around and find the woman . . . but then what? Kill her?

"She see you guys?" asked the man in the back, who'd seen only the flash of the woman's face.

The guy with the bottle said, "She was looking right at me. Goddamnit."

"Nothing to do," the leader said. "Nothing to do. Get out of sight. Shit, it was only one second . . ."

And they went on.

Weather had seen the man with the bottle, but paid no attention. Too much going through her head. She went on to the physicians' parking, got a spot close to the door, parked, and hurried inside.

The tall man got back to the utility closet, pulled off the raincoat and pants, which he'd used to conceal his physician's scrubs: if they'd been seen in the hallway, the three big men with a doc, somebody would have remembered. He gathered up the scrubs abandoned by the big men, stuffed them in a gym bag, along with the raincoat and pants, took a moment to catch his breath, to neaten up.

Listened, heard nothing. Turned off the closet light, peeked into the empty hallway, then strode off, a circuitous route, avoiding cameras, to an elevator. Pushed the button, waited impatiently.

When the door opened, he found a short, attractive blond woman inside, who nodded at him. He nodded back, poked "1," and they started down, standing a polite distance apart, with just the trifle of awkwardness of a single man and a single woman, unacquainted, in an elevator.

The woman said, after a few seconds, "Still hard to come to work in the dark."

"Can't wait for summer," the tall man said. They got to "2," and she stepped off and said, "Summer always comes," and she was gone.

WEATHER THOUGHT, as she walked away from the elevator, *No point looking at the kids.* They'd be asleep in the temporary ICU they'd set up down the hall from the operating room. She went instead to the locker room and traded her street clothes for surgical scrubs. Another woman came in, and Weather nodded to her and the other woman asked, "Couldn't sleep?"

"Got a few hours," Weather said. "Are we the only two here?"

The woman, a radiologist named Regan, laughed: "No. John's got the doll on the table and he's talking about making some changes to the *table*, for God's sakes. Rick's here, he's messing with his saws. Gabriel was down in the ICU, he just got here, he's complaining about the cold. A bunch of nurses . . ."

"Nerves," Weather said. "See you down there."

She was cool in her scrubs, but comfortably so: she'd been doing this for nearly fifteen years, and the smell of a hospital, the alcohol, the cleaners, even the odor of burning blood, smelled like fresh air to her.

No point in looking at the kids, but she'd do it anyway. There were two nurses outside the temporary ICU, and they nodded and asked quietly, "Are you going in?"

"Just a peek."

"'They've been quiet," one of the nurses said. "Dr. Maret just left."

Moving as silently as she could, in the semi-dark, she moved next to the babies' special bed. When you didn't look closely, they looked like any other toddlers, who happened to be sleeping head-to-head; small hands across their chests, eyes softly closed, small chests rising up and down. The first irregularity that a visitor might notice was the ridges in their skulls: Weather had placed a series of skin expanders under their scalps, to increase the amount of skin available to cover the skull defects—the holes—when they were separated.

There was really no need for her to look at them: she simply wanted to. Two babies, innocent, silent, feeling no pain; their world was about to change. She watched them for a minute. The one named Ellen sighed, and one foot moved, and then she subsided again.

Weather tiptoed out.

THE OLD MAN in the pharmacy was moaning, the woman trying to talk, and the old man heard the woman fall down against a chair, after trying to get up, and then somebody was rapping at the service window and they both tried to scream, and they were loud but muffled. He was chewing at the duct tape on his mouth, and finally it came loose from one side and he spat it away from his face.

"Dorothy, can you hear me?"

A muffled "Yes."

"I think I'm hurt bad. If I don't make it, tell the police that I scratched one of the robbers. I should have blood on my hand."

She replied, but the reply was unintelligible. He'd been working on the tape on his wrists, and eventually pulled one free . . . He tried to get up, but was too weak. He couldn't orient himself; nothing seemed to be working. He fumbled at the tape over his eyes, failed to get it free, moaned, moaned . . .

More time went by and the old man felt himself going dark; didn't know what was happening, but his heart was pounding and he told himself, calm down, calm down. He'd had heart and circulatory problems, clots, and he didn't need a clot breaking free, but his heart was pounding and he was sweating and something was going more wrong than it should be, more wrong than rolling around on a tile floor gagged and blinded and beaten. Hurt bad.

Then the door rattled and he shouted and he heard an answering shout, and he shouted again and Dorothy tried to scream through her gag, and some time later the door rattled again, and he heard it open, and somebody cried out, and then more people were there.

He blacked out for a moment, then came back, realized he was on a gurney, that they'd put a board on him, they were moving down a hallway. Somebody said, a few inches from his face, "We're moving you down to the ER, we're moving you."

He said, as loud as he could as the world faded, "I scratched him. I scratched him. Tell the police, I scratched him . . ."

THE OPERATING ROOM had been reworked for the separation operation. Maret had stripped out all the general surgery stuff, put in more lights, brought in the custom table. The table had been made in Germany, and lined with a magic memory foam that would adapt to the kids as their bodies were moved this way and that.

Sara and Ellen Raynes were joined at the skull, vertically, but slightly turned from each other. If an observer was standing at Sara's feet, looking at her face, and Sara was looking straight up, then Ellen's face was upside down and rotated to the observer's left. Imaging studies, done by Regan and her associates, indicated that their brains were separate, but they shared a portion of the dura mater under the skull, a kind of fibrous lining that protected and facilitated the drainage of venous blood from the brain.

The incoming blood in the arterial system was good in both babies; but if the blood couldn't be drained away, and recirculated, it would put increasing pressure on the brains, eventually killing them.

Sara and Ellen were eighteen months old. Their parents had known the babies were conjoined before birth. The option of abortion had been proposed but rejected by the parents, Lucy and Larry Raynes, for religious and emotional reasons. The children had been delivered by cesarean section at seven and a half months. Sara had been born with a congenital heart defect, which further complicated matters.

*

10

Weather pushed into the OR and found three surgeons working with the baby doll—a life-sized, actual-weight dense-foam model of the Raynes twins. They had it on the table and were rolling it against the foam.

"So . . . no change," Gabriel Maret said.

Maret was a short man, with a head slightly too large for his body, the size emphasized by a wild thatch of curly black hair, shot through with silver. He was dark-eyed, olive-complected, with a chipped front tooth. He favored cashmere in his carefully tailored, French-cut winter suits, and the women around the hospital paid close attention to him: he *was* French, and the observing women agreed that his accent, in English, was perfect.

Maret had come to dinner with Lucas and Weather every week or so over the winter, enjoying the kids and the family life. He was divorced, with four children of his own. He and his wife still shared an apartment in Paris, and, sometimes, he said, a bed. "It's insane," he said. "She is more stubborn than one of your mules."

"More stubborn than you?" Weather had asked.

He considered the question: "Maybe not that stubborn," he said.

He and her husband, Lucas, who got along improbably well, once spent an hour talking about men's fashion, nearly driving Weather crazy with the inanity of it. She'd said, "Fifteen minutes on loafers? Loafers?"

"We were just getting started," Lucas said. She wasn't sure he was joking.

"So . . . no change," Maret said.

"Not as long as everything goes right," said John Dansk, a neurosurgeon. "If we run into trouble splicing the six vein, if we lose it, we may have to take out another piece and that means rolling Sara this way and Ellen will torque back to the right."

The six vein was a vein shared by the twins. They'd tie it off on Ellen's side, and attempt to splice it into the five vein on Sara's, the better to move blood out of Sara's brain. The vein numbers simply came from imaging charts prepared by the radiologists.

"So what are you suggesting?" Maret asked. He glanced at Weather: "You are gorgeous this morning."

11

"I know," she said, to make him laugh. As did the other women around him, she liked to make him laugh.

Dansk scowled at them and said, "I'm suggesting that we slice a few wedges out of the base of the mold, so that we can use them as shims if we have to brace one of the kids."

"Why not have a nurse hold her?" Maret asked.

"Because we might be talking a couple hours, if worse comes to worse."

"You know how much that mold cost?" Maret asked.

"About one nine-thousandth of your annual salary," Dansk said.

Maret shrugged. "So, we cut a few wedges. Why not? If we need them, we have them, and if we don't, it won't matter."

"Should have thought of this before now," said Rick Hanson, an orthopedic surgeon who would make the bone cuts through the kids' shared skull. He seemed shaky; he'd invented a half-dozen little saws for this operation and would be the focus of a lot of attention. Because of the way the children's skulls intersected, they formed a complex three-dimensional jigsaw puzzle—basically, an oval ring of bone—of which he'd be removing only a few pieces at a time. Normally the cutting would have been done by the neurosurgeon, with drills and flexible wire saws. Hanson, from Washington University in St. Louis, had developed his own set of electric saws matched to jigs—cutting templates— for complicated bone cuts. Maret had decided that Hanson's technique would be ideal, and would make it possible to prepare perfectly fitted composite plates to cover the holes in the babies' skulls.

"We're just nervous," Maret said now. "That's normal." Maret was the team leader, the one with all the experience. He'd done two other craniopagus separations, one in France, one in Miami. Of the four children involved, two had survived—one from each operation. When he talked about the work, he talked mostly about the children who'd died.

ANOTHER DOC PUSHED into the room, followed by a second one. They had all kinds—anesthesiologists, radiologists, neurosurgeons, cardiologists, plastic and orthopedic surgeons, and a medical professor who specialized in anatomical structures of the skull, as it pertained to

12

craniofacial reconstruction. They had twenty nurses and surgical assistants.

Weather said to Dansk, the neurosurgeon, "If you want to cut those wedges, you better get it done: they've got to start cleaning the place up."

Dansk said, "I'm on it," and, "I need a scalpel or something. Anybody got an X-Acto knife?"

ABOVE THE TABLE, in an observation room behind a canted glass wall, people were beginning to filter into the stadium seating.

A nurse came into the OR—one of the sterile nurses—and said, "I wanted to see if we could make the move one more time."

She wanted to practice breaking the tables apart, so that when the final cut was made, and the twins were separated, they could be moved to separate operating areas for the fitting of the new composite skull shells.

"Why don't we visually check the linkage . . ." Maret began.

It was starting; Weather didn't think it, but she felt it, felt the excitement and the tension starting to build. She worked almost every day, cutting, sewing, cauterizing, diagnosing. This was different.

She thought, Remember to pee.

THE RAYNES TWINS were a rare and complicated medical phenomenon. Craniopagus twins comprise only about one percent of conjoined twins. Because of the rarity of the condition, experience with separation surgery was limited. One of the twins, Sara, suffered from defects in the septum of the heart—the wall that divides the right side of the heart from the left side—and the defects were already causing congestion in the circulatory system.

The type of surgery usually favored for craniopagus separation might take place over several months. The most critical part of most operations was doing a staged separation of the brain's blood-drainage system. Each operation would isolate the drainage systems a bit more, and would allow the bodies to create new bypass channels.

In the Rayneses' case, surgeons feared that a protracted series of operations would weaken and possibly kill Sara, which would also threaten the stronger Ellen, especially if Sara were to go into a rapid decline.

The additional factor in the Rayneses' case was that the conjoined area was relatively small—the hole left behind in the babies' skulls after the separation would be no bigger than the diameter of an orange. That meant that a single operation was possible—even with some shared venous drainage, it was thought that one continuous operation would be the best chance for saving both twins.

The surgical team would do the separation, and once separated, the team would break in two, each working on an individual twin. The joint surgery was expected to last up to twenty hours.

The team was committed to saving both twins.

WEATHER DID AESTHETIC, reconstructive, and microsurgery. Her availability in Minnesota, and a paper she'd done on a thumb reconstruction, had caught Maret's eye when he began to consider the Raynes twins.

In Weather's case, a young boy had caught his thumb in a hydraulic log-splitter: the thumb had been pulped. After the wound healed, Weather had removed one of the boy's second toes, and used the toe to replace the thumb. Since a thumb represents a full fifty percent of the function of the hand, the reconstruction gave back the kid the use of his hand. As he used the new thumb, it would strengthen and grow, and eventually come to resemble a normal thumb, except for the extra knuckle.

As part of the eleven-hour operation, Weather had hooked up two nerves, two tiny arteries, and two even smaller veins—veins the size of broom straws. The photomicrographs of the sutured veins had particularly attracted Maret's attention. The more veins that could be hooked up, the better off the twins would be—and Weather could do that work, even on the smallest vessels.

He'd also been attracted to her sheer stamina: eleven hours of microsurgery was a super-marathon. He sold her on the idea of joining the team, which also made her available to study the twins, to get to know the parents, and to place the skin expanders under their scalps.

WEATHER HAD TURNED away from Maret and the argument—*Remember to pee*—when they heard a commotion outside the operating room.

"What is that?" Maret asked. Dansk had just come back with a large scalpel, and he turned to look. A few seconds later, an anesthesiologist named Yamaguchi burst into the room. He looked, Weather thought, like someone who'd just come to the emergency room to see his child: panicked.

He said, urgently, to Maret, Weather, and the others, "It's off. The operation's off. We've got, we've got . . ."

Weather caught his sleeve and said, "Slow down, slow down."

"It's off," Yamaguchi said. "Some guys just raided the pharmacy and cleaned the place out. Everything is shut down. Everything."

Maret's face clicked through a series of expressions, from "Is this a joke?" to astonishment: *"What?"*

"Some guys with guns," Yamaguchi said. He was flapping his arms, like a loon trying to take off. "Robbers. They robbed the pharmacy. The police are here. There's nothing left, they took everything . . . That old guy who works there, the one who wears the surgical hat . . ."

"Don," said Weather.

"Yeah, Don—he's hurt pretty bad. They're taking him into the ER."

"You must be shitting me," Maret said with a non-Gallic precision, looking around at his astonished crew.

ALAIN BARAKAT STOOD at the back of the emergency operating room, mask dangling around his neck, watching the work: the surgeon was cursing at the nurse, who was fumbling the gear, and they were all watching the blood pressure on the old man dropping and the surgeon was saying, "Get it in there, get it in there, get some pressure on it," and the nurse stood on a chair and lifted the bottle of saline and somebody else said, "Two minutes for the blood." The surgeon said, "I don't think we have the time, I don't think we've got it . . ." and the anesthesiologist said, "We're losing him, man," and the doc said, "Fuck this, I'm going in," and he cut and cut again and again, going in through the beginning of a brutal black bruise on the old man's belly, and the anesthesiologist said, "Hurry it up, man," and the surgeon said, "Ah, Jesus, I've got no blood, I got no blood here," and he hurled the scalpel into a corner and it clanged around and he said, "It must've been his goddamn kidneys. Let's see if we can roll him," and the nurses moved up to help with the roll and the anesthesiologist said, "Man, he's arresting."

Barakat, standing in the corner, said, "Shit shit shit shit shit shit . . ."

One minute later, the old man was gone. No point in trying to restart the heart—there was no blood going through it. They all stood around, shell-shocked, and then the surgeon said, "Let's clean up."

One of the nurses said, "We had no time. He was going too quick."

They all looked at the body on the table, worn Adidas sneakers pointed out at forty-five degrees, chest flat and still, the bloody gash on the gut. The anesthesiologist turned to get something and saw Barakat, a tall man, standing in the corner, hands pressed to the sides of his head, and the anesthesiologist said, "Wasn't you, man. You did good. Everybody did good. He was gone when we got him."

And Barakat thought: *Now everybody will be here. Now the police will tear the place apart.*

Because he really didn't care about the old man.

THE SEPARATION TEAM was standing around, repeating what Yamaguchi had said, when Thomas Carlson, the hospital administrator, came hurrying down the hall. Carlson was wearing his white physician's coat, which he often did on public occasions, to remind people that he had an MD in addition to the MBA; but for all that, not a bad guy, Weather thought.

He went straight to Maret: "Gabe, you've heard."

"I've heard there was a robbery."

"Unfortunately. The problem is, we've also got a man down. He's hurt pretty badly, and we won't have access to your drugs—any drugs, except in an absolute emergency, and then we'll be crawling around on the floor trying to find them. The place is completely wrecked. They threw everything out of the lockers, what they didn't take."

"So: everybody is here," Maret said.

"But you're going to have to wait," Carlson said. "God, I'm sorry, man. But this is an incredible mess. As long as the kids are stable . . ."

Maret nodded: "Well. I guess we can wait."

*

WEATHER AND MARET went together to tell the Rayneses. The parents were waiting in what the team called the "separation lounge," once a meditation room, which had been converted for family use and for team conferences.

The Rayneses were sitting on a couch, looking out over a table full of magazines: neither one was reading. They were in their early thirties, and except for their sex, as alike as new marbles: honey-blond, tall, slender, from the small town of New Ulm in southern Minnesota. Larry worked in a heating and air-conditioning business owned by his father; Lucy worked at the post office. Neither had lived outside of New Ulm. Both of them spoke fluent German, and went to Germany every summer, to hike. They had no other children.

They'd conferred with Maret on the separation process, but had worked more with Weather than any other physician, because of Weather's involvement in the preliminary surgery.

They were astonished by the news. "What does it mean? It's off? For how long?" Lucy Raynes blurted. "I mean . . . ?"

"We'll go tomorrow," Weather said, patting her arm. "Same time. This whole thing is so bizarre . . . there are police everywhere, I guess. The girls are fine, no change for them."

"I can't believe it," Larry Raynes said. "After we got this far . . ."

His wife put an arm around his waist and squeezed him: "We'll be okay. It'll be all right."

OF THE TWO RAYNESES, Lucy was the most demanding of information, had studied the details of the separation, used terms like "superior sagittal sinus" and "calvaria," read medical papers on other separations. She'd spoken to the media on a number of occasions, both televised and print. Larry, on the other hand, mostly talked about timing, and the children's development, and often, to Weather, seemed to simply want to get it over with. He wasn't stupid, but swept along in a current too strong for him, part medical science, part circus. He wanted to go home.

Maret had warned everybody about the circus. "Whenever this is done, we get the media, because of the drama and the sympathetic

17

aspects. You have to be prepared. In Miami, we had reporters following the surgeons home, knocking on doors, waiting in the streets."

Now he said to the Rayneses, "I'll talk to the media in ten minutes or so. I'd like you to be with me."

Larry Raynes said to his wife, "You go. I'll go sit with the kids."

Weather left them talking, and went back to the locker room to change back into her street clothes.

By THE TIME she got back, most of the team had drifted away. The OR nurses were shutting the place down. Weather stopped to talk with her surgical assistant, when one of the team's cardiologists, Alan Seitz, who'd been called to the ER, came ambling down the hall, looking distracted. "What?" Weather asked.

"That Don guy died," Seitz said. "One of the robbers kicked him to death. Broke up his kidneys. He was soaked in Coumadin. He bled out before we could get anything going. We were dumping fluid into him fast as we could, nothing to do."

Weather stepped up and gave him a squeeze. Seitz was an old friend. "Nothing to do. You only do what you can."

"Yeah." Seitz looked around and said, "I mean, Jesus Christ: kicked to death. In the *hospital*."

2

LUCAS DAVENPORT CRACKED his eyes at nine o'clock and did the calculation: Weather should be done with the initial part of the operation. She'd be removing one of the expanders, and also making the first cuts down to the skull itself. If it had gone off as scheduled, at seven-thirty, she'd be drinking a cup of coffee, while the bone-cutter went to work.

All right. Interesting.

He lay under the blankets for a couple of minutes, listening: nothing to hear. Might be snowing again. Lucas had helped the architect put the house together, and had isolated the bedroom suite at the north end, away from the other bedrooms, and the kids. Weather had imported a baby monitor, so she could hear Sam wake in the night, but the monitor was quiet: the housekeeper would have Sam in hand, by this time.

Get up.

He rolled out, dropped to the carpet, did a few push-ups, a few sit-ups, picked up two twenty-five-pound dumbbells and did a hundred curls with each arm. In the bathroom, he brushed his teeth and shaved, watching himself in the mirror. Still in good shape, even after a lot of hard years. But it was something he'd have to work on, he thought, as he got to fifty—once the tone is lost, it's tough to get back.

Still had all his hair, dark, but threaded through with gray. His face was too white after three months of Minnesota winter gloom, showing scars and dimples from fifteen years of hockey and twenty-five years of cops; he'd kept the winter weight off by playing basketball, his cheekbones showing beside his hawkish nose. At least he didn't smoke. He could see the smoke eating into guys like Del.

He was standing in the shower, lathered up with Weather's body wash, when she called from the bedroom—"You still in there?"

"One more minute . . ." he shouted back. Surprised: he hadn't expected to see her until sometime in the evening. He rinsed off the body wash, gave the ugly bits a final scrub, climbed out and found her standing in the doorway.

She reached across to the towel bar, pulled a towel free and handed it to him. "The operation was canceled because a man got murdered in the pharmacy and they took all the drugs."

"What?" He was dripping, and started to dry down.

She said, "Mmm, you smell like spring rain."

"What?"

"There were about a million media people there, all the cable networks, and Gabe had to go out and tell them the hospital got held up and they murdered Don Peterson by kicking him to death."

Held up his hands: "Wait-wait-wait. I can't listen to this naked."

"Ah, God, this is the third most awful day of my life," she said, but she popped him on the ass as he went by.

Lucas got his shorts on and pulled a T-shirt over his head. "Now. Start from the beginning."

"Okay. The hospital pharmacy got robbed. One of the pharmacists was beaten up so bad that he died. Guess who's running the investigation for Minneapolis?"

He shrugged. "Who?"

"Your old pal Titsy."

Impatient, didn't want to hear about it: "Weather . . . just tell me."

She backed up and sat on the bed as he dressed: "Okay. I got there on schedule . . ."

THE BROTHERS Lyle Mack and Joe Mack, Mikey Haines, Shooter Chapman, and Honey Bee Brown sat in the back of Cherries Bar off Highway 13, looking at an old tube TV balanced on a plastic chair, the electric cord going straight up to a light socket. The room smelled of sour empty beer bottles and wet cardboard. Three nylon bags full of drugs sat on the floor behind them, and Lyle Mack said, "You dumb fucks."

"What was we supposed to do? The guy was calling the cops," Chapman said. Haines, who'd done the kicking, kept his mouth shut.

Honey Bee stared at them, as she worked through a wad of Juicy Fruit the size of a walnut. She said, around the gum, "You guys could screw up a wet dream."

Lyle Mack was sweating, scared, and thinking: *Too many witnesses.* Too many people knew that Joe Mack, Haines, and Chapman had raided the pharmacy. He and Honey Bee, the three of them, anyone they may have talked to—and there were probably a couple who'd taken some hints—plus the doc, and maybe the doc's pal, the square doc, whoever he was.

"Tell me about the woman in the Audi," Lyle Mack said.

"She rolled in as we were rolling out. She might not connect us," Joe Mack said. "She saw me, I think, but who knows? Our lights was in her eyes. She was blond, she was short, was driving an Audi. Could have been a nurse."

"She totally saw you, dude," said Haines, trying to take some pressure off himself. Christ, he'd kicked that dude to death. He didn't know what he thought about that. Shooter had once killed a spade out in Stockton, California, but that was different. "That dude that died, it was like totally a freak accident. They said so on TV, he was on some meds that made him bleed. Wasn't me. I kicked him a little."

"Punted the shit out of him," said Joe Mack, passing back the pressure.

"The old fuck scratched me," Haines said. "He was hanging on."

"That was after you kicked him," Joe Mack said.

Lyle Mack asked, "How bad you hurt?"

"Aw, just bled a little, it don't show," Mikey said.

"Let me see," Lyle Mack said.

Mikey pulled up his pant leg. "Nothing," he said. He looked like he'd been scraped with a screwdriver, a long thin scratch with some dried blood.

The TV went back to the morning show where some crazy woman was talking about making decorations for Martin Luther King Day from found art, which seemed to consist of beer-can pull-tabs and bottle caps. They all watched for a minute, then Joe Mack said, "She's gotta be on something bad. You couldn't do that, normal."

Lyle Mack pointed the remote at the TV and the picture got sucked into a white dot. He scratched his head and said, "Well, now."

Honey Bee cracked her gum. "What're we gonna do?"

"Lay low," Lyle Mack said. "Dump the dope at Dad's farm. Put the guns in with the dope—they could be identified, too. Nobody touches anything for a month. You three . . . no, Joe Mack, you better stay here. Honey Bee can give you a haircut. Cut it right down to a butch."

"Aw, no," Joe Mack groaned.

Lyle Mack rode over him: "Mikey and Shooter, you go out to Honey Bee's. When Joe's cleaned up, me'n him'll come over. I think the three of you better get the hell over to Eddie's. Hit a couple bars every night, let everybody see you, until nobody knows exactly when you got there, and then you can say you were over there a week before this shit happened."

"Man, it's fuckin' freezin' over there," Haines said. Eddie's was in Green Bay.

"It's fuckin' freezin' here, and we can trust Eddie, and this shit wouldn't have happened if you hadn't kicked that old man to death," Lyle Mack said. "So shut up and go on over to Eddie's. Wait until night. Get over to Honey Bee's right now, until it's dark. Don't stop for no food, don't get no beer, don't let anybody see your faces. We don't want anybody sayin', 'I saw him the day it happened.'"

"What about, you know . . ." Chapman glanced at the packs full of drugs. "This was supposed to pay us something."

Lyle Mack got to his feet, a short heavy man in a black fleece and jeans. He went out to the front of the bar and came back three minutes later with a thin pile of fifty-dollar bills. He cut the pile more or less in half and gave one stack each to Haines and Chapman. "You go on, now. That's two thousand for each of you. It'll keep you for a month, at Eddie's. After we sell the shit, you'll get the rest."

"Green Bay, dude," Haines moaned.

"Better'n Oak Park Heights," Chapman said. Oak Park Heights was the state's supermax prison.

They all looked at each other for a moment, no sound other than a hum from a refrigeration unit, and Honey Bee's gum-chewing, and then Lyle Mack said to Haines and Chapman, "So—take off. I'll get over there soon as I can. You can get some pizzas from the freezer and take a couple cases of beer."

"Biggest score we ever did," Haines said.

"Yeah, but you had to go and fuck it up," Lyle said.

HAINES AND CHAPMAN got four pizzas and two cases of Miller, and shuffled out through the back, off the loading dock. Their 2002 Trans Am was leaning against a snowdrift, and Lyle Mack stood on tiptoe, looking out of the garage door windows, watching as the two got inside, still watching until the car turned the corner.

Then he turned back to Joe Mack and Honey Bee and said, "Honey, go get me a hot fudge sundae."

"What?" Her jaw hung open, and he could see the wad of gum; it looked like a piece of zombie flesh. She was a good-lookin' woman, Lyle Mack thought, who ruined it all when she did something like that, and she did something like that all the time.

"A fuckin' hot fudge sundae," he said, patiently. "Get me a hot fudge sundae. Put the hot fudge in the microwave so it's really hot."

She shook her head, looked at her watch—it was five minutes after eight o'clock in the morning, a weird time for a hot fudge sundae, but she got up and wandered off to the front of the bar. Lyle Mack walked behind her, shut the door, and turned back to Joe.

"You crazy fuckers," he said, shaking his head. "You couldn't have done worse if you'd shot a cop. You dumb sonsofbitches."

"That fuckin' Mikey," Joe Mack said. "And I don't think sendin' us to Eddie's is gonna do much good. How many times have you heard about Shooter killing the colored dude out in California?"

Lyle Mack shook a finger at him. "That's why they aren't going to Eddie's."

"They aren't?"

"We got no choice, Joe. That old fart scratched Mikey," Lyle Mack said. "That means the cops got DNA on him. You remember when Mikey fucked that high school chick over in Edina and the cops came and made him brush his gums? That was DNA. About two minutes from now, they're going to come looking for him, and they'll give us up bigger'n shit."

Joe Mack thought about that for a few seconds, then a frown slowly crawled over his face. "If you're talking about killing them, I mean, fuck you. I'm not killing anybody," Joe Mack said. "I mean, I couldn't do it. I'd mess it up."

Lyle Mack was nodding. "Me and you both, Joe Mack. We gotta get hold of Cappy."

"Ah, man." Joe thought about Cappy for a minute, and then thought about getting a drink.

"Got no choice," Lyle Mack said. He listened toward the front of the bar for a minute, then said, "Don't tell Honey Bee about this. She likes those boys, and she'd get upset."

"What if Cappy . . . I mean, Shooter and Mikey is his pals."

"I don't think anybody is Cappy's pals," Lyle Mack said. "Cappy is his own pal."

*

23

OUT IN THE Trans Am, Haines said, "Hope Honey Bee's got Home Box Office."

"Gotta stop at the house first," Shooter said.

"Lyle said—"

"It's Lyle that worries me," Chapman said. "I could see him thinkin'. He's worried about us."

"About us?" Haines didn't understand.

"About us givin' him up. I could see his beady little eyes thinkin' it over. So he sends us out to Honey Bee's, which is so far out in the country a goddamn John Deere salesman couldn't find us. Why is that? Maybe he wants to get us alone and do us."

"But he said we can't be *seen*," Haines whined. "He said we're going to Eddie's."

"Well, he's sorta right about not bein' seen, but we gotta take the chance," Chapman said. "We gotta run by the house, grab the guns, and then we can take off. Turn the furnace down. If we was going to Eddie's for a month, we'd at least turn the furnace down. Take the shit out of the refrigerator. Take us two minutes."

The chrome yellow Trans Am fishtailed around the corner; a great car, in the summer, but with its low-profile, high-performance rubber, a pig on ice.

LUCAS FINISHED DRESSING, checked himself in the mirror: charcoal suit, white shirt, blue tie that vibrated with his eyes. Weather said, "And now, something occurred to me this very minute. When I was going in the parking ramp, a van was coming out really fast. We almost ran into each other."

"You weren't driving too fast, were you?" Of course she was; he'd given her a three-day race-driving course at a track in Vegas, as a birthday present, and she'd kicked everybody's ass.

Weather ignored him. "The man in the passenger seat looked like a lumberjack or something. One of those tan canvas coats that lumberjacks wear. Long hair, brown-blond, down on his shoulders, and a beard. He looked like a Harley guy. Big nose. That was just about . . ." She rubbed her forehead, working it out, and said, "That must have been just about the time of the robbery." She looked up: "Jeez, what if that was the guys? The driver looked the same way. I didn't see him so well, but he had a beard . . ."

Lucas held up a finger, picked up his cell phone, sat on the bed, and punched up a number. A moment later, said, "Yup, it's me, but I can't talk because my wife is standing about a foot away."

"Hey, Marcy," Weather called. Marcy Sherrill was a deputy chief with the Minneapolis cops: Titsy.

Lucas said, "What we need to know is, what time exactly did this whole thing happen? What time did it start, and when did it end?"

Marcy: "I don't think this is for the BCA."

"Listen, just shut up and tell me, and then I'll tell you why I want to know," Lucas said.

He listened for a moment, turned to Weather and said, "Between five-thirty and five-forty, right in there."

Weather said, "Lucas, that was . . . I mean, that was *exactly* the time I got there."

Lucas went back to the phone: "You know Weather is on the surgical team that's separating the twins? Yeah? So she pulled into the parking ramp right then, and saw a van coming out, and the face of a guy in the passenger seat. Said he looked like a lumberjack, blond or brown hair, down on his shoulders. Beard. Yeah, saw him pretty clearly. Saw the driver, too, not so well, but he had a beard. They were moving fast, and a little recklessly. Said the passenger was wearing like a yellow lumberjack coat."

"Tan canvas," Weather said.

"Tan canvas coat," Lucas repeated. He listened, then put the phone down and asked, "You get any impression of size?"

Weather closed her eyes for a minute, then said, "Yes. He was a big guy. Bigger than you. Taller, I think, and heavier."

Lucas passed it on, listened again, and said, "All right. How about . . . ten o'clock? Is ten good?"

When he hung up he said, "The robbers were three guys, wearing blue orderly scrubs, but the woman in the pharmacy doesn't think they were orderlies. They were apparently wearing the scrubs over street clothes. They were wearing heavy boots and ski masks, but the woman

25

thought that at least a couple of them had beards. One of them was a really big guy. We need to talk to Marcy. Probably do a computer sketch, see if they can figure out who the guy was."

"Probably nothing, though," Weather said, as though she regretted telling him about it.

"Maybe not," he said. "But hell, you've got the day off. The kids are out of the house—let's go hang out. Talk to Marcy, do lunch. Hit a boutique. I could use a new suit or two for spring."

She nodded, quickly, and repeated, "It's probably nothing."

LYLE MACK SAT in his tiny loading-dock office and thought about it for a minute, then got on the cold phone and called Barakat. He said, "We gotta talk."

"Why should I talk to you? My hands are clean," Barakat said. "You and that bunch of idiots are in trouble. I'm walking away. I know nothing. Why are you calling me? You know the police can follow phone calls—"

"I ain't stupid, we all got cold phones. You gotta get one, too."

"What?"

Lyle Mack was patient: "Go down someplace and buy a phone and a card and give them a fake name, if you gotta give them a name," Lyle Mack said. "You can get them at the grocery store. Some grocery stores. You can go to Best Buy."

"I'm telling you, I am out of all this—"

"Man, you were *there*. You can't walk. And I got your goods," Lyle Mack said.

"I'll get them some other time," Barakat said.

"Look. When the guys were going out the ramp, some chick was coming in. Black Audi convertible. Blond. She saw one of the guys, and we want to know who she is, just in case. They think she was probably a nurse."

"How am I going to find out? I'm not a mind reader," Barakat growled. "What am I supposed to do, walk around asking people who saw *the killers* coming out of the ramp? How am I supposed to know that? That somebody saw somebody?"

"Just *listen*," Mack said patiently. "People will talk about this for weeks—just listen. You don't have to fuckin' *investigate*."

Long silence. Then, "If she's a nurse, she was working the day shift," Barakat said. "There are probably a hundred Audis out in the ramp right now. So, I can keep an eye out tomorrow. If she's a shift worker, she should be coming in about the same time. That's all I can do."

"And listen around," Lyle Mack said. As an added attraction: "The goods we got for you. It's the best I've ever seen. It's like a hundred percent gold."

ALAIN BARAKAT hung up and wandered into the kitchen. Glanced at his watch; had to get back.

He was tired: he'd just worked the overnight shift, and was continuing straight through the day, with only the hour-long lunch break. He'd already used half of that, and had come home hoping to find a package inside the push-through mailbox.

Hoping against hope.

The box was empty. Lyle Mack still had the goods. The knowledge of that would drive him crazy, he thought: and sooner or later, he would be over there begging for it.

Barakat lived in a modest brick house in St. Paul's Highland Park, a street of tidy houses and neatly shoveled sidewalks and kids and yellow school buses coming and going. His father had bought the house for him, but carefully kept the title for himself, part of the family's move out of Lebanon. They were investing in real estate—houses and farmland— socking away gold coins, buying American educations for the kids.

The price of American houses had never gone down, his father had told him. A year later, when prices started going down, the old man had title to at least thirty houses in the hot markets of California and Florida. He was losing his shirt and he'd cut Barakat's allowance to five thousand a month. He said, "You're a grown man now and a doctor. You can be rich if you work."

"I don't want to be a doctor," Barakat had said. "I don't want to be in St. Paul. This is not Lebanon, Pops, this is like the North Pole. It was minus twenty here the other day."

27

"Men have to work. That's what men do. Finish the residency, then go where you like. Move to Los Angeles. What I know, is, I'm cutting back. You live on five thousand a month, or you go hungry."

But Barakat couldn't live on five thousand; couldn't feed the habit for five thousand. The financial problem had led to his involvement with the Macks, a solution he'd suggested himself. The whole thing had seemed so simple.

Now this.

And the blond woman.

If the blond woman was the same one he'd seen in the elevator— and he'd have bet she was, she had to have been coming down from the parking ramp, and the timing was right—then he had a problem, too. He had no reason to be back there at that time of day—the emergency room was at the far end of the hospital, and nothing at the back end was even open. If she'd picked out one of Lyle Mack's guys, and was asked if she'd seen anyone else . . .

He dropped in an armchair and propped his head up with his hand. Thought about the blonde, and about the goods: Lyle Mack said he had the goods. Fire in the blood; needed the goods, despite what he'd said. Why had he said he'd get them some other time? He needed them now . . .

Think about the blonde.

Arriving at that time of the morning, she had to be staff, and medical staff, not administrative. If she'd been an emergency case, she would have gone down the street, instead of up the ramp. If she was a nurse, she had a rich husband—nurses didn't drive Audis.

A doc? Maybe. There were lots of women docs.

His brain switched tracks again. Mack *had* the goods. All he had to do was pick them up. They were right *there.* Like a fat man thinking about a doughnut, he thought about the heft and feel of a big bag full of powder cocaine.

The keys to the kingdom of glory. He'd been sober for three days, and he didn't like it. Though he'd read that there was no real physical dependency—he wasn't shaking or seeing snakes—the psychological dependency was just as real. Without the coke, without money for the coke, he was living a drab, colorless existence, a life of shades and tints. The coke brought life, intelligence, wit, excitement, clarity: primary colors.

He looked in his wallet. Nine dollars, and he hadn't eaten in a day. Had to eat. Had to get the goods.

THE MINNEAPOLIS police department is in the city hall, which is an ungainly, liver-colored building that squats in the Minneapolis glass-and-steel loop like an unseemly wart. Marcy Sherrill was slumped in her office chair, door closed to a crack. Lucas poked his nose in, called, "Hello?" He got what sounded like a feminine snore, so he knocked and tried again, louder this time. "Hello?"

Marcy twitched, sat upright, and turned and yawned, disoriented.

"Ah, jeez . . . come on in. I dozed off." She half-stood, then dropped back in her chair, dug in her desk drawer for a roll of breath mints, popped one.

Marcy was a tidy, athletic woman, forty or so, who'd never had a problem jumping into a fight. Dark-haired and dark-eyed, she and Lucas had once, pre-Weather, spent some time together—or as Marcy said, forty days and forty nights. She'd later had a lengthy, contentious affair with a local artist, then married a medium big shot at General Mills.

And quickly produced James.

James was just back to preschool after a bout with the flu, she said, as Lucas and Weather settled into visitors' chairs. "I've been getting about two hours of sleep a night," she said. "As soon as he got better, he started running again. He never stops. He starts when he gets up, he runs until he drops, he sleeps like a log, then he starts running again."

"Same with Sam," Weather said. "Sam is starting to learn his letters now . . ."

They one-upped each other for a minute or two, on their respective kids' looks, intelligence, vigor, and overall cuteness. When they were done, Lucas scored it as a tie, though, of course, Weather was correct. Sam was the superior kid.

"SO WHAT do you think about this Don Peterson guy?" Lucas asked. "What'd you get?"

"The killing was pretty straightforward," Marcy said. "The killer probably didn't mean to do it. Kicked the guy a few times. According to Baker—"

"Baker's the nurse," Weather said.

"Yeah. Dorothy Baker. She was doing inventory on the drugs. She couldn't see anything, or say anything, because they taped her up, but she could hear everything. Peterson got a hand free, somehow, tried to slip his cell phone out and call nine-one-one—Baker heard the robbers talking about it—but he fumbled it and got caught. One of the guys kicked him a few times, in the back, and in the chest. That broke him up. He bled to death, internal bleeding around his kidneys. They got him to the emergency room before he died, but he only lasted a few more minutes. He was on Coumadin; there was no way to stop the bleeding."

"So this Baker—"

Marcy held up a hand, cutting him off. "You know what Peterson did? Took some balls, but he did it on purpose. When the guy started kicking him, he grabbed him, probably on his leg, and scratched him. He told Baker what he'd done, and on the way down to the ER, he came to and told one of the docs. That he scratched this guy. He had blood on his hands, skin under his nails."

"DNA," Lucas said. He'd never met Peterson, but he was suddenly proud of the guy. "That's terrific . . . if we can find the guy who did it."

"Yeah: we find him, we've got him," Marcy said.

"She hear anything else? Baker?" Lucas asked.

"Yes. Interesting stuff. These guys were talking as they cleaned the place out, and she said they sounded kind of dumb—like street guys," Marcy said.

"Black, white?"

"White, four of them. She saw their hands—hands of three of them, anyway. Big guys, wearing ski masks. Their hands were rough, like they worked outside. They sounded dumb, but they knew exactly what they were doing. More interesting is the fourth guy, and what she didn't hear. Or see."

"What didn't she hear?" Weather asked.

"She didn't hear anybody knock on the door, because nobody did,"

Marcy said. "The door just popped open and there they were, all over Baker and Peterson. The fourth guy stayed out of sight until they were on the floor."

"That door should have been locked," Weather said.

The door *was* locked, Marcy said. It locked automatically, and to prevent that, it had to be deliberately disabled. Peterson was already inside when Baker got there, and she used her key to get in. "She's absolutely sure the door was locked, because when she put her key in, she didn't turn it far enough, didn't click it, and when she tried the handle, it was still locked and she had to twist the key harder. So it wasn't disabled."

"The robbers had a key," Weather said.

"Yes. Plus, the fourth man stayed out of sight until both Baker and Peterson were blind. Baker said he came in and pointed out specific lockers . . . and she thinks she might have heard his voice before. She said he sounded like a doctor, but she didn't know who. If so, that's why they taped their eyes—they would have recognized the fourth guy. Maybe even if he wore a mask. He's the inside guy, who got the key for them."

"Interesting," Lucas said. "You're pushing that?"

"Of course. We're pushing everything," Marcy said. "We looked like goofs this morning. All the TV stations were there, a couple cable networks, for this operation on the twins—and we had to cancel it because our *hospital* gets knocked over? It's like when the I-35 bridge fell in the Mississippi: people ask, what the hell are you doing, your bridge fell down? Now they're asking, 'Your hospital gets held up? Your *hospital*? What's going on up there?'"

"Hard to believe it's a doctor," Weather said.

"Why? I've known a couple psycho doctors," Lucas said.

Marcy nodded: "Don't even get us started on nurses." She stood up and said to Weather, "Let's get you going on that drawing. I'd like to get it on the noon news."

As they were walking down the hall, Marcy added, "I want you guys to take it a little easy until we've got them locked up."

"Why's that?" Lucas asked.

Marcy said, "Well, Weather saw them—so they probably saw *her*."

31

Lucas stopped in his tracks: "I never thought of that." He looked at Weather. "I'm so dumb. That never occurred to me."

HONEY BEE had once been a professional hairdresser, so she offered Joe Mack a choice of styles: greaser, punk, industrial, skater, Mohawk, or military sidewall.

"We don't want a rearrangement. We want something so different that nobody'd dream that some long-haired guy might have been him," Lyle Mack said. "Cut it all off. Right down to the scalp."

"Ah, man . . ."

But she did it, using a couple of plastic attachments on a barber's clipper, and took his hair down to a quarter-inch, Joe Mack sitting on a toilet with a towel around his neck. That done, she lathered him up and, using a straight razor, gave him the most sensuous shave of his life, not only because he was scared of the razor, which added a certain *frisson* to the proceeding, but because either her left or right tit was massaging his either left or right ear, depending.

"You think Mikey meant to kill that man?" Honey Bee asked.

"No way," Joe Mack said. "He's just . . . dumb."

Honey Bee nodded. Mikey was dumb. And violent. Unlike Joe Mack, who was just dumb. Mikey might not have meant to kill the old man, but he probably enjoyed it. Give him a month or two, and he'd be bragging it around, just like Shooter and the black dude in California.

When she was done with Joe Mack, he washed off his face and looked at himself in the mirror. Christ: he looked like a German butcher, big, red, wind-burned nose sticking out of a dead-white face.

"What do you think?" Honey Bee asked.

"Ah, man . . . Not your fault, though." He rubbed his head. "Bums me out."

She went to the back door, peered through it. Lyle Mack was in the back, moving stuff around. She turned back to Joe Mack, hooked the front of his jeans. "You could come upstairs, later, if that'd make you feel better."

Joe Mack's eyes cut toward the door. Lyle would be really upset if he found out that Joe was screwing his girlfriend. Maybe.

"He's way in the back," she said.

"Yeah, but still . . ."

"I don't mean right this minute."

"Well . . ." He stepped close to her, slipped his hand up under her skirt to her underpants. She wore white cotton underpants, and for some reason, that really wound his clock. "That'd help, Honey Bee. I mean, I'd really appreciate it. I'm feeling kinda low."

THEY BACKED away from each other when they heard Lyle Mack coming back. Lyle pushed through the swing door, took in Joe and said, "Whoa."

Joe Mack rubbed his head again and said, "I look like I just got out of the joint. I look like they been sprayin' me down for head lice."

"Better'n taking a fall on the old guy," Lyle Mack said. "You know, you look about ten years younger."

"Yeah?"

Lyle Mack turned to Honey Bee and said, "I need you to run out to Home Depot and get some stuff. I got a list."

"I gotta get the wieners started," she said.

"I'll get the wieners. I want you out of here," Lyle Mack said. "Like, now. Don't come back for an hour."

She looked at him for a minute, then said, "More trouble."

"I don't want you to know about nothing, 'cause then you can't get hurt," Lyle Mack said. He followed her around, being nice, gave her a squeeze—she was in a huff—and got her out the door and on the way.

When she was gone, Joe Mack asked, "What was that all about?"

"Cappy's coming over," Lyle Mack said.

CAPRICE MARLON GARNER dreamed of flying alone out of Bakersfield, up through the mountains, straddling his BMW, wind scouring his shaved scalp, sand spitting off the goggles, slipstream pulling at his leathers; and then down the other side, in the night, toward the lights of Tehachapi, then down, down some more and boom! out into the desert, running like a streak of steel lightning past the town of Mojave, blowing through Barstow to the 15, then up the 15 all the way to the lights of Vegas, coming out there at dawn with the lights on the horizon, the losers heading back to LA in the opposite lane . . .

Pulling up to the city limits, getting gas, sitting there with the BMW turning over like silk, and then boom! back down into the desert, the BMW hanging at 120, the white faces of the people in their Audis and Benzes and Mustangs, like ghosts, staring out at the demon who whipped by them in the dawn's early light . . .

The ride was the thing. The world slipped away—work, history, memory, dreams, everything—until he was nothing more than a piece of the unconscious landscape, but moving fast, a complex of nerves and guts and balls, bone and muscle and reaction.

And he dreamed of sitting up on a high roof in Bakersfield and looking out over the town, the roofscape, the palm trees and mountains, the hot dry wind in his face. Sitting up there, it felt like something might be possible. Then you'd smell the tar, and realize it wasn't.

And he dreamed of the men he'd killed, their faces when he pulled the trigger. The BMW had come from one of them. He'd put the shotgun to the man's head as he signed the papers, whining and pleading and peeing himself, and when the papers were in Cappy's pocket, boom! another one bites the dust. The Mojave was littered with their bones.

He'd killed them without a flicker of a doubt, without a shred of pity, and enjoyed the nightly reruns . . .

SOMETIME IN THE early morning, the Minnesota cold got to him, and he stirred in his sleep. Eventually he surfaced, groaned and rolled over, the images of California dying like a match flame in a breeze. He'd kicked off the crappy acrylon blankets, and the winter had snuck through the ill-fitting windows, into the bed. He'd unconsciously pulled himself into a fetal position, and now the muscles of his back and neck cramped up like fists.

He groaned again and rolled over and straightened out, his back muscles aching, pulled the blankets up to his chin, and listened: too quiet. Probably snowing again. Snow muffled the sounds of the highway, of the neighbors. He caught sight of the alarm clock. Nine o'clock. He'd been asleep since six, after a three-day run on methamphetamine and maybe a little cocaine, and work; they were all mixed up in his mind, and he couldn't remember.

He was still tired. Didn't want to get up, but he swung his feet over the side of the bed, found the pack of Camels, lit one in the dim light that came through the window shade. Sat and smoked it down to his fingers, stubbed it out and trudged to the bathroom, the old cold floorboards flexing under his feet, the room smelling of tobacco and crumbling plaster and peeling wallpaper.

THE ONLY bathroom light was a single bulb with a pull string. Cappy pulled on it, and looked at his face in the medicine cabinet mirror. Picked up some new lines, he thought. He was developing a dusty look, with a slash from the corner of his nose down toward his chin. Didn't bother him; he wasn't long for this world.

Today was his birthday, he thought. One more year and he could legally buy a drink.

He was twenty years old, on this cold winter morning in St. Paul Park.

AFTER COMING BACK to Minnesota, he'd stopped in his hometown, looked around. Nothing there for him. He looked so different than he had in junior high, that it wasn't likely that even his father would recognize him.

But one guy had. A kid he'd grown up with, named John Loew. Loew had come into the SuperAmerica as Cappy was walking out. Cappy had recognized him, but kept going, and then Loew had stopped and turned and said, "Cap? Is that you?"

Cap turned and nodded. "How ya doin', John."

"Hey, man . . . you really . . ."

Cappy gave him the skeleton grin. "Yeah?"

". . . look different. Like a movie guy or something. Where've you been?"

"You know. LA, San Francisco, West Coast."

A woman got out of a Corolla and came walking over and asked, "John?"

Loew said, "Carol. This is Cap Garner. We grew up together, went to school together."

The woman was Cappy's age, but he could tell she was also about eighteen years younger: a woman that nothing had ever happened to, a little heavy, but not too; a little blond, but not too; a little hot, but not too. She looked at Cappy with utter disdain and said, "Hi, there."

Cappy nodded, threw his leg over the BMW, and asked Loew, "So what're you doing? Working?"

"Going to Mankato in business administration. Finance." He shrugged, as if apologizing. "Carol and I are engaged."

Cappy pulled his tanker goggles over his eyes and said, "Glad it's working for you, John."

John said, "Yeah, well," and stepped toward the store. "Anyway . . ."

"Have a good day," Cappy said.

Riding away, he thought, *Isn't that just how it is?* This guy grew up next door, he's going to college, he's got a blond chick, he's gonna get married, he's gonna have kids, and not a single fuckin' thing will ever happen to him. Except that he'll get married and have kids. For some reason, that pissed him off. Some people go to college, some people go to work throwing boxes at UPS.

MINNESOTA WAS GRINDING him down. Before the last cold front came through, he'd taken the BMW for a ride down the highway, and in fifteen minutes, even wearing full leathers, fleece and a face mask, he'd been frozen to the bike like a tongue to a water pump.

He needed to ride, he needed to do something, but he had no money. None. His life couldn't much be distinguished from life in a dungeon: work, a space for food and drugs, sleep, and work some more—with nothing at the end of it.

He smeared shaving cream on his face and thought of California; or maybe Florida. He'd never been to Florida. Had been told that it was lusher and harder than California—meth as opposed to cocaine—with lots more old people.

And he thought again about the liquor store. Big liquor store in Wisconsin, next to a supermarket. He'd been in just before closing on a Friday night, nobody else in the store, and he'd paid $12.50 for a bottle of bourbon, fake ID ready to go.

They never even asked: he looked that old. But more interesting was that when he'd paid with a fifty, the checkout man had lifted the cash tray to slip the bill beneath it, and there'd been at least twenty bills under there, all fifties and hundreds. With the five, tens and twenties in the top, there had to be two thousand dollars in the register.

Enough to get to Florida. Enough to start, anyway.

He caught his eyes in the mirror and thought, *Stupid*. Every asshole in the world who wanted money, the first thing they thought of was a liquor store at closing time. They probably had cameras, guns, alarms, who knew what?

No liquor stores, Cappy. Have to think of something else.

Some other job.

He was staring at himself, thinking about the bed, when the phone rang.

He picked it up, and Lyle Mack asked, "That you, Cappy?"

CAPPY SAT in the back of Cherries and looked at Lyle Mack and said, "So that fuckin' Shooter told you I kill people."

"He made it pretty clear. Didn't exactly say the words," Lyle Mack said.

"That could get you locked away in California," Cappy said. "Maybe get you the needle."

"That's exactly the reason we have a problem with Shooter. He talks," Lyle Mack said.

Cappy, his voice flat: "Ten thousand dollars?"

"Five thousand each."

"Then what?" Cappy asked.

"What do you mean?"

"You can't just leave them laying out there," Cappy said. He'd had some experience with the disposal issue.

"We'll . . . dump them somewhere."

Cap sat staring at Lyle Mack for a long time, his flat crazy-man stare, until Mack began to get nervous, then said, "Fifteen."

"Aw, man, we don't have a lot of cash," Lyle Mack said. "C'mon, Cappy, we're asking you as a brother." Lyle Mack had never contracted

37

for a murder, and he was jumpy as hell. Joe Mack sat next to him and kept rubbing his face, as though he couldn't believe it.

"Fifteen is the brother price," Cap said. "I need a new van."

"You can't get a new van for fifteen," Joe Mack said.

"Well, it's not a new-new van, it's new for me," Cap said.

Joe Mack leaned forward. "Tell you what. I'll sign my van over to you. It's worth that, Blue Book. Perfect condition. Dodge Grand Caravan Cargo, three years old, good rubber, twenty-eight thousand actual. It's got XM radio and a drop ramp for bikes, it's got nav. It'd be perfect for you."

"How's the tranny?"

"The tranny's perfect. Never been a glitch," Joe Mack said.

"I gotta Dodge; it's been some trouble," Cappy said. But he was thinking: Florida.

"Everything got some trouble. But in vans, the Dodges is the best," Joe Mack said.

Cappy stared at Joe Mack, then said, "I'd want to look it up in the Blue Book."

"Be my guest," Joe Mack said.

"And two grand in cash. I gotta eat, too."

Lyle Mack, staring into Cappy's pale blue eyes, realized what an insane little motherfucker he really was.

THEN THEY got practical, and Lyle Mack called Honey Bee on her cell phone: "You still at Home Depot?"

"Just got back in my car."

"I thought of a couple more things we need," Lyle Mack said. "Run back and get some of those contractor clean-up bags, okay? Like big garbage bags, but really big. And some Scrubbing Bubbles, and, uh, you know, some of those rubber kitchen gloves."

"So when am I the goddamn maid around here?"

"Well, you're right there at the store, goddamnit, Honey Bee . . ."

They'd sent Cappy down the street to wait at the Log Cabin Inn, and picked him up after Honey Bee got back. Honey Bee would open the bar: "You didn't start the wienies. They're still gonna be cold when we open."

Lyle Mack shook his head. "Honey Bee, I'm just so . . . *busy*. You know we've got some trouble. Help me out, here."

When Lyle had gone out the back, and Joe Mack was getting his coat on, he tried to cheer her up by squeezing her butt, and giving her a little leg hump, but she wasn't having it: "Get out of here. Go get busy."

HONEY BEE had a horse ranch thirty miles south of St. Paul, though as ranches went, it was on the small side—forty acres. But Honey Bee liked it, and so did her three horses. The Macks were not horse persons themselves; their attitude was, if God had meant people to ride horses, He wouldn't have invented the Fat Bob.

They rode out in Joe Mack's van, so Cappy could hear it run, with the Macks in the front seats, and Cappy on a backseat with a shotgun that he'd brought from home. Joe Mack said to his brother, "I totally know where you're coming from, you know, with this thing—but I gotta say, I kind of like these guys, when they're not being assholes."

"But they're assholes most of the time," Lyle Mack said. "Now look at this. We have a perfect job, big money, no trouble, and now what? Now we're looking at a murder. I mean, fuck me. Murder? And they keep lettin' you know about that eggplant that Shooter killed out in California. You can't sit down and have a beer without them hinting around about it. It's gonna be the same thing here."

"You're right about that," Cappy grunted. The Macks had told him about the bind they were in; not because they wanted to, but because he said he needed to know. "I didn't know him but two minutes when he started ranking me about it."

"So we shouldn't have used them," Joe Mack said.

"Well, you're right. You know? You're right," Lyle Mack said. "We made a mistake. There they were, handy. I shoulda gone, it shoulda just been me and you and the doc, but you know I'm no goddamn good in the morning."

They both thought about that—and the fact that Lyle Mack was too chicken to have gone in—and then Lyle Mack added, "We made a mistake, and now they're going to have to pay for it. I gotta say, it's not fair, you know, but what're we going to do? They'll flat turn us in, if they get in a pinch."

"Bother you?" Joe Mack asked Cappy.

Cappy shook his head. "Don't bother me none, long as I get the van."

THEY RODE along in silence for a while, looking at the winter countryside, then Lyle Mack said, over his shoulder to Cappy, "One thing I gotta tell you. If they're sitting on the couch in the front room, it's a purple couch, we gotta get them off it. We can't shoot them on that couch. Honey Bee would have a fit. We need to get them up on their feet."

"Not on the couch," Cappy said.

"It's velour, and it's brand-new," Lyle Mack said. "If we do them on the couch, the couch is toast. She'd be really, really pissed. She just got it from someplace like Pottery Barn. One of those big-time places."

"Okay."

Joe Mack asked, "What do you think about the van? Pretty nice, huh?"

"It's okay," Cappy conceded. He looked in the back. With one rear seat folded, he could get the BMW in there, no problem.

They were coming up to the turnoff, and as they came down off the blacktop onto the gravel road, Lyle Mack said, "Okay, listen, I got an idea."

HONEY BEE's house wasn't much, an early twentieth-century clapboard farmhouse with a front porch that was no longer square to the rest of the structure, and a round gravel driveway big enough to circle a pickup with a two-horse trailer. The barn was newer, red metal, with a loft for hay. A detached garage was straight ahead, an exercise ring off to the left.

They pulled in, and the Macks climbed out of the van, opened the side door and took out the big bag of Home Depot stuff. Instead of walking up to the house, they walked back to the barn, talking loudly. Lyle Mack slipped on what might have been a big puddle of frozen horse urine—it was yellow, anyway, and ice—and they went to the barn door and Lyle Mack went inside while Joe Mack waited outside. Joe Mack said to Lyle's back, "I'm gonna be sick. I think we oughta call it off."

"Gone too far," Lyle Mack said. "Just hold on. It's your ass we're trying to save."

A minute later, Joe Mack said, "Ah, shit, they're coming," and Lyle Mack said, "Uh-huh."

Outside, Joe Mack called, "Lyle's looking at one of the horses. Honey Bee's worried that one of them got something."

Lyle Mack heard a reply, couldn't quite make it out, and then, closer, heard Shooter Chapman say, "Horse's supposed to be good eatin.' I saw on TV that the French eat 'em."

"Yeah, the fuckin' French," Joe Mack said, friendly. His face was white with the stress, and he could feel the words clogging in his throat.

Then Haines said something and Lyle Mack didn't understand quite what it was, just that Chapman and Haines were walking up. He stepped outside and saw the two men coming up to the van with its open door, his brother frozen like a statue.

Haines glanced at the open van as he passed and said, "Hey . . ."

Cappy was right there with the shotgun. He shot Haines in the face and, without looking or waiting or flinching, pumped once and shot Chapman.

Both men went straight down. Cappy stepped out of the van, pumped again, stepped close, carefully, kicked Chapman's foot, looked for a reaction, got none, kicked Haines. Then they all looked around, like they were sniffing the wind: looking for witnesses, listening for cars. Nothing.

"They're gone," Cappy said. "No couch, no problem."

"Okay," Lyle Mack said. His heart was beating so hard that he thought it might jump out of his chest. Chapman and Haines looked like big fat bloody dead dolls, crumpled on the beaten-down driveway snow. Shooter might have looked surprised, but the surprise part of his face was missing, so it was hard to tell. Mikey had a hand in his pocket and Lyle Mack could see the butt of a pistol in his fist. Joe was leaning against the barn, with a stream of spit streaming out of his mouth.

"Look at this," Lyle Mack said to Joe Mack. "They got guns. I bet the motherfuckers were going to kill us. Can you believe that? Can you believe it?"

41

"Well, yeah," Joe Mack said, spitting again. "They were probably thinking the same way we were."

They looked at the bodies for a few more seconds, and then Lyle Mack said, "Well, I'll get the garbage bags. We won't need the Scrubbing Bubbles. See if there's a shovel in the barn, we should scrape up any ice that's got blood on it."

Joe Mack went into the barn and found a No. 5 grain scoop, which would be okay for the snow, and scraped it away, though it was hard work; the blood just kept coming. Lyle fished the wallets out of the two men's pockets, retrieved the money he'd given to Chapman, and passed it to Cappy. "Your two thousand. It's my money, not theirs. I loaned it to them this morning."

Cappy nodded and took a drag on his Camel. Lyle said, "And don't go throwing that Camel on the ground. You always see in cop shows where somebody finds a cigarette butt."

Cappy nodded again, and Joe and Lyle put on the gloves and together rolled the dead men into the contractor's bags, while Cappy sat in the van door and watched. When they hoisted the bodies into the back of the van, thought Joe Mack, they looked exactly like dead men in garbage bags.

"Don't want to go driving around like this," Cappy said.

"No, we don't," Lyle Mack said. "I know a place we can dump them. I got lost one day, driving around. Way back in the sticks. Won't find them until spring, or maybe never."

To his brother: "Joe Mack, you take their car, drop it off at the Target by their house."

They scraped up the last bit of blood, wiped the grain scoop with a horse towel, and threw the towel in another bag, along with the rubber gloves. "Burn that when we get back to the bar," Lyle Mack said. "Take no chances."

"How far to the dump-off spot?" Cappy asked.

"Eight or nine miles. Back road, nobody goes there. We can put them under this little bridge. Hardly have to get out of the van. No cops, no stops."

"What about the woman that saw me?" Joe Mack asked.

"We gotta talk about that," Lyle Mack said. He looked at Cappy.

"What woman?" Cappy asked.

3

SAME TIME, SAME STATION, doing it all over again.

Weather slept less well, with the anxiety of the prior day weighing her down. Again she got up in the dark, dressed, spoke quietly with Lucas, and went down to a quick breakfast and the car. Driving down the vacant night streets, to University, along University to the hospital complex. Nothing in her mind but the babies.

Alain Barakat waited for her, one flight up from the security door he'd opened the morning before, freezing in his parka, smoking. The place was a nightmare; dark, brutally cold. Barakat had grown up in the north of Lebanon, with beaches and palm trees. That he should wind up in this place . . .

When he finished here, one more year, he would move to Paris. He'd gone online and found that his American medical certificate was good in France, though there would be some paperwork. Paris. Or maybe LA.

Only one good thing about Minneapolis: he could still get Gauloises, smuggled down from Canada. No: two good things.

The cocaine.

He took a long drag and thought about going back inside. Fuck this. He had nothing to do with anybody being dead.

BUT OF COURSE he did. The whole thing had been his idea. He'd seen a chance to steal a pharmacy key, and he'd taken it, without even knowing why at that moment. Or maybe he'd known why, but not how . . .

Barakat had started with cocaine at the Sorbonne, buying it from a fellow student who was working his way through college. He'd tried other stuff, uppers, downers, a little marijuana, a peyote button once, but none of it did it for him: the idea wasn't less control, it was *more* control.

That's what you got from the cocaine.

It had helped him through med school, but after that, in Miami, getting cocaine had not been a problem. Once in Minneapolis, for his residency, he'd asked around, found a guy who was recommended as a source for decent marijuana, the imported stuff down from Canada. A guy like that knew where to get cocaine.

So he bought his coke from a dealer named Lonnie, and then from a redneck named Rick, who took over Lonnie's route when Lonnie moved to Birmingham. Then Rick got hurt in a motorcycle accident, hurt really bad, and Barakat went stone cold sober for a week and a half, and it almost killed him.

One day Joe Mack showed up on his porch with a free baggie of blow. Like the cocaine Welcome Wagon.

"Our friend Rick said you were one of his best guys, but he's gonna be out of it for a while . . ."

At that point, Barakat was spending eight hundred dollars a week on cocaine, with no way to get more money. He hung at eight hundred, until one late night he was waiting at the pharmacy window, the key already in hand, and thought, *They've got no protection, and I know the guys who could take it away from them.*

It all seemed so simple. And it should have been.

Now HERE he was, freezing his ass off, trying to set up an assassination. Not simple anymore. Not uninteresting, though, if only he'd been working with a competent crew. The whole concept of crime was interesting: the strong taking from the weak, the smart from the stupid. A game, with interesting stakes . . . if only he hadn't been working with the Macks.

At twenty minutes after five o'clock, a black Audi convertible rolled up the ramp, headlights bouncing when its tires bumped over expansion joints. The car swooped into a reserved parking place in the physicians' area. Five seconds later, a short blond woman got out and started toward the exit door opposite Barakat.

Had to be her—the same woman he'd seen in the elevator. He let the door close: he couldn't allow her to see him again. Even being in

44

the same part of the building, where she might see him by accident, could trip off a memory.

He waited, nervous, stressed, sweating in the freezing cold, and when she'd gone through the door, went after her. And as he went, the thought crossed his mind: fix it now. Take her. She was a small woman in a deserted building, he could break her neck, who'd know what happened?

Just a thought, but it stayed with him. He might catch her at the elevators . . . but when he got there, she was gone. A little feather of disappointment trickled across his heart, his gut. He could have done it.

So now, the question remained. Who was she, and where was she going?

She was early for most docs. They wouldn't normally arrive until sometime after six. On the other hand, the Frenchman's surgical team was supposed to start separating the twins . . .

He went that way.

THIRTY PEOPLE milled in the hallway outside the special operating theater. Like most of the other docs, he'd found an excuse to look the place over—the special double operating table, the intricate anesthesia setup, the newly painted, sign-posted floor, an attempt to better choreograph the movements of the massive operating team, to keep the sterile and the non-steriles separate, even as they walked among each other.

He saw the blond woman, still in her long winter coat, talking to Gabriel Maret, the Frenchman. Maret was listening closely. She had to be somebody important.

Barakat was an emergency room doc, not on the team, or anything close to it, and all the team members knew each other, so he couldn't risk joining the crowd. What he could do, though, was climb into the small observation theater above the OR. If you wanted a seat, all you had to do was get there early. One of the team members would be narrating the surgical procedures for the observers. The woman, if she were central to the work, would be introduced.

LUCY AND LARRY RAYNES were with the children, who were still awake, but about to be moved to the operating theater. Sara saw

Weather and her eyes misted up. She was still a baby, but she recognized the woman who'd caused her pain in the past. She began to cry, softly, and then Ellen started, not yet knowing why.

Lucy Raines bent over them, comforting them. Larry flapped his hands around, helplessly, and said to Weather, "They're about to give them something."

Weather nodded: "We're not the only ones who feel the stress. They're babies, but they know something is happening."

Ellen pushed against the sides of the hospital bed, and that torqued Sara, who stopped crying and thrashed with her hands. The babies could hear each other talking, but had never seen each other.

Larry said, "We just talked to Gabriel, he said everything was going smoothly."

"Yesterday was like a freak accident," Weather said. "Everything now is just like it was yesterday—maybe better. Maybe some of the nervousness got burned off."

"I felt terrible about that guy," Lucy said.

"So do I." Weather bent forward and kissed Sara on the forehead. "It's hard, baby," she said.

AN HOUR LATER, the twins were rolled into the OR, sedated, but not yet fully anesthetized. As the two anesthesiologists worked to position them, to rig them with the drip lines and to take a final look at the blood chemistry, to check their monitors, Maret wandered over to Weather and said, "It's time. No problems with the pharmacy this morning."

Weather nodded and followed him into the scrub room. A few seconds later, Hanson, the bone-cutter, followed them in, with his resident; the surgical assistant stood waiting behind Weather. They scrubbed silently, until Maret said, "That first day of practice, we started with Vivaldi. If no one objects . . ."

"Perfect," Weather said. She'd always had music in her ORs. "Start with 'Primavera.'"

"Your choice," Maret said, smiling at her. "You're okay?"

"Anxious to get going," she said. Her part, her first part, would be routine, nothing more than she did every day: cutting down to bone, cauterizing the bleeders, rolling back the scalp. Then, she'd get out of the way until the bone-cutter was done.

An anesthesiologist stuck his head in: "We're set. You want to say go?"

Maret looked at the team members in the scrub room, pursed his lips, smiled, nodded and said, "Go."

THE OBSERVATION THEATER was packed: team members had the first choice of seats, but after that, it was first-come first-seated, as long as you had the right ID. Barakat looked around: the watchers weren't just residents, but included a lot of senior docs on their own time. He was at the back, in the highest row of seats.

Down below, three nurses and two anesthesiologists clustered around the two small bodies joined at the skull; so close to perfection, and yet so far. Each was an attractive child—if there'd been another inch of separation, they'd have been just fine. Now they lay on the special table, brilliantly lit, cradled in plastic, asleep, their eyes covered and taped, the bottoms of their faces isolated in breathing masks.

The scrub room doors opened in, and a small woman led a first group into the OR. A man sitting in the first row of the observation theater said into a microphone, "Doctors Gabriel Maret, Weather Karkinnen, Richard Hanson. Dr. Karkinnen will begin . . ."

She was masked, hatted, robed, gloved and slippered, wearing an operating shield over her eyes; but she was the woman from the elevator and the Audi, Barakat thought. Right size, right shape. Now that he knew her name, he could Google her, just to be sure.

The narrator said, "For those who just got here, the first procedure will be to open the scalp at the point of conjoin, to remove the first expander, and to prepare the bed for the initial craniotomy."

The surgical lights were miked. Barakat could hear Karkinnen talking with her surgical tech as they prepared the tools on a tray at her left hand. Karkinnen bent over the babies, with a surgical pen, her head blocking Barakat's view of what she was doing. Then Karkinnen straightened and asked an anesthesiologist, "Where are we?" and the anesthesiologist took a few seconds and then said, "We're good. Sara's heart looks good."

Karkinnen: "Dr. Maret?"

Maret looked around and said, "Everybody . . . may God bless us all, especially the little children. Weather, go ahead."

With Vivaldi playing quietly in the background, Weather took the scalpel from the surgical tech, leaned over the skulls of the two babies. She'd used a surgical pen to indicate the path of the incision, and now drew the scalpel along it, the black line turning scarlet behind the blade.

ALL SKIN has its own toughness and flexibility, and from post-puberty to old age, there was so much variation that you never knew quite what you'd get when you made the first cut. Sometimes it was saddle leather, sometimes tissue paper. Older people often had papery skin, and so did the young, though it was different.

Cutting into the twins was like cutting into a piece of Brie; Weather had noted that in earlier operations and no longer really paid attention to it. There was almost no separation between scalp and bone. She cut the first jigsaw pattern, got one little arterial bleeder, burned it, then slowly peeled the skin away from the incision. The room was suffused with the scent of burning blood, not unlike the smell of burning hair.

Her first part had taken twenty minutes.

She hadn't done much, but at the same time, she thought, everything: they were under way. They could still turn back, but the bonecutter was right there, with his custom surgical jigs. Once they were in, turning back would be more complicated.

"I'm out," she said.

"Looks good," Maret said. "Perfect."

SEPARATING THE TWINS was not a matter of simply cutting bone and then snapping them apart. The venous drainage inside the skull had to be carefully managed, or blood pressure would build in the babies' skulls and damage their brains, and likely kill them.

The brains themselves were covered by a sheath of thin, tough tissue called the dura mater, which acted like a seal between the brain and the skull, and channeled the blood away from the brain. The dura mater, in most places, was thick enough that it could actually be split apart—like pulling a self-stick stamp off its backing—leaving each brain covered with a sheet of dura mater.

However, the imaging had shown that there were a number of veins that penetrated the dura mater, and rather than returning to the original twin, instead drained to the other twin. Those veins had to be tied off, and, in the case of several of the larger ones, redirected and spliced into other veins that drained to the appropriate twin.

To get inside, Hanson would fit a custom-made jig, or template, around the join between the twins' skulls. During the course of the operation, he would cut out a ring of bone, with what amounted to a tiny electric jigsaw. When the twins were taken apart, the holes in their skulls should be precisely the shape and thickness of pre-made skull pieces made of a plastic composite material.

Before that could happen, Hanson had to take out the bone, and then Maret, a neurosurgeon, and a couple of associates, would probe the physiology right at the brain, to make sure there was no entanglement of the brains themselves. Imaging said that there was not; if there had been, the shorter operation would have been impossible. When they'd confirmed the imaging, and that the dura mater stretched across the defect, they would begin separating the tissue, and splicing veins.

Weather's surgical tech started giggling at the scrub sink and said, "I was so scared. I did three little things and I was completely freaked out."

"I was a little nervous myself," Weather said. "Are you okay?"

"Oh, sure. It's just that everybody's up there watching. Everybody important. What if I dropped a scalpel on your foot?"

"I'd have to have you killed," Weather said.

The nurse started giggling again, and it was infectious, and Weather started, though it was unsurgeon-like. They'd just stopped when Weather said, "Couldn't you see it? Sticking out from between a couple toes? What would I say? Ouch?"

They started again.

WEATHER STRIPPED out of the sterile gown, head-covering, shoe covers, and surgical gloves, and tossed it all into disposal baskets and walked down to the lounge where the twins' parents were waiting.

They both stood up when Weather walked in, and she smiled and said, "It's going. I made the first incisions, and Hanson is getting started on the entry."

"How are the girls?" Larry asked.

"They're strong. Sara's heart is fine. This next part will take a while . . ." The parents nodded. They had a time line, knew about what each procedure would take. The bone-cutter would be working for a couple of hours, followed by the neurosurgeons.

After talking with the parents, Weather left them in the lounge and walked down to the cafeteria for a cup of coffee and a roll. Several members of the team were there, called or waved to her when she came in; she went to the line for a roll, then joined them.

Barakat had come in well behind her, watching, got a slice of pizza and a cup of coffee, careful to keep his back turned when she might look his way. When she was seated, he carried his tray to a table behind her, his back to her. A few minutes later, after some chatter about the twins, she was telling her friends about doing an artist sketch for the police, of the man coming out of the parking structure.

Barakat finished his coffee, checked the time. Too early for a civilized call, but the Macks weren't civilized, and Lyle Mack said to call as soon as he knew who she was.

WEATHER WAS IN the gallery when the operation started going sour. The first indication was simple enough, when the anesthesiologist said, "We're looking at a little thing with Sara's heart, here."

Maret nodded to an associate and backed away from the table. "What can we do?"

He and the anesthesiologist began talking about it, and the cardiologist came in and looked at all the numbers on all the machines. He wasn't sterile, so he stayed back, watching.

The anomalies continued to develop. The cardiologist ordered medication to steady the rhythm of Sara's heart, but the medication began to slow Ellen's, and finally the cardiologist told Maret that they needed to move the children to intensive care, where they could be taken off the anesthesia and treated for the heart problems.

"You see no alternative?" Maret asked.

"We could go a little longer, but then, if Sara really gets into trouble, it could take longer to bring them both back . . . we could wind up with an emergency." An emergency most likely meant Sara would die.

"Damnit." But Maret acceded, looked up: "Weather, we'll need to close up here."

"ANOTHER FIVE THOUSAND, and all you have to do is make the one ride," Lyle Mack told Cappy. They were back in Cherries, Cappy an hour out of bed. "We've got a bike spotted for you, a Yamaha sports bike. Almost new, perfect condition. Owner keeps a spare key in a magnet box shoved up under a flap behind the seat. Joe will drop you at his garage. The guy doesn't come home until eight o'clock. You ditch the bike after the ride, Joe'll pick you up. Clean, quick."

Cappy's eyes slid over to Joe Mack. "Saw your picture on TV. Like you used to look."

"I saw it; it don't look like me. Like I used to look," Joe Mack said.

"Not exactly, but it had all the right parts in the right place," Cappy said.

"Once this woman's gone, it's no problem. Can't identify somebody on the basis of a drawing-thing if the witness is gone," Lyle Mack said.

"The thing that bothers me, a little bit, is the spotter," Cappy said. "You know . . . that's another guy. I thought we were cutting down on the number of guys who know."

"Well . . . maybe we can talk about that sometime," Lyle Mack said.

Cappy smiled his minimalist smile, a slight widening of his narrow lips. "I was thinking about it at work. This could be like a job. I could be, like, you know, one of those *eliminators*."

"You could be," Lyle Mack said. He scratched his head, and like any small-business man, got thinking about the bureaucracy of it. Nobody ever thought about the bureaucracy, but that's most of what any small business was. He said, "I don't know how you'd set it up. You know, find guys who need the work. If any one of them folded up, you'd go down with them. But we ought to think about it. If there was some way to do it, you could sure make some bucks."

"I wish . . ." Joe began. Then, "I'm not sure we oughta be doing this. This is like, remember that Walt Disney cartoon with the tar baby? It's like we're getting more stuck in the tar baby."

Lyle Mack took a quick circular pace, his jowls shaking, and he said, "Joe . . . She saw ya, goddamnit. We gotta do something about it, while we got the chance." He looked at Cappy: "By the way, I got a question. That goddamn shotgun, even cut down . . . how you gonna manage that?"

"Not using the shotgun," Cappy said. He took a revolver from his pocket, wrapped in Saran Wrap, turned it sideways so the Macks could look at it. "Got it in Berdoo. Perfect bike gun. Can't touch it, because I wiped it."

"What the hell *is* that?" Lyle Mack asked.

"It's the Judge," Cappy said. "Three .410 shells with Four-O buck-shot, that's five pellets the size of a .38 in each shell. And two .45 Colts in the other two chambers. Gotta get close, but I won't do it unless the barrel's touching her window glass."

"Dude," Lyle said, "you got the *equipment*."

As HE AND JOE went over to get the bike, Cappy thought about killing people for money. Well, what was the difference between that and kill-ing a guy for his bike? Maybe that was when he crossed some kind of line—the first guy he killed, he did almost out of self-protection. Later on, he did it because it was interesting.

He'd seen all kinds of killing on TV, ever since he could remember—crime movies and war movies, cop shows, people being killed every way you could think of. Machine-gunned and executed and shot with long-range rifles and stabbed and strangled and poisoned and electro-cuted and beat with baseball bats, *everything*. Real airplanes flying into real buildings, guys blowing themselves up on the news.

You'd always get some news chick telling you how bad you should feel about it, but Cappy didn't feel much of anything, except interested, and neither, he thought, did the news chick. Or anybody else. It was entertain-ment, was what it was, and in real life, it was kind of *more* entertaining.

Like riding a bike too fast: you didn't know exactly what was going to happen. It was almost like he was killing people in a movie, except more. Like you see Bruce Willis cap somebody, that's how much he felt it, times ten. Times a hundred. He liked rerunning it, when he'd pulled one off, but he liked rerunning Bruce Willis movies, too.

The thing is, it was intense.

But, Lyle Mack was right. How would you get in touch with the people who needed the work done? Maybe you could find some big Mafia guy and contract out for it. Have to think about it.

"HERE WE GO," Joe Mack said, as they turned down an alley. He pointed out the garage: "The white one with the red doors. I'll drop you off right in front of it. Nobody can see us, unless they're right in the alley. Got to get in and out quick, though."

Cappy nodded. "I can do that." He reached under the seat and pulled out a Penney's bag with the handgun in it. "See ya."

He seemed really calm, Joe Mack thought, as he dropped him. Joe Mack could hardly hold on to the steering wheel, and every time he closed his eyes, he saw the smiling faces of Mikey and Shooter, followed by a fade-in of the dead faces. It was creeping him out. He planned to drink a lot that night, so he'd get some sleep.

In fact . . .

He fished a pint of bourbon out from under the seat and took a pull. Looked both ways for cops, and took another one.

AT THREE O'CLOCK in the afternoon, the sun was already dipping toward the horizon. Weather came out of the parking garage, looked both ways, took a left, down toward the I-94 entrance. She'd take it only a mile or so to the Cretin Avenue exit, then head south.

She was tired. She needed to get home and take a nap. The surgery she'd done hadn't been difficult, but the stress around the operation was taking a toll that she really hadn't expected. It wasn't the work, it was the talk afterward. The fact was, they could go in and dissect the dura mater from Sara's brain in a half hour or so; they could finish the bone cutting, take out the dura mater, leave it with Ellen, close up, and Ellen would be good.

Sara would die. In medical papers, they would say that a patient was sacrificed so the other could live. Sacrificed. Nice. The idea of making that decision made her skin crawl. Separating the dura mater, so that each baby could drain blood back into the venous system, was the time-eater. The neurosurgeons were advancing toward each other a millimeter at a time, sorting veins, saving everything they could.

But if something went too wrong . . .

JUST NEEDED A NAP, she thought. The surgery could resume in the middle of the night, if Sara's heart function improved. Or, if it worsened enough that they were compelled to let Sara go, and attempt to rescue Ellen.

As she came out of the parking garage, she glanced in her rearview mirror and saw the biker break away from the curb a block behind her; paid no attention, saw the stoplight ahead turn yellow, and floored the accelerator, clipping the red light as she went through. She kept the speed up down the block to the next light, and caught an odd motion in her rearview mirror; the biker had flat run the red light, and had almost been taken out by a car coming through.

Asshole.

She made a right and was on the long sweeping entry ramp, accelerating as she went. She liked to drive fast, and felt, as a surgeon, with a surgeon's reflexes, that she was entitled to; and she'd had that race training, although there had been some knocks and bumps over the years . . . unforeseen circumstances, she claimed in her own defense . . . like when she drove through the garage door. She smiled, thinking of Lucas as he came running out of the house. He'd wanted to kill her, but had pretended to be totally calm about it, and understanding.

COMING DOWN THE RAMP, she saw the biker again, leaning into the turn, coming fast. Since she'd be getting off quickly, she stayed in the right lane.

She merged with traffic, pushed her speed to sixty-five, and in her left mirror saw the single headlight weave between cars in the right and the right-center lanes, two hundred yards back but coming very fast now. Too dark to see much.

As the bike came up beside her, she glanced back, saw the face shield, black leathers. He was on her back quarter-panel when he took his left hand off the clutch and pulled something from beneath his jacket.

She could feel him focused on her window, still coming, saw him lift his hand, in a peculiar way, and of the thousand things that might have occurred to her, only one rang true: she was a cop's wife and she thought, *Gun.*

She flicked the car left, into his lane, and at the same instant she hit the brakes on the Audi, hard, and the bike flicked left and surged past her, the rider, snapping his head around, dropped whatever it was, tried to grab it with his clutch hand, lost it, and she still thought, *Gun,* and she yanked the wheel left and fell in behind him, and with a surge of road rage, floored the accelerator again.

She hadn't had time to process it, but instinct told her that this was one of the guys from the robbery, one of the guys who killed Don, and now they were after her: and she was not the turn-the-other-cheek sort.

Though the Audi was fast, it was no match for the bike. The rider glanced back, saw her coming and took off, the front wheel lifting off the ground. She got the impression of a small man. The people from the hospital were supposed to be fairly big . . . but there was no doubt about what he'd tried to do, not in her mind.

She stayed with him for a few hundred yards, but he sliced up the white line between two cars and was pulling away when the Cretin Avenue exit came up.

She swerved onto it, up to the top, turned right, stopped beside the golf course, unsnapped her seat belt and turned to watch traffic, as she pulled out her cell phone and punched in 911.

"Is this an emergency?"

"My name is Weather Karkinnen, and I'm a surgeon. A man just tried to kill me. He's on I-94 going east toward Snelling on a motor-cycle. He's going really fast . . ."

LUCAS SHOWED up fifteen minutes later.

Weather had driven around the golf course to the clubhouse. She parked, went inside, told the restaurant manager that she was waiting for police. The first cops arrived two minutes later; in the interval, she'd called Lucas.

"I'm pretty sure," she told him on the phone. "Whatever it was, the gun, if it was a gun, he dropped it, and then he took off."

"You know where he dropped it?" Lucas asked.

"Just after 280. Right there . . . maybe three or four hundred yards east," she said.

"Okay. Any chance he saw where you went? That you're at the club?"

"No. I called nine-one-one, and then came right here to wait for the police," she said.

"Stay there, stay inside. I'm coming."

WHEN THE FIRST St. Paul cops showed up, they were skeptical. When she explained that she might have seen the face of one of the robbers who took down the hospital, they became interested. When she mentioned that Lucas was her husband, and that she had some familiarity with assholes, and this particular asshole may have dropped a gun on the highway, they got busy.

Lucas arrived in the truck, shouldered past the cops and asked, "You okay?"

"I'm fine." She was fine, but she could see that he was not. He was white-faced with anger.

He turned to one of the cops and said, "Did you get somebody to look for a weapon?"

The cop nodded. "We're rolling on it. We've got a highway patrol guy to block off 94, and two of our cars down there with him. It's gonna be a mess, though. Rush hour."

Back to Weather: "The guy you saw yesterday. He's got to be the robber. What kind of a bike was it? Anything you recognize?"

"It wasn't a Harley, that's all I know," she said. "The guy's legs were behind him, so he was leaning over the handlebars. When he took off, the front wheel came right off the ground. He was wearing a black helmet. But he was kind of a small guy, I think. That's the impression I got."

"Crotch rocket," one of the cops said. "The highway patrol guy had a stop just east of downtown, and when Miz Davenport called, they passed the word to him and he was looking for the bike. Nothing came through, so the guy got off somewhere."

"Not many bikes at this time of year," the other cop said. "Too much snow and ice."

"Clear right now," Lucas said.

"On I-94 it is, but you wouldn't want to cut any corners on the back streets," the cop said.

Lucas nodded: the cop was right. "Had any reports of stolen bikes?"

"We'll check."

LUCAS TURNED BACK to Weather. "We've got to lose you until we find the guy. We could put you in the University Radisson. . . ."

Weather shook her head. "Nope, nope. I need my sleep, and I need to be at home, with the kids, and I need to get to the hospital at the right time every day. And maybe in the middle of the night."

"How're the twins?"

"Sara's heart is a problem," Weather said. "They're working on it now, but the stuff they need to give her causes problems for Ellen. So—maybe we'll be good tomorrow."

"Tired?"

She shrugged. "Not terribly—but it could get bad if this goes on for a few days. We knew it might, but hoped it wouldn't. That's why I need to be at home."

Lucas said, "What would you think about a house guest?"

She shook her head. "Lucas, I don't want Shrake or Jenkins bumbling around the house. I mean, those guys could fall on the piano and break it."

"I called Virgil. He said he would be here in an hour."

She nodded. "Virgil would be okay. Besides, it sounds like it's settled."

"Yes, it is," he said.

She recognized the tone. They both had tempers, and they had learned to recognize when the other was putting his/her foot down, when things had moved beyond negotiation. She nodded: Virgil it was.

LUCAS CALLED the cops' supervisor, an old friend named Larouse, who said he'd call with any news. "You want a car outside your house?"

"You don't have to park it, but if you'd cruise it pretty steadily, that'd be good."

"We'll check every movin' dog," Larouse said. Then, "Hang on a minute." There was a moment of silence, then Larouse was back. "We've got a gun. A Taurus revolver. Listen to this: it's loaded with three .410 shells and two Colt .45s. Got run over about two hundred times, but the shells are still inside. Maybe we'll get something off them."

They talked for a couple of more minutes, then Lucas signed off: "Get back to me, man."

Weather had been listening and she asked, "Good news?"

"Well, you weren't hallucinating—they found the gun."

"I knew it."

"It's all beat up. Got run over a lot. They're running it back to the lab. They'll check the shells for prints and then ship them over to us and see if we can pull any DNA."

"Doesn't sound too hopeful."

"Hey: if there're prints on the shells, Lodmell will pull them up. And I believe the guy'll be on record. You don't send somebody out with a man-killer and a crotch rocket if he's a virgin."

"A man-killer?"

He looked at her: "You got lucky."

"Not just lucky," she said. The two cops had gone off a way, and she told him about flicking the Audi into the biker's lane, causing him to fumble the gun, and about going after him with the car.

"Crazy woman," he said, and wrapped an arm around her head, in a headlock, and gave her a noogie.

But he was scared.

THE NOOGIE made her laugh, at least a bit, and then Lucas went off to talk to the cops again, leaving her, and suddenly, for the first time in years, she flashed back to a winter day with a motorcycle crazy named Dick LaChaise, at Hennepin General Hospital in Minneapolis.

LaChaise and two killer friends had come to town looking for Lucas, because Lucas had led a major crimes squad that had killed LaChaise's wife and sister during a bank robbery. LaChaise had taken Weather

58

hostage at the hospital. Lucas had come to negotiate in person, to talk LaChaise out of killing her.

At least, that's what Weather had thought, and LaChaise, too.

But as soon as LaChaise moved the muzzle of his pistol an inch from Weather's skull, a concealed sniper had shot him in the head. Weather went down, covered with blood, brains, and fragments of skull.

She hadn't been able to stay with Lucas after that; it had taken years to get back. But they *had* gotten back, and now here was another motorcycle hoodlum coming for her on the highway, and suddenly she was there again, in the hallway, and LaChaise's head was exploding behind her . . .

"No." She shook it off.

She might flash back again, she thought, but she wasn't having it, this time. She'd worked all through it. LaChaise was dead, and this had nothing to do with Dick LaChaise or Lucas Davenport.

Lucas touched her on the shoulder. "You okay?"

"Yeah. Yeah."

"You look like you've seen a ghost."

"I suddenly got scared," she said. "Before, I was too busy to be scared."

CAPPY SWORE and tried to grab the gun, fumbled it, then heard the scream of an angry engine, looked back, and realized that the bitch was coming after him. He hit the accelerator, felt the rush as the front wheel lifted free, cut down a center line and was gone. He watched her lights and saw her swerve left, and she was gone up the off-ramp. He took the next one, quick right at the top, then a left, down through the dark streets, careful about the leftover snow, and the black ice at intersections. Three blocks from Central High School, four minutes after he made the attempt on Weather, he stuck the bike between a couple of parked cars, walked a crooked route down to Central, watching his trail, to where Joe Mack was waiting in his van.

"Missed," Cappy said, climbing into the passenger seat. "Bitch saw me and came after me with her car. Goddamn near ran me down. I lost the fuckin' gun."

Mack stretched his neck, looking out of the van in all directions: "You're clean? Nobody's behind you?"

"Nah, that part went fine. Dropped the bike, walked away, nobody saw my face with the scarf and all."

"The gun . . ."

"Gun's clean, too. Hated to lose it, though. I needed that gun. I never fired a shot. I dunno."

Two minutes and they were back on I-94, headed east. Joe Mack said, "I'm thinking about going over to Eddie's. You know? Got some guys who'll say I've been around for a couple weeks, had the haircut all the time."

"Yeah?" Cappy wasn't too interested. He was thinking about what had happened; the lack of respect. And he'd noticed the alcohol that Joe Mack was breathing all over him: that didn't seem right. Your pickup guy shouldn't be getting drunk.

He said, "That bitch tried to run me down. I was coming beside her, running good, and all of a sudden, she like, jukes into my lane. I god-damn near ran up her tailpipe. I got only one hand on the handbar, and I freak and I drop the gun, but I get back on top of the bike and the next thing I know, she's about six feet behind me and coming for me. What kind of bitch is that?"

"The thing about Eddie's is, you know, you ever been in fuckin' Green Bay?"

"I oughta kill the bitch for free, after that," Cappy said.

"What?"

Cappy looked at him and realized that Joe was dead drunk. "Pull over," he said. "Let me drive."

CAPPY DROVE back to his room, in an old house in St. Paul Park, and Joe said he was fine, took the keys and headed back to Cherries. Lyle was waiting in the back.

"No go," Joe Mack said. He told Cappy's story, then shook his head. "I think we made a mistake bringing Cappy into it. If this chick talks to the cops, they'll be looking at bikers. Before, they weren't looking at bikers. If they start showing her pictures, I might turn up."

Lyle Mack said, "I didn't think of that."

Joe Mack said, "You know, maybe we're not smart enough to pull this off. Maybe we oughta run on down to Mexico for a couple years."

Lyle Mack looked around at the bar: "But what'd we do with Cherries?"

Joe Mack said, "I don't know. Once, you said, we maybe should sell it to Honey Bee. On paper. You know, to keep our names out of it. Maybe—"

"Aw, man. We gotta do better'n that." Lyle cocked an ear to the front room, where "Long Haired Country Boy" was booming out of the jukebox. "How could we leave this?"

A SNOW FLURRY had just crossed the Mississippi when Virgil showed up. He got out of his truck and a squad car pulled to the side of the street and two cops rolled out, and Lucas stuck his head through the front door and yelled, "He's good."

The cops waved and moved on. Virgil, watching them go, said, "Heavy."

Virgil was a tall man, nearly as tall as Lucas, but wiry, with shoulder-length blond hair like a surfer's. Lucas, on the other hand, was heavy through the shoulders, and dark.

Virgil lifted a duffel bag out of the truck and came up, and Lucas stepped out on the porch. "They sent a guy after her on a Yamaha sport bike," he said. "St. Paul found it ditched off Snelling Avenue. He picked her up right at the hospital, so they must have a spotter inside. He had a handgun that fires .410 shells. The idea was to pull up beside her and put the barrel one inch from the window and blow her out the other side of the car."

"Who's the owner of the bike?"

"A guy . . . Dick Morris. St. Paul checked him out. He says the bike was stolen from his garage while he was at work, and the St. Paul guys believe him. He's pretty straight, a business guy—he seemed pretty scared when he found out what was going on. He rides with a couple clubs, lots of people knew about his bike."

"The shooter who came after Weather would have to be a good rider," Virgil said. "Good rider with a good bike gun, who knew what he was doing."

Lucas said, "I think so."

"You had some trouble with the Seed," Virgil said. "Weather was involved."

"A long time ago," Lucas said. "And this gun came out of California."

"Still."

Lucas thought about it, and then said, "It's the robbery. I doubt they even know who she is. Still, could be a Seed guy with the gun. They've got some kind of deal with the Angels, they've been coming across the river."

The Bad Seed was a Wisconsin club, originally out of Green Bay and Milwaukee; the Angels dominated the Twin Cities.

"All those guys are getting old, they're merging," Virgil said. "I've seen Banditos over on the West Side, riding with their colors."

"Hmm. Don't think we need to bother Weather about it," Lucas said. And, "You got your gun?"

Virgil smiled. "I knew you were going to ask." He patted his side. "Right here, boss. And I got a twelve-gauge in the truck. I'll get it later."

As they went back inside, Lucas asked, "You know what she did? After she saw the gun?"

"What?"

"Tried to run his ass down," Lucas said.

"Semper fi," Virgil said.

INSIDE, LUCAS introduced Virgil to Marcy Sherrill, who'd stopped to talk about the attempt on Weather. "She's a deputy chief over in Minneapolis," Lucas said.

They shook hands and Virgil said, "Yeah, we met a few years ago—the Yellow Peril thing," Virgil said. "Don't know if you remember. I was working with Jim Locke, before he retired."

"I remember," Marcy said. "Jeez, that must have been six or eight years ago."

Lucas said, "I don't remember—"

"I think that was after you got kicked off the force, and before you came back," Marcy said. "Some asshole . . ."

"Louis Barney," Virgil said.

"Yeah—Louis X. Barney . . . He stole a bunch of five-gallon cans of methanol from some race-car guy's garage. He told the judge that he just thought it was alcohol. And he figures what the heck, the winos wouldn't know any different. He blended it with pineapple juice and started selling it on the street. We had four people go blind, and two people die, before we caught him."

Virgil: "Wonder if he's out yet?"

"He got twenty years . . . but I think that was under the old two-thirds rule . . . so not yet, but he's getting close."

"Pretty stiff, for a semi-accident," Lucas said.

"The judge didn't believe him," Marcy said. "Barney was a drunk himself, but *he* didn't drink any of it."

WEATHER CAME IN, carrying a coffeepot, followed by the housekeeper with a tray full of cookies, and Weather kissed Virgil on the forehead and messed up his hair, and said, "Your nose looks fine." And to Marcy: "The last time I saw him, he had this big aluminum thing on his nose. From a fight."

"I read about it," Marcy said. "The buried car thing."

"How you doin'?" Virgil asked Weather.

"I've been thinking about it, and thinking about it, and thinking about it," Weather said. "You know what? I *can't* think about it. I've got too much to think about already, with this operation. So I'm not going to pay any attention to it. I'm going to let you guys take care of me."

"Good plan," Marcy said. "If they come again, we'll get one. Could break it for us."

"They spotted her in the hospital. Somebody in the hospital set it up," Lucas said.

"I think so," Marcy said. "We're putting hammerlocks on everybody. We're pushing it—we've pulled people off about everything else."

"So there's no reason for me to jump in," Lucas said.

She smiled at him. "Nope. No reason at all."

As they were shutting down for the night, with the kids asleep and the housekeeper in her apartment, Weather already gone back to the bedroom, Virgil was jacking triple-ought shells into his twelve-gauge and he said to Lucas, "There *is* a good reason for you to jump in. You're the second smartest cop in Minnesota. They can always use more of that."

"I'm always a little sensitive around Marcy," Lucas said. "She used to work for me, you know."

Virgil snorted. He knew about their history.

"Hey . . ."

"The point remains," Virgil said. "Never hurts to have a little more IQ on the job. Fortunately, you got me."

IN THE WINTER, Weather slept in a variety of ankle-length flannel night-gowns, and on really cold nights, she wore socks, even though it was no colder in the bedroom on really cold nights than on halfway-cold nights. When Lucas got back to the bedroom, she was wearing a man's wife-beater undershirt that clung to her body and was low-cut enough to show the rim of her nipples at the top; and white bikini underpants.

Lucas said, "Oh, God. I'm so tired, too."

"Poor baby," she said. "Let me help you with your shirt."

Another thing that Lucas liked about Weather, right from the start, was that when it came to sex, she knew what she wanted, and how to get it, and one thing she *didn't* want was excuses. So they rolled across the bed, talking and sometimes laughing, stroking this, pulling on that, and Weather wound up on top, straddling his hips, and said, like she might say to an overanxious horse, "Steady, boy," and "Whoa, slow down," and "Easy, there," and she rode up and down and up and down, chewing her lower lip, still wearing the shirt, but now rolled up above her breasts, moving like she wanted to, until she got to the orgasm part, and then she made a sound like a tiny steam whistle from a miniature paddle-wheel boat, urgently signaling a need for more firewood, Ooo, Ooo, Ooo, Ooooooo . . .

Then, after a few moments of lying with her head on his chest, with some aftershocks, she said, "Okay, go ahead. Pay no attention if I look at my watch."

"You're in no shape to read a watch, even if you were wearing one," Lucas said, rolling her onto her back. "Brace yourself, Bridget . . ."

When they were done, she asked, "You think it's a bad sign when you're funny when you're having sex?"

"Depends on what you're laughing at," Lucas said. "That wouldn't apply to myself, of course."

"I'm serious."

"I'm too screwed to be serious. So, why don't you shut up? Or, tell me something."

"What?" In the dark, turning toward him.

"Are you really not scared?"

"Background scared. But I'm not going to dodge. I'm going to do what I do."

"Not gonna fight it, not going to play us."

"No. I'm going to think about the twins, I'm going to take care of them, I'm going to put everything else out of my mind, and I'm going to let you guys take care of me."

CAPPY WAS asleep when he heard the knock on the door. He came awake in a rush, startled—nobody ever knocked for him, or even knew where he lived. It didn't sound like a cop's knock—or what he thought a cop's knock would sound like. He looked at the clock: after eleven.

Another knock.

He rolled out of bed, went to the door, left the chain on, opened it, and peeked out. Joe Mack was standing in the hallway with a sack.

"Got a sack for you," he said. More bourbon breath.

Cappy looked at him for a moment, then closed the door far enough to take off the chain, opened the door and backed up. Joe Mack stepped inside, looked like he might say something like, "Nice place," but the place was such a shithole that the comment would have been absurd, so he swallowed it and instead said, "Here."

He thrust the bag at Cappy, and Cappy took it, felt the weight, knew what it was.

He took it out: a Taurus Judge.

"Where'd you get it?"

"Up here, they got anything you want in the way of guns, if you look around. This was stole from over in Minneapolis. So it's hot, but if the cops chase you down, you say you bought it from a guy on Hennepin Avenue, you know, for self-defense, because you live in such a dangerous place."

Cappy nodded, asked, "You want a smoke?"

Joe said, "Nah, I gotta run. Got stuff to do." He left, leaving behind a cloud of alcohol breath.

The boy had it bad, Cappy thought. He got back in bed with the gun, happy, turned the cylinder, popping out the shells, dropped them on the floor, slipped the gun under his pillow. He lay awake for a few minutes, listening to the *zzzzz* of the electric clock, then drifted away, the hard lump under his head, relaxed and comfortable as a woolly sheep.

4

JOE MACK LEANED close to Lyle Mack and muttered, "Will you look at the tits on the—"

"Shut up, for Christ's sake. And stop fuckin' staring at them," Lyle Mack said. "You'll freak them out."

"They're freakin' *me* out." And Joe Mack couldn't stop staring.

Joe and Lyle Mack were out of their comfort zone, wandering through the University of Minnesota's student union, baby blondes all over the place, sweaters and wool slacks, rosy cheeks. They were . . . dewy, with tits. But it wasn't just that: it was that there were so *many* of them.

Joe Mack had never done dewy. Ever. Or, as far as he could remember, ever been on a college campus.

LIKE TROLLS in a sorority house, the Macks traipsed through the first floor and down to the basement food court, where they found Barakat sitting in a corner, nursing a cappuccino. He was wearing a white dress shirt, buttoned to the top, and a scowl, and he shivered occasionally, though his forehead was shiny with sweat. An Arctic-level parka was sitting on a bench seat beside him.

Lyle Mack pulled up a chair and leaned forward and said, "This wasn't necessary."

Barakat leaned toward him and pitched his voice down, and snarled at them. "I'm going to tell you a one-minute story. My father, my family, is Christian, in Lebanon. This means nothing to you Americans, but to us, it meant that we had to struggle in a sea of Palestinians and Syrians who hate us. We had to defend ourselves."

Lyle Mack said, "Yeah, yeah . . ."

Barakat wagged a finger at him. "Listen: I know about your silly fucking motorcycle gangs. Your Seed. Sometimes you kill one person, or two persons, these Outlaws. When I was five years old, in Lebanon, there was fighting in Beirut. Our people took a company of Hezbollah, from the basement of a department store. They gave up, or we would have burned them to death with gasoline from a tank truck, so they gave up. Huh? You understand? They surrendered. They thought, a few days in a prison camp until a cease-fire. So we, the Christians, took them out three at a time, shot them in the heads, threw them in a hole. Sixteen men. I sat on my roof eating Armenian apricots and watched. My father, my uncles, my cousins. It was like directing traffic: stand over here, stand over there, bang-bang-bang. You know what I did? I ate the apricots and laughed.

"We are here in the United States now, and start businesses. This and that. Some hard businesses. I have called my cousins, and I have told them that I have some business trouble, and that if I disappear, or if I am killed, you will kill the brothers Joe Mack and Lyle Mack from Cherries Bar. You got that? They understand business trouble; and they will do it. I told them, be safe, do it any way you can, but if you can, make it hard for them. One of my uncles, Timor, claims he once got the entire skin off a Hezbollah fighter before the man died, using nothing but a straight razor as a skinning knife. I don't know if I believe he succeeded, but I believe he tried to do it."

They sat staring for a minute, then Barakat said, "I deeply hope you believe me, because it is true. Because you stupidly killed this man in the hospital, I think that you might try to eliminate me as a witness against you. Do not do it. I promise you, there are worse things than prison."

Lyle Mack's eyes were popping out. He said, "You're telling us that somebody else knows about the job? Maybe a whole bunch of people?"

"No, no. They don't know why they will kill you, only that they must," Barakat said, shaking a finger at them. "For the family."

"Ah, crap, Al, we weren't gonna hurt you," Lyle Mack said, leaning back in the booth, putting on his best Bible-salesman's smile. "I mean, you're in as deep as we are, so we don't have to worry about you talking. If the cops crack this, we'd all go inside for the rest of our lives."

"Yes. Well, I didn't take the chance." Barakat leaned forward again. "Now: I would not sell the merchandise here. In Minneapolis. The police will be looking for it everywhere, I am thinking."

"Let us worry about that," Lyle Mack said. "First of all, we've squirreled it away—"

"Squirreled? What is this?"

"We've hidden it. Really good. Second of all, we have clubs all over the country. We'll repackage the good stuff in a couple months, when the heat's died down. Move it along to three or four different places, tell them to take care when they push it out on the street. Nobody'll know where it came from. It's not a problem."

Barakat stared at them for a moment, then leaned back, his eyes dark, and asked, "Where's my payment?"

Lyle Mack tipped his head at Joe Mack, who glanced around, then produced what looked like a brown-bag lunch and pushed it across the table. Barakat hefted it and said, "That's no kilo."

"It's a half," Lyle Mack said. "We've got nothing so far, except some shit we're afraid to move. Soon as we move it, you'll get the other half."

"The deal was—"

"The deal was that we'd hit the place, clean it out, start selling it two days later and pay you off," Lyle Mack said. "But I don't have thirty K sitting on a shelf, and this whole fucked-up guy, the guy who died, this has changed everything. Don't worry: we want to keep you happy. But it'll be a while. Maybe a couple months. No longer."

"Two months," Barakat said. "All right, two months." He stuffed the bag in his parka pocket, then said, "Here is something else for you to think about. Sometimes, you get hurt, you motorcycle people. And you do not want to go to the hospital, because then the police will know. I am one very good emergency room specialist. I can help you—and your friends, people you recommend—and nobody has to know about it. Think about that. I am of more value alive."

"You're really worried," Lyle Mack said.

"Of course I'm worried," Barakat said. "You killed this man out of stupidity. You could kill me out of stupidity. Or because you think you're being smart. I don't want your mistakes to kill me."

"Don't know if I'd care to get operated on by a guy with a fuckin' orangutan on his back," Joe Mack said.

Barakat's eyes flicked to Lyle Mack, then back to Joe Mack. "Orangutan?"

"Really big monkey," Joe Mack said.

Barakat shook his head: "What? Monkey?"

"Forget it," Lyle Mack said. "It's an old American joke." He stood up, jerked a thumb at Joe Mack, who pushed away from the table and stood.

"See you around, Doc," Joe Mack said. "Try to . . . relax."

"Wait, wait," Barakat said. "What about the woman?"

"Just keep cool," Joe Mack said. "We're working on that."

"But what happened? I haven't heard anything," Barakat said.

"You did just fine. The deal wasn't quite right, and our man called it off," Lyle Mack lied. "We're thinking over some other possibilities. So stand by, and we'll get back to you."

"I don't want to have anything to do with it, anymore. You people . . ." He flicked a hand that said, *You people are flies.*

Lyle Mack jabbed a finger at him: "You might have to. She got a good look at Joe. If they pull his picture, she could bite us on the ass. We need her tracked; we'll get back to you on that."

"She's on the twin-separation team . . ."

"You said that. We don't give a fuck," Lyle Mack said.

"That means that she'll be here every day for the next few days. One of the twins is having heart problems. The operation is taking longer than they thought. So . . . you know where she'll be. Every morning she comes, at the same time. I can't help you much more than that."

"We'll get back to you," Lyle Mack repeated.

They sat staring at each other for a minute, then Joe Mack said, "You know, Al, if we don't get her, and she fingers me, and it's your fault . . .

well, we won't worry so much about your fuckin' family, then. I'd be looking at thirty years."

"Worse things than jail," Barakat repeated.

"Something for you to remember, too," Joe Mack said. "I got a chain saw in my garage. You hang me up, I'll cut you in half, the long way, balls first."

More staring, then Barakat said, "If you need some specific thing, call me. On my cell, all the time. But don't call me from your bar, or from your houses."

"We got clean cells," Lyle Mack said.

Barakat slid out of the booth. "And don't call me Al," he said. He walked away.

On the way out of the student union, Joe Mack asked Lyle Mack, "You believe that thing, about skinning the guy alive?"

"Hey, they're fuckin' Arabs or something," Lyle Mack said. "Who knows what they'd get up to?"

"You know, he's a harder guy than I thought," Joe Mack said. "I don't think he was kiddin' about all that."

Barakat walked the bundle of cocaine out to his car, locked himself in, checked the ramp, then unrolled the sack and took out the Ziploc bag inside. Half a kilo: it looked right. And pure, crystalline white. Gorgeous. The Macks had said that it would be straight, unstepped-on; he'd believe it when he tried it.

And he'd try it now. A terrible risk: anyone could come along. Somebody could be walking down the ramp, quietly, see him in the car . . . but he was going to do it anyway.

He took his briefcase off the passenger seat, opened it, took out a paperback book with a slick cover, closed the briefcase and put it on his lap. Looked around again. His hands were shaking as he shook a pile of coke onto the paperback. The pile was the size of the last joint on his little finger. He dipped his little finger into it and tasted it. Tasted fine.

Still a little worried. Coke was sometimes cut with strychnine to boost the rush—that's what he'd heard, anyway. What if they'd added a little extra? But it tasted fine . . . and clean. Coke was cut with lactose, mannitol, lidocaine, dextrose, all kinds of other shit. He looked at the little pile, felt the cold sweat on his forehead.

Mentally flicked back to the Beirut story he'd told the Macks: all bullshit, an accumulation of legends he'd picked up from kids at school. But he was worried about the Macks.

He looked again at the pile of cocaine. Didn't matter if there was strychnine in it, he thought. He couldn't wait. He fished the cafeteria straw out of his pocket, made a last check, and snorted the stuff up.

One minute later, the world had changed.

First the rush, like electricity running through his nerves; then the power, the brightness, the focus.

Better than sex.

THAT NIGHT, Adnan Shaheen let himself into Barakat's house, called out, "Alain?" Shaheen was a short man with a fuzzy, bushy mustache, dark-complected, soft brown eyes. He was wearing a parka over a white, hip-length physician's coat. He was in his first year of residency in internal medicine. "Alain, are you there?"

Barakat's car was in the driveway. Instead of an answer, Shaheen got a thump from the back bedroom. Like a body hitting the floor.

"Alain?" He went back, down the hall. "Alain?" Pushed open the bedroom door. Barakat was sitting on the floor, back to the bed, his head back, eyes closed, saliva running over his lips and down his chin. He was wearing a sleeveless undershirt, boxer shorts, and over-the-calf socks. His shoes were on the floor between his legs.

"Ah no," Shaheen said. He grasped the hair at the sides of his head, as though he were going to tear it out.

"Go away," said Barakat.

Shaheen ignored him, squatted on the rug next to the other man, switched to Arabic. "What is it? Cocaine? What have you taken?"

Barakat opened his eyes. "Maybe . . . too much. Better now." He giggled. "Pretty bad an hour ago. That was very, very crazy. You know. My blood was . . . on fire."

Shaheen stood up and turned on the bedside lamp, and Barakat shouted, "Off . . . turn it off!"

Shaheen turned the lamp off, but not before he saw the baggie of cocaine on the nightstand. A lot of cocaine. Too much.

"Where did you get this?" he asked. He poked a finger at the bag, but was careful not to touch it.

"Got some money."

"Not this much money," Shaheen said. "Three days ago, you borrowed two hundred dollars from me."

"Go away," Barakat said.

Shaheen looked at him for a long moment, then said, "If your father knew, he might disown you."

"So don't tell him," Barakat said. He waved his arms around, struggling to get up. His eyes were black as coal. "Gotta get something to eat."

"Sit on the bed. I'll get you something . . ."

Barakat shook his head, as if to clear it. Shaheen walked out of the bedroom, down the hall, and into the kitchen. Opened the refrigerator: empty, except for a bottle of olives. Checked the cupboards, where Barakat sometimes kept cereal. Nothing. There was no food in the house.

He went back to the bedroom, where Barakat was staring down at his shoes. His sport coat was thrown over a chair, and Shaheen picked it up, took Barakat's wallet out of the breast pocket, opened it. Ten or fifteen dollars, a five and a wad of ones.

"You have no money for food, even," Shaheen said. "Where did you get this cocaine? What have you done?"

"Fuck you," Barakat said in English. He pushed himself up, went to the cocaine, picked up the bag, pushed it in the drawer of the nightstand. Then, "You know what I need? I need falafel. A lot of falafel. I need three kilos of falafel, right now. And coffee. Lots of coffee."

"You have to go to work . . ."

Barakat shook his head. "I'm on day shift for two weeks."

SHAHEEN AND BARAKAT had grown up together, Shaheen's family as servants of the Barakats; servants for generations. While Barakat was fouling out at one private school after another, Shaheen was thriving. He won a scholarship to the American University of Beirut, to study biology, the first of his family to finish high school, much less go to college. Barakat went off to Paris, wedged into the anything-goes foreign division of the Sorbonne, where he majored in women, wine, kief and cocaine.

Shaheen had spent a jobless year after graduation, his biology degree almost useless in a country that was falling apart. Then one day old man Barakat came to see him and they struck a deal.

Barakat was floundering in Paris. Five years, no degree in sight. Shaheen would go to Paris, move in with him, get him through school, get him through the medical exams, get him into a medical school in the U.S.

Get him through it, no matter how . . .

And Shaheen would go with him.

A journey of seven years, but they'd done it. They struggled, cheated, fought with each other, and Barakat—who was smart enough, if lazy—managed to scrape through. Shaheen did very well. Not quite as well as he would have on his own, because he was studying for two, and if anyone had found out how they'd cheated on virtually every test they took, they'd both be out on their ears.

But now it was almost done. Once through their residencies, they'd go their separate ways—Shaheen back to Miami, he thought, Barakat back to Europe, or perhaps LA. Someplace warm, where he wouldn't have to work too hard.

If, Shaheen thought, the American cocaine didn't kill Barakat first.

THE TWO BEST falafel places in St. Paul were closed, and they wound up at a McDonald's on University Avenue. Barakat couldn't go inside because the lights were too bright, so Shaheen went in, bought two Quarter Pounders with cheese and two large fries and a strawberry shake for Barakat, and a chocolate shake for himself. They ate in the parking lot, Barakat wolfing the food like a starving man. And he might be starving, Shaheen thought, watching him. All the money was going on dope.

"You'll need a stomach pump," Shaheen said as Barakat finished the second burger.

"I'm okay," Barakat mumbled through the last of the beef.

"So you got more money from your father?"

"Mmm. Not yet. Next week. You get catsup?"

"In the bag," Shaheen said.

Barakat found the three little packets and squirted them on the fries, started stuffing the fries in his face.

Shaheen thought about it. A few days past, he'd loaned Barakat money for food, though he suspected it would go for dope. And there'd been no sign of food in the house. Now he said that his father's check wasn't due for a week.

He had a big bag full of cocaine, and had apparently spent most of the evening snorting it. Not an eight-ball, but a big bag full of it. So where did he get what felt like a full pound of cocaine?

Shaheen thought about it, and the idea came upon him like some dark miasmic fog rising out of a swamp. He tried to push it away, but it wouldn't go.

He leaned close to Barakat—so close that Barakat frowned, and pulled away, his face turned so Shaheen could see his eyes. Shaheen said quietly, "Tell me you know nothing about this robbery at the hospital."

And he saw, in a flash, the truth in the other man's face . . .

Shaheen sagged and turned away and said, "Oh, no."

"I didn't. I didn't," Barakat insisted. "I use the cocaine, but I had nothing—"

Shaheen cut him off with a wave of his hand. "I've known you every day of my life," he said. "When you lie, I see it in your face. What have you done? Why have you done this?"

Barakat leaned back against the car door and said, "If you tell anybody, Addie, I'll kill you. I'll kill you like a dog."

SHAHEEN DROPPED HIM off at his house: "You have nine hours before your shift begins."

"I'm okay."

"You're not okay. You're a drug addict. You need treatment," Shaheen said.

"Forget it. I'll take care of it myself," Barakat said.

"Allee . . ."

"I'm okay," Barakat said, and he went into the house.

IN THE EARLY MORNING, he took only a small hit as he got ready for work: just enough to cool him down. Hair of the dog, as the Americans said. The small hit was enough to get his brain moving again, and he thought: Joe Mack, Lyle Mack, Weather Karkinnen.

Two separate problems, the Macks on one side, Karkinnen on the other.

If Joe Mack were to die, the threat would be mostly gone—even if Karkinnen identified him, the cops could get no further. Not unless Lyle Mack did something really stupid, like keep the drugs in his basement.

An additional thought: the Macks had a killer. So that was one more person who knew. How many were there, on the Mack side of the equation? Hard to tell. Did the killer even know about him? Barakat worked through it: the Macks didn't necessarily have to tell him, but the Macks were not the most reliable, he thought. He should have seen it before, but he'd been blinded by the idea of a mountain of cocaine.

Then there was Karkinnen. She'd had a good long look at him, could put him in the wrong part of the hospital at the wrong time.

One more hit before he left for work, and just a twist in a little Saran Wrap for lunch. He put the rest of the cocaine in a shoe in his closet.

The Macks. The Macks were a problem. Karkinnen was a problem only as long as the Macks were around. If Joe Mack were to die, though . . . or both of them, for that matter . . .

The idea pleased him; but he still wondered if the Macks, despite their denials, despite their slow-moving minds, had worked through the same equation.

5

WEATHER WALKED QUIETLY down the stairs, sensed a presence, stepped sideways and looked into the kitchen. In the reflected light from a hallway sconce, she could see Virgil Flowers sitting on his sleeping bag in the arch between the dining room and the kitchen. From there, he could see both the front door and the back. A shotgun was lying on the floor behind him.

"Did you get any sleep?" she asked.

"Yeah, I'm fine," he said. He yawned.

She suspected that he was lying; that he'd spent the night prowling the first floor with his gun. "I'm going to make some coffee, and there's a coffee cake in the freezer. I could stick it in the oven. Ready in twenty minutes?"

"Great, thanks. I need to brush my teeth. Don't open the curtains in the kitchen."

"I don't think—"

"Don't open the curtains," he said. He said it with the same hard tone that Lucas sometimes used; not something she often saw in Virgil, though she knew it must be there.

She nodded. "Okay."

Virgil asked, "Would there be enough coffee cake for another guy?"

"There's enough for six," she said.

"Jenkins has been wandering around outside. I might give him a call."

"Ah, you guys . . ."

Guys with guns, taking care of her. She hadn't flashed on the sniper killing again, but it was back there, somewhere, like Grendel, waiting to crawl out of its cave.

LUCAS CAME DOWN the stairs a moment later, wearing jeans and a sweatshirt, looking sleepy. He was carrying a shoulder holster with a .45. Virgil, just off his cell phone, said, "Jenkins thought he'd stop by."

Lucas nodded, taking Jenkins's behavior for granted. He dropped the .45 on the kitchen counter, and a minute later, Jenkins knocked on the side door. Virgil let him into the mudroom, a big man, cold, blowing steam. He said, "Four below," and, clapping his gloved hands, said, cheerfully, "Looks like everybody's up and at 'em, huh?"

"Ah, Christ," Lucas said. Early mornings disagreed with him, unless he was coming from the dark side.

Weather got the coffee going and Lucas got the oven preheating, and Virgil went off to the guest bedroom with his Dopp kit while Jenkins shed his coat and rubber overshoes, and put two 9mm Glocks on the end of the kitchen table.

With the coffee going, Weather went to the phone and punched in a number, identified herself and asked, "Are we on schedule? Thanks." She hung up and said to Lucas: "We're on schedule. Sara's stable. Don't know if she'll stay that way, but we're going to do it."

They ate the coffee cake, and argued about politics and medical care. The morning felt almost like an early fishing trip, a bunch of people sitting around eating unhealthy food.

Then Weather looked at her watch and said, "Better go."

Lucas and Weather took Lucas's SUV, on the theory that if somebody was still shooting for Weather, they might not know where she lived, or what other vehicles she had access to. Jenkins led the way in his personal Crown Vic, followed by Lucas in his SUV, with Virgil trailing behind in his 4Runner. Instead of going to the hospital parking ramp, they went to the front entrance. Jenkins parked, put a BCA placard in the front window, and held the door for Weather as she went in, with Lucas a step behind her.

"So I'm good," she said, when they were in the lobby. "See you guys this afternoon?"

"I think I'll hang out for a while, see who comes by," Jenkins said. Virgil came in.

Lucas said, "Maybe I'll get a bite in the cafeteria."

"I'll come with you," Virgil said.

Weather looked at them: "You're going to stay here all day, aren't you?"

Jenkins shrugged: "Maybe."

Virgil said, "Not me. I'm going back to your place and crash."

"I don't think it's necessary—" Weather began.

Lucas cut her off: "You do the surgery, we'll do the bodyguarding."

*

THEN THERE was the deal with the chickens. But not just any chickens.

Arnold Shoemaker, the farmer, was either blessed with, or cursed by, exotic fowl. He wasn't quite certain which.

He didn't buy them, he accumulated them. Somebody would come by, hearing that Arnold would take them, and they'd drop them off—unwanted family pets, stray birds, leftovers from farms that were going down. Cuckoo Marans, Golden Penciled Hamburgs, Leghorns, Buttercups, Red Caps, Blue-Peckered Logans, assorted bantams and guinea hens, he had them all.

He ate the few eggs they produced, when he found them fresh, but never ate the chickens. They ran in and out of the old barn in the winter, and he'd feed them table scraps and ground corn, and leave them on their own to peck up gravel out by the road and bugs in the barn.

The fact was, they made him happy to look at. It was nothing short of remarkable, he thought, how so few people realized how good-looking a chicken could be. Better-looking than parrots, by a long way. No contest.

Arnold was up before dawn, into town, had breakfast at the diner, where the waitress called him "hon" and knew to bring the Heinz 57 sauce for his scrambled eggs and home fries cooked in sausage grease; the combo gave him gas, but the taste was unparalleled, and Arnold lived alone, except for the chickens and his yellow Lab, so the gas wasn't a critical problem, though the dog sometimes got watery eyes.

The sun was just over the horizon when Arnold topped the hill on the way home, and came down to Minnie Creek and saw the coyotes break out from under the bridge and into the trees. He went on by, but he could see them at the edge of the woods, watching the truck with their silver eyes.

Coyotes loved the taste of a tender young guinea hen. Arnold's young guinea hens. He lost a half-dozen birds a year to the coyotes—he'd find an explosion of feathers outside the barn and another old pal was gone. And the dogs were getting more and more aggressive.

So Arnold parked the car in a hurry, hustled inside, put on his insulated hunting boots and cold-weather hunting jacket, opened the gun safe and got out the Savage .223 with the nine-power variable scope. Back outside, he headed straight down the driveway, across the road, across Dornblicker's field, over a hump and down toward the creek. The land sort of swole up, as Dornblicker said, before it dropped down to the creek, and the swole covered Arnold's approach.

He crawled the last few yards on his elbows and thighs, slithering over the snow. At the top, he lay still for a minute, then two, then carefully, slowly, pushed up. Four coyotes down by the creek; cold breeze in his face, so they couldn't smell him. Maybe they found a roadkill deer, Arnold thought.

He pushed the rifle forward. He was 130 yards out, but the coyotes were big animals compared to woodchucks. He eased off the safety, picked out the biggest mutt, let out a breath, squeezed . . .

BAP! The shot echoed across the freezing winter countryside, and three of the coyotes broke for the trees. One of them jumped, and fell.

Arnold worked the bolt action, watching the tree line, looking for a second shot, but the coyotes were gone. He stood up, slung the gun over his shoulder, and walked down through the crunchy snow to look at the dead one.

Thirty feet out, he saw the garbage bags and thought, *Goddamnit.* Every once in a while, somebody who didn't want to pay garbage fees would throw sacks of garbage and trash in the roadside ditches. Half the time, it was full of hazardous waste—paint cans, old TVs, insecticide. Stuff you had to pay to get rid of.

Ten feet out, as he was looking at the dead coyote, the muzzle of his gun on the mutt's head, he saw the shoe.

And then, through a hole in the second garbage bag, a single, frozen, blue eye, wide open.

Lucas was sitting in the hospital cafeteria, reduced to reading a tattered copy of *The Onion*, nearly delirious with boredom, when, at three o'clock, Marcy Sherrill called and said, "I'm having carrot sticks and low-fat yogurt for my afternoon snack."

"I'm proud of you," Lucas said. "Can I hang up now?"

"No. I've got something that might interest you, out of Dakota County. A farmer down there found a couple fresh bodies in garbage bags under a bridge. Their wallets were gone, but one of them had an envelope in his pocket, a gas bill, with his name on it. Charles Chapman, aka 'Shooter' to his pals in the Seed. The Dakota deputies ID'd the other one as Michael Haines, Chapman's housemate. Both of them are on the computer, both of them are members of the Seed. Both of them were wearing jeans, biker boots, and tan Carhartt work jackets."

Lucas hunched over the table, and Jenkins, across the table, perked up. "Man . . . that's *interesting*."

"They took the bodies up to St. Paul, and we called an ME's investigator and asked him to take a peek at their legs. Their arms and faces had been ripped up by coyotes, but their legs were okay. Haines has three scratches down the back of his left leg, just above his Achilles tendon. They look like fingernail scratches."

"Now we're getting somewhere," Lucas said. "I'll get Weather home, then I'll head over to the office and talk to the gang guys. Goddamn, this could break it."

"But if two out of the three are dead . . ."

"The other one, the one still alive, is a smart guy. He had to get rid of the other two for security reasons, after Peterson died. Maybe the smart guy knew what it meant when Haines got scratched. The assholes are getting onto DNA."

"The ME's sending DNA samples over to your lab, if we could get them to hurry it up a little," Marcy said. "The samples from Peterson's fingernails are already there."

"Well, you know, they keep telling me that chemistry is chemistry, but I'll call them," Lucas said. "I'll tell you what: shutting this down would be a load off my mind."

"I think *we* can shut it down," Marcy said. She leaned on the *we*, meaning Minneapolis.

"I'm not going to bullshit you, Marcy. We've got the gang guys and the files," Lucas said. "I'm going to take a look, see what's what, and go talk to whoever I need to talk to. This is my wife they're screwing with."

Long silence. "Take it easy. Talk to me."

"You know me," Lucas said.

*

WEATHER HAD REOPENED the sutures in the twins' heads, and the neu-rosurgeons got back to work, slowly, millimeter by millimeter, splitting the dura mater into separate sheets. By two in the afternoon, they were halfway done.

"We're showing some heart," the anesthesiologist said.

Maret stopped and peered at Sara.

"Not Sara. It's Ellen," the anesthesiologist said.

They got Seitz, the cardiologist, in. "Her blood pressure is too low," he said, looking at the monitors. "Too low . . . goddamn it, she's gonna arrest."

Then things got quick: Seitz put some chemicals into her, steadying her heart, and avoided arrest, but then Sara started looking shaky.

Seitz: "You've got to get out now. We've got to get her blood pres-sure up, but we can't let Sara's get too high. We need to get them in the ICU again."

Maret said, "If we could get another hour or two . . ."

The cardiologist shook his head. "We'd lose one or the other. They can't tolerate any more of this."

"Damn. Everything else is going so well . . ." Maret said. He looked at a clock, then up at the observation wall.

"Dr. Karkinnen . . . how long will it take you to close?"

Weather was in the front row, Jenkins two rows behind her. "Half hour."

"Scrub up, and we'll back out."

THE BABIES looked like little pale meat loaves under her bloody gloves, faceless, masked and taped, the edges of the skin on their head drying and raggedy now, their personalities submerged. At times, it was like working on a couple of logs; and then they'd come back, and be chil-dren again. She moved fast, with Maret leaning on her elbow, pulling the kids together again. People in the room silent, watching, regretful. For every day they didn't finish, death got closer, for one or the other or both.

WHEN WEATHER had finished, and gotten back into her street clothes, she walked with Jenkins back out to the front lobby. Marcy

Sherrill was waiting with Lucas. Marcy took mug shots of Haines and Chapman from her briefcase and passed them to Weather.

"Is either one of these the guy you saw?"

Weather shook her head. "I don't think so. The guy had real thick hair, down on his shoulders, almost . . . How'd you come up with these guys?"

"Somebody murdered them. One of them has scratches on his leg; and they're members of the Seed."

Weather shuddered. "They may be the guys who did the holdup, but I don't think they're the one I saw. Could have been the driver—all I saw of him was a beard."

Lucas said to Marcy: "This might not be bad: it means we've still got a handle on our third guy."

VIRGIL WAS SITTING on the front porch, in the cold, eating a Hostess cupcake, when they got home. Jenkins stopped at the curb behind a brown Cadillac and Lucas turned up the drive and took the truck straight into the garage.

Jenkins came crunching up the driveway and asked Virgil, "Shrake inside?"

"You know anybody else with a brown Cadillac?"

"He got a deal on it," Jenkins said.

"I should hope." Virgil finished the cupcake and led the way in. Lucas and Weather came in through the back, and they all met in the kitchen, where Shrake and Letty, Lucas and Weather's fifteen-year-old daughter, were playing gin rummy at the breakfast table.

Shrake was a big man, as big as Jenkins, in shirtsleeves, with a .40-cal Smith in a shoulder holster. He was staring fixedly at his cards, and Weather asked, "Who's winning?"

"Don't bother us," Letty said. "If he goes out, I've got to take off my bra."

Shrake jerked bolt upright, looked from Letty to Weather, mouth open, recovered and said, "Jesus Christ. It's dangerous just being around her."

"You got no idea," Lucas said. "So listen up, guys, we got a break—"

"What about me and my bra?" Letty asked.

"That's your problem," Lucas said. "Now either shut up, or go away."

LUCAS LAID IT OUT: the Minneapolis cops were focusing on the hospital, but the BCA had the gang files. "So we're on it. We're cooperating, but I'm going after it full-time. Virgil, Jenkins, you guys stay with Weather. Shrake, I want you hanging around, keep loose. If something comes up, I'll call you."

Weather said, "You don't think this has anything to do with . . . that other time? With the Seed?"

Lucas shook his head: "That's ancient history. Those guys were nuts, everybody knows it. Nope: this has to do with the hospital. They've got themselves in a crack now, and they're trying to get out."

Virgil said, "You think somebody in the hospital was involved, an insider, right? Maybe Weather, or me, or somebody else, could talk up the idea that the Seed guys might be coming after him. Maybe break him out."

Letty said, "Put it on the ten-o'clock news."

Lucas shrugged: "We could try, but I don't see anybody confessing. We've got three murders now. More likely somebody'd quit his job and head out. That's something we could look for."

"Need to talk to other gang squads where the Seed and the Angels have branches," Jenkins said. "See if anybody dumps a load of commercial pharmaceuticals on the street."

"That we can do," Lucas said. "What else?"

"Roust the Seed," Shrake said. "Kick some ass. Keep an eye on Weather."

6

THE BCA HEADQUARTERS was in a modern building out in a St. Paul residential area, the parking lot mostly empty at six o'clock on a cold winter night. Lucas let himself in, climbed the stairs to his office, dropped his coat, and walked down the hall. Frank Harris was sitting in his office, in the dark.

"You asleep?" Lucas asked.

"Thinking," Harris said. "And my eyes are tired."

Lucas settled into a visitor's chair. "You know the situation."

"Yeah, and I'll give you everything we've got," Harris said. He was a slim shadow, in a suit and tie, on the other side of the desk. "But I don't like it. I wouldn't do it if it wasn't your wife."

"I don't need any inside sources. I don't need any of your guys, I won't give anything up. What I need is names: I'll generate my own information," Lucas said.

"If you talk to a smart guy, and a few of them are pretty smart, they'll get an idea of how deep our information is," Harris said. He didn't particularly like Lucas, and Lucas knew it, and knew why.

Harris was a third-generation cop, had struggled to get out of a suburban police force and into the BCA, had hustled his way up through the ranks, lived on his seventy-five thousand dollars a year, married when he was twenty, had three kids. Lucas had parachuted into a top spot, helped by political muscle, and worse, was rich, drove a Porsche, once had a reputation as a serious womanizer, and still got more than his share of face time with the media.

Now Lucas shook his head. "No. Two or three names—it's nothing. Especially if I go in dumb, and thrash around. I swear to God, Frank, we're not going to burn you. We just need a place to start."

"Well, don't get hurt," Harris said. He leaned forward and pushed a paper file across the desk. "Shred it when you finish reading it. If it got out, it'd be a goddamn disaster. If you need another copy later, I can print another one."

Lucas took the file and stood up. "Thanks, Frank. I owe you."

Sometimes, he thought, walking away, you do favors for people you don't like, because you're cops. Just the way it was.

SHRAKE WAS SITTING in Lucas's office, waiting, and Lucas shut the door behind himself, sat down and opened the file. Maybe two hundred pages, printed out in color: surveillance and source reports, photographs, mug shots and rap sheets. They covered the Hells Angels and Bad Seed, with miscellaneous stuff on the Outlaws, Banditos, and Mongols.

Lucas cut the stack of paper roughly in half and pushed it across to Shrake. "Read. Mention anything that looks like anything—especially with the Seed."

THE ANGELS were the main biker gang in the Cities. The Seed didn't have a clubhouse, but ran out of a bar called Cherries, south of the river, the reports said. The Seed had a working treaty with the Angels, and Angels members were welcome at Cherries. On the other hand, the report said, the Seed also had some alliances with the Outlaws in Illinois, and might then be a trusted communications link between the two bigger rival gangs.

Money for the gangs came from drug dealing, fencing, and miscellaneous small-time street crime, although most of the members also had jobs, and membership turnover, outside a core group, was heavy.

"The thing is, these guys are perfect for the hospital job," Shrake said. He had rap sheets for the two dead Seed members, Haines and Chapman. "They fit physically, the clothes are right. The Seed has gang contacts both west with the Angels and east with the Outlaws, and they've always moved drugs: they've got the retail connections. Haines and Chapman both have robbery convictions; Haines did time in Wisconsin, Chapman in California. Haines has a crim-sex no-pros because the girl backed off, but he's in the database, one, two, three DUIs, small amounts of marijuana . . . Chapman has three assaults, one conviction, juvie record of assault, had a weapons charge that was dealt . . . small amounts of dope. Assholes. Completely likely to hold up a pharmacy."

"That no-pros is why they killed Haines. Somebody knew he was in the database, and that after we processed Peterson, we'd have him," Lucas said. "They were afraid he'd flip."

LUCAS FOUND a reference to the owners of Cherries, Lyle and Joseph Mack, brothers, who'd been patched in the Seed in the early nineties;

and another reference to their father, Ike Mack, who'd been a Seed member in the sixties. A surveillance photo of Lyle Mack showed him sitting on the steps of a bar, surrounded by beer bottles, taken after the autumn river-run of 2006.

"We need to talk to this guy—he'd know all the locals," Lucas said, pushing the photo across the desk.

Shrake picked it up. "Short and chubby. He wasn't at the hospital."

"But he'd know Chapman and Haines, and I'll bet we get the DNA back on Haines."

He thumbed through the rap sheets, found sheets for both the Macks. "Huh. Criminal possession of stolen goods. Two different busts for each of them, they dealt on all of them. Maybe involved in some sports betting, small-time bookies. Joe Mack has three DUIs over ten years. Looks like they've run a couple bars, one up by Hayward, another in Wausau. Showed up here about eight years ago, bought Cherries. They get a few complaints every year, noise, parking problems. Have some hookers going through, but not regular. Used to have a porno night . . . More like dirtbags than hard guys. But they're merchants. They buy and sell. They seem to be close to the center of the Seed."

He pushed a copy of a mug shot of Joe Mack across the desk: six years old, it showed a big man with a ponytail, clean-shaven.

They continued reading, and a half hour on, Shrake said, "There are a hundred killers out at Stillwater who we could turn loose, and they'd never in their lives commit another crime. If we replaced them with a hundred of these guys, we'd have to find new jobs. You get these guys with ten offenses, mostly ratshit stuff, they deal on it, they walk. You *know* they did ten times that many that never got reported or they never got caught on."

"Just having a good time, Saturday night," Lucas said.

"Yeah. Murder, rape, robbery, assault, extortion, fighting, drugs, prostitution, criminal sexual assault, domestic assault, drunk driving, you name it," Shrake said. "Makes my teeth hurt."

"You've never had a problem with a fight," Lucas said.

"Pretty big difference between a fight during an arrest and an assault," Shrake said.

"You're sounding self-righteous."

"Got me on that," he said.

They read for another half hour, trading sheets back and forth, putting down names, and then Lucas looked at his watch.

"Getting to be prime time out at Cherries," he said.

CHERRIES LOOKED like a suburban split-level house, but larger, a frame building with a blacktopped parking lot out front and along the west side, and a loading dock with a dumpster in back. There were ten or twelve vehicles in the parking lot when they arrived, and only one was a sedan—the rest were SUVs, pickups, and Ford and Chevy commercial vans, every one with a trailer hitch. Snow was piled up on the perimeter of the lot, and Budweiser and Miller neons hung in the visible windows.

Lucas pulled the Lexus around so the lights played off the tags of the two vehicles parked in front of the loading dock. Shrake checked the tag numbers against a list and said, "Yup. That's them. Elvis is in the house."

Lucas pulled up tight in front of the two vehicles and parked. Shrake took a pistol out of his belt holster and put it in his side coat pocket. "Joe and Lyle," he said.

"Watch your back," Lucas said.

They got out, crunched around the bar to the front door. The air smelled of barbeque and auto exhaust from the highway, and they could hear the thump of a country song. Cold; lots of stars, but cold. Shrake said, "'Bubba Shot the Jukebox.'"

"Huh?"

"That song. Mark Chesnutt." He pulled the door open and held it, and Lucas led the way in.

Just a run-down bar-type bar; fifteen booths and a dozen tables, a bar with a few stools, a jukebox, the odor of snowmelt and wet wool and beer and barbeque beef and tacos, a whiff of illegal cigarette smoke. Two waitresses, both with push-up bras under T-shirts—one of Barack Obama's face done up as the Joker in the Batman movie, the other with the slogan "Ride It Like You Stole It"—were working the booths. A redheaded female bartender in a frilly white blouse was talking to a big man hunched over the bar.

Lucas and Shrake didn't look like the rest of the clientele. They had no facial hair, and they were wearing white-collar-worker winter coats, unbuttoned; like, unbuttoned so they could get at a gun. Every other male had some kind of hair on his face, and a parka hanging off a hook at the end of his booth. Talk dwindled as Lucas led the way to the bar, Shrake a couple of steps behind.

"We're with the state police," Lucas said to the bartender. "We need to talk to the Mack brothers."

The bartender looked at the clock, then shook her head. "You missed them. They left here half an hour ago."

"I wonder why they left their cars in the parking lot?" Lucas asked. He leaned across the bar. "Go get them. And mention that we've blocked their cars in. And if we don't talk to them now, we'll talk to them downtown. This is just a friendly visit, but it could get pretty fuckin' unfriendly if they want it that way."

She looked at Lucas for a minute, then at Shrake, said, "Asshole," dropped her wet bar towel on Lucas's hand, turned and walked through a door into the back.

Lucas wiped his hand on his pant leg and said to a waitress, "Nice place."

She ignored him.

The big man whom the bartender had been talking to asked, "What's up?"

"You know Mikey Haines or Shooter Chapman?" Lucas asked.

"Maybe. I remember the names. Sort of. What'd they do?"

"They got themselves shot in the head with a shotgun," Lucas said. "Found the bodies this morning."

The big man's face pulled together. "Are you shittin' me?"

"Do I look like I'm shittin' you?"

"Didn't see anything on TV," he said.

"Didn't make the evening news, but it'll be on at ten," Lucas said. He looked at a television set in the corner, which was showing a hockey game. "Took a while to identify them."

The big man finished his beer in one gulp, wiped his mouth on his sweatshirt sleeve, and said, "I gotta get out of here."

"Why?"

"Look, I don't know nothin' about nothin'," he said. "I really don't. But if somebody's startin' a war, I don't want to be sittin' here suckin' on a Budweiser."

Two more guys got out of a booth, pulling their coats on as they headed for the door. Shrake put out a hand. "Friends of Haines and Chapman?"

"Never heard of them," one said, and they were gone.

A SHORT MAN, whom Lucas recognized as Lyle Mack, followed the bartender out of the back, an aggrieved look on his face. "Now what?"

"We're investigating the murders of Shooter Chapman and Mikey Haines," Lucas said.

Mack registered what looked everything in the world like shock. The bartender, eyes wide, put both hands to the sides of her face, her mouth open. Her lips working, no words coming out. If they were faking it, Lucas thought, they deserved Oscars.

"What?" Mack got the first response out.

"Is your brother around?" Lucas asked.

"He's in the can . . . Uh, shit, come on back. We can talk in the office."

He turned and went through the door, heading into the back. Lucas and Shrake walked around the end of the bar past the bartender, who asked, "How were they killed? Are you sure they were murdered?"

"They were shot with a shotgun and put in garbage bags and thrown under a bridge," Shrake said. "If it wasn't murder, it was a really weird accident."

They went through the door behind the bar, heard Lyle Mack yelling at his brother, up a set of stairs. "The cops are here—they say Shooter and Mikey been killed. Come on out of there."

And he turned back and said, "Come on to the office."

The office was a small plywood room attached to the loading dock; one chair behind a desk and two chairs in front of it, two filing cabinets, an old computer, and a new multitask print-fax-copy-scan machine.

Mack took the desk seat and Lucas sat down while Shrake leaned in the doorway. "You know them?" Lucas asked.

"Sure. They're members of the club," Mack said. "I bet the fuckin' Mongols had something to do with this. We're okay with everybody else."

"You know any Mongols? They're pretty thin around here," Shrake said.

"Well, who else . . . ?"

"Lyle, don't give us any shit. I've had some dealings with the Seed in the past, and people got killed, and I've got very little patience with you guys," Lucas said. "You push dope and you used to do a little strong-arm robbery and you ran a couple massage parlors and I know all that shit. So what I want to know is, were Haines and Chapman hustling meth or coke? Who were they selling it to? Did they owe somebody? Were they scared?"

Shrake stepped back and let another man through the doorway, Joe Mack, who had a lean, pale-white face and lantern jaw, with a black do-rag on his close-cropped head. If he'd had a gold hoop earring, Lucas thought, he could have played Long John Silver.

"They're dead?" Joe Mack asked. His eyelids were half-closed, and he smelled of alcohol.

Lyle nodded at Lucas and said, "This guy is giving me a lot of shit. He thinks they were dealing dope."

Joe Mack registered astonishment so profound that Lucas almost laughed, and Shrake did. He said, "Dope?" as though it were inconceivable.

"Let me 'splain something to you guys," Shrake said. "This is a double murder, at least, and maybe a triple. We think they were the guys who knocked over the pharmacy at University Hospitals three days ago, and kicked the pharmacist to death."

Lyle Mack: "No . . ."

"And you're bullshitting us, right now, is what you're doing," Shrake continued. "That's accessory after the fact on three murder-ones, which is just as good as doing it yourselves. We'll shake it all out, and you'll go to prison . . . if you keep bullshitting us."

Lyle Mack shook his head: "All right. Shooter and Mikey could be assholes. We know that. But we don't know anybody who'd kill them for it."

"The Mongols would," Joe Mack said to his brother.

"Aw, for Christ's sakes, forget the Mongols," Lucas said. "We're gonna prove Haines did the pharmacy, by tomorrow. Then we're gonna come back here with a flamethrower, if we don't get some cooperation. This is their club. This is where they hung out, where their friends were. So: Who were they running with? They hang out with any hospital people? What?"

Lyle Mack said, "Listen . . . we're bar owners. We make money at it. These guys are customers, but they're not good friends or nothing. They always come in together, they hang together. And you know, they bullshit with the guys, but they were partners. They hung with each other."

"They gay?" Shrake asked.

Joe Mack snorted. "I don't think so. They were Seed. Seed don't take gays."

"No gays, no sex perverts of any kind," Lyle Mack said.

"When was the last time they were in?"

The two brothers looked at each other, and then Lyle Mack said, "Could have been Saturday. I'm pretty sure they were here on Saturday night."

"Did they seem nervous, or worried, or scared?" Lucas asked. "Were they hanging with anyone new?"

Lyle Mack exhaled, looked at his brother, back at Lucas, and said, "Listen, if we, you know . . . if we talk to you, this gets out, we're done. The place gets wrecked, we get the shit beat out of us, or killed."

"We don't talk," Lucas said.

"If the information is good," Shrake added. "If it's not good, we might talk."

Lyle Mack said, "Saturday night, they were hanging with Anthony Melicek and Ron Howard. Drank a few beers. They were on the Deer Hunter for a couple hours."

"The Deer Hunter?" Shrake asked

"Game machine," Joe Mack said.

"Where do we find these guys?" Lucas asked. He was writing their names in his notebook.

"I don't know," Lyle Mack said. "You've probably got their addresses. Or Ron's, anyway. He's on probation, some kind of thing with his old lady."

"You mean, he beat her up," Lucas said.

"No, no. I mean he and his old lady are on probation," Lyle Mack said. "I'm not sure exactly what they did, but they might have been selling stuff."

"Stolen stuff."

"Maybe. If you tell anybody we told you this . . ."

"Who else did they hang with?"

"Man, they hung with each other . . ."

THEY HAD two names, and not much more; and assured the brothers that they would hang around in the parking lot, talking to customers coming and going, so that Melicek and Howard wouldn't know where their names had come from.

Lucas stood up, took a card out of his wallet, and dropped it on the desk. "If you hear anything, it would behoove you to call me. No motorcycle big-shot bullshit, burning the card or any of that; just a quiet call. Nobody will know, and it might be useful to you sometime, to have a guy you can call. If you know what I mean."

SHRAKE LED the way out, Lucas a step behind; when they'd gone through the door into the front, Lyle Mack said to Joe, "We're in a lot of fuckin' trouble, Joe."

Joe Mack said, "We oughta get out of here."

"Can't," Lyle Mack said. "If it was only a robbery, we might get out of town. Murder, they'd come after us. Come after you. We gotta find that chick and shut her up."

THERE WERE still fifteen or twenty people in the bar, but in clusters now, four and five together. From behind the bar, Lucas called, "Can I have your attention? Anybody here know Mikey Haines or Shooter Chapman?"

Dead silence.

"I know some of you must be their friends, if they had any friends," Lucas said. "Somebody took them out and blew their faces mostly off, with a shotgun, and I would like any opinions anybody's got about that."

More silence, then one voice, "We got no opinions."

Shrake said, "If you get home and find out you got an opinion, about who may be executing Seeds, you call the Bureau of Criminal Apprehension and ask for Agent Shrake. S-h-r-a-k-e. Shrake."

"The reason you should do that is, being a tough guy is just fine, but if somebody's shooting you in the back of the head with a shotgun, from an ambush, like they did with Shooter and Mikey, tough isn't good enough," Lucas said. "So you got any ideas, it might be your own life you're saving."

THEY DID SPEND fifteen minutes in the parking lot, grabbing people as they came and went—mostly went—but got no more names.

"Can't talk to us in public," Shrake said. "Gang law."

"Talk about the cold shoulder," Lucas said. "My shoulder's frozen all the way down to my ass."

"Let's go. Look up those other two guys," Shrake said. "We can come back if we need to."

Lucas looked back at the club. Lyle Mack was staring out a window at them, his head visible from the neck up, like a bust of Beethoven, or somebody.

Tony Soprano, maybe.

BACK IN THE CAR, Shrake got on his phone and got addresses for Anthony Melicek and Ron Howard, the two men named by Mack as friends of Chapman and Haines. Howard lived in Cottage Grove, a suburb to the southeast, and he *was* on probation, for theft. Melicek lived in the opposite direction, on the edge of downtown Minneapolis, not far from the Metrodome.

"Howard," Lucas said. He punched Howard's address into the SUV's navigation system, and they headed east. As they drove, Shrake called around until he found Howard's probation officer, a woman named Melanie. They talked for a few minutes, and Shrake rang off.

"She says Howard and his wife got caught stealing eight hundred and sixty board-feet of walnut and cherry from a wood specialty place in Shakopee. Got caught loading it onto their pickup. She says there was an argument about money he'd given them for some wood, and he told the cops he was just taking what he was owed. She said he was probably right about what he was owed, but he broke through a back door, so there it was. They both got probation. He had some arrests six or eight years back when he was running with the Seed, drugs, firearms, did some county-jail time over in Wisconsin. She says he's not a problem."

"Good. I'm not in the mood for a big deal."

"Neither am I." A minute later: "I wish Weather wasn't involved. I mean . . . you know."

"Yeah, and she won't budge, either," Lucas said. "She'll be over at the hospital every day. Marcy's not getting anywhere inside the hospital. I might have to go over there with my nutcracker."

"I've done hospitals before," Shrake said. "You know what the problem is? Doctors. No offense, you know, about Weather being a doctor . . ."

"S'okay."

"They're so sure they know everything. They were the smartest kids in high school, which is how they got in premed, and they were the smartest guys in premed, which is how they got in med school, and then they get this big piece of paper that says, 'Yup, you're the smartest,' and they truly believe that shit. They will tell you everything you need to know about your job. They never answer questions—they'll tell you that you don't need to know that answer. You need to know the answer to something else."

"Hey, I live with one," Lucas said. "And she's a surgeon. They're worse than everybody but the shrinks."

"And you gotta shrink for your best friend . . ."

"Almost intolerable," Lucas said. "Goddamn Weather, if I didn't love her, I'd choke the shit out of her about twice a day."

"To say nothing of your goofy daughter," Shrake said. "No offense again, but she really does scare me. Sometimes, she acts like a forty-five-year-old narc."

Lucas laughed and said, "The sad thing is, I've never been happier."

"Well, that's nice," Shrake said. "I mean, that really is. That makes one."

"One what?"

"Happy cop."

HOWARD LIVED in a rambler-style single-story house halfway down a hillside, brown fiberglass siding with a two-car garage on one end; bright light was shining through the three windows in the garage door. A pickup and an old Camry were parked in the driveway.

Lucas looked at the dashboard clock: ten-forty-five. Not too late. Shrake had taken the pistol of his pocket and put it back in its holster, and now took it back out and stuck it in the pocket. "Better safe," he said.

Lucas rang the doorbell, and a moment later a woman came to the door and peeked out behind a chain. "Who is it?"

"We're with the Bureau of Criminal Apprehension . . . state police," Lucas said. "We're talking to people who knew Mike Haines and Shooter Chapman."

"Oh . . . jeez. Just a minute." She pushed the door closed and the chain rattled, and she said, "Ron's in the shop. We thought somebody might come by."

"You're Mrs. Howard?"

"Yes. Donna." She was using the female nicey-nice voice, submissive, scared by cops. She looked pleasant enough, a round woman with brown hair and dark eyes and a prominent mole by the corner of her mouth. Lucas smiled at her and stepped inside, carefully shuffled his feet on the mat inside the door and she said, "Oh, don't worry about that. He's this way . . ."

He followed her through the small kitchen, past a dining table and through a garage door. The garage had been converted into a woodshop, with a table saw, band saw, drill press, and lathe fixed to the floor, and a long workbench with wood-cutting tools along the far wall. Howard was working over the lathe, wearing goggles and earmuffs; his back was turned to them. The air smelled of fresh-cut wood, and a stack of wooden bowls sat along one wall of the shop.

Donna Howard flipped a switch on the wall, a quick on-and-off, and a light flickered and Howard backed away from the machine and turned around, saw them, hit a kill switch. He pulled off the goggles and headset as the machine wound down; he was holding a nasty-looking chisel. He saw them check it out and hastily put it aside. "Police?"

THEY SAT in the Howards' small living room. Howard started right out with an explanation of the burglary they'd been convicted of. "I hadn't been in trouble for years, since I was a kid. But I gave those assholes twelve hundred dollars for the wood I needed, and they kept putting me off. If I don't produce, I don't eat. They wouldn't give me the money back, either, said they'd already ordered the stuff and the supplier was having problems and all of that. Bullshit. So I made the mistake. Two mistakes—I took Donna with me."

"The judge knew all that, so he went easy," Donna Howard said.

"Did you ever get your money back?" Shrake asked.

"Yeah . . . but the lawyer cost us two thousand, and we were lucky to get off that easy. Tell you what, soon as it was settled, I put the word out on the Internet. Won't be many guys going out there for their turnin' wood, I can tell you."

Lucas said, "I understand you guys were talking to Shooter and Mike last week."

"Yeah. A friend called and told us about them being dead. He was down at the bar when you were there," Donna Howard said. "I've never known anybody who was murdered."

"How well did you know them?"

Howard shook his head. "I've known them since we were all kids, running around in the woods in Wisconsin. They never grew up. I rode with the Seed for a while, but you know, it gets to be a lot of bullshit. People hassling you, cops coming around. Some of the guys were enormous assholes. Ridin' was fun, you know, impressing the squares and then . . . you wonder why the hell you're drunk all the time and living out of a shitty apartment. So I got a straight job and met Donna, and we eventually started the business. But we still go up to Cherries three or four times a year, talk with the older guys. That's about it."

"So you wouldn't know what they were up to." Lucas let a little skepticism show in his voice.

"No, we really don't." They sat silently for a moment, then Howard said, "They were always trying to hustle something up. Usually, it was like buying stuff from drug guys up in Minneapolis. Stolen stuff, computers and cameras and stuff. About a million iPods. They'd sell them to high school kids for ten bucks each."

"They'd done some time for robbery . . ."

"Yeah, but they weren't any good at it," Howard said. "Fact is, Shooter was sort of a chicken, and Mikey was just dumb."

"Pulled off a pretty slick robbery up in the Cities," Shrake said. "We think they're the ones that knocked over that hospital pharmacy."

"Really?" Donna Howard looked surprised. "That doesn't sound like them. They were more the Saturday-night liquor store guys."

"Didn't a guy get killed?" Ron Howard asked.

"Yeah, they kicked a guy, and it turned out he was on some blood thinner because of his heart," Shrake said. "He bled to death internally. They got him to the emergency room, but the docs couldn't stop it."

"God, that's awful." Donna Howard put her knuckles to her teeth. "I can't believe they did that."

"Could have been accidental," Lucas said. "The guy tried to sneak out a cell phone, and they kicked him a couple times. But, you know, you're robbing a place, and somebody dies because of it, it's murder."

Ron Howard grunted: "I can believe they did *that*. Kicked the guy. That's just another screwup. I just can't believe they thought of it— holding up a hospital. How much did they get?"

Lucas said, "Nobody really knows. Street value, maybe anything up from half a million."

Howard laughed: "Man. Those guys were small-timers back in grade school. No way they pulled off a half-million-dollar robbery."

More questions, met with a general lack of information: the Howards, Lucas decided, really didn't know much about Chapman and Haines. When they ran out of questions, Howard asked one.

"Who told you about us? Had to be somebody at Cherries, right?"

"We talked to quite a few people, looked at some records and stuff, your name was in there," Lucas said.

Howard looked at him for a moment, then down at his knuckles, which showed a small, damp cut, the kind woodworkers got. He said, "I'll tell you what, Officer, you're bullshitting me, right? I mean, I haven't ridden with those guys for years, but here you are, real quick. Had to be Cherries."

Lucas shrugged. "What difference does it make?"

"It pisses me off," Howard said. "Those guys knew we'd gotten in trouble, so they sicced you on us. And they're making chumps out of you. Anybody who knew us, and knew those guys, knew we didn't have much to do with them. We're just old acquaintances. We'd talk to them, but it was all old-time stuff. Everybody knows I'm straight."

"Did you see the artist's sketch of what the pharmacy robber looked like? Should have been on the ten-o'clock news."

They both shook their heads. "Don't watch the news anymore. It's just too depressing."

"The third guy on the robbery, would have been a pal of Haines and Chapman. Big guy, lots of hair, beard."

"That's about ninety percent of the Seed, right there," Howard said.

Donna Howard asked, "It's not my place . . . it wasn't the Macks, was it? The ones who gave you our name?"

"I really can't say, Mrs. Howard," Lucas said.

"Then I can't tell you what I was going to tell you," she said.

They all looked at each other, and Shrake started with, "Listen, there've been a bunch of murders, and you could get yourselves in serious shit—"

Lucas held up a hand, shutting him off. He said to Donna Howard, "The people who gave us your name said that if we let their name out, you'd tell the rest of the Seed members and that would be the end of them."

"Oh, bullshit," Ron Howard said. "We're not gonna get somebody killed because of this. Then we *would* be in trouble. All I want to do is keep the business going, and that's hard enough."

"Do not pass along what I'm going to tell you," Lucas said. "Or we'll be back in your faces."

"Who was it?" Donna asked.

"We spent some time interviewing the Macks, who . . . described who was talking to whom last weekend."

"I knew it," Donna said to her husband. To Lucas: "It's the *Macks* who were closest to those two. The Macks. The word is, you steal something good around the Cities, the Macks will get rid of it for you. They're the whole . . . *heart* . . . of everything that goes on there. If somebody at Cherries was in it with Shooter and Mikey, it was the Macks."

Ron Howard bobbed his head. "That's like it is," he said. "Shooter and Mikey practically lived at Cherries. And if somebody was stupid enough to kick a guy to death by accident, it probably was Mikey."

"And if you were looking for somebody who might dream up a deal like robbing a hospital, it'd be Lyle Mack," Donna Howard said. "He's always thought he was a big operator."

"How about Joe Mack?" Shrake asked.

"Joe . . . is a little simple. He pretty much does what he's told. But he's not a mean guy. He wouldn't kick anybody to death," she said.

Now it was late and bitterly cold and getting colder, but because Anthony Melicek lived only ten minutes from Lucas's house, across the river in Minneapolis, they decided to drop in, see what was what. See if another finger pointed at the Macks.

Melicek lived in an apartment in an old house not far from the Metrodome; the navigation system in the Lexus was pretty good, but the addresses were so cut up that Lucas took them down the street at ten miles an hour, looking for street numbers. They were getting close when Shrake said, suddenly, "Hey. Whoa. Stop. Back up."

"What?" Lucas looked over at him. Shrake was looking out the passenger-side window, back behind the truck.

"This guy we just passed. I want to look at him. He's right over there. Back up."

Lucas backed up a hundred feet, and Shrake popped the door and hurried across the street. There was little light, but Lucas saw him talking to a black man in what looked like jeans and a tight black jacket. There was a staggering tussle for a moment, and Lucas popped his door, ready to run over, but then Shrake yelled, "Open the back door. Open the back door."

He had the guy in an arm-bar and was hustling him across the street.

As they came up, Lucas realized the man was not wearing a tight black jacket. He wasn't wearing anything at all above his waist.

"Jesus."

"Better get him to the ER," Shrake said. "He's fucked up."

Shrake was in the backseat with the man, who began shaking violently, and Lucas did a U-turn and Shrake took off his coat and put it on the man and said, "We need to move right along." And he said, "Sit up, take a deep breath, take a deep breath, come on, man, deep breath, now don't do that . . ."

"Ah, jeez, don't let him barf," Lucas said.

"Better hurry."

Hennepin General was ten or twelve blocks away, and Lucas ran all the lights going in, piled up to the ER and ran inside. A nurse looked up and asked, "What?" and Lucas said, "I'm with the BCA. We need a gurney in a hurry, we got a guy in bad shape out in my truck."

The ER people piled out and put the man on the gurney and a couple of docs came and took him away. Lucas left his name and office number, and told the nurse where he'd picked the guy up. Shrake added, "He's got some bad shit inside him. He didn't even know he wasn't wearing a coat."

THEY WERE BACK outside and Lucas said, "That's your good deed for the year."

"If he hadn't walked under that light . . . he walked under that light and I thought, Man, that's *skin*," Shrake said. "I kind of didn't believe it, but I had to look."

"I'll put you in for something. A medal, or something. Or we could get the guys to chip in, buy you one of those family packs of Cheetos."

"I'm countin' on ya," Shrake said.

MELICEK CAME to the door in a pair of yellowed Jockey shorts, a brown T-shirt, and red velvet bedroom slippers. He was a short, fat man with a receding hairline and a brush mustache. A cigarette hung from his lower lip, and he was scratching his stomach. He looked at Lucas and Shrake and said, "Just what I needed. Makes my day complete."

He stepped back, a mute invitation, and Lucas followed him in, Shrake a step behind. Melicek had one room, plus a bathroom with an old cast-iron tub visible through an open door. A bed was stuck along one wall, an easy chair next to it, facing a flat-panel TV. There were two kitchen chairs at a table next to a refrigerator; there was no stove, but a microwave sat on a sink counter. The place smelled like pizza, tobacco, marijuana, bananas, and wallpaper mold. A single window looked out over a porch roof to the street.

"Mike Haines and Shooter Chapman," Lucas said.

"That figures. The dumb shits finally got themselves shot by somebody, huh?" He took the easy chair, and pointed the cops at the kitchen chairs.

"Smoke a little dope, there, Mr. Melicek?" Shrake asked.

"Yeah, but not enough to worry guys like you," he said. "I don't know anything about what Mike and Shooter were doing. I talked to them last week, we had a couple beers."

"You still run with the Seed?"

"Not right at the moment. Me and my ex-wife used our home equity loan to buy new bikes. Then everything went in the toilet, and U.S. Bank got the house and the bikes, and my ex–best friend got the wife. Maybe U.S. Bank is starting a gang. They got enough bikes."

"What do you do for a living?" Shrake asked.

Melicek snorted. "What does it look like? Nothin'. I was doing assembly until that shut down, then the unemployment ran out, so now I'm on welfare."

They thought about the perils of negotiating a capitalist economy for a moment, then Lucas said, "Three guys went into the University Hospitals and robbed the pharmacy, got away with maybe a half-million in drugs. Mike and Shooter were two of them. What we're asking around is, who is smart enough to figure out how to do that, and also mean enough to shoot his own pals?"

Melicek tilted his head and said, "The same guy who is smart enough to figure out I talked to you guys, and mean enough to come over here and kill my ass."

"We're talking to a lot of people—in fact, we got your name from other members of the Seed, who said you were friendly with Haines and Chapman."

"Well, *I* didn't do it," Melicek said. "If I had a half-million in drugs, you think I'd live in a shithole like this for one more minute?"

"Maybe . . . if you were being smart about it," Shrake said.

"If I was that smart, I wouldn't be living in a shithole like this in the first place," Melicek said. He squinted at Lucas: "Who'd you talk to about me?"

Lucas shook his head.

"It was that fucker Lincoln, wasn't it?"

Lucas took out his notebook, wrote, "Lincoln," and said, "Thank you."

"Hey, I didn't tell you anything . . ."

They pushed him, not getting much more than "Lincoln," and finally Lucas asked, "What exactly is your relationship to the Macks?"

"I'm one of their beer drinkers," he said.

"You think the Macks could have had anything to do with the robbery?"

Melicek opened his mouth to answer, thought better of it, and shut his mouth again.

"I take that as a big 'yes,'" Lucas said.

"I'm a little pissed about Mikey and Shooter. They weren't bad guys, you know, under it all," Melicek said. He was leading up to something.

"Come on, spit it out," Lucas said. "You know you want to."

"You know that picture the cops put out on the robbery? To the TV stations?" Melicek asked. "They say the witness saw him?"

"Yeah?"

"It sorta looks . . . not exactly, but if you talked to them, you oughta know as good as I do . . . it sorta looks like Joe Mack. At least, to me it does."

Shrake and Lucas looked at each other, then Lucas said, "The guy we met, who said he was Joe Mack, had a skinhead cut and a clean shave."

"What?"

"Just about bald," Lucas said.

"Then he got that way since the weekend," Melicek said. "Last time I saw him, he, well, he looked like that drawing."

Shrake said, "If you weren't short, fat, and male, I'd kiss you on the lips."

"Hey, that's okay," Melicek said. "I can live without it."

7

BACK AT LUCAS'S OFFICE, late now, they went to the computers, looking for Joe Mack mug shots, found his driver's license ID photo—and Melicek had been telling the truth. When the ID photo was taken, Joe Mack had a full head of hair and a curly reddish-blond beard. Lucas pulled the photo up as a .jpg, called Letty, his daughter, a night owl, on her cell phone, and said, "I'm going to e-mail you a .jpg. Get your mom to look at it. Get her on the phone."

"I think she's in bed."

"Ah, poop."

"But she says she's not working early tomorrow. I could get her up."

"See if she's sound asleep. If she's not, get her up."

He sent the photo along and then Letty came back and said, "She wasn't asleep. She's coming."

"You got the photo . . ."

She said, "Not yet," and then yelled, "Mom? Mom! Come here."

A minute later Weather came on, sounding sleepy, and asked, "What photo?"

"A guy who could be your robber," and in the background, he heard Letty say, "Got it."

Weather said, "Hang on," and then, a moment later, "Jeez, Lucas, that could be him. I'm not a hundred percent sure, but it looks like him. I mean, I'm sixty percent."

"All right. Is Virgil still there?"

"Yes. He's in the front room. Jenkins comes and goes—he's cruising the neighborhood in his car."

"What time do you go in tomorrow?"

"They're holding the kids in the Intensive Care. They reevaluate at nine o'clock. I need to be there for that."

"Good. We'll get some sleep. I'll be home in twenty minutes."

He checked the time, decided not to call Marcy. There wouldn't be much to do in the middle of the night. He'd call her first thing in the morning. To Shrake, he said, "I'll drop you, you can get some sleep, and meet me back at my place at eight-thirty. Call Jenkins, tell him I'll be home in fifteen minutes, and he can take off, too. If he wants to come along, we'd appreciate seeing him at eight-thirty."

Shrake nodded, pulled his cell phone, and speed-dialed Jenkins. "We're going after Joe?"

"I'll talk to Marcy tomorrow, decide what we want to do. Weather couldn't give us a hundred percent, based on the photo, but she thinks it looks like him. We'll have to talk, before we hit him."

Shrake nodded, got Jenkins up. "Got a break, big guy. Well, you know, I was doing the investigating. Davenport was backing me up . . ."

SNOW WAS SPITTING down the street when they got to Lucas's place, small nasty hard crystals that ricocheted off the windshield and over the top. Jenkins's Crown Vic was parked in front of the neighbor's house, a curl of exhaust coming out the back, and its headlights flicked a couple of times when Lucas turned in the driveway. Lucas blinked his own lights, paused to let Shrake out, said, "See you tomorrow," eased around Virgil's 4Runner, and pulled into the garage.

Inside the house, Virgil was standing by the kitchen arch when Lucas came in the back door; he and Letty had been watching television when they saw the lights in the driveway. "It's quiet," Virgil said. "Weather's in bed. What's the story on the photo?"

Lucas peeled off his coat and told Virgil and Letty about the day. When he was done, Virgil said, "It sounds like ninety percent that he's the guy, forty percent that we could convict him."

"Yeah, but these guys aren't exactly geniuses, either," Lucas said. "We'll set up surveillance with the gang guys and the Minneapolis cops, then we go in tomorrow and bust Joe's chops. See what he does. Maybe we'll panic him."

"I'll stick with Weather," Virgil said. "She thinks she'll be downtown all day."

Lucas said, "Don't forget, there has to be an inside guy. Stick close."

"Close as they'll let me," Virgil said. "They get antsy about guns."

Letty said, "Mom's pretty worried about the twins. She was talking to Gabriel tonight about which was worse, going slow or going fast. She says if they guess wrong, Sara's going to die."

"She's a little more involved this time," Lucas said.

"A lot more involved," Letty said, nodding. "She's not even thinking about somebody trying to kill her. She thinks that's all over, or that you guys will take care of it. She's, like, totally focused on the twins."

IN THE MORNING, Lucas called Frank Harris, the BCA gang guy, and told him what they'd learned.

"Pretty interesting," Harris said. "What do you want to do?"

"My other guys are either working nights, or are covering Weather," Lucas said. "I can pull Del Capslock, have him help out, but I won't be able to get him until later. We could use one more BCA guy. I'll get Minneapolis to kick in a guy."

"I'll send Dan Martin over. He knows most of the Seed guys by sight."

When he was done with Harris, Lucas called Marcy Sherrill at home, filled her in. "Do we have enough for a search warrant?" she asked.

"Not yet. I went over it with Weather. She says it could be him, but she wouldn't swear to it in a court."

"So what do you want to do?"

"Jack him up," Lucas said.

"I'll come with you."

"I thought you might. Listen, we're thinking we should leave a team behind, in case we stir something up. If you've got a guy . . ."

THEY GOT LETTY off to school, and Sam went with the housekeeper to toddler playtime at the Episcopal Church, and Virgil, Lucas, Shrake, and Jenkins did the caravan down to the hospital. Jenkins would stay with Virgil and Weather, they decided, while Shrake and Lucas went over to Minneapolis, where they'd hook up with Marcy and one of her investigators, and Martin, the BCA gang investigator.

Marcy showed up in her ass-busting outfit, lady-cop slacks with Spandex panels and shoes that looked like women's flats, until a closer look revealed the Nike swoosh on the back and a wedge-shaped aluminum toe—pants and shoes that you could run and fight in. She had her gun clipped on her hip, under a green military-style sweater with nylon elbow patches, which complemented her dark hair and eyes.

After everybody was introduced, with a certain amount of dog-sniffing—Lucas didn't know Phil Dickens, the detective she'd brought along, and the Minneapolis cops hadn't known Martin—they agreed that Lucas, Marcy, and Shrake would confront Joe Mack, while Dickens and Martin bracketed the front and back doors, close enough that they could be called for help, far enough away that they could watch the bar after Lucas, Marcy, and Shrake left, in case the Macks did something interesting . . . like try to run.

"We're not expecting an arrest, unless he blurts something out," Marcy said. "We're hoping he reacts somehow. Does something that'll give us something."

"Do we know where he is right now?" Shrake asked.

"No. The first thing we need to do is nail down his location," she said. "The bar doesn't open until three o'clock, but Lucas gets the idea that he's there quite a bit of the time. We check the bar first, then go on over to his apartment in Woodbury. The cops there know we might be coming."

THE SUN was climbing out of the deep well of winter, but it was still brutally cold. Old saying: As the days get longer, the cold gets stronger. Still, if Lucas pretended hard enough, he could smell the early edge of spring. Something, somewhere, was beginning to melt—probably, he thought, in Missouri. Just not here.

The five of them went in four cars, Lucas and Shrake together, Marcy, Dickens, and Martin in separate cars, out of Minneapolis, through St. Paul, south on I-35E. They'd made the turn south when Lucas's cell phone burped: Marcy, calling from her car.

"What's up?"

"We got the lab report from your DNA people," she said. "We got a match on Haines. He was the guy scratched by Peterson."

"Excellent. We're tying it up," Lucas said.

"I'm going to use it on Mack," she said.

THE BAR in daylight looked like most crappy bars look in daylight: crappy. Purple paint and concrete block and dirty snow piles and neon signs; though it might be possible to believe that you were honky-tonkin' if you only saw it at night; in daylight, it was clear that you were actually arm-pittin'.

Martin and Dickens set up first, one watching the back of the bar, the other the front. Martin called Lucas and said Joe Mack's van was parked in back, along with an SUV owned by a Harriet B. Brown and a fifteen-year-old Chevrolet owned by a guy named Lenert from Rochester.

"I'm running Brown and we're not coming up with much. She's thirty-nine years old, blue eyes, a hundred twenty, five-six, lives down in Dakota County. Got a couple speeding tickets in three years. Lenert, I've got nothing."

Lucas passed the word to Marcy. "Good. Let's go straight in."

They went straight in, parking in empty spaces on either side of the front door, and found the door open. A woman behind the bar called, "We're not open yet," and Marcy said, "We're police. We're here to talk to Joe Mack."

"Uh . . ." The woman's eyes flicked toward the door to the back. Another man, who had been working on one of the game machines, stopped working to watch. Lucas asked, "Who are you?"

He said, "Uh, Dan Lenert . . . Mid-State Vending and Games."

"Okay." Lucas turned back to the bartender. "We were here last night, we know the way."

Shrake asked, "Are you Harriet Brown?"

"Honey Bee Brown," she said. "I had my name changed. How'd you know that?"

"Ran the plates on your car," Shrake said. "You're the bartender."

"Uh-huh. What's going on?"

Lucas was already behind the bar, headed for the door, Marcy a step behind him. "We're investigating the Haines-Chapman murders."

"*What?*"

No question that she was shocked. Lucas stopped and asked, "Did you know them well?"

"Well, sure, but the last time I talked to them . . . Christ, it was only a couple nights ago. They said they were going to Green Bay. They had a friend over there who had a job for them."

"Who was that?"

She shrugged. "I don't know. But they're *dead*?"

"Yes. I'm sorry."

"God, the brothers are gonna be *freaked*," she said.

"They know," Lucas said. "We told them last night."

"They *know*? They didn't even tell me?"

Lucas said, again, "I'm sorry."

Brown turned on her heel and pushed through the swinging door into the back, and Lucas looked at Shrake and Marcy, shrugged, and followed her.

The back of the bar was cold, with the loading dock door open. A beer distributor's truck was parked in the garage-door opening, and a heavyset man in a Budweiser shirt was moving kegs and cases in and out of the storage area on a dolly. They turned the corner, to the small office.

The door was closed, but through the window they saw Joe Mack sitting inside, facing a skinhead on the other side of a desk. They were both looking up at Honey Bee Brown, who was screaming at Joe Mack. They could hear the screams, but couldn't make out the words. Lucas said to Marcy, "That's him behind the desk," and he saw Mack look up, see them, and say to the skinhead, though he couldn't hear the word, "Cops."

The skinhead turned to look at him—a prematurely bald twenty-five or so, Lucas thought, a white kid with ghetto eyes and work muscles, rather than gym muscles. His flat blue eyes looked at Lucas without fear or sympathy, and he shook his head and tapped some papers on the desk. Honey Bee started shouting again, but the skinhead said something that shut her up. She turned and stormed past them, tears running down her cheeks, saying, as she passed, "What a bunch of fuckin' fuckers."

Marcy watched her go: "Must have one of those fuck-words-a-day calendars," she said.

Lucas knocked on the office door, and Joe Mack stood up and opened it.

"We need to talk to you," Lucas said. "Now."

"Just finishing up," Joe Mack said. "I sold my van."

Lucas recognized the titling papers, and nodded. The skinhead asked Joe Mack, "We all done?"

"Take it all down to the DMV, and it's yours. Gotta get insurance right away, though. I'm calling my insurance company today and canceling mine."

"Do that, but I think my other insurance covers me for thirty days," the skinhead said.

"Don't fuck it up. Throw some extra boxes if you got to," Joe Mack said.

The skinhead stood up and squeezed past Lucas. "Pardon me," he said. His voice was toneless, nothing implied at all. He walked past the Budweiser guy, hopped off the ramp, jingling the keys Joe Mack had given him.

"SO WHAT'S UP?" Joe Mack asked.

The ramp was cold, so Lucas, Marcy, and Shrake squeezed into the small office and closed the door. Marcy took the visitor's chair, while Lucas stood against the wall and Shrake against the door.

Marcy identified herself, and then said, "You know these guys." She waved at Lucas and Shrake. "So, Joe. We talked to a bunch of people last night, and some lab people this morning, and a witness to the robbery at University Hospitals, and your name kept coming up. First of all, we identified Michael Haines with a DNA test as one of the men who robbed the hospital. We got a whole bunch of people to tell us that you and your brother are the people closest to Chapman and Haines, and that you and your brother are the most likely people around to move a big load of drugs out of the Cities down the Seed pipelines to the Angels on the West Coast or the Outlaws on the East Coast. And lastly, we've got a witness who saw you coming out of the parking garage at the hospitals, and who has identified you from a photo on your driver's license. We know all about the haircut and the shave, and when you got them. We thought you might have something to say about that."

Joe Mack was staring at her with increasing fascination, and when she finished, sat with his mouth open for a few seconds, then said, "That's bullshit." But he said it with the peculiar downcast despondency that said he did do it; and that they all knew it.

Lucas relaxed: almost done here. "Joe, this is a murder charge. But there's a lot of other stuff going on. Somebody's trying to kill the witness, but that won't happen now. We've got her totally hidden and covered—and if you're not in on that part, we can probably cut a deal with you. If you *are* in on that part . . . then, you know, you do the crime, you do the time."

There was a knock on the door, and Shrake leaned forward, away from the door, opened it a crack and said, "We're having a private meeting here." Honey Bee Brown got her face wedged in the crack of the door and said to Joe Mack, "You asshole, Shooter and Mikey are dead. What kind of bullshit deal is that? They were our *friends*, but you just don't give a shit." She started to cry.

Joe Mack said to her, "Aw, Honey, I don't know what the fuck is going on. These guys say Mike held up the hospital."

Shrake said, "Miss Brown, Honey Bee, we need to have some privacy here, we're interviewing—"

From behind them all, the Budweiser guy called, "Hey, Joe—you gotta sign the invoice. I'm running late."

Joe Mack said, "Oh, for Christ's sakes," and he said to Shrake and Lucas, "This'll take one minute." Honey Bee stepped back and Joe Mack stepped around the desk to where the Budweiser guy was waiting with a slate computer, and he said to Joe Mack, "Okay, we've got sixteen . . ."

And Joe Mack was gone. He stepped past Lucas, cleared Shrake, and suddenly sprinted past the Budweiser guy through the crack of daylight between the back of the truck and the edge of the garage door and off the dock.

The move was so unexpected that he was gone before the cops got out of the office, and then Lucas, going after him, crunched into Honey Bee and then the Budweiser guy, and Lucas and Honey Bee went down. Shrake, who was faster than Lucas anyway, was out the door, Marcy two steps behind him. Lucas scrambled to his feet and got through the door quick enough to see Joe Mack vault a fence that separated the back of the bar from a neighboring house, and disappear.

Shrake was thirty or forty yards behind him, but running in boots and a heavy coat, and losing ground fast. Marcy was farther back. Shrake clambered over the fence and kept running, while Lucas swerved toward the street and ran past the surveillance car where Martin had just hit the ground and shouted, "Was that him?"

"He's running," Lucas shouted. "Get in the car, get in the car . . ."

As soon as the woman cop began to talk, Joe Mack began to panic, his heart up in his throat. *They knew.* They had a witness, they knew about the haircut, moving the drugs, the whole works. The minute he saw the daylight, the Budweiser guy standing there with the invoice in his hand, he bolted. He didn't think about it, he ran.

Joe Mack was fast. He'd been a sprinter in high school, and he wasn't wearing heavy winter stuff—he was wearing the light jacket and gym shoes he wore in the back end of the bar, where it was on-and-off warm, with trucks coming and going.

Now, on the run, he needed to get inside. If he didn't, he'd freeze. He ran through a block of backyards, and then another, zigging and zagging around houses and garages and fences and parked boats and hedges, got tired, turned downhill to his left, made it across a street, and another one . . . ran past a house, jumped a fence, collided with a birdfeeder, vaulted another fence in a right-angle turn, ran along a hedge and a garage.

And there was Jill MacBride, getting into her minivan.

Mack hit her in the back, and she screamed but he lifted her with brute strength across the driver's seat, picked up the keys she'd used to open the van's door, and shoved the keys in the ignition and slammed the door and screamed at her, "Shut up, shut up, shut up . . ." and backed out of the driveway. Ten seconds later, he was down the block and around the corner. In his rearview mirror, he saw a man sprint across the end of the street, running in the wrong direction.

The woman was sobbing, and she cried, "Don't hurt me, don't hurt me," and Joe Mack took a long breath and said, "I'm running from the cops. I've got a gun. Fuck with me and I'll kill you in one second." He didn't have a gun, but he was scared enough that he sounded as though he might. MacBride stayed in the foot well.

She was half upside down, her purse on the floor under Joe Mack's feet. He picked it up, dug through it, stuck her wallet in his pocket. He'd need the money. The van rolled up to a red light. He ignored it—no traffic coming—and made a left turn and headed west, then a right, and another left, and he was on Highway 13 headed west again, toward the airport.

He had to think, but couldn't seem to. He couldn't go outside or he'd freeze. He saw the airport sign.

THEY GOT a ticket and parked in the top of the parking structure. Joe Mack said, "Get out of there and get in the back."

MacBride clambered out of the foot well and between the two seats and into the back, and Joe Mack said, "Lay down," and then, "I'm gonna go outside and make a call so you can't hear it. If you stick your head up, or try to get out, I'll chase you down and kill your ass. If you stay here, you'll be okay. You understand what I'm telling you?"

"Yes . . ."

Joe Mack got out of the van and took his cell phone out of his pocket and called Lyle Mack. When Lyle answered, Joe said, "Jesus Christ, I'm in fuckin' big trouble, man."

He told Lyle what had happened: "They know everything. They know about the haircut. They got me."

"So you kidnapped a fuckin' woman, you fuckin' idiot?" Lyle was screaming at him. "They might have been bullshitting you, but now they got you for kidnapping."

"I didn't kidnap her. She's right in the van, she's right here, she's fine, I'm gonna let her go," Joe Mack said.

"Don't do a fuckin' thing," Lyle Mack said. "Stay right there and keep her with you. I'm gonna call Cappy and have him pick you up. Then I gotta call the cops."

"What for?"

"To turn you in, you dumb shit. If I don't turn you in, they'll get me, too. I'll call them and tell them you called me, but I won't tell them where you're at."

"What about me?"

"Like you said the other day—you're headed for Mexico. Or Panama. You're gone, man."

LYLE MACK, hurrying, not thinking, dug his clean phone out of the pocket of his old army uniform in a back closet and called Caprice Garner. "I can do that, but it'll cost you another five grand," Cappy said, when Lyle Mack explained the situation. Cappy was out test-driving his new van.

"Five grand. That's fine. But I'm gonna have to owe it to you. We've got all that stuff we took out of the pharmacy, that's worth way more than five grand. But you'll have to be patient."

"Hey, I'll wait," Cappy said. "For a while, anyway."

"Deal," Lyle Mack said. He put the clean phone in his pocket and called his lawyer on the house phone. They talked for two minutes, and then the lawyer said, "I don't want to hear any more right now. Wait till the thing has settled down, then come see me."

That didn't help. He started to pace: he felt caged, like an animal. Joe Mack might have finished them off.

JOE MACK sat in the van and talked with MacBride: "Look, I don't want to hurt you, and I won't. But the cops are . . . framing me. I took off. I freaked out and grabbed you, which I know I shouldn't have done, but now I'm in trouble for that."

"I won't testify against you, if you let me go," MacBride said.

Joe Mack wasn't the sharpest knife in the dishwasher, but he knew she was lying the moment the words were out of her mouth, and he almost laughed. "You'd turn me in the minute you got loose," he said. "I know that, you know that . . . when my buddy gets here, we're heading for Canada. There's good jobs up there, and they don't care who you are. Just be a little bit patient, and then you can tell the cops whatever you want."

He told her about working in the bar, and how the cops were trying to frame him for holding up the hospital. "We did not do that," he told her. "We did *not*. We got a good business, why'd we want to go around breaking into a hospital? But we're in an unpopular group, you know? The Seed? Have you heard of us?"

She shook her head.

"Well, we're really called the Bad Seed of America, Inc. We're a motorcycle club that got started in Milwaukee and Green Bay back, you know, a long time ago. My dad was a member . . ."

He told her about riding with the Seed, and she told him about getting laid off by the West Metro Credit Union. "I've got a job interview tomorrow at Macy's, in the credit department . . ." She had two daughters, she said, and was separated from her husband, but hoping to get back together after they worked out some issues. She was a sincere-sounding, dark-haired woman, and Joe Mack liked her well enough, though she was not really his style, too thin and small-breasted, with the beginnings of a satchel ass.

"I was just going to pick up Stacy when . . . you know. They're going to wonder what happened to me . . ."

CAPPY GARNER parked in the green ramp and took the elevator down, walked through the underground plaza, found the blue ramp, and went up to the top level, pulled on a watch cap, turned up his collar, walked across the open top level, his hands thrust in the pockets of his new navy pea jacket. Joe Mack saw him coming and said to MacBride, "Here's my buddy. Now you stay down and everything will be okay. He can be a badass, so you don't want to see his face."

"I'll stay down," she promised.

Joe Mack got out of the van and Cappy came up and asked, "She inside there?"

"Yeah, but I made her stay down, so she couldn't see your face."

Cappy looked around the deck. "Don't see any cameras."

"No, but they'll figure out who done it anyway. She'll tell them."

"No, she won't," Cappy said. "Lyle says we get rid of her."

Joe Mack was taken aback. *"What?"*

"Get rid of her. Doesn't nobody but her know you grabbed her, so if we get rid of her, you're in the clear."

"Well, Jesus, we can't just . . . I mean, she's a nice lady."

"Little shit's gotta fall in everybody's life," Cappy said. He grabbed the van's side door to pull it back.

"Come on, Cappy," Joe Mack said. "Don't . . ."

"Already got a contract," he said. He pulled the door back. MacBride was lying on her stomach, and she looked at him, startled, and then asked, "Who are you?"

"I'm Cappy," Cappy said. He crawled into the van and pulled the door most of the way shut. Joe Mack, outside, shouted, "Goddamnit, Cappy . . ."

Cappy crawled over to her and she tried to crawl away, seized with desperation, and Cappy grabbed her left arm and yanked her halfway over on her back, but she struggled to get back on her stomach. He hit her once, hard, in the back of the head, and her face bounced off the floor, and the next time, when he yanked her over, she turned, and he lurched over her hips, one knee on each side. He tried to reach for her throat, but she cut at him with her nails, and he hit her again, on the side of the head, dazing her, and then got his thumbs under her chin.

He'd never strangled anybody, and thought there couldn't be too much to it, but she bucked and fought him, and his thumbs kept slipping off her windpipe; she tried to claw him again and he lost patience, hit her in the forehead, then caught her arms and pinned them with his legs, and went back into her throat, with his thumbs, and squeezed . . .

She was a thin woman, with no fat to protect her neck, and he felt something pop and her eyes widened and she stopped struggling and began to shake, and then her eyes rolled away.

*

JOE MACK thought Cappy would shoot her or something, but after a second, heard MacBride start to scream, the scream suddenly cut off. Mack ran a few dozen yards away from the van, stopped, looked back at it, paced this way, then that, then ran back and pulled the door open. Cappy was sitting astride MacBride, strangling her. His hands were bleeding, where she'd scratched him, but she was all done with that. Her eyes had rolled up in her head, and her body had gone into a dead-shake. Cappy was riding her like a horse, a strange, stretched grin on his face, teeth showing. He held her until she was gone, then looked at Mack with his pale eyes, smiled, and said, "See, nothing to it."

"You're not going to kill me, are you?" Joe Mack asked.

"Why would I do that?"

"I thought maybe, you know, Lyle said something."

Cappy shook his head. "Nope. Didn't say nothing to me."

Joe Mack looked at MacBride's body and thought, *Man, she looks really dead*. She really *was* dead. A few minutes ago, she'd been talking about her daughters.

"We gotta go," Cappy said. "I'm parked in the Green Ramp."

"Where're we going?" Joe Mack asked, as they headed for the elevators.

"You're going over to that horse place, to start with. Hide out there for a few days."

Joe Mack said, "I don't know—Honey Bee was pretty pissed about Mikey and Shooter."

"Yeah, but she can't talk about it, because she was in on the hospital stickup. That's murder for her, too. So you hide out there, let your hair grow a little bit, maybe put on a mustache, and we'll clean up this witness woman, and then, you know . . . head for the border."

"Yeah . . . yeah." Joe walked along for a minute, then said, "Excuse me. I gotta puke."

8

Lucas, Marcy, and the others circled through the neighborhood, on foot and by car, looking for Joe Mack, confused for a few minutes about exactly which town they were in. They finally settled on Mendota Heights and they got a couple of Mendota Heights cars out, but there were only a half-dozen cops on duty. The chief, whose name was Mark Grace, was a little pissed about the ruckus, until Lucas explained that they'd thought it'd be a routine interview.

"We were putting some pressure on the guy. We didn't think he'd do anything that stupid," Lucas said. It sounded lame in his own ears. "We sorta fucked up, but not really."

"Yeah, yeah," Grace said. "I guess it happens. The question is, is he holed up in somebody's house?"

"We don't know," Marcy said. "He got lost in those houses back there, and he could have gone anywhere."

"But not too far—he didn't have a coat," Lucas said.

"You look for tracks?"

"Yeah, but there are a lot of tracks. When we lost sight of him—"

"Guess we start knocking on doors," Grace said.

"Problem is, half the people in town are at work," one of the other Mendota cops said. "If he's got a gun on somebody, and nobody answers the door, how're we gonna know he's inside?"

Everybody looked at Lucas, who said, "You know what? We won't. So let's not do that. Could we just get a couple of your cars roaming around the streets? Put some pressure on him and let him run. He'll run sooner or later. He's not smart enough not to."

They argued about that for a while—the chief pointed out that somebody might be held hostage, and if they knocked on doors, they'd at least eliminate places where they knew he wasn't—but finally agreed that cruising was the best option, until something better came along. They were still talking about it when Lucas got a call from the BCA duty officer.

"You got a guy name of Lyle Mack calling you about his brother, who he says you're chasing."

Lucas took the call, and Lyle Mack said, "I got a call from Joe. He said you guys scared the shit out of him and he ran away."

"Where is he?" Lucas asked.

"I don't know. Someplace around here," Lyle Mack said. "He said he ran until he couldn't run anymore and then he went down to a shopping center where he saw a cab letting a guy out, and got a ride downtown. He said he bought a coat at Macy's, and he's leaving town."

"Don't lie to me, man. We're past that," Lucas said.

"Hey—I'm not," Lyle Mack said. "I'm telling you what he said. He said he ran for it because you accused him of sticking up the hospital, which he didn't, and you're trying to frame him, and he's heading out. He said *hasta la vista*, and he's gone."

"How is he gone? We saw him selling his van this morning."

"Yeah, and he's got a pocket full of cash from it, and Joe Mack's got friends," Lyle Mack said. "I told him I was gonna call you, because there was no point of both of us getting in the shit. He said 'go ahead.'"

"Where are you?" Lucas said. "We're coming to see you."

"I'm on my way to the bar. I'll be there in five minutes."

Lucas got off the phone and told the chief that it'd be good to keep a car or two roaming around, but that he believed Joe Mack was gone.

SHRAKE AND THE BACKUP COPS went to Joe Mack's address, while Marcy and Lucas waited at the bar for Lyle Mack. While they waited, they pushed on Honey Bee.

"When you came back there, you said to Joe Mack, 'They were our friends,' or something like that," Lucas said to her. "It sounds like you thought Joe had something to do with them being dead."

Honey Bee had had a little time to think about it, and she said, "No, I don't think Joe . . . Listen, they were friends of mine. They were friends of Joe and Lyle. They came here every night, and when they had the money, they were good tippers. Good guys. I couldn't believe those assholes didn't tell me they were dead. Like they were nobodies. Like they didn't care, it was like a bigger deal to pay the Budweiser guy."

"So why'd he run?" Marcy asked.

"I don't know—I don't know what you guys said to him. You must've scared him," she said. "Joe's a good guy, but he's not smart. Lyle's always taken care of him. I think you must've said something that panicked him."

"We told him we thought he helped rob the hospital," Lucas said.

Honey Bee flipped her hands in the air. "Well, that would have done it. Listen, the one thing Joe knows for sure is that cops frame people. He says he was framed twice, already."

She'd thought about it, but she overdramatized her answers, giving them the odor of lies. Lucas smelled it, and so did Marcy.

Lucas said, "As far as we know, there were no women involved in the robbery at the hospital. If you know something about that, and you're lying to us, you could go to jail as an accessory after the fact to a triple murder. That's thirty years, Honey Bee, and I'm not fooling around. This is a bad thing."

"I'm not lying," she said, with her best earnest, honest face. But she was.

Quick test: Lucas asked, "When did Joe get the haircut and shave?"

She hadn't seen it coming, and she said, "Uh . . ." and she looked from one of them to the other, and finally went with the truth. "Couple days ago, I guess. Listen, I don't know why. He does that every once in a while."

LYLE MACK came steaming through the door, looked at the three of them and said, "What happened? What happened? What'd you say to Joe? He's so scared he's peeing his pants. For Christ's sakes, Joe's a little retarded. What'd you tell him?"

Mack was scared. They all sat in the front of the bar, in the stink of the weenie machine, arguing about what Joe Mack was up to, and Lyle Mack insisted that his brother had nothing to do with any holdup. He rapped his knuckles on the table. "He doesn't do that shit. We got a good business here. And Joe Mack is not a violent guy. He doesn't like violence."

"Hey, we got his records," Marcy said.

119

"They don't tell the whole story."

"Oh, horseshit," Marcy said. "And we understand you're a branch of eBay."

"Hey. That's a lie. Anybody tell you that, send them to me. I'll set them straight."

"So where's he going?" Lucas asked. "Joe?"

Lyle Mack shook his head: "I don't know. LA, maybe. Mexico? He's a good mechanic, I suppose he could head up to Alaska or Canada."

"Has he got a passport?"

"Yup. He does. But he doesn't carry it. And if you've got cops over at his apartment, then he's not going to get it. But you know LA—if he wants to go to Mexico, he can. You can buy real passports on the street corner for a thousand bucks."

"What about Joe's haircut and shave?" Lucas asked. "You must have asked him what all that was about."

"I don't know what that was all about," Lyle Mack said. "Time for a change, I guess."

"Right."

Lucas took a call bounced off the BCA office from Grace, the Mendota Heights chief of police.

He said, "We got a call from a preschool teacher. One of the kids' moms was supposed to pick her up two hours ago, and they haven't been able to find her. Doesn't answer her cell, nobody home. Supposed to be super-responsible . . . and her house is three blocks from Cherries. She was supposed to pick up her kid about ten minutes after Joe Mack ran, and the school is about five minutes away. Never called to say that she'd be late or had a problem. She would have been leaving the house just about the time he ran."

"Sonofagun," Lucas said. "You got somebody on the way to the house?"

"Yeah. The preschool lady is there, with the kid. They say there was no answer at the door, but the back door was open, so they went in. Nobody home. The minivan is gone. Crock-Pot is on. I mean, maybe it's nothing."

"Maybe the Pope's a Presbyterian," Lucas said. "I'm heading over there. You got the tags for the car?"

"Uh, we're getting that," Grace said.

"Call the duty guy at the BCA when you get them. I'll have him set up to put them out everywhere."

"You think he's got her?"

"I do." Lucas took down the woman's address and rang off and said to Lyle Mack, "Your brother may be in really deep shit. I'm telling you, man, if you know *anything*, you better cough it up. Or we're gonna hang you, I swear to God."

"Man . . ."

THEY WERE out the door, and Lucas filled Marcy in on the possible kidnapping. Marcy said, "I'm going to get a warrant for a phone tap."

"Okay."

"Didn't have probable cause. Now we've got a lot of circumstantial, plus he's a runner, and we've got a possible kidnapping. And we know he calls his brother."

"So get it," Lucas said. "Problem is, every jerkwater on the planet has a disposable phone."

ON THE WAY OVER, Lucas called the BCA duty officer and told him to expect the call from Grace; and Marcy got the wiretap going. Two cop cars were parked in front of the house, and Grace arrived as Lucas and Marcy were walking up the driveway.

The house was a modest, dirty-white ranch with a detached garage; the garage door was open. It was more like five blocks from Cherries, than three, but also made sense for a runner, Lucas thought. Joe Mack had threaded around houses to stay out of sight as long as possible, then made a long hard zig downhill to his left.

THE TEACHER'S name was Marti Stasic. MacBride's daughter, four-year-old Stacy, a tiny black-haired girl with a smudge of tears under her eyes, held on to one of Stasic's index fingers.

Stasic said, "She was *never* late. Never. We had Brenda for two years, and now Stacy for almost two, and in all that time . . . never."

She said that she'd personally driven Stacy back home because she was afraid that "something had happened" to Jill MacBride. "I was almost afraid to come in the house."

Marcy asked, "Was the garage door open when you got here?"

"Yes, it was. That's . . . well, it looked to me like she left in a hurry, like she was running late to the school. So I called there before I called you, but she still hadn't shown up." She glanced down at Stacy: "I just hope . . . you know."

The other daughter was still in school, first grade. Grace said, "We'll get somebody over there when school gets out, if we haven't found her."

Stacy asked Lucas, "Where's my mom?"

"We're looking for her, honey," Lucas said, and he touched the top of her head with his fingertips, and felt the anger starting to build. To Stasic: "What about Mr. MacBride?"

"Jill and Frank are divorced. He has an apartment over in Minneapolis, I guess. I know he comes to see the kids pretty often," Stasic said.

Stacy said, "Where's Mom?" and she started to cry again.

Lucas said to Marcy, "Can you . . ."

Marcy nodded: "Right now," and she stepped away with her phone. To Stasic: "Frank MacBride? Do you know where he works?"

"He works for the federal government, but I don't know what he does. I really don't know him very well," Stasic said.

Marcy talked to somebody in Minneapolis, and finished by saying, "I want to hear back inside of ten minutes. I mean, like *now*."

Grace asked, "You need to check anything here? Inside?"

Lucas shook his head: "No—you guys have been through the house, right?"

"Top to bottom." He tipped his head and said, "C'mere."

Lucas followed Grace out the door and around the house. The snow was thin and hard, crunchy, with strips of frozen grass showing through. "Look." Grace pointed at a single line of footprints in the crusty snow, coming across the backyard from the house behind it.

"Okay," Lucas said. "Don't let anybody get near them: we'll want some photos, and some crime-scene guys. I'll make the call."

"Getting nasty," Grace said.

LUCAS AND MARCY left, and as they were going, they both turned back to look at the kid, and then walked away. "If Joe Mack did anything to that little girl's mom, I'll kill him," Lucas said. He was not joking. He said, "Keep that under your hat."

Marcy said, "Listen, it wasn't *us*. We were talking to him, had him right there, and he *runs*. That's crazy. He just outran us. It happens. It's like . . . I don't know what it's like."

"Ah, man," Lucas said. "I was just thinking that. How many people you got? How many can we put on it?"

They ran through the resources, and Marcy asked, "What about Lyle Mack? No way his brother was in this deep and Lyle didn't know about it. I got the feeling he's the brains behind the operation, whatever brains there are."

"I don't want to mess with Lyle at this point," Lucas said. "I want him sneaking around. Why don't we get your guy, and Martin, and put them on Lyle? See where he goes and who he talks to. At least for the rest of the day."

She nodded: "Let's do that. What else?"

"Well, I'm gonna stop downtown at Macy's and see if anybody who looks like Joe Mack bought a coat. Get a guy calling around to the cab companies to see if anybody picked him up. Get the highway patrol and all the local agencies looking for MacBride's van. There's a chance we'll need some DNA, so we get a warrant for Joe Mack's apartment, or wherever, and get what we can, and start processing it. See if we can find anything from the hospital robbery."

"That works," she said.

They rode along in silence for a while, and then Lucas said, "The longer we go without hearing from MacBride, the more likely it is that he killed her. Goddamnit. Goddamnit."

*

BARAKAT KNEW he had to stay down, at least for a while. He'd nearly killed himself the night before with the orgy of cocaine, to say nothing of the McDonald's meal afterward. One of the other docs asked him if he was ill, when he came in, and he mentioned the burgers. "All I wanted was a falafel," he said, with a sickly grin.

His body felt as though somebody had beaten him with a broomstick. He felt old, creaky in the joints, and like there might be something wrong with his heart rhythm. When he got up in the morning, he'd taken a couple of quick snorts, and then resolutely put the rest of the coke back in the shoe.

He got to the hospital an hour before his shift began, went to the reference library, got an open computer, went to the Internet and began searching for Weather Karkinnen's home address.

He got a hundred and twelve hits on Google, and all but a handful of them referred to Weather; Karkinnen was not a common name. He crunched through the listings: papers, reports, civic honors. And way, deep down, from years back, a report of a shoot-out at Hennepin General Hospital, Karkinnen taken hostage by members of the Seed, freed with a single shot by a sniper.

Barakat recoiled. How could that be? The Seed? The same gang? He looked for other stories about the shoot-out. Never found an address, but found a reference to her husband, who'd set himself up as bait for the sniper in the hospital. A police officer?

He switched his search to "Lucas Davenport" and got more than four thousand hits. He read through the length of Davenport's career: the man was a killer, and controversial, but somehow had climbed into an influential post with the state police.

They were hunting the wife of a state police investigator . . . and a killer.

He was still working through the files when Lyle Mack called. He answered on the way to the library door, and in the hallway, hissed, "Are you insane? You can't call me—"

"I'm on a safe phone, I'm in my garage. We've got big problems. The cops are all over us, and that dumb shit brother of mine ran. They don't know anything, I don't think, but he kidnapped a woman when he was on the run."

"Kidnapped . . . *Kidnapped?*"

"He was scared and he was running, and the cops don't know he took her. At least, they can't prove it."

"What do you mean, can't prove it? She'll *tell* them." Silence from Lyle Mack, and Barakat caught on: "Oh, no, no. Oh . . ."

"Listen. We got one chance," Lyle Mack said. "We've got to nail down that woman doctor. We're looking for information . . ."

"I'll give you some information," Barakat said. "She's the wife of a state police officer. If we touch her, they'll never give up. Never give up."

There was another long moment of silence, and then Lyle Mack said, "We don't have any choice at this point. Do you have her address?"

"No, but I didn't look for Davenport—that might be her married name," Barakat said.

More silence, then, "You're not joking with me."

Barakat: "Of course I'm not joking, you idiot. Why would I joke? This whole insane program—"

"Davenport is one of the investigators on the case," Lyle Mack said. "He was here. I just talked to him."

Barakat's jaw flapped, but no sound came out, until he managed, "Did you know? The Seed and Davenport?"

"What are you talking about?"

"The Seed took Weather Karkinnen hostage, trying to assassinate Davenport. He had your man shot by a sniper. They killed . . . the police killed . . . five or six Seed members."

"That was *him?*"

"Yes. That was him. Go to the Internet, it's all there."

"Ah, man. Listen: You gotta get a clean cell phone. Buy one at a Wal-Mart, with cash. Call me at this number . . . We *need* that address."

"You *don't* need that address. They come here in a *convoy*. She has bodyguards. They must be bringing her from home. You're going to assassinate a half-dozen police officers now? You're going to invade her house and shoot it out with men who have machine guns?"

Another space, then, "No. I guess not."

"I have some advice for you, my fat friend. If something were to happen to your brother, then it would all be done. Would it not?"

"He's my brother," Lyle Mack said.

Barakat sensed equivocation. "If your brother kidnapped some-body, then he is going to prison for a long time. A living death, anyway. Be better, not to be kept in a rat cage for the rest of your life."

"I'm gonna get him to Mexico," Lyle Mack said. Again, Barakat thought he sensed a tentativeness.

"If you just—"

"I'm not going to talk about it. Take down this number . . ." Barakat took down the number for Mack's clean phone. Mack added, "Get yourself a clean phone. Use a fake name and address. They won't ask for an ID. And if we can't get at Weather what's-her-name at home, then we'll have to do it at the hospital. Watch her."

And he was gone.

TWO FLOORS DOWN, Weather was working on a cancer patient, a quick job transferring skin from buttocks to arm to cover a wound created by the removal of a lesion from a blood vessel. She was humming along with Shostakovich's *Jazz Suite #2*, thinking of nothing much more than getting a nice suture line, when Maret pushed backward through the OR door, holding a mask to his face.

"What's up?" Weather asked.

"We've heard from Spacy, and he said that we should probably push through the operation tomorrow. He needs to get Sara isolated so he can work on her heart. They're evaluating her for a possible op within a few days after we finish. A week, maybe."

"Okay." She'd been expecting something like this. Juggling the requirements of both children had become increasingly difficult. "I can be here anytime."

"There's no point in starting this evening—too many people scat-tered around. But we are tentatively on for seven o'clock tomorrow."

"I'll be here."

He left, and one of the nurses asked if she'd heard any more about the killer who'd kicked the pharmacist to death.

"Nothing more. My husband is out chasing him today. I should get an earful when I get home."

"How can that happen in a hospital?" the nurse asked. She was a young blond woman, three years out of school.

"All kinds of weird and awful things happen in hospitals," Weather said. "Now listen to the nice music, and let me finish this arm."

BARAKAT WANDERED onto the surgical floor, nodded at a nurse at the monitoring station. "I've been trying to watch the separation work as much as I can. Is it on for tomorrow?"

The nurse had recognized him as a doc, both from passing him in the hallways and from the ID clipped to his jacket. She'd had other inquiries, and never even thought about the question: "Yup. Seven o'clock. Get there early for a good seat."

"The whole thing is so cool, huh?"

They chatted for a couple of minutes; Barakat was tall, dark, handsome, and convivial. The nurse liked him for all of that. He patted her hand as he left: "Thanks for the info. Maybe I'll see you up there."

Nice guy, she thought. *Definitely husband material.*

LUCAS LEFT MACY'S with a bag of short-sleeved golf shirts—January in Minnesota, how far away could summer really be?—and the information that the menswear department hadn't sold any coats at all that morning. By January, everybody in Minnesota already had one.

9

LUCAS WAS LEANING against Joe Mack's refrigerator with a Diet Coke in his hand, watching with little interest the two men from the BCA crime-scene crew. Joe Mack lived in a nice-enough but bland apartment with all-eggshell walls, in a singles' complex in Woodbury, a suburban town six miles from Cherries.

Joe had decorated the place with framed posters of Harley-Davidsons and *Playboy* Playmates. He had a stereo/TV system that occupied an entire wall in the front room, and a swinging-singles wet bar with every kind of North American alcohol known to man. No scotch. One of the crime-scene technicians had a Janis Joplin album playing on the stereo, a nice quiet background to nothing much. They'd found two ounces of marijuana in a baggie in the refrigerator. They'd tag it, and if needed, it could be used to hold Joe Mack, but with an outstanding charge of kidnapping, the dope wasn't lighting anybody's fire.

A DNA specialist had already come and gone. It seemed likely that Joe had been sleeping alone, since there was only one pillow on his bed. The pillow provided a harvest of curly, auburn hair, and the sheets a couple of semen stains that should, altogether, provide excellent DNA.

They also found two pistols, a 9mm Beretta and a Colt .45 with full clips, and several boxes of ammo, a twelve-gauge shotgun and three boxes of shells, a scoped .22 rifle, a scoped .30-06 rifle, a broken taser, and a paintball gun with a bag of balls. They took them away, but except for the taser, they were really nothing more than any Wisconsin boy might have in his closet. That included the dope.

"Now here's something really interesting," one of the techs said. He was in the bedroom, across the hall from the kitchen, kneeling next to Mack's bed. The other tech came down the hall from the front room and Lucas asked, "What is it?"

The tech turned and sat down with a magazine in his hands. "The February 1990 *Playboy* with Pamela Anderson. The gatefold is worn, but intact."

"Whoa." The second tech drifted into the bedroom to look over the first tech's shoulder.

"Think it could be a clue?" Lucas asked.

"It's a clue to something, but I'm so old I can't remember what it is," the first guy said. "Look at this: thirty-six, twenty-two, thirty-four. This woman was in exceptionally good shape."

"I'm not so big on blondes," the second tech said.

The first tech looked at him with pity and said, "Loser."

After a bit, Lucas said, "We're not going to find anything here, are we?"

*

HE WAS GETTING READY to leave when his cell phone rang, and he looked at the screen: Marcy.

"Yeah?"

"The airport police looked at their tag file, and they found out that Jill MacBride's van came into the Blue Ramp about forty minutes after Mack ran. They went looking for it and found it up on top. Door was unlocked. MacBride was inside. Looks like she was strangled."

Janis was singing that "freedom's just another word for nothin' left to lose," and Lucas said, "I, uh . . . Ah, crap."

"I'm going down there. We'll get crime scene on the way. Are you still at Mack's?"

"Yeah. Not much here. Got the DNA going. I'll see you over there."

THE SADNESS CAME ON like a wave. He'd never met the woman, but he'd seen the kid, and there was another kid still at school. Weather was talking about having another kid, looking for a daughter, and he wouldn't mind, Lucas thought. Tough to have too many daughters.

What about the girls, Joe? And in a way, he couldn't believe that Mack had killed the woman—he'd seemed like a screwup, but didn't have the hard edge of somebody who could throttle a woman in cold blood. On the other hand, the questioning might have triggered a psychotic state. If that were the case, then he could have strangled MacBride without really understanding what he was doing; from a terrible need just to remove her. That would also explain the irrationality of it. He must've known that they'd put it together, that they'd be after him.

Or maybe he was simply too damn dumb.

Janis echoed in his head as he climbed into his car, and he thought, *No.* Not Right. *Dead* is just another word for nothing left to lose.

DEL CAPSLOCK was leaning against the barrier wall, watching crime-scene techs working through the white van, when Lucas pulled onto the top level of the Blue Ramp. A couple of airport cops were observing, and Marcy was standing at the van. Del was wearing a Russian Army greatcoat, a black watch cap and galoshes, and looked like a guy who might have been hired to shovel the snow.

Lucas parked and Del ambled over and said, "Shrake told me about what happened this morning, and then Everson mentioned this deal."

"You look at her?"

"Yeah. Not much to see," Del said. "I guess you know who did it."

"Guy named Joe Mack," Lucas said. "He's one of the guys who stuck up the hospital, and probably killed the other two guys who were with him. Dumb sonofabitch."

"You're looking pretty grim."

"I'm feeling pretty grim," Lucas said. "Woman had a couple kids, and we met one of them. A preschooler. Cute. Scared for her mom. And herself."

"Ah, jeez."

MARCY HAD NOT TURNED to look toward Lucas, so he and Del walked up behind her and Lucas touched her shoulder and asked, "How you doing?"

"I'm okay," she said. She glanced at him, then peered back into the van. "But we got him. More blood, and it's not hers. Same deal as at the hospital—she tried to fight whoever it was, scratched him."

Marcy stepped back a foot or so, and Lucas leaned past her. The dead woman was on her back, her legs spread, her eyes still open. Stiff, either with rigor mortis or the cold.

The anger bit at him again. Not necessary: a woman dead because of nothing. Lucas backed away, then asked to the technician's back, "You see any other damage? Head wounds? Was she hit with anything?"

"She might have been hit a couple times," the tech said. "She's got some abraded skin on her cheek and forehead, but she died from strangulation."

"Was a cord used, or . . ."

"Looks like fingers," the tech said. "Like he crushed her windpipe with his thumbs. Really dug in."

"Raped?"

"No sign of that. Her clothing is fine."

"So he just killed her," Lucas said.

"Looks like it."

"Okay. We need to go over every inch of the van. We need everything you can get from the driver's seat and the passenger seat . . . We need to know if she drove over here, or if Mack did."

"Okay." The tech sounded annoyed: of course he would do that. Lucas backed out.

"What are you thinking?" Marcy asked.

"What Lyle Mack said—that Joe took a cab into town, went to Macy's. I went to Macy's, up to the men's department. There were two salespeople up there and neither one remembered anybody like him."

"Did you think they would?" Marcy asked.

"I wanted to check. He's gotta get a coat from somewhere. Anyway, they hadn't seen him. It's possible he carried the coat to another checkout desk. I'd want to see the receipt before I believed it, but it's possible."

"And the point is . . ."

"The point is, Joe didn't seem like this big an asshole." Lucas waved at the van. "He seemed like this hang-out guy. He seemed like a 'how ya doin'?' guy. He might do a burglary, he might strong-arm somebody, he'd steal something if he thought he wouldn't get caught, but . . . not this. This freaks me out."

"He was panicked. Something cracked. I mean, look at the guy in the hospital. Somebody kicked him, didn't mean to kill him . . . dumb guys, trashing around," Marcy said. "How many times have you seen it? A hundred?"

"Yeah, yeah. It's just that everybody keeps saying what a basically good guy he was." He looked back at the van. "I'll tell you what—that wasn't done by a nice guy. He looked right into her eyes and choked the life out of her."

THEY WERE still talking when Virgil called: "We're leaving the hospital."

"Nothing happened with the kids?"

"Nope. Sara's still got problems. They're now saying they could go tomorrow."

"How's Weather?"

"She's okay, but it's wearing on her," Virgil said. "There are

Minneapolis cops over here, talking to people who might have been around when the pharmacy got hit. It's pissing people off."

"It's a murder investigation."

"I know, but a lot of the people over here, especially the docs, are pretty busy, and they figure what they're doing is pretty important. I mean, it *is* pretty important. So . . . A couple people have made remarks to Weather, because they know she's involved."

"Fuck 'em," Lucas said. "When'll you be back?"

"Fifteen minutes."

"See you there."

LUCAS MENTIONED the cop-doctor tension to Marcy, who shrugged. "Not much to do about it. I'll tell the guys to go as easy as they can, but no easier."

Del said, "They oughta ask why somebody would hold up the pharmacy."

"For money," Marcy said.

"But how much? I saw in the paper that they were estimating the loss at a million or so . . ."

"Less than that," Lucas said. "That's if you count every last nickel on every last pill at street level . . ."

"But say a million. Just for argument's sake. So, wholesale, on the street, a half-million, or less. If there is somebody involved at the hospital, that's at least four people, and probably more."

"Lyle Mack makes five," Lucas said. "He's too short to have been one of the robbers."

"Whoever," Del said. "So, say five guys, because the math is easier. Say they've got direct retailers—they'd get half of the half-million. That means these five, if they divide it evenly, it's fifty thousand each. How many big-time docs need fifty thousand so bad that they'd hook up with a bunch of dumb-ass bikers to rob a pharmacy?"

Marcy said, "I see what you mean. We were working on the doctor angle because a witness thought it might be a doc. We'll start looking further down the food chain . . ." She looked back at the van, then at Lucas. "As soon as we nail down Joe Mack, we go after Lyle Mack with a flamethrower. Joe Mack, when he gets a lawyer, won't say anything. He's toast, no reason to. Can't plead out on this thing. But Lyle. Lyle could talk, with the right encouragement. Or get Joe to. Put the finger on the guy in the hospital."

"It's a plan," Lucas said.

DEL FOLLOWED Lucas home. On the way, Lucas thought about Marcy: she was a good cop, but she might have been on the street a little too long, or a little too long for her personality. The murder of Jill Mac-Bride hadn't affected her much—not as much as it affected Lucas, anyway. Another bad day in the life, but something she'd adjusted to. Lucas could blow off some murders easily enough, but some of them dug into his heart.

MacBride's murder made him furious. Why had it happened? How could it happen? How could chance stack up like that, how could they drive a crazy man to run at the precise moment a woman was getting into her van to pick up her daughter at school? It sometimes seemed to him that there was an invisible hand behind it all, and it wasn't a beneficent hand. Evil in the world . . .

WHEN LUCAS, with Del a hundred feet behind, arrived at Lucas's house, they found Jenkins leaning against the back of his Crown Vic, in the street, red lights flashing on the front grille and above the back bumper. He had a shotgun on his hip, muzzle pointed up at the sky, like a poster for a Rambo movie, if Rambo had ever worn a parka and winter boots. Lucas stopped at the entrance to the driveway: "What's up with the gun?"

"Virgil's idea. If somebody's scouting the place, we want them to know we're armed to the teeth," Jenkins said. "If they make a run at her, we don't want it here, with the kids in the house and the house-keeper and all."

"Probably scaring the shit out of the neighbors," Lucas said.

"So what?"

"All right. Don't freeze your ass off," Lucas said.

"I'll be inside in a couple minutes," Jenkins said. "We figure if they're scouting the place, they probably followed us."

Lucas pulled into the garage, saw Del stop at the mouth of the driveway and get out, to chat with Jenkins. Making a show out of it.

WEATHER WAS APPALLED by the murder of Jill MacBride. "Did we do something?"

Lucas shook his head: "No—except that Marcy and I didn't run Joe Mack down. Pure chance. And this whole thing came out of kicking that poor bastard to death in the hospital."

They sat for a moment, as Del stomped through the mudroom door. Then Virgil said, "Maybe we caught a break. With Joe on the run, Weather doesn't mean much anymore, as a witness. All she can do is identify a guy we already know is guilty of murder."

Lucas said, "That's true. It's a hard way to get there, though."

"Does that mean that everybody's going home?" Weather asked.

Lucas shook his head. "Not until we get Joe. He's so goddamn deranged, he might still be looking for you. We'll get somebody to Photoshop our pictures of him and paper the hospital with him. But his brother says he's on the way to Mexico. Maybe he is."

Letty had an unpaid, part-time job as an intern at Channel Three, fixed by an old friend of Lucas's. She said, "If nobody minds, I'm going to call in the murder. We can still get it on the six."

Lucas said, "Just the murder. None of this—what we're talking about here."

She left to make the call, and they sat staring at their coffee for a while, then Lucas sighed and said, "The kids never bothered me so much when I was younger. Back then, it was just another routine tragedy. I remember working the disappearance of a couple little girls, back in the eighties. I was still in uniform, they put me in plainclothes, temporarily, to ask questions. Most exciting thing I'd done. But it's really started to bother me the last few years."

"Well, it's how you got Letty," Del said.

They all looked after the girl; could hear her talking on the family-room phone. Lucas said, "She's got the scars. She was hurt worse than any of us know."

Virgil said, "I'm getting pretty tired of guarding Weather's body. If you don't mind, I'm going to lounge around the hospital a little bit. Chat with people."

"You might piss off Marcy," Del said. "She gets a little territorial."

"She can live with it," Virgil said. "I've talked to their guys, and they haven't gotten a thing. Maybe, you know, something would pop up."

"How are the babies?" Lucas asked Weather.

"Better. We could go back in tomorrow."

"They won't get at her when she's operating, or when she's with that crowd," Virgil said. "She can buzz me when she's done. Otherwise, I'm just sitting in the cafeteria, eating Jell-O."

"All right," Lucas said. "Chat with people. Try not to piss off Marcy's guys."

"What are *we* gonna do?" Del asked.

Lucas told them about Marcy's plan to go after Lyle Mack, when Joe Mack was caught. "We're gonna pick him up, take him downtown, sweat him . . . let him hire a lawyer, whatever. He could give us the insider at the hospital, or tell Joe to. We've got everything on Joe, nothing on Lyle, so maybe Lyle'll save himself."

Del said, "The other thing we could do is, start figuring out who Joe Mack's friends are, and busting their chops. Somebody's hiding him."

"Unless he's in Mexico," Weather said.

"Marcy's got the feds looking for him," Lucas said. "Both the Canada crossings and the Mexican ones. We can't do that—all we can do is look around here."

LYLE MACK TURNED the bar over to Honey Bee at nine o'clock and headed home. Felt odd to be leaving so early. He watched his rearview mirror, wondering if the cops were following him, or had bugged him somehow. Saw lots of cars, but had no idea if anybody had followed him.

He lived in a shabby but quiet neighborhood a mile from the bar, a three-bedroom rambler with a dry basement and a two-car garage off the alley in back. He put the car in the garage, went inside the house, walked around turning on lights.

Turned on the TV.

"Goddamnit." He was scared. He went into the kitchen and turned

135

the lights off, then went back and tried to watch a late-night sports channel. Gave it half an hour, then went to bed. He lay there, unable to sleep. Lay there for eight hours, looking at the clock every fifteen minutes. Knew he must have slept part of the time . . . was asleep when the alarm went off at five o'clock.

He got out of bed, drunk with exhaustion. Using his clean phone, he called Cappy. "Where are you?"

"Wal-Mart parking lot."

"Let's do it."

"Call me when you're set," Cappy said.

He got dressed in the dark, and when he got his coat and gloves on, he looked out through the crack between the front-room curtains, up and down the street. He saw no vehicles that didn't look like they belonged. He doubted that they were watching him, but . . .

"Oh, Jesus," he said. He was scared. He went anyway. Out the back door down the sidewalk to the garage, into the garage, groping past the truck to the back door, then, after getting his guts up, out the back door and into the alley.

Nobody in sight: a cold, dark night in January, looking down a narrow alley toward the street a half-block away. He listened for a moment, heard nothing but distant cars on I-494, and headed toward the street.

When he got there, he stopped beside a hedge and punched Cappy's number on his speed-dial. The phone rang and Cappy said, "Ten seconds."

Ten seconds later, Cappy's van came around the corner. Not Joe Mack's old van, but Cappy's old van—and stopped at the mouth of the alley. Lyle Mack crawled in and said, "So fuckin' cold. You get off work?"

"Yeah, I did. First day I ever missed," Cappy said. "Told them I had the flu."

"Whatever," Lyle Mack said. He pointed. "Go that way."

Cappy did a lot of turns through Mack's neighborhood, saw nothing behind them. They drove out to Cherries, stopped a block away, and Lyle Mack got into Joe Mack's old van. They headed into St. Paul, Cappy a half-block behind Lyle Mack.

*

BARAKAT was waiting.

Lyle Mack pulled into Barakat's driveway and Cappy parked in the street, and he and Lyle Mack went to the side door. Barakat jerked the door open, and they filed in, and Lyle Mack could see that Barakat was furious.

"What the fuck is going on?" he shouted. "Your brother kidnapped and strangled some woman? You guys are crazy."

"Ah, Joe fucked up bad," Lyle Mack said. "We've got him hid out."

"They'll get him," Barakat said. "He's all over TV."

"They won't get him," Lyle Mack insisted. "We got a guy named Eddie coming over from Green Bay. He's gonna drive him down to Brownsville. He's . . . going away."

Barakat stared at him, eyes cold as black glaciers; just a thin patina of white under his nose. He was flying, Lyle Mack realized. He was high as a kite. Lyle Mack said, "This is Cappy. He's gonna come with you."

Barakat's attention shifted to Cappy. "You as dumb as the Macks?"

"Hope not," Cappy said. His voice was mild, and he smiled, the corners of his mouth turning up. His eyes were dead as planks.

"I hope to God," Barakat said. He inspected Cappy for a moment, then nodded. "You could be an orderly. You got the look. We gotta talk before we go in."

"Lyle said that you could teach me how to act like a hospital guy."

"It's not rocket science," Barakat said. "I got a map for you and other stuff. A key. A place you can hide if you need to."

"Cool," Cappy said. To Lyle Mack. "You best get back. Leave the van . . ."

". . . right up from the SuperAmerica. By the pink house."

"Don't put it on the plow side. It might snow."

"Don't worry . . ." Lyle Mack glanced at his watch. "I'm outa here."

WHEN HE WAS GONE, Barakat said, "We have to leave in a half hour. So let's sit, and I'll tell you where you can go, and walk you through the map."

"You got a little blow under your nose. In the whiskers," Cappy said.

Barakat wiped his face with his hand and said, "Thanks. You want a taste?"

"Well, yeah. If you got some extra."

"Just a taste," Barakat said.

They had two or three tastes, and Cappy banged around the kitchen, going with the flow, talking like he didn't usually talk; told Barakat about living in Bakersfield, and riding his bike to Vegas and LA. Barakat told him about growing up in Lebanon and the war with the Party of God. "Goddamn, this is good shit," Cappy said, after a while. "You don't operate on people when you're high, do you?"

"I don't operate on people. When somebody needs to be operated on, we call a surgeon."

"So what do you do?"

"Whatever," Barakat said. He said, "I can't believe that idiot kidnapped that woman. Then killed her. I mean, if you want to get hunted down like a dog . . ."

"He didn't kill her," Cappy said.

"He didn't? Who did?"

Cappy raised his hand. "I did."

Barakat fixed on him, then stepped sideways to the kitchen table and sat down. "How'd you do that?"

CAPPY WAS TAKEN ABACK. Nobody wanted to talk about that. But Barakat seemed straight enough. Intent.

"Well, Lyle called me up and says Joe has this big problem . . ." He told Barakat about driving over to the airport parking structure, about getting lost, about finding the van, about crawling in and strangling MacBride. Barakat took another hit of the cocaine and passed another one of his twists to Cappy, who unwrapped it and snorted it as the punctuation at the end of his story.

"Okay, so you're saying that she was already on her back when you went in there?"

"Sort of on her side, looking at me, and when I got in there she started to roll over and I thought she was going to scream or something, so I slap my hand over her mouth and pull her around and jump up on top of her and get her by the throat . . . my thumbs in her throat."

"Did she fight?"

"A little bit, but it's more like she was trying to get a grip on the floor of the van, or something."

"Were her eyes open?"

"Oh, yeah, right until she died," Cappy said. "They were like, huge. Like bubbles."

Barakat scratched his throat and then said, "Makes me hard."

"Yeah, me too, sometimes," Cappy said.

"I don't mean really . . ." Barakat said hastily.

"Well, either did I, but I'm saying, I know what you mean," Cappy said.

They were both lying and they both knew it. A spark of camaraderie, something not often felt by either of them.

BARAKAT SHOWED HIM a drawing of the hospital and gave him a key. "This only works for one door, which is this closet." Barakat tapped the map. "I've got to let you in. I tried to get the outside door key, but they watch them. Getting out is just a push-bar."

Cappy looked at the key. "So the key is just about useless."

"No, not at all. If you've got to hide, you can get in there and pull the door shut. There are about a million doors and they're all locked, most of the time. Could give you a break. The thing is, nobody uses the closet. It's empty. You can leave your clothes there and put on the scrubs . . . Scrubs are hospital clothes."

"Okay," Cappy said. Barakat seemed really smart to him.

"I got an ID for you. I'll show you where to clip it on," Barakat said. "The picture doesn't look too much like you, but you can say you cut your hair off. Nobody looks at the pictures anyway, if you keep walking."

They talked about it for another fifteen minutes, then Barakat looked at his watch. "You know, you're catching on pretty good. You *are* pretty smart. But we gotta get going. Get over there, on the fourth floor—you'll go past some signs that say patient parking, and then physicians parking, and then you're in general parking, probably on the fourth floor but maybe the fifth. Just wait. When I can get loose, probably a half hour after I get in, I'll come open the door for you."

"Okay."

"If you really want to go," Barakat said.

There was something in the tone of his voice that made Cappy look up. "I thought that was the deal. Get the chick."

"That's the deal, except for one thing," Barakat said. "That is, it's crazy dangerous. She's got this cowboy-looking guy with guns who goes around with her. Her bodyguard. He's always out in the hall. I got his name and checked on him, and he's known to be a killer. So's her husband."

"Don't mean much to me," Cappy said.

"It should. It means they're in the same business you're in, and they've had more practice," Barakat said.

Cappy thought about it for a minute, then raised his eyebrows. "Okay. Something to think about. So? You were leading up to something."

"Look. It wouldn't do you any good to kill me. Nobody knows I'm involved, or even suspects I'm involved, except you and the Mack brothers. I can't tell anybody, or I go to prison forever." He shuddered at the thought, and let Cappy see it. He didn't mention Shaheen. "But. Instead of going after this woman, who's going to be hard to get at, if something were to happen to Joe Mack? If Joe Mack died, there'd be no link."

And he thought, *If Joe Mack were dead, even if the woman remembered seeing him in the elevator, they wouldn't be able to prove anything.*

"Lyle would figure it out," Cappy said. "He'd be pissed. Those brothers are tight."

Barakat took the point: if Joe Mack were killed by Cappy or Barakat, maybe he could find a way to turn them in, without paying the penalty himself. He said, "What if something were to happen to Joe Mack *and* Lyle Mack?"

Cappy grinned at him. "You really *are* an asshole."

"Listen to me, Caprice," Barakat said, shaking a finger at him. "The Macks are dealers. I know these kind of people. Joe Mack will try to deal if he gets caught. What does he have? He has you and me—me for the hospital, you for the lady in the van. If he deals . . . maybe he gets off with fifteen years. Maybe less."

"I think they're too scared of me."

140

Barakat shook his head. "Scared now. Scared if they're locked in a jail, with more bikeists in there?"

"Bikers . . ."

"Bikers. They'll have friends in prison," Barakat said. "We won't. They *will* deal us. That's all I worry about now. I pray that Joe Mack is killed by the police, but I'm thinking, for both of us . . . maybe we could make it happen."

"What's in it for me?"

"I have no money," Barakat said. "I'm slave labor at the hospital, until I finish. Then there are possibilities. But one thing we know. We know that the Macks have a million dollars of medical-quality drugs. If you would help, if we could find Joe Mack . . . I could get him to tell us where they are. I know they are not yet moved."

Cappy thought again. Then, "How'd you do that? Get him to talk?"

Barakat spread his hands: "I'm a doctor. I have scalpels."

"I GOTTA THINK about it some more," Cappy said.

"But you're not saying 'no.'"

"Well, you got some good points," Cappy said. "I hadn't thought about . . . you know, they could sell me out for doing the woman. I mean, hell, except for the guy they kicked at the hospital, I'm the only one who's killed anyone."

They both pondered it for a minute, then Barakat said, "This is a very interesting name that you have. 'Caprice.' In English it means an unpredictable action, does it not?"

"I don't know," Cappy said. "I don't know if it's a real word in English."

"Yes, it is. I remember it, because it's also a word in French—a kind of musical composition."

"You can speak French?"

"Yes. And Arabic."

"Huh." Cappy was impressed. "All I know is, my old man told me I was named after an 'eighty-two Chevy."

Barakat smiled at the idea—naming your son for a car—then glanced at his watch. "If we're going to go, we have to go now."

"Better go," Cappy said. "Tell the truth, I'd like to catch that bitch somewhere. She almost ran my ass over. Just couldn't believe it; cut me off, then almost ran me over."

Barakat laughed: "LA car talk," he said.

He was quite taken with Caprice, and slapped the boy on the back as they went out.

INSIDE THE HOSPITAL, Barakat led him to the closet, showed him how to wear the orderly's uniform, clipped the ID on his chest. "If anybody asks, you work in sanitation, and your boss, whose name is Rob Jansen, gave you a map and told you to spend the morning learning the hospital. Stay out of the basement. Jansen's office is there."

Easy enough to do.

Cappy ghosted down the hallways, patients, doctors and nurses, visitors, coming and going, all the time: people lying on gurneys, in wheelchairs, shuffling down the halls, sometimes towing bags of saline mounted on wheeled racks; people staring out of hospital rooms, watching television; beeps and boops from equipment, chimes from elevators, more laughter than you'd think.

He got a quick sandwich in the cafeteria, actually helped move a patient from one floor to the other, on a cart. Pushed a guy in a wheelchair to an elevator, took him to the cafeteria, the guy breathing oxygen from a bottle on the back of the chair, who said, when they arrived, "Thanks, son."

He thought at first that the other orderlies would look him over, but nobody paid any attention to him; after a while, he began to get the feeling that he was effectively invisible. He asked about, and located, the special operating room for the twins. Barakat had told him about the overhead observation room, and he found that, looked it over. Thought: Can't take her here.

There'd be too many people around . . .

Started on an idea.

If he could wait in a doorway, on a hall where she'd pass by, he could shoot her, slam the door, block the door somehow, and run for it. The place was such a tangle of hallways that if he worked out an escape route in advance, he'd probably make it out . . .

But that meant watching her for a while, so he'd know where she went. And watching her meant that a lot of other people would see his face around.

Maybe he could simply wait for the twins' operation, and watch her. When she got ready to leave the hospital room, he could run down the stairs, shoot her when she came out—thirty feet or so—step back into the stairwell.

If he'd stashed a piece of two-by-four in the stairwell ahead of time, he could wedge it between the door and the bottom step, and that would block the door as effectively as a padlock.

He could then run up or down the stairs, mix with the other uniforms, and disappear into the crazy maze of hallways.

Be out of the place in four or five minutes.

Maybe.

10

VIRGIL, LUCAS, and Shrake saw Weather safely into the hospital, all the way to the women's locker room. "Do not go off by yourself," Lucas told her. "Virgil can be there in one minute. Don't get a Coke or a candy bar. Just call him."

"I will," she said, but she said it in a way that made Lucas turn back to her.

"Weather, if you don't, I'll be sincerely pissed off. I mean it," he said. "There's a guy in this hospital who might be trying to kill you."

"I'll call," she promised.

A pretty blond nurse, carrying a load of fresh scrubs, had piled up behind them, and she said to Lucas, "We'll take care of her."

"I'd appreciate it," Lucas said. "And I want you to rat her out, if she cheats. This is serious stuff."

The nurse nodded, paused as she passed Virgil, and said, "How're you doing?"

Virgil said, "How're you doing yourself?"

"I'm doing fine . . ."

Weather hooked her by the arm and said, "Don't flirt with the hired help," and they went inside, the nurse turning to wiggle her fingers at Virgil, who wiggled back.

Lucas said to Shrake, "She didn't say, 'How're you doing?' to us."

Shrake said, "She was saying it to me, but that fuckin' Flowers jumped in front of me."

"I'm so hot," Virgil said. He touched a thigh with a fingertip and made the steam sound: "Chhhh."

Lucas covered his eyes in mock embarrassment, and Shrake laughed and said to Virgil, "You're so fuckin' gay."

LUCAS AND SHRAKE drove back across town to the BCA to meet with an agent named Lannie Tote, a gang-squad guy who specialized in the Seed, and Del. They picked up Del, who was talking to Lucas's secretary, and found Tote in Frank Harris's office. Tote was a thin man, a runner, who dressed in conservative gray suits with white business shirts and dark blue neckties with American flag pins on the lapel. He had a reputation for being conservative and Christian and competent.

Lucas told them what had happened to that point. They knew the outline, but not the details. When they were done, Harris asked, "Where are you on Joe Mack? Eighty percent?"

"Ninety-nine percent," Lucas said. "What we need, ideally, is a guy we can really put the screws on. We need to get a biography of the Macks. We need to know who they hang with, who'd be likely to stick Joe up in the attic, even knowing what he's done."

"Have you talked to their old man? Ike? He'd do it," Tote said.

"Where's he at?" Lucas asked.

"Up by Spooner. Got a place back in the woods. Works at an auto-parts store in town, does custom work on old Harleys. Does some welding."

"A bad guy?" Del asked.

"You know, small time," Tote said. "All the Macks are small time. Lyle is the pinnacle of Mack achievement. There was a rumor that Ike used to cook up some meth and move it through his boys, but quit when it got too hot. I'm pretty sure he buys stolen bikes, takes them apart, uses the parts on his custom jobs."

"You got anything we could use as a lever?"

Tote shook his head. "We don't pay too much attention to him—he doesn't run with the gang guys anymore. Too old, and what . . . mmm . . . eight, nine years back, he had to lay his bike down, up on Highway 53. Busted his legs in about twenty places, and his pelvis. He gets around, but he's pretty hobbled."

Harris showed a thin smile: "So if he runs on you guys, you can probably catch him."

"Not funny," Shrake said.

Lucas asked, "Who else, guys? I'd like to get a name where you've got a lever. Somebody who'll spill his guts."

"Ansel Clark," Tote said, after a moment's hesitation. "I was going to hold him back until I had time to really debrief him."

"What's his story?" Del asked.

Clark, Tote said, was locked up in the state penitentiary at Stillwater. He'd gotten a five-year sentence for an armed robbery in Forest Lake, in which a bypasser had recognized him. The bypasser hadn't recognized Clark's accomplice, but Clark had given him up for a sentence reduction. "He's not a popular guy. Every time Clark gets a new TV, somebody'd shoot it full of WD40 and it'd be ruined. The prison guys turned the cell around, so the set's on the back wall, but he's already lost three of them, and he's got no money, no family or friends on the outside to get him one."

"He needs a TV," Shrake said.

"He's pretty desperate," Tote said. "The last time they had a lockdown, all he had in his cell was an old AARP magazine and a picture dictionary. Didn't even have anything with which to . . . entertain himself."

"No stroke books," Shrake said.

LUCAS WAS friendly with the head of the department of corrections, who hooked him up with an assistant warden at Stillwater.

"If anybody sees him talking to you, he'll have bigger problems than he already has," the warden said. "But come on; I'll figure out something."

Lucas and Del went together, a half-hour ride, checked in, and got with the assistant warden, whose name was Jon Orff. Orff came down to the entry hall to get them, led them back through a maze of offices.

"I had the guy who's in charge of disciplinary action pull him off the job," Orff said. "He's down in an isolation unit. Should be okay."

They rattled down through the prison, through security gates, to isolation, a bunch of human-sized metal lunch boxes. Orff had the guard pop the electronic lock and they went in. Clark, a heavy, soft-looking man with a small brown mustache, was lying on the bunk, feet crossed, staring at the ceiling. He sat up when they came in.

"Now what?" he asked. He had one uncontrolled eye that would wander toward the outside edge of his eye socket, then pop back to the center.

"We're cops," Lucas said. "We need to talk to you about some friends of yours."

"Ah, man, they're gonna break my arms out there," he said.

"That's why we were careful about putting you in here. And you'll stay for a couple days," Orff said.

"What do I get?" Clark asked. His eye wandered off.

"I'll leave two hundred fifty dollars with Jon, earmarked for a TV," Lucas said.

Clark brightened, but then tried to frown. "That's it?"

"That's it," Lucas said. "We're not asking you to talk about anybody in here. We want to know about the Mack brothers."

"I'm gonna have to have something more," Clark said.

"There is no more," Del said. "We're buying this TV out of our own pockets. The courts aren't involved, the prosecutors, nobody. We can't do a thing for you, except the TV."

"How about some lunch money, some—"

"Nothing," Lucas said. He looked at his watch. "If you pick out a cheap TV, you can have the rest of the two-fifty. Start talking, or we start walking. We don't have time to screw around."

Clark scratched his mustache, arched his eyebrows, and said, "Be a hardass. Okay. I don't know what I can tell you . . ."

"How well do you know the Macks?"

"Pretty good. We used to hang together, years ago. When they were just getting started with Cherries. I'd still go by a couple nights a week, when I was in the Cities."

"Joe Mack is on the run, on a kidnap-murder," Del said. "Who'd put him up? Who'd hide him?"

"You know about his dad over in Wisconsin . . ."

"Yeah, Ike. We're headed that way."

"You know . . . murder-kidnap doesn't sound like Joe. Was he high on something?"

"Not as far as we know. He did it cold—strangled a woman. Mother of two little daughters."

"Jeez. That *really* doesn't sound like Joe. You sure you got the right guy?"

"Yes. He flipped out," Lucas said. "Look, you haven't earned a TV set yet."

"A guy named Phil Lighter, who lives west of here, somewhere," Clark said. "West of Stillwater. He drives for a limo service over in Minneapolis."

"How are they connected?" Del asked.

"Old friends. Go back to school. This one time, some school-kids found a dead wolf with his tail cut off, and they called the game wardens, and somebody said Phil had been driving round with a bushy tail on his car, and they went looking for him," Clark said. His eye wandered off, he blinked, and it popped back. "The story was, Phil went down and hid out with Joe for the rest of the winter and spring. By the summer, when he went back home, the wardens, you know, they'd given it up. They didn't have any real proof, and the case was so long gone, they'd just moved on, I guess."

"So he owes Joe," Orff said.

"Well, that was a long time ago. But, you know what I mean. They're that kind of buddies. I mean them crick dicks, they get pretty harsh if you go killing a wolf."

"Who else?" Del asked.

"I only know one more where he might hide, this guy named James . . ."

WHEN THEY WALKED out of the prison, leaving behind an envelope with $250, Del said, "This James guy sounds like a figment of somebody's imagination. But I'd like to talk to Lighter."

"Yeah." Lucas looked at his cell phone: call from Virgil, a half hour past. Lucas punched the redial and Virgil came up.

"You oughta come over here," Virgil said. "I got somebody I want you to hear."

"Weather's okay?"

"Yeah, she's doing something right now. Some kid was messing around with a nail gun, and nailed his face."

"Be there in half an hour," Lucas said.

VIRGIL WAS SITTING in the lounge reading a *Men's Journal* when Lucas and Del walked in. He dropped it on the couch and stood up and stretched and said, "Weather just called me. She's done, but she has to hang around for a while—she needs to talk to some parents about care, and stuff."

"So what's up?" Lucas asked.

"Come on back," Virgil said. "I got to chatting with this woman, this nurse, who was in the pharmacy when the old guy got kicked to death."

"Baker," Lucas remembered.

"Yeah. Dorothy." Virgil led them down a couple of corridors, to a small office full of nurses looking at clipboards and files. He spotted Baker, who was staring at a computer screen, and called, "Dorothy . . ."

Baker saw him, smiled, walked across the room, and Virgil held the door so she could step into the hallway. Virgil said, "Let's go down to the lounge in Imaging."

They found a waiting area for people lined up for CAT scans; nobody there, and they took chairs, and Virgil introduced them. Then Virgil said, "So I was talking with Dorothy, here, about the idea that one of these guys was a doctor. I asked her why she thought he might be a doctor."

He nodded at Baker, who turned to Lucas and Del and said, "I didn't really remember why I thought that, until I was talking to Virgil . . ." She patted Virgil's arm. ". . . and then I remember, when we were going over everything, word for word, that one of these men asked, 'What about this?' And the other man said, 'Lortab. It's hydrocodone with acetaminophen.' The way he knew that, and the way he said, 'a-seat-a-min-o-phen,' which is this funny-looking word if you don't say it all the time, made me think he was a doctor." She hesitated, then said, "Maybe."

"The next thing is, Dorothy told the Minneapolis cops that he had some kind of an accent. The guy who came in later, who they didn't see. So, I'm pretty good with accents . . ."

She laughed, and patted his arm again. "Every one of his accents sounds exactly the same. Like Wile E. Coyote."

"That's not what you said at the time," Virgil said.

"But she's right," Del said.

Baker said, "Virgil got me laughing, and then we were trying out all those accents, you know, Mexican, German, French. And I thought, you know, he did sound like a French guy. But I couldn't swear to it."

"And that's about it," Virgil said to Lucas. He turned to Dorothy. "You've been great. Thank you."

"If there's anything else, just call," she said.

When she was gone, Virgil said, "I believe her about the doctor thing. Del says, why would a doc go down for that little money? But I just believe her. She talks to doctors and nurses and administration people and orderlies all day, and if she said the guy was a doc, I believe it. Then, when she decided that the accent might have been French . . ."

Lucas took a minute to get it: Gabriel Maret.

He said, "Ah, boy. Do we know where Gabe was, when Weather arrived?"

"He got there a couple minutes before she did," Virgil said. "He was still in street clothes. They were talking outside the OR."

"Now I don't know what to do," Lucas said. "And I don't buy it, Virgil—he's a good man. Not only that, he's got a load of money."

"For sure?"

Lucas made a face, then, "Well, that's what I understand."

"Okay. But I thought I should run it by you. You're the big guy."

Lucas said, "Let's see how many more Frenchies there are in the hospital. Medical people who know how to say a-ceet-oh-my-a-fin."

Virgil corrected him, "A-seat-a-min-o-phen."

"Let's see how many there are," Lucas said. "Christ, I don't even want to mention this to Weather. She's gonna go ballistic."

"You could chicken out—tip Marcy's investigators, let them take the heat," Del said.

Lucas: "I suppose."

"But not really," Del said. "It's our find. We oughta run with it."

"What Del said," Virgil said.

Lucas nodded, then grinned at them: "Not gonna let those clown shoes from Minneapolis take it away from us, huh?" He thought for a moment, then said, "Okay. But I'm not telling Weather about Gabe. He's a friend of ours."

"Somebody ought to mention it," Virgil said.

Lucas looked at him, and said, "Yeah. Somebody should."

VIRGIL WOULD START looking for people with French accents who worked in the hospital, Lucas decided, since he was there most of the day anyway. "I'll get Shrake and Jenkins to haul Weather back home, so you can stay late," Lucas told Virgil. "Del and I are gonna jack up a guy named Lighter."

LUCAS AND DEL had called Lighter's name in to Lucas's secretary, Carol, and asked her to run him through the NCIC. On the way back across town, she called with the bad news, and Lucas put it on the speakerphone.

". . . charged six times with assault, two possession of controlled substances, which was speed . . . note in the file says he's a steroid guy, weight lifter. Spent most of his twenties working as a bouncer over on Hennepin Avenue, got too old for that, now he's a driver for Blackjack Limousine Service."

"How old?" Del asked.

"Thirty-seven. He spent two years in Stillwater for beating up a

Minneapolis cop named Lancaster after a Rolling Stones concert back in 'ninety-nine. He said he didn't know Lancaster was a cop, thought he was trying to crack security lines around the Stones."

"I remember that," Lucas said. "Don Lancaster. He had a fractured skull, or something."

"That's it. Lighter's alibi failed to hold up because Lancaster was wearing a uniform at the time."

"That's a bad alibi," Del said.

"Yes. He's been remanded for drug treatment a couple times, all the way back to when he was a juvie, but it looks like it didn't take," Carol said. "You guys be careful."

LIGHTER'S PLACE was a junkyard: three or four acres of buckthorn, scrubby red cedar, and weeds, punctuated by the rusting hulks of eighties and nineties cars, rotted-out snowmobiles, trashed trail bikes, all surrounding a two-story house covered with thirties-era gray tar shingles.

A deck, a few years old, stuck incongruously out of one side of the house, next to an anachronistic sliding-glass door. An oversized charcoal grill, made out of a metal barrel cut in half, sat on the deck, with the cooking implements still hanging on the side. A Jeep and two Oldsmobiles, though older and rusting out, sat in the driveway and appeared to be in running condition.

"If this guy doesn't have six pit bulls, I'll kiss your ass," Del said.

"I don't see any stakes in the yard," Lucas said.

"You watch," Del said. "Six."

They got out and both of them touched their guns, then Lucas led the way to the front door through the crunchy snow. He knocked on the aluminum storm door, and there was a thump inside, as if somebody had fallen off a couch, and a minute later, the inner door opened a crack, and a woman put her nose in the crack. "What?"

Lucas held up his ID: "Bureau of Criminal Apprehension. We need to chat with Phil Lighter."

"Phil's working," the woman said.

"Would you mind opening the door?" Lucas asked. "I can't hear you."

She opened the door a foot or so. She was a heavy woman with a bad hairdo, played-out blond streaks over natural brown. She was wearing a sweatshirt that said *If I wanted to talk, I woulda worn underwear.* "Phil's working," she said again.

"When do you expect him back?"

"Pretty soon," she said. Pause. Then, "You best not be here when he gets back."

"Why's that?" Del asked.

"Because he really doesn't like cops, and he's really pissed off right now," she said. "He was supposed to drive for some rock band, and they blew him off. He called a half hour ago. He's on his way back." She opened the door another inch and peered down the road. Nothing.

"I guess he has a problem when he gets pissed?" Del suggested.

"Yes, he does. I'd say he was a sweetheart under it all, except that under it all, he's an asshole."

"Sounds like the relationship isn't working out," Lucas said.

"Well, you know." She shrugged. "He's a warm body at night."

"How many pit bulls you got?" Del asked.

"Well . . . none. We got a cat."

Lucas said, "We're not here to hassle him. We're really looking for an old friend of his, Joe Mack. Joe's not around, is he?"

"I guess not. Not after he fuckin' strangled somebody," the woman said.

"Hasn't even called?"

"No . . . uh-oh. Too late."

Lucas and Del looked down the road and saw a several-year-old Cadillac rolling toward them, in a hurry. Not a limo.

"I thought he drove a limo," Del said.

"He doesn't get to bring the work cars home," she said. The door went back to the one-inch crack. "That's his car." And she shut the door.

LIGHTER WAS in the driveway one minute later. He climbed out of the Cadillac, a huge man wearing a navy pea jacket, white dress shirt, black pants, white socks, and a massive scowl.

"Who're you?" he asked, marching around the nose of Lucas's truck.

"Bureau of Criminal Apprehension," Lucas said. "We're looking for Joe."

"Haven't seen him," Lighter said, and he cruised past Lucas on his way to the porch. He was four inches taller than Lucas, six-seven or -eight, with a heavier build. Lucas could feel the weight when he hooked Lighter's arm.

"Take the fuckin' hand off, man," Lighter said, and Lucas let him go.

"Not a social call, Phil," Del said. "We're talking about kidnapping and murder. If you've got Joe in the house, if you know where Joe is, you're not getting any mercy."

"I haven't talked to Joe in a couple weeks," Lighter said. His face was red, and getting redder. He was about to blow, Lucas thought.

"Take it easy, Phil," he said. He gave himself a few more inches of space. "We're not saying that you had anything to do with it. We're just asking you, politely, if you've seen him, and we're telling you the consequences if you're lying to us. We know he's an old pal of yours."

Lighter stepped closer to Lucas and jabbed a hand in the general direction of Minneapolis. "You know what those fuckers just did to me? I was supposed to get two hundred bucks, plus tips, today. I turned down other work, and I get there and they tell me to go fuck myself. The fuckin' supervisor's ass-fuck brother-in-law got the job, and I can't say a fuckin' thing or they'll fire my ass. I been working there for ten fuckin' years . . ."

"Hey, man, we know nothing about that," Del said, his hands out, and down, trying to make peace. "We're just asking . . ."

". . . ten fuckin' years. And you know what I figured out after all that time, the one big thing? The one huge fuckin' thing?" He held a thick index finger in front of Del's nose, in a "one."

"What's that?" Del asked, and Lucas winced. Some questions were best left unanswered.

"I really, really HATE fuckin' cops," Lighter said, and he launched himself at Del, who'd moved a step forward.

Lucas gave him a hard elbow as he went by and they both lost their footing and fell, and they rolled and Del was yelling, "Hey now, hey now," and then both Lucas and Lighter were on their feet. Lighter launched a roundhouse punch that would have knocked Lucas's head off, and Lucas dodged it and grabbed his arm, but his arm was like a fence post and Lighter yanked it free and hit Lucas on the forehead with a backhand and Lucas went down again, not hurt badly, but his city shoes gave him no traction in the snow.

As Lucas was rolling and scrabbling back to his feet, Lighter went after Del and Del hit him, hard, in the chest, with no effect at all—a heavy wool coat was like armor on a guy as big as Lighter—and Lighter grabbed Del by the shoulders and head-butted him, and then Lucas was on Lighter's back, trying to get an arm around his neck.

Lighter twisted round and round, and Lucas hung on, best he could, and Lucas, in the spinning, saw Del, his nose pouring blood, coming back into the fight. Lighter suddenly screamed and went down, sideways, and Lucas saw Del coming through on a low roundhouse kick, which had taken out one of Lighter's knees.

Lucas tried to pin him, but Lighter threw him off and grabbed one of Del's legs and pulled him into the pile, and Lucas half-stood and hit Lighter on the side of the face, hard as he could. Lighter let go of Del, and Del, jerking away, sprayed blood over Lighter's face, and Lighter came back at Lucas, snarling like a dog.

Del shouted "fuck it" and ran away. Lucas didn't know what had happened except that he was on his own, ducking and rolling, faster than the other man; now on Lighter's back again, hanging on for dear life, on the ground, in the bloody snow.

He and Lighter rolled over once and then again, with Lighter trying to pull Lucas's arms free from his neck, then Del was back and he shouted, "Roll him once more," and Lucas pushed with one leg and rolled Lighter faceup, on top of Lucas, and then Lucas heard a metallic WHANK and Lighter groaned and jerked and pushed against Lucas, and there was another WHANK and Lighter went slack.

Lucas rolled him over one last time, with the last of his strength, and Del, looking crazy, his face a mass of blood, stood there with the cast-iron briquette shovel from the charcoal grill. "Bend his arms back, let's get some cuffs on him."

They did, and then sat there in the snow for a minute, Lighter blowing bubbles of blood into the snow, and Lucas asked Del, "How bad?"

Del said, "My whole face hurts."

Lucas said, "Thanks, man. He was kicking my ass."

Del laughed and licked blood off his lips. "We gotta call somebody. I'm not hauling this asshole back to town."

"Need to get you to a hospital," Lucas said. He fumbled out his cell phone and punched in 911. A woman asked, "Is this an emergency?"

WHILE THEY SAT in the snow and waited for the Washington County deputies, the woman came out on the porch and said, "You took him. Didn't think you could."

"Piece of cake," Del said.

THE WASHINGTON COUNTY deputies showed up with an ambulance, and one cop car and the ambulance headed to the hospital in St. Paul, Del riding with the cop.

Lucas and the other deputy decided that since the assault took place at the house, they could look around to see if there was evidence that might apply to the crime. They walked through, found a bag of marijuana in the refrigerator and added that to the list, and a bottle of a hundred or so little white pills in the Cadillac, which they agreed was speed, and bagged up for the lab.

They also bagged both Lighter's cell phone and the woman's. Her name, she said, was Butch. Alice, really, but nobody called her that. "Joe never called," she said. "I'll tell you, Phil probably would've helped him out, if he called, but he never called."

No Joe.

The cop asked Lucas, "How bad are you hurt?"

"I'm okay. He backhanded me."

"You're limping."

"I don't know what happened, but the sole of my shoe came off," Lucas said, lifting one foot off the ground. Four hundred and fifty bucks of Italian calfskin, and the shoes looked like suede rags after a car wash.

"Man, I'm glad *you* took him on. Somebody was going to have to do it, sooner or later. I was afraid it was gonna be me," the cop said. "So, what do you want to do?"

"I'll write up my part, you write up your part. Del can handle the arrest . . . you can do the search . . . whatever." He stood up, bent over and touched his toes, then bent backward. Aches and pains. "I'm tired. I'm going home."

WHEN HE GOT HOME, Shrake eased out the back door, took a look at Lucas and said, "Holy shit. What happened to you?"

"Tap dancing with a steroid freak," Lucas said. "Del got his face messed up. He's down at Regions."

"How bad?"

"They've got him sitting in the waiting room, waiting, so apparently it's not so bad. He hit the guy with a shovel."

"With a shovel?" Shrake's face lit up. "Man, I miss all the good stuff."

"Yeah, well, I need a shower."

"Listen. Weather's on the warpath," Shrake said, his voice dropping. "That's why I snuck out. Virgil told her what was going on, with the Frenchman, and she freaked out."

"Ah, man. Just what I needed."

Shrake said, "If you wait a minute, I'll get a shovel out of the garage."

Made Lucas smile, for the first time since the fight.

WEATHER WAS WAITING in the kitchen, arms crossed under her breasts in what Letty called the "You're goin' down" pose. That fell apart when Lucas dragged in, and she said, "Oh my God—what happened?"

"Fight," he said. He detected the possibility of some sympathy, so he added, "Del's down at Regions. Guy head-butted him, eyebrows got ripped up, just about bit through his lip. Saved my ass. The guy was crazy, a goddamned Frankenstein's monster. Del hit him in the face with a shovel."

"A shovel?"

"Twice."

Shrake, who'd come in behind Lucas, chortled, and said, "Twice? That's my boy."

Weather looked past Lucas and snapped, "Shrake, go play the piano. I need to talk to Lucas. Privately."

Shrake stepped hastily across the kitchen and out, and Weather turned back to Lucas and asked, "Really—you're okay?"

"I'm okay. I need to take a shower. I got blood on my coat and it has to go to the cleaner's, and my shirt and pants are probably ruined, and my shoes are gone."

"So what? You've got more clothes than Brooks Brothers," she said. "Are *you* hurt? Your forehead's all scraped."

"I'm fine. Del's not so fine. I mean, nothing serious, but he's gonna be in some pain," Lucas said. "The thing is, it was all pointless. The guy freaked and jumped us because he was pissed off about losing a limo-driving job. Ah, Christ, I stink. I had the guy all over me. I smell like the ass-end of a limo driver."

Weather crossed her arms again. "Virgil told me about the French-accent thing. If you think for one second that Gabe had anything to do with it . . ."

"I don't think it for one second," Lucas said. "I've already got Virgil looking for other people with French accents."

"Well, that's just fine," Weather said. "Virgil told me that. He also told me that he didn't want me alone with Gabe, which means he's thinking about Gabe. I was screaming at him: at Virgil. But he wouldn't budge. You know what he gets like."

Lucas thought, silently, *Good*. "I'll talk to him."

"Do that," she said. She looked at him for a second, and said, "Don't go telling him behind my back that he's doing the right thing."

"I won't," Lucas lied. They could hear Shrake playing "White Christmas" on the piano, and it echoed strangely through the house. "Listen, you want to come up and wash my back? I'm sorta hurtin' here."

"No, because then you'll try to jump me, to make sure you're still alive. I'm not sure that I'm not still pissed off at you."

157

"Looking for some comfort," Lucas said, trying to put a little pathos into it.

"Well, I'm going down to Regions and comfort Del," she said. "I bet Cheryl's freaked out. You call Virgil."

"Take Shrake with you." Shrake was banging out "Silent Night" with a jazz beat. He only knew how to play the piano one way, and only knew Christmas tunes, so that was what you got—honky-tonk Baby Jesus.

"And Jenkins," Weather said. "Jenkins is out driving around the block again. This whole thing is driving me insane."

"Crazy is better than dead," Lucas said. "That's my rule of thumb." He sniffed himself again. "Jesus, that guy smelled bad. You know? Some people just stink."

11

TWENTY MINUTES BEFORE Barakat's shift was due to end, a kid was brought in from a back-street traffic accident. He had a couple of cuts on his forehead, probably from airbag shrapnel, and his stomach "felt really bad."

Barakat ran him through the hospital's blunt trauma protocol and learned that he'd been using a laptop in the passenger seat, and when the car hit the truck, the laptop had been jammed into the kid's gut. Barakat thought, Liver, and talked to the shell-shocked mother for a minute, then got the scans going, woke up the radiologist and cranked up a surgeon, just in case.

By the time everything was in place, he was running almost two hours overtime, for which he would not be paid. He went back to the locker room, changed clothes, and did a twist of coke to pick himself up. Hated overtime.

He did another twist, washed his face, got his shoes on, and headed out. On the way, a senior medical guy slapped him on the back and said, "Nice call. The boy's going into the OR right now."

"That's great," Barakat said. "I had a feeling that something was going on in there." A little self-aggrandizement, combined with discreet, comradely sucking up, just might get him to Paris.

Or LA, anyway.

BY THE TIME he got to the parking ramp, it was fully dark and colder than it had been in the morning. The wind was coming from the northeast, which, he'd learned from watching local weather programs, meant it might snow. He shivered against it, pulled his coat collar closer, and hurried to his car.

"Hey, bro."

Cappy was there, getting out of a white van a few spaces down from Barakat's car. Barakat stiffened: Had Cappy told Lyle Mack about their discussion that morning, and Lyle sent Cappy to resolve the problem? There was nobody else in the ramp; they were alone in the dark.

Barakat said, "You know, you're parked in a physician's space. That's a good way to get noticed."

Cappy came slouching up. "Don't worry, I'm not here to hit ya." And he grinned: "That's what you were thinking about, weren't you?"

Barakat bit back a direct answer. "What's that weak cigarette you're smoking? It smells like a sewage-plant fire."

Cappy looked at his cigarette: "Just a Camel."

"Give me that," Barakat said. He took the cigarette, dropped it on the ramp, ground it out with his foot. "Try one of these." He shook out a Gauloise. "Smuggled in from Canada," he said. The relief was surging through him like a flood tide.

He held his lighter and Cappy took a drag: "Holy shit."

"So did you see her?" Barakat asked.

"Yes, I did. I even followed her home," Cappy said. He let the harsh smoke drift out through his nostrils: better than a hit of NyQuil. "She's got three bodyguards, at least, and they've got shotguns and I suppose their pistols and all. If I'm going to do her, I'll have to figure something out."

"Listen to me, Caprice. You must be maximum careful," Barakat said. "I agree, it may be necessary, for your own satisfaction. This is what men sometimes have to do."

"She sorta punked me," Cappy said.

"This is what I am saying." Barakat paused, then said, "I need something to eat. There's a diner in St. Paul, we could talk."

Cappy said, "Sure." He took a drag on the Gauloise. "Give me another one of those, hey?"

Barakat took one for himself and gave the pack to Cappy.

THEY GOT a booth at the Snelling Diner, and after the waitress had taken their orders, Barakat held up a twist and said, "I gotta use the men's room. I'll be right back." He went in the men's room, into the toilet stall, sucked up the twist, wiped his nose, checked himself in the mirror before he went back out. Back in the booth, Cappy asked, "You got another one of those?"

Barakat said, "One more," and pushed the twist across the table. Cappy took it and went back to the men's room, and two minutes later, was back. "That's better'n Wheaties," he said.

"I don't know . . ."

"Never mind. Anyway, I've been thinking about Joe and Lyle. Those rascals hired me to get rid of this doctor chick and this kidnap chick and Shooter and Mikey, who was supposed to be their friends, and you know what? I was thinking about what you said, and you're right. They'll try to do me in, when I finish with the doctor chick. If I do her, then I'd be the last link, huh? Or you would be."

Barakat ticked a finger at him: "Now you are thinking correctly. But . . ."

"But?"

"You, my friend, may have to kill the woman anyway. I don't know; maybe you don't think so. Women are nothing. Nothing. I don't care if she's a surgeon. That's just some . . . bullshit. But still: it would not do your dignity any good to let this woman pass."

"I gotta think about it some more," Cappy said. "I kind of got a plan."

He explained, and Barakat thought the same thing that Cappy thought when he looked into the mirror: this boy is not long for the world. He didn't say that. It would be useful, though, if he took Karkinnen with him, when he went. He asked, "Have you heard any more about the Macks?"

Cappy scratched his chin, his eyes wandering away for a moment. "I talked to Lyle," he said. "I might know where Joe is. Lyle sent Shooter and Mikey out to his bartender's house. The bartender's like his girl, but I think Joe might be fuckin' her, too. Anyway, I think that's probably where he is. It's way out in the country. Nobody would ever find him out there, unless they were told about it. That's where we took Mikey and Shooter."

The waitress came with their shakes, burgers, and fries, and when she was gone again, Cappy asked, "So what do you think?"

"I think we go after Joe," Barakat said.

"If we take Joe, we might have to take Lyle. They're pretty tight."

Barakat said, "So?"

The coke was on top of both of them now, and they were stuffing the fries into their mouths, eyes bright, faces animated. "Do that, we gotta figure out where they put that dope," Cappy mumbled through the potatoes.

They snarled through the rest of the meal, and when wiping their hands and faces with paper napkins, Barakat asked, "Why didn't you take Joe when you could have? At the airport?"

Cappy raised his eyebrows, shook his head. "Hell, you know, I wasn't thinking about it. I was there to do the chick. I had a contract, you know, with the brothers: so I went and did it. I only got to thinking about it later, when you brought it up. If it wasn't for the doctor chick, and then the kidnapping, I'd let it go. Trust that they'd keep their mouths shut, and that we could ride it out. That's not going to happen, now. If they catch Joe without killing him . . ."

"We better get him," Barakat said.

Cappy suggested that they would have to wait until the next day: "Honey Bee usually goes home about seven o'clock. If she's there, she adds to the problem."

"All right, but tomorrow . . ." He stopped, and looked around. "We should talk about this somewhere else. My place is two minutes from here."

THEY WENT to Barakat's and Barakat brought out the cocaine again, still far enough from a shortage that he didn't worry about it. The coke helped with that attitude, steadied him with its cold clearheadedness, its chemical confidence, the sense of potency.

They started to argue.

"You go in there with a gun, you can't pussy out," Cappy told him. "The second that Joe figures out what you're doing, he'll be all over you. He's a tough guy, you know. A little stupid, but he can fight. Strong as an ox. You gotta put the gun on him and keep it there."

"No worry," Barakat said. "I'm no pussy."

"You know what does it? It's that accent, you know?" Cappy said, his eyes glowing. "It's kind of a pussy accent. What kind of accent is that, anyway?"

"There's nothing pussy about my accent," Barakat said. "I'm Lebanese, I speak French, you know, I have a French accent in English."

"You an Arab?"

"No. I am a descendant of the Phoenicians. The Arabs come from Arabia. My family, we were in Lebanon since Adam."

"Whatever the fuck all that means," Cappy said. He lit one of the Gauloises and added, "I just hope you don't pussy out."

Barakat stared at him for a second, then jumped out of his chair and stormed into the bedroom. Poured coke into his hand, pulled it through his nose in a burst that was as cold as an icicle. Snatched open the closet door, and found the gun. A minute later, he was back with the .45. "You think I'm a pussy?" he demanded.

"Whoa, whoa, whoa," Cappy said. He pulled his feet up on the couch. He'd always thought that he wasn't long for this life, but he didn't want to cut it any shorter than necessary.

"I'm not a pussy," Barakat said. He wiped his face and nose with his free hand. "You fuckin' American gangsters, you think you're the only people who can do this. You know nothing at all." He yanked the magazine out of the .45, tested the spring with his thumb, and slapped it back in the butt and jacked a shell into the chamber, pointed the barrel at the ceiling.

"You think—"

"Dude—"

Barakat pulled the trigger, and the gun went off with a deafening explosion, and a trickle of plaster fell from the ceiling. Stunned, they both stared at the small hole above their heads.

"Dude," Cappy said, and then he started laughing. Barakat didn't join in; he got angrier.

"Let's go," he said. He pushed the gun into the front of his pants.

"Gonna shoot your nuts off," Cappy said. But he stood up.

Barakat frowned—an "Oh, yeah" frown. He took the gun back out, checked the safety. "This is, they say, cocked and locked. Let's go."

"Where are we going?" Cappy asked.

"You a pussy?"

"I'm smoking this fuckin' cigarette, ain't I?"

They took Cappy's van, with Barakat behind the wheel. He'd taken a small baggie of coke, and he snorted another pile off the back of his hand and passed the baggie to Cappy. "Pussy," he said, and he laughed, and turned north, and reached out, clicked the radio on, pushed the first tuning button and got a rock station. Cappy sat almost silently, except for the sniffing, and watched the streetlights go by. Two blocks before they would have gotten to the I-94 entrance ramp, Barakat turned east, down the dark streets, toward St. Paul's downtown.

Snow was filtering through the trees, and the streets were empty. Four blocks, five, around a couple of blocks, past a closed market and a couple of open bars, town houses, apartments, back through the residential area. They crossed Lexington, still going west, when they saw the man walking alone down the sidewalk. He was wearing a parka, and carrying some kind of bag.

"Pussy," Barakat said. He stopped the van, pulled the pistol from his pants, undid the safety, got out of the van, shouted, "Hey, mister. Hey, mister."

The man stopped, looked at him, slipping and sliding across the street; tall thin white man on ice.

"What's up?" Black man with a briefcase. For some reason, the briefcase irritated Barakat. An unwarranted assumption of status.

He pointed the gun at the man's chest and said, "This," and pulled the trigger. There was a bang, and a lightning flash, and the gun jumped in his hand, and the man went down. Barakat ran back to the van and they were off.

Cappy was laughing hysterically. "You crazy fuck, you crazy fuck, you shot that motherfucker . . ."

"Am I a pussy? Am I a pussy? Tell me . . ."

They jogged out onto Snelling Avenue and idled back toward Barakat's place. A block or so away, Cappy said, "That was cool, but you know what? I could use another bite to eat. I don't know. Let's go someplace else, get another sandwich."

"I would like a doughnut," Barakat said.

"You're right. Let's get a doughnut. We could go to Cub. They got good doughnuts."

"Maybe two doughnuts," Barakat said.

Virgil Flowers had the sense that things were out of control, that they didn't know what was going on. He could see the same worry reflected in Lucas. Virgil had taken three pillows off the living room couch so he could sleep in the doorway between the living room and the kitchen, where he could intercept any traffic coming into the house, from any direction. Weather thought that was ridiculous, and made Lucas help Virgil carry the couch to the same place, so he'd have an easier night.

Easier, but still not easy. He woke with the unfamiliar sounds in the house, and he woke when he heard a car turn into the driveway at four in the morning. He looked at his watch, in the dark—paper delivery. He rolled off the couch and peeked out the window, recognized the car, and then the paper hit the porch with a solid thunk, and the car was backing away. He sat for another two minutes, watching. Nothing moved, and he went back to sleep.

At six, he woke again when he heard movement: Weather was up and about. Virgil went quietly back to the guest bathroom, washed his face and brushed his teeth, then out to the front porch to get the papers.

Lucas and Weather came down together, quietly, not to wake the kids, and found him reading at the kitchen table. At the same moment, another car pulled into the driveway, and Virgil checked: "Shrake," he said. He could see light snow coming down, in Shrake's headlights. Still dark as pitch. "It's snowing."

"That's great," Lucas said. "I love getting up in the middle of the night when it's snowing."

Shrake came in: "Good morning, everybody."

"Shut up," Davenport said.

Virgil: "I'm gonna shave and take a shower."

"Anything in the papers?" Lucas asked.

"Some poor bastard got shot off Snelling. He was walking home from his job. Somebody shot him in the chest. Paper says there was no robbery . . . says he was an interior decorator guy, working late on some remodeling plans. St. Paul says it looks like a random shooting."

"Poor guy," Weather said. "Why would anybody do that?"

"Gangs," Lucas said. He yawned, stretched, and said, "Doesn't have anything to do with us, anyway."

"And that's a good thing," Shrake said. "Are we talking coffee?"

12

WEATHER WAS HEADED out to the car when her cell phone rang. Gabriel Maret: "Go back to bed. Sara's got problems again. I'll be down in the cafeteria about nine o'clock, maybe you could come by."

"Are you at the hospital now?"

"All night. They're cycling. Sometimes they're fine, and then they start to deteriorate. Blood pressure is a problem. I'm going to take a nap, and we can talk about what to do at the staff meeting."

"I'll see you at nine o'clock."

LUCAS AND SHRAKE were looking at her: "They put it off?" Lucas asked.

"The kids are in trouble. We're going to meet at nine. I'll tell you what, we're getting to the point where we'll have to go no matter what. They can't be hung up like this."

Weather went to their home office to work on correspondence, Lucas went back to bed, Shrake went out to drive around the block, and Virgil turned on the TV. Nothing to do but wait . . .

GABRIEL MARET looked busted. He sat at the cafeteria table with a cup of coffee, talked with Mark Lang, one of the neurosurgeons, and Geoff Perkins, a cardiologist, and when Weather and Virgil came in, he waved and pointed at a chair. Virgil peeled off, taking a chair where he could see the room. Weather sat next to Maret, and he said, "Still have the gunslinger, yes?"

She sighed and nodded. "Yes."

"He looks like a cowboy," Maret said, watching Virgil. "He's watching us, I think."

"Probably. He's a little obsessive," Weather said.

"With those boots and jeans, he would do very well with French women," Maret said. "Unless he's gay?"

"No. He's definitely not gay," Weather said. "He does disgustingly well with American women. He sometimes has Lucas writhing in jealousy."

"Ah, well. He will fall, sooner or later," Maret said.

"He's already fallen several times," Weather said. "So: are we going?"

Maret shook his head: "Maybe late this afternoon—I've asked everybody to be ready. Tomorrow morning is more likely. But Geoff is saying that the kids are in a tailspin. Is that the word? Tailspin?"

"That's right, but it's not good," Weather said. She looked at Perkins. "What's happening?"

He shrugged. "The operation is putting too much pressure on Sara's heart. To take the pressure off, we slow it down and drop the blood pressure. But that gets on Ellen's heart, too, and she's not handling it well."

"So what are we doing?" Weather asked.

"We're going to try a couple more things, try to balance out the chemistry, get back to stable," he said. "This afternoon's a possibility, but tomorrow's more likely. Still not a sure thing."

"We've got to wait it out," Maret said.

"But the trouble is not going away," Perkins said. "You might have to make a decision."

Maret knew what he meant: "No. I'm not going to lose Sara. We can pull it off."

A tear started in one of his eyes, and Weather thought, *No way did this guy rob the pharmacy . . .*

THEY TALKED for half an hour, going over and over the possibilities and probabilities, until it began to seem pointlessly obsessive: they knew what the options were. Maret finally tossed his plastic coffee cup at a wastebasket, bounced it in, and said, "I'm going to look at the kids again."

Weather went over to Virgil and said, "To reiterate, Gabe had nothing to do with anything, except helping the kids. You're doing no good, sitting there staring at him under your eyebrows."

"What next?" Virgil asked. "Back home?"

"There's a small chance we could go this afternoon, so I have to hang around. When will you get that list of French people?"

Virgil looked at his watch. "Now, I guess. They should be open."

"I'll come along," Weather said. "I'd like to look at the list."

MARCY SHOWED UP at the BCA with two cops named Franklin and Stone. Lucas and Franklin knuckle-tapped, old pals. Stone was new to detective rank, but had spent five years with the Minneapolis SWAT; he and Franklin had brought SWAT gear. Shrake and Jenkins were planning to ride together, in a BCA truck. Marcy rode with Lucas.

"We'll pick up the Washburn deputies in Shell Lake. The sheriff's coming along—Bill Stephaniak," Marcy said. "They're set to pull the warrants, but won't do it until the last minute, so word doesn't get around."

"They all set on a judge?"

"Stephaniak says the judge would sign a ham sandwich if you put it in front of him."

"Always nice to have one of those," Lucas said.

THE TRIP to Wisconsin took two and a half hours, north up I-35 to Highway 70 through Rock Creek, across the St. Croix River to Grantsburg, Wisconsin, through Siren, to Spooner, and then to Shell Lake; a convoy. The snow wasn't deep, but had taken on a cold, gray midwinter edge, stark against the near-black evergreens and barren broadleaf trees. They filled the time catching up with each other's lives; and Lucas was pleased that she seemed happy with hers.

"The kid is just way more than I ever expected," she said. "I'm getting so I hate to go to work."

"How many years you got in?"

"Eighteen—I'm a long way from retirement. James says if I want to quit, I can. It's not like we need the salary."

"But what would you do? Is being a mom enough?"

"That's what I keep asking myself. Right now, it's yeah—it's enough. The question is, will it be enough in two years, when he goes to school?"

"And you don't want to get your ass shot before he grows up," Lucas said. "You want to be here to see that."

"Yeah." They looked out the windshield for a while, then she said, "But you're not exactly backing off, and you've got Sam."

"Might be different for a guy," Lucas said. "Work is . . . what we do. Like mom is what women do. Not to be a pig about it."

"I'll deny it if you ever tell anybody I said it," Marcy said, "but I know what you mean."

IN SIREN, Lucas said, "You can still see where the tornado came through."

An F3 tornado had ripped the town in 2001, a half-mile wide at points, with winds up to two hundred miles an hour.

"I have a friend from Georgia," Marcy said. "He was up here when it happened, saw some TV stuff about how the Siren warning siren didn't go off. He says, 'There was no sy-reen in sy-reen.'"

*

168

COMING INTO POONER, Lucas said, "I've got to take it easy through here—the place is a speed trap. They already got me once."

Marcy got on the phone and called the Washburn sheriff. When she got off, she said, "They're walking the warrants up to the judge."

Shell Lake was five miles south of Spooner, and the Law Enforcement Center just off the highway. They collected Shrake, Jenkins, Franklin, and Stone in the parking lot, trailed inside, and hooked up with the sheriff, a bluff, former highway patrolman with a clipped gray mustache, pale green eyes, and a non-uniform rodeo belt buckle. "Dick'll be back in a minute with the warrants. I told the judge we'd have something coming up to him . . . You folks want coffee? We've got a Coke machine down the hall."

Stephaniak said that Ike Mack was working—the sheriff had sent one of his office workers down to the store to take a look. "I suggest I have one of my boys go along and serve him copies of the warrant, and ask him out to the house. We'll give ourselves about a fifteen-minute jump on him, so we can see what's what out there."

Marcy said, "Sounds good to me," and Lucas nodded.

Shrake asked, "Is Ike going to be a problem?"

"I don't think so. He's . . . tired. He's turned into an old guy. I think he mostly wants to be left alone. With his stolen bike parts, of course."

"But if Joe's out there . . ."

"That would be a whole 'nother problem. Though, I can't say I remember Joe as being all that violent. Not that I doubt these things you got going. But I never saw it in him."

"I can't think of another way our woman would have gotten strangled," Marcy said. "We'll know for sure tomorrow. We've got a rush DNA going."

"Well. People change. Maybe they get desperate," Stephaniak said. "Now. Look at this. I printed this out this morning, and as far as I know, it's up-to-date."

He pushed an eleven-by-fourteen photo across his desk, and the Minnesota cops clustered around: a satellite view of an isolated house sitting off a blacktopped road. The photo had been taken in late September, with the trees in full autumn colors.

In the center of the photo, they could see the roof of a house, surrounded by a farmyard, more dirt than grass. A woodlot bordered the west edge of the house's lot, with farm fields on the south and east, and the road on the north. Another building, probably a garage, stood on the west side of the house, with a narrow, silvery metallic roof extending out the back of it—probably a covered woodshed, or lean-to. Another, even smaller building stood on the south side of the house. An old chicken coop, or something like it, Lucas thought.

"Small place, nine acres. Two-story house, nothing much to look at. The garage there is good-sized—he uses it as a shop to work on his motorcycles. But it's not gonna take long to go through it. What you see is what there is."

"What we have to worry about is that Joe is laying up in there, and he's got a deer rifle and starts blowing holes in us," Shrake said. "So do we sneak up on him, or go in fast?"

"We send your two SWAT guys, with two of our SWAT guys, in through the woods." Stephaniak tapped the woodlot. "They check the garage. It's heated, so Joe could be in there. If he's not, they break through the side door—our guys have a crowbar—and get lined up at the front door. From there, it's only about thirty or forty feet over to the side door of the house. I'll call the house, and at the same time, they rush it. They'll be inside before Joe can get a gun . . . with any luck."

THEY WORKED through the plan for a couple of minutes, then another, older, deputy came in. The sheriff said, "Hey, Dick. You get 'em?"

The deputy nodded. "We're set."

Stephaniak said, "Let's rock."

THE FOUR SWAT guys armored up and took the BCA truck, which was unmarked and had Minnesota plates. The rest of the crew staged in the empty parking lot of a barbeque joint four miles from Mack's place.

Stephaniak had given radios to all five vehicles involved. Franklin called after a few minutes and told them that the roads were clear all the way out, and a few minutes later called to say that they'd left the truck and were about to make the approach to the back of the garage. "We've got a couple fences to cross, so we'll be ten minutes," he said.

They rolled out of the parking lot a couple of minutes later. Two miles down the road, Franklin called again: "We're at the back of the garage. No cars inside. Can't see anybody inside. Ron's at the door, we're taking the door out. Okay, we're inside. Nobody here. No loft, we can see the whole place . . . Make the call."

Stephaniak, riding in the lead SUV, made the call as they turned into Mack's driveway, and Lucas saw the SWAT guys rush the house, hit the door. A minute later, they were all out, on the snow, behind the trucks, and Franklin came out on the porch and waved.

"Nobody home," Marcy said, disappointed.

"Goddamnit, I hope he's not on his way to Mexico," Lucas said.

"Let's look at the phones, see who's calling him," Marcy said.

"Ike's on his way out," Stephaniak said. "My guy says he didn't seem surprised."

THE HOUSE SMELLED like home-canning; like pickles and creamed corn and cigarette smoke. Like an old single guy living out in the woods. Shrake and Jenkins, with the Minneapolis cops, ran the search, moving quickly and efficiently through the house, from attic to basement. Marcy went for the phones: Mack used handsets that listed calling numbers, and she took them down in her notebook. As she wrote, she called to the other cops, "Nobody mention the phones to him. Nobody mention that we looked at them. Ignore them. We want him to use them."

Lucas asked, and she said, "Half-dozen calls from the Cities since the hospital. None of the numbers go to Lyle or Joe."

Lucas wandered through the house with his hands in his pockets, then out on the porch, to the garage. The garage had three overhead doors and was set up to handle two parking spaces and a motorcycle shop. There were pieces of three or four older Harleys around, and one complete frame, but without handlebars or wheels. Nothing of interest.

He checked the woodshed, supposed that something might have been concealed under the three or four face-cords of hardwood, but if so, it hadn't been concealed since the hospital robbery. Snow had been blown in from the sides and had crusted over the lower layers of wood. Not much way to fake that.

Farther back, a cop was looking into what had been a chicken house. He walked away, shook his head at Lucas, and said, "I'm going to walk the perimeter, see if there are any tracks heading back into the woods."

A cinder-block incinerator sat next to the chicken house, and Lucas went that way. There were fresh ashes, signs of burned garbage—orange peels, the odor of burned coffee grounds. Lucas looked around, got a short downed tree branch, and stirred through the debris.

Came up with a partially burned piece of black nylon fabric. Heavy, with a piece of charred strap across it. Like a nylon bag.

The robbers, Dorothy Baker had said, had come in with black bags; had dropped the bags on the floor before they'd taped up Baker and Peterson.

Lucas stirred a bit more, started finding more fragments. Stood up, walked back to the house: "Marcy, Bill . . ."

Marcy and the sheriff came over, and Lucas showed them the strap. "Looks like it came off a nylon bag. The ashes are fresh."

"Dorothy Baker . . ." Marcy began.

Lucas nodded, and said to Stephaniak, "The nurse who was in the pharmacy said the robbers brought big black nylon bags, or packs, to carry the drugs. There are more pieces out there in the ash. We need your crime-scene guy to go through it."

"It's suggestive," Stephaniak said. He meant, *That doesn't prove much.*

"It'll worry them," Lucas said. "If it's the bags, it'll help crank the pressure. And if we find there's more than one bag, then we'll know. The shit came through here. Ike's involved. That's always a help."

The sheriff nodded. "I'll get my boy on it."

A deputy said, "Ike's here."

IKE WAS A STOUT MAN, but hard fat, beer-belly fat, with a shiny red bald head and black-plastic-rimmed glasses on a full nose; with little yellow shark teeth under the nose, and water-green shark eyes. He was wearing a sixties army parka over a T-shirt. He was angry but was suppressing it: he'd dealt with the cops before.

Marcy held up her badge and said, "We're picking up evidence that your boys were here with the drugs. We're talking about murder, Ike. You're, what, sixty-five? We'll slam you in Stillwater for thirty years if you're in on it. So: where's Joe?"

"I ain't seen him." He put on a phony wild-eyed look, appealing to the cops. "I *ain't* seen him. He ain't been here. He knows better'n to draw the shit down on his old man."

Lucas said, "We're gonna get him, Ike. He's killed three or four people now. We're tearing the country up, and he's gonna fall. And when we get the lab results back, on these straps, your ass is grass."

"You find any dope? You won't find dope here, nosir. You'll find some Millers, but there's no dope. I don't allow it."

"Well, shoot, Ike, you made meth for ten years," one of the deputies said. "Everybody in the county knows it. You could smell it all the way down to Barronett."

"I don't know anything about any meth—"

"Ah, bullshit, you're wasting our time, Ike," Stephaniak said. "You could cooperate for fifteen seconds and we'd let you skate on the murder."

". . . Maybe . . ." Marcy said.

"Maybe," Stephaniak agreed. "But if you don't talk to us, and we find out you been hiding that boy, or that you know where he is . . ."

"You went and burned the bags out in the incinerator, but you didn't burn them well enough," Lucas said. "We'll get them identified by the witness, and you're done."

Ike didn't ask, "What bags?" but said, "I don't know everything that goes in the fire. If Joe was up here, he didn't tell me. I work all day. I don't know everything that happens out here." He wiped his nose with the back of his hand, sniffed, and said, "I'm old. I'm gonna go lay down. If you don't mind."

"Put a cold rag on your head and think about it," Marcy said. "If you talk to us before I leave, we can deal. Once we're gone, you're toast. You get no second chances."

Ike looked around at all the cops, shook his head, muttered "fuckin' . . ." and stalked through the house to the back bedroom.

When he was out of earshot, Stephaniak said to Lucas, "You were right about the bags. That's them, and he knows it."

IKE WAS IN the bedroom for fifteen minutes, then came out, got a beer, and sat in a platform rocker in front of the television and watched the cops take the place apart. No drugs. No anything, but the bag straps from the incinerator.

Marcy got her coat on, said to Ike, "We're leaving. Your last chance is walking out the door."

"Don't let it hit you in the ass," Ike said.

WEATHER AND VIRGIL got the names of French-passport employees. Virgil called Jenkins, who'd been down in the cafeteria, and went off to talk to some of the employees. Jenkins showed up, leaned against a wall. Weather put a copy of the list in her briefcase, and then went down and found the Rayneses, Jenkins tagging behind. She'd thought the Rayneses seemed shell-shocked before, and they weren't getting better.

"Those poor little babies," Lucy Raynes said. "They hurt so bad, I can see it in their eyes. Sara knows what's going on, I can see it, she knows her heart isn't working right. She's really scared."

Weather explained about pain control, ground that Maret had already been over, but she wasn't convincing because she really didn't know for sure what the twins were experiencing. They might be, she thought, in some kind of inexpressible pain, though the cardiologist said they were comfortable. But then, he didn't know, either, Weather thought. "God, this is awful," she said aloud. "We'd hoped to get through it in a hurry, but Sara's heart . . . We should finish tomorrow. I really believe we will. We were ready to go this afternoon, but they started doing better. By this time tomorrow, we'll be done, and then the medical guys can really get in there with individual treatments . . ."

"Just want to get done," Larry Raynes said. "Just . . . over."

WEATHER FOUND a spot in an empty waiting lounge and took the paper out of her briefcase and looked it over: seventeen names, French nationals working in the hospital. All French nationals, not just doctors, of whom there were four.

She knew one of them, vaguely, an ENT guy who thought he was also a plastic surgeon. He had, in Weather's estimation, bungled a nose job or two or three. One of them, a black woman who found herself with a nose the size of a peanut, had been referred to Weather for help. Weather had reworked the nose, but the result, while better, had still been poor.

In general, Weather decided, if some French doc had to fall on a robbery charge, he was the one she'd pick. Not because she really thought he'd done it, but because it might save somebody's nose.

Jenkins was reading *The Complete Idiot's Guide to the Middle East Conflict*, and she stood up and said, "Give me a half hour. I need one more consult."

"Right here?"

"Upstairs."

"I'll come along."

"Jenkins . . ."

"Look, if you get killed, Lucas is gonna pound me on my annual review. Okay?"

THEY TOOK the elevator up two floors, and she left him sitting in a broken-down corridor chair while she went into the office of the head of surgery, a woman named Marlene Bach. Bach's secretary's desk was vacant, but Weather could see the other woman sitting in her office, her back to the door. She knocked: "Marlene?"

Bach turned in her chair and called, "Come on in, Weather."

Bach was a tall, thin woman, with a small head and dark hair, which gave her somewhat the aspect of a stork. She usually had a yellow No. 2 pencil stuck behind one ear, and had a reputation for efficiency and speed in the operating room. And, the OR nurses said, she listened to classic Whitesnake while she worked.

She had pinned a half-dozen large-format photos of a burn victim onto a corkboard on her office wall. The torso was nude, and the top half was covered with snarky black burns. Weather looked at them and said, "Electrical?"

"Yes. Blew him right off a power pole," Bach said. "He was hanging upside down for fifteen minutes before somebody went up after him."

"He gonna make it?"

"I don't know. He's forty-four, he's got fifty percent third-degree burns. Gonna be close." Rule of thumb: if the burns covered more of your body than your age deducted from one hundred, you'd probably die. Forty-four deducted from one hundred was fifty-six. Close.

"Looks like a lot of work," Weather said. She sat down and said, "Listen, I have a personal concern."

Bach nodded. "I heard. Somebody's trying to kill you. Or tried to, anyway."

"Yes. There's been some talk that the person in the pharmacy, who opened the pharmacy for the robbers, was a physician, and the witness thinks he might have had a French accent. And you know who I thought of . . ."

"Halary," Bach said. "You really think . . . ?"

"Not really. But I was wondering what you think? You know him better than I do."

"He's a weasel, but I don't believe he'd do anything like that," Bach said. "For one thing, his wife's a dermatologist with a big practice out in Edina. He really wouldn't need the money."

"I didn't know that," Weather said.

"And he's not a bad ENT, if he'd lay off the plastic surgery," Bach said. "I know that thing with the noses irritated you."

"Not as much as it irritated the owners of the noses," Weather said. And she said, "Hmm. How about a guy named Albert Loewe? Supposed to be a . . ."

Bach was shaking her head: "Got hit by a car a month ago. In a supermarket parking lot. Broke both his legs. He was a mess, and he's still in casts."

"All right. Look, check this list. You know anybody else?"

Bach knew two more people on the list, a male nurse and a third doc named Martin, but she didn't know either of them well enough to make a judgment. "Let me ask around."

"Discreetly," Weather said. "This guy did try to kill me."

"I'll be very discreet," Bach said. "I'm too good-looking to die." She looked back up at the burn photos. "Unlike Bob. Bob's not too good-looking to die."

OUT IN THE HALL, Jenkins asked, "You done?"

Weather said, "Yes. A burn victim. We'll be moving some skin around on him, if he makes it through the next couple weeks."

Didn't want to worry him, to think she was investigating.

THAT NIGHT, at the dinner table, Lucas told them about the proposed raid on Mack's place. "If Weather weren't going to the hospital every day, I'd back off," he said. "We know who did it—it's the whole damn Mack family, plus Haines and Chapman. We'll never prove anything about those bags, but we know what they were, and why they burned them. The drugs went through Ike's place, and from there, probably over to the Seed headquarters in Milwaukee, and down to the Outlaws, and they're probably all over Illinois and the East Coast by now."

"Still gotta find the guy in the hospital," Virgil said.

"All we have to do is nail one of the Macks—any one of them—and we'll get him."

"Could be done with the hospital tomorrow," Weather said. "I cleared out two weeks, just in case. If we get it done, we could take off for a week."

Lucas's eyebrows went up, and he said to Letty: "Disney World."

She stopped with a fork spun full of spaghetti, halfway to her mouth, and said, "Instead of St. Paul in January? I'd buy that."

"You'd be willing to leave the case?" Weather asked Lucas.

"My main concern in this, is you. If we take off, and nobody knows where we are, what're the Macks going to do? They won't have any way to find you," Lucas said. "If you're done with the babies, we could take off."

"I think we will be," Weather said. "One way or another, we can't wait much longer."

13

BARAKAT WALKED down the hall in his stocking feet and took a seat in the ER next to an unconscious woman with a temperature of 104; a saline bag hung overhead and was dripping into her arm. Another doc was looking at her chart. Barakat sniffed at one of his shoes, said, as he pulled it on, "I require some shoe spray . . ." And, "So, what do you think?"

"You started the antibiotics?"

"Yes. She was here two days ago with a urinary tract infection and we gave her a prescription, but I think she didn't fill it. She has no insurance and probably no money, looking at her, so I think she tried to get along without the pills and it got away from her."

The other doc nodded and said, "No pain?"

"No. The woman who came with her said this one kept getting hotter and sleepier and finally fell asleep watching TV, and then she couldn't wake her up when it was time to go to bed."

The other doc nodded and snapped the chart shut and said, "Willing to bet you're right. Wish I could talk to her."

"If I'm right, she'll be talking in an hour," Barakat said. "No sign of lung congestion, so I don't think it's the flu . . ."

They talked about some other possibilities and then the other doc said, "You got a kinda froggy accent. Are they talking to you, too?"

"What? Froggy?"

"French accent," the doc said. "There's a cop asking around for French accents, and now one of the docs is asking around. Because of that guy who got killed, you know, in the pharmacy."

Barakat suppressed a shrug and said, "I have not heard. Anyway, my accent is already Lebanese, not French. The fucking French, they are the most responsible for destroying my country."

"Didn't know that," the doc said. He looked back at the patient. "Goddamn women get the weirdest diseases up there. You know? We oughta have a wazoo guy working full-time."

"You've seen the other one? Rosemary something?"

"Nope. What's that about?"

"Either a bad sprain or a broken navicular. She was in yoga class, doing some pose, and she fell and put her hand down. She's in imaging, should be back anytime. Barry has her chart . . ."

CAPPY WAS WAITING in the parking garage. "We have trouble," Barakat said. He popped his car door and threw the briefcase in the back.

Cappy looked sleepy. "What kind?"

"A cop is looking for somebody with a French accent. Also, this woman doctor is now going around the hospital, telling everyone. They will come to me."

"So what?"

Barakat looked at him. "So . . . it's a problem."

"Don't tell them the truth, dude. No problem. Tell them you don't know what the fuck they're talking about."

Barakat thought, *She'll recognize me.* "You're right. I'm being a woman."

"Don't ask for an attorney. Get pissed off. You're a big-shot doctor, right? No cops can talk to you like that."

"My friend, you are smarter than you look," Barakat said. "When I move to Paris, or LA, you should come along. We will be partners in crime."

They took Barakat's car, a three-year-old Subaru, for the four-wheel drive, and Cappy asked, "So, did you bring some tools?"

"A scalpel, duct tape, and I took a hammer from the maintenance shop. I was careful. I took an old one; they have several."

"Have you thought about how we do it?"

"Yes, we go in. You shoot him in the knee, and we fall on him."

"Fall on him?"

"Jump on him. Attack him. Immobilize him with the duct tape. Then I set to work. I cut his pants here . . ." He touched his groin. "I tell him, the first thing I do is, I take off one ball. Then I take off the penis, and then the other ball. I tell him, I take one ball before we ask him anything, to show him that I will do it . . ."

"That's cold," Cappy said cheerfully.

"With any luck, we don't need the second ball."

"What if Honey Bee's there?" Cappy asked.

Barakat did the shrug again: "We don't need her, yes? We don't need her."

THEY DROVE SOUTH on I-35, and thirty minutes later, cut east and south, through thinning suburbs, away from the lights. Cappy read off the turns as they came to them, and finally they left the highway for snow-covered tarmac road, down the valley and around the curve, and saw Honey Bee's place, white-on-white, with the snow in the fields, under the blue glow of her yard light.

Hardly a light in the house: a yellow glimmer from the kitchen, which looked like an alarm light, or a candle.

"Nobody home," Cappy said. "Ain't that a bite in the ass?" He was annoyed: all dressed up and nowhere to go.

"Maybe he ran," Barakat said.

"He was talking about going to Green Bay. Somewhere in Green Bay," Cappy said, remembering the vague conversation after the attack on the doctor chick. "He even said where—but I don't remember that part."

"This is a misfortune," Barakat said. Then, "There's more than one way to . . . I don't know the word . . . flay? Flay a cat?"

"Skin a cat," Cappy said. "What you got in mind?"

Barakat said, "Well, there are *two* brothers. . . ."

They went and knocked on Honey Bee's door, but there was no answer, and in the last dying light of day, they turned the car around and headed back to town.

AT BARAKAT'S PLACE, they got into the cocaine, clicked around the television, ate a pizza, and had a long, intricate, dope-fueled discussion about their childhoods. "I don't really think you should kill your old man, because it's not the right thing to do," Cappy announced at one point. "That's why I stay away from Rochester. 'Cause if I saw that cocksucker, I'd shoot him down like a yellow dog."

"My father, he has money, but does he give it to me? No. It's mine by rights," Barakat said. "He got it from his father, who got it from his father. But with my father, it stops. He tells me everything. He tells me to do this, and I must do this. He tells me to do that, to be a doctor, and here I am, a doctor. Do I want to be a doctor? No, I do not. Not much. Huh? Every day, I have my finger in somebody's rectum. Is this a way to go through life? I am living in Paris, and I see other sons, whose fathers are not so greedy, and they are living very, very well. And the women. The most beautiful women in the world, and do I get them? No, I do not, because my father is so greedy, so small."

"Where does he live?"

"West Palm Beach, in Florida."

"Tell you what, when we get done with this, we go to Rochester, you kill my old man, and then we go to Florida, and I kill your old man," Cappy said. "My old man owns a recreational equipment business, and I'll fuckin' inherit. And you'll fuckin' inherit. We'll both be fuckin' rich."

"My friend," Barakat said, pausing for a twist, "we have a deal. Huh. I kill your cocksucker father and you kill my cocksucker father and we go to Paris."

Cappy took a hit and a thought occurred to him: "You don't like being a doctor. That's scary, you know, having a doctor working on you who doesn't like it."

"Well, I don't like it much, but . . ." Snort. "I am really a very good doctor, huh? I know what I'm doing. But I don't like it. I have seen one asshole too many."

At two o'clock in the morning, they watched the last drunk roll out of Cherries, pause in the parking lot to light a cigarette and zip a parka against the cold, and then drive away; two minutes later, a bartender came out, walked around to the side, got in his car, and disappeared.

"Let's go," Cappy said. They got out of the van and walked across the back parking area, where Lyle Mack's car was parked next to the dumpster, the last car at the bar. They climbed the back stoop to the door, then stepped sideways into a shadow of the loading-dock door.

Ten minutes, and a light went out; and another. "He's coming," Cappy muttered.

"Finally. My hands are freezing."

They both unconsciously shuffled their feet. A minute later, Lyle Mack came out the back door, turned to pull it shut. Cappy jumped across the space between the loading dock and door, hit Mack in the back, slammed him through the door and into the bar.

Barakat was a step behind, with his .45. Cappy was on Mack's back, Mack facedown on the floor, trying to do a push-up. Barakat slammed the door closed, and in the dark, pressed the muzzle of the .45 against Mack's head and said, "Stop, or I kill you."

Mack went limp. Cappy said, "Lyle, we need to talk."

LYLE PLEADED and moaned and argued, but they taped him up with duct tape, awkward in their heavy winter gloves, and then Lyle asked the question, "Why?"

"The thing is, man, this whole deal has gotten too complicated, and sooner or later somebody is going to talk, and then you're going to sell us out," Cappy said. "So we decided we had to move."

"Man, I can't sell you out," Lyle Mack said. "If I sell you out, I go to jail for thirty years."

"Yes, yes. Now. We need answers to two questions," Barakat said. "Where is the dope? And, where is your brother?"

"Well, fuck you," Lyle Mack said, nearly choking on the words. "You're gonna kill me anyway."

"But maybe not," Barakat said. "You don't want to hurt Joe, because he is your brother. But if Joe disappears, then who can touch us? Then, we believe you. You won't sell us out, because there is no reason. You take revenge on us, you send yourself to prison. We will kill your brother, and then the woman doctor cannot reach us, and maybe you plan revenge, or maybe you choke on his death, but you don't sell us out."

"About the dope," Cappy said. "We're not going to see any of that. That's gone, isn't it?"

"No. We hid it good. We gotta wait, guys—"

"Bullshit, wait," Barakat said. "Now, Lyle, I think you will tell us where the drugs are, and where your brother is. How hard this will be, you decide." He emptied his pockets—the scalpel, the hammer, two vinyl gloves. He took off his winter gloves, pulled on the medical gloves. "Now, I will tell you. You do not believe what we will do to you, so before you answer the question, I will cut a ball off. Huh? One ball. You will still be able to fuck later, with one ball. But if you do not answer after the ball comes off, then I cut off your penis and then the other ball. Then, I work with the hammer. Huh?"

"Oh, man, don't do that. I'll tell you," Lyle Mack said. "Joe's on his way to Mexico. Our friend Eddie picked him up this afternoon. They should be in Wichita tonight. The drugs, we hid up north . . . "

Barakat held up a hand. "Maybe I believe you. But I cut off one ball anyway, huh? Just to show you." He wiggled his fingers and picked up the scalpel.

Cappy said, "Let's get him in where it's warmer," and they dragged him like a sack of potatoes across the loading dock and through the door into the bar itself, his head bumping on the doorjamb. Cappy got a chair and said, "Roll him," and when Barakat rolled him, Cappy put the chair across Lyle Mack's chest, one of the crossbars over his neck, another cutting into the fat man's gut. Cappy sat in the chair and said to Barakat, "Go 'head."

Lyle Mack began to weep: "Man, please, please, don't do this, man, please . . ."

ANYONE WALKING by the bar, bareheaded and listening, might have heard the screams, but then again, they might not have; there was just enough wind to carry the sound away.

14

LUCAS GOT UP EARLY, with Weather, then went back to bed for a while, and finally rolled out at seven o'clock, two hours before he usually did. He got cleaned up, ate breakfast, played chase-the-tennis-ball with Sam, and then sent Sam and the housekeeper off to the grocery store. As she went, the housekeeper said, "You should take the truck today. There's a storm warning."

"Yeah? When's it supposed to get here?"

"They were saying tonight. I can't see it on the radar yet, but it's coming."

Lucas went to look at the TV. The storm was still winding up over western South Dakota. Brought up the computer in the den, checked again: heavy snow tomorrow, starting with flurries around dawn, with rapidly falling temperatures. Ten to fifteen inches of snow possible in the next forty-eight hours. The Black Hills were being pounded.

He went out and told the housekeeper, "Not until tomorrow, they're saying."

She said, "Somebody's here."

A car pulled into the driveway, and he looked and saw Jenkins getting out. He let him in the back door, and then heard Shrake arrive, and let him in, too. "Gonna storm tomorrow," Shrake said. He was holding a box of sticky buns. "What're we doing?"

"Marcy's getting an arrest warrant for Lyle Mack. We're a little thin on cause, but we think he's talking to Joe."

"Prepaid cell," Shrake said.

"That's what we think. We can get the cell phone as part of the arrest, and then . . ."

"We've got real probable cause," Jenkins finished.

They had coffee and two sticky buns each, and talked about the fact that none of them smoked anymore, and how enjoyable it had been, and then Marcy called: "I got two pieces of news, one of which I should have had a long, long time ago, but you jerks held out on me."

"And that is?"

"With your new equipment, with a high-priority case, you can do DNA in twelve hours."

"Didn't know that," Lucas said. "You get it back?"

"Yes, we did. Guess what? Whoever strangled Jill MacBride, it wasn't Joe Mack."

"What?"

"Got some weird shit going down, big boy. Get your crew cranked up, and let's go see Lyle Mack. If Joe didn't strangle her, maybe he didn't kidnap her—and he's got no reason to run."

"Well, bullshit," Lucas said. "I don't know what happened, but Joe grabbed her. I mean, if he didn't, it'd be like a zillion to one."

"You know what? A perfect solar eclipse is a zillion to one. But I've seen one."

"I don't believe it."

"Hey, I was there."

"Not the eclipse. I don't believe that Joe didn't snatch her. When will you get here?"

"Fifteen minutes—leaving here in two."

MARCY'S NEWS gave them more to talk about, but in the end, they couldn't figure out what it meant. She arrived in her husband's truck, came in, looked at the box on the table and said, "I'll bet you didn't save a single—"

"Ah, but we did," Shrake said. "In fact, we saved two."

"I'm watching my weight," she said.

"I've been watching it, too," Jenkins said. "I gotta tell you, it's looking pretty good."

"Spoken like a true connoisseur," Shrake said, and they bumped knuckles.

Marcy said, "Mental note: don't hire Jenkins and Shrake when Davenport finally fires them."

Lucas said, "Yeah-yeah. Let's knock off the bullshit and get over to Mack's. Take the buns with you."

"Yeah, take your buns with you," Shrake said.

Marcy gave him a delicate finger and asked Lucas, "Tell me what you think about the DNA."

"I have no idea," he confessed. "Maybe more people are involved than we thought. Maybe, well, we know there was one guy at the hospital . . . maybe when we get him . . . I don't know, Marcy. Did the DNA rule out Lyle Mack, too?"

"Unless they're adopted brothers, with different parents. They don't look too much alike—I guess we could ask."

"They don't look much alike, but they both sort of look like Ike," Lucas said. "They weren't adopted."

THE RIDE to Mack's took twenty minutes: Marcy left her truck in Lucas's driveway and rode with him, the better to eat the sticky buns—both of them—and drink her coffee. "Is Weather working on the twins?"

"Not sure. They're better, but they might get a little better if they go another few hours, or another day. It's a mess. If they don't move soon, one of them's going to die."

"Man—sometimes it's better being a cop."

"Yeah. Like when we were talking to MacBride's kid," Lucas said.

"Jesus, Lucas: you still got that depressive thing going, huh?"

"You don't?"

"Not like you. For me, MacBride getting murdered was seriously annoying. That's different," she said. "You gotta handle the rage, big guy."

THEY'D PLANNED to take Mack at his house, but the place was locked up, and when they looked in the garage windows, the garage was empty. While they were looking, a car pulled into the driveway next door, and Marcy hustled over and talked to the driver, an old guy, and then hustled back. "Neighbor's been up since six, and didn't see or hear anybody over here. He says Mack usually goes to work around ten."

"Jeez, I hope he didn't skip," Shrake said.

Lucas shook his head: "Ah, he's probably just out early. Like us. Let's check the bar."

AND MACK'S CAR was parked next to the dumpster behind Cherries. They got out, and Shrake and Jenkins walked around to the front, while Lucas and Marcy went to the back door. The door was locked, and they banged on it, with no response. Lucas looked around, couldn't see a camera. Banged on the door again.

Shrake came around the corner and said, "It's all locked up, up front, but the neon's turned on. The 'Open' sign."

"You bang on the door?"

"Yeah, but it's locked."

A cop car pulled into the lot, and a uniformed officer got out, looking at them, talking on a radio. Marcy said, "Poop," and walked over to him, her badge out. They talked for a minute, then Marcy waved them over.

"We're going to get his push bar right up by a front window," she said. "Shrake, you're the tallest, see if you can look in."

The cop pulled up to the bar, and Shrake stood on his push bar, using a hand to block reflections. After a moment, he said, "Well, I can see . . . yeah."

He hopped down.

"What?" Marcy asked.

"I can see a leg on the floor on the other side of the pool table."

"A leg. Like he's hiding?"

"Like he's dead," Shrake said.

THE CITY COP wasn't sure of the technical entry procedure, so Jenkins took a long switchblade out of his pants pocket, punched a hole in the front-door glass, and flipped the interior lock. Lucas led the way in, Marcy a step behind.

Lucas called, "Mack?" but then they walked out of the main bar area and saw the body on the floor next to the pool table. A wooden chair sat over Mack's neck and chest, with a wooden crossbar at his neck, so that somebody sitting on the chair could keep Mack from sitting up or twisting away. His hands and feet were taped. He had a hole in his forehead, with burn marks around it, and a puddle of blood under the head and the legs. The front panel of the pants had been cut away, and Mack's groin was a mass of jellied blood.

"Aw, man," Shrake said.

Marcy asked, "What's that?" pointing at Mack's stomach.

Jenkins bent over, then straightened up and stepped back. "I do believe that's the gentleman's testicle," he said.

The city cop, gagging, mumbled something about calling it in, and dashed for the door. They stood there, the metallic smell of blood infusing the air, and listened to him retching in the parking lot.

Then Shrake said, "You know what? When they did this, somebody was sitting in that chair, looking right down at his face."

LUCAS GOT everybody moving, BCA crime scene, the ME's investigators, while Marcy called her chief. Lucas went into the back and found Jenkins in the office, with plastic gloves on his hands, going through Mack's parka. "Anything?"

"Cell phone, I think. I can feel it, but I can't find the pocket." The pocket was under a hidden zip flap, and Jenkins pulled it out, turned it on, and said, "This is probably it: it says it's got seventy-five minutes of talk-time left."

"Need the numbers, right now," Lucas said. "Incoming and outgoing calls."

"Got it."

Marcy came in: "Lucas: what do you think?"

"We're back to square one. We don't know what's happening. Mac-Bride is killed by somebody we don't know, Mack is tortured to death. Joe didn't do this, so . . . there's gotta be somebody else. Probably a couple or three of them."

"Another gang?"

"Don't know. We've got a mystery guy at the hospital. We don't know about him."

She said, "I wonder if the Macks had *anything* to do with it—the robbery, and all of it."

"Sure they did," Lucas said. "If they didn't, then why that?" He nodded toward the front room. "They cut on him until they got what they wanted, and then they stopped and killed him. If they were just doing it for pure pleasure, they could have gone on for a while. And then there's Haines and Chapman, and we know they were good friends with the Macks . . . and I still believe that Joe had something to do with MacBride. Maybe this is about the drugs. Maybe somebody figured out the Macks had the drugs, and came after them. You know what? I bet the drugs are still around."

LUCAS NEVER liked the writing of reports, but did it; in this case, he could unload most of it on the Mendota Heights cop, and he did that, too. Weather called at eleven o'clock and said, "We're still on hold, but the kids are getting stronger. May go another day."

"It's gonna snow tomorrow," Lucas said.

"We're planning to operate *inside* the hospital, not on the parking ramp."

"Ah. That's so clever." He told her about Lyle Mack, and she said, "Worse and worse. All because some guy got mad and kicked poor old Don Peterson."

LUCAS TOLD MARCY, "I'm going to call Ike—notify him, and see if we can pry anything out of him. Maybe this'll loosen him up."

The place was getting crowded, with Grace, the Mendota Heights chief, two more local cops, crime-scene and ME investigators. Lucas called the Washburn County sheriff, Stephaniak, told him what had happened, and asked, "Where'd you say he worked? I need to notify him."

"Better you than me," Stephaniak said. "I've done that a few too many times."

He looked the number up in the local directory, read it off, and Lucas dialed.

A man answered, a little tired: "Larry's."

Lucas said, "I'm a police officer from Minnesota. I'm trying to reach Ike Mack on a family issue. Can I speak to him?"

After a few seconds of silence, the man on the other end said, "Ike didn't show up today. Don't know where he is."

"Does that happen a lot?"

"No, it doesn't. He's pretty reliable, when he's not drinking, and he's not drinking. Unless he started last night," the man said. "I've been calling him on his cell, and there's no answer. What'd he do?"

"Nothing—this is a family emergency. Do you have a home phone number for him?" Lucas asked.

"He doesn't have a home phone, only the cell phone. He usually has it with him."

Lucas got the number, dialed it, got no answer. He called Stephaniak again and said, "Ike didn't show up this morning. What happened here was pretty bad. Is there any way you could send somebody over to his house, take a look?"

"You think somebody might have come up here?"

"His son was tortured," Lucas said. "Like they were interrogating him. They may be looking for those drugs from the hospital. Maybe they stashed them at Ike's, out in the woods or something . . . Anyway, if you could take a look."

"Ten minutes," Stephaniak said. "I got a guy patrolling over that way."

LUCAS ASKED the techs if anything was coming off the body, and one of them said, "It's gonna sound weird, but I wonder if one of them was sniffing cocaine while they were cutting on him. There's this little sprinkling of powder on his legs. Doesn't look like dirt, or plaster . . . it's not ground in, it's just sitting there."

Lucas had to look closely to see it, a fine-grained, beige sprinkle.

"Doesn't look like coke."

"I agree. I've taken samples."

Lucas said, "You know my wife's a surgeon?"

"Yeah, plastic surgeon, right?" The tech was with the BCA, and they'd worked together on a number of cases.

"Yup. And she brings home surgeon's gloves, from time to time, like when she's going to paint things. And she gave me some for my shoe-shine box. The thing is, they've got this very fine powder in them, to get them on and off easier. It looks like this stuff. When you get to the lab, check that."

"The guy's testicle looks like it was removed with something very sharp. Like a scalpel. Not like a bar knife."

Lucas patted the guy's shoulder a couple of times: "And we're looking for a doctor, somebody who could have set up the hospital robbery."

JENKINS CAME BACK: "We got a full list downtown on the incoming and outgoing calls. Most of them are to one number, and five of those were in the couple hours after Joe ran."

"That's him," Lucas said.

"The last call from that number was at eleven o'clock last night," Jenkins said. "It went through a cell tower in Emporia, Kansas. It's right on I-35."

"He's running."

Marcy said, "Maybe I should call him. You guys might scare him. If he's running, we want to engage him before he throws the phone out the window."

"So figure out what to say," Lucas said. "Let's give him a ring."

THEY WERE GETTING ready to make the call when Stephaniak called back on Lucas's phone: "I don't know all the details, but Ike was killed, apparently last night, in his house. Multiple gunshot wounds to the face. You know out back, in the yard . . . over toward that old shed?"

"Yeah. By that incinerator."

"Yes. My deputy says there are a bunch of ABS stacks from the septic system, but one of them is a fake. There's a stack, and a lid set in the ground, and when you lift it out, there's a concrete sewer tank underneath it, but it's dry. Somebody pulled the stack up last night. There are four big waterproof plastic bins, military surplus, laying on the ground next to the tank. Empty. Probably where they stashed the drugs. There's still a box with thirty or forty handguns in the tank, oiled up and sealed in Ziploc bags, and a lot of ammo. Looks like Ike was dealing guns on the side."

"Yup, that was the dope," Lucas said. "That's why they tortured Lyle. You got a crime-scene crew that can do DNA?"

"We do. We're talking to the guys in Madison. They'll get a crew up here. I'm going out there in two minutes."

"Look for DNA," Lucas said. "Anything that seems worth processing. Was Ike tortured? Interrogated?"

"Nope. The deputy says it looks like they walked in the front door and shot him in the face."

MARCY CALLED JOE MACK from Lyle Mack's office and got him on the second ring. She said, "Joe? This is Marcy Sherrill, the police officer who was talking to you when you ran. Listen to me: Lyle's been killed. He was killed last— Listen to me, Joe. He was killed last night. Somebody— *Listen to me.* I'm calling on Lyle's cell phone. That's how we got your number.

"Listen, whoever did it . . . I'm so sorry to tell you . . . whoever did it apparently went north and killed your father, too. Sheriff Stephaniak up there says whoever did the shooting took the top off a septic tank out back that was dry, and that there were a bunch of boxes where we think somebody hid the drugs. That's what they were after."

She was talking fast, trying to reel him in.

"Listen, Joe: we need to know what you know. We know you didn't do this, and we know you didn't kill Jill MacBride, because we got DNA from her body that says somebody else did it, not you. We need to know who you think did it. We need— Joe, okay, I'm on Lyle's cell phone, call me back. Call me back . . ."

She looked up at Lucas: "He's gone."

"He listened for a while, though," Lucas said. "Maybe he'll call you back."

JOE MACK SAT STUNNED, and Eddie, a gray-faced forty-something man with a red ponytail and acne-pocked face, said, "Maybe they're bullshitting you, man. Maybe they were trying to keep you on the phone, so they could see where we are."

He looked up in the sky, as though scanning for black helicopters.

Joe Mack said, "I don't think she was bullshitting me, man. I don't think so." He began to weep, sitting in the passenger seat, both hands wrapped around the phone. Eddie didn't know what to say, because he'd never seen Joe Mack weep. Joe stopped, after a minute, and wiped his eyes, and said, "We gotta go back there."

Eddie said, "Aw, Jesus, man, we're halfway there. We gotta be in Brownsville tomorrow."

"Got to go back," Joe Mack said. "I got business I gotta do."

"Man, the cops are looking for you all over."

"Eddie, goddamnit, I know who done it. If they're dead, I know who done it."

Eddie exhaled, then said, "Look, do me a favor. Throw that fuckin' phone out the window. We can use mine. We can get another one at Wal-Mart . . . but throw it out the window before somebody pulls us over and shoots our asses."

JENKINS CAME IN from the front room: "Phone company says it came out of a cell on the Kansas Turnpike north of El Dorado . . . so he's still headed south, and pretty fast."

"Need to figure out where he got a car," Lucas said. "We saw him selling his van to that skinhead. He must've had a way to get another car. We need to run it down."

"That bartender . . . Honey Bee? She seemed pretty tight with the brothers," Jenkins said. "Why don't I pick her up, see what she has to say?"

"Good idea," Lucas said. "I'll come with you."

"You know where you're going?" Marcy asked. "And how'll I get back to my car?"

"Shrake can take you. And Honey Bee—there've gotta be employee records here somewhere, with her address," Lucas said, looking around the office. "The thing is, we've got to stash her somewhere. If she knows anything, this guy, or these guys, will think about it, and go after her."

ON THE WAY SOUTH, to Honey Bee's house, Lucas called Virgil at the hospital and told him what had happened, and about the powder on Lyle Mack's body.

"You think our guy at the hospital is taking out witnesses?" Virgil asked.

"Don't know. But we need to find him."

"We got nothing to work with, except that accent thing," Virgil said. "I'm thinking about it, but I got nothing right now."

"How about the kids? Are they working?"

"They're meeting now. We'll find out in a few minutes."

HONEY BEE WAS SHOVELING horseshit when the cops arrived. She heard the car, looked out through the crack between the door and the jamb, and saw the dark-haired detective, the one who'd been questioning Joe when he ran, walking toward her front door. He stopped, stooped, picked something up, looked at it, and put it in his pocket. What?

For one second, she thought about hiding; or running: she had an image of herself riding across the back pasture and into the trees. A dream. Stupid.

They'd be coming, and she licked her lips, and said to herself, "I don't know what you're talking about. I don't know anything." Should she smile at them? Or look scared?

She took a breath, saw the dark-haired man knocking on the door, took another breath and pushed open the barn door and called, "Hello?"

HONEY BEE CAME walking across the driveway with a guilty look: that is, her face seemed to be searching for an appropriate expression, and not finding it. She was wearing a torn nylon parka, knee-high green-rubber barn boots, and rubber gloves, and said, "I was shoveling . . . manure."

"I do that a lot," Jenkins said.

Lucas introduced himself and Jenkins, again, and then said, "I'm afraid we've got some fairly harsh news."

Her mouth dropped open, and she said, faintly, "Joe?"

Lucas shook his head and said, "I'm sorry, but Lyle Mack was killed last night."

She froze, then slowly lifted her hands to the sides of her head, then broke and screamed, "Lyle? Lyle died? Oh, God . . ." She sank to the ice-covered ground and began sobbing, and Lucas squatted next to her and said, "We know you were close friends. But we need to get you inside, now, and we need to talk about this. We think there are some reasons for you to be worried."

He wasn't sure she'd heard him, or understood him. She continued sobbing, then looked up and cried, "You're sure? Lyle?"

Lucas said, "Yeah." His eyes drifted away from her, and he picked up several pieces of straw from the ice, twirled them in his fingers, and put them in his pocket. "Yeah, it's him."

*

THEY GOT her inside, and somewhere along the way she stuttered, "We thought we might get married someday," and "Was it a heart attack? He always ate those goddamned hot fudge sundaes."

They sat her in the kitchen and Jenkins asked if he could make her some coffee or tea, and she said yes, and Jenkins got cups and Folgers instant and stuck them in the microwave. Lucas said, "Ms. Brown? I know you're upset, but listen, Lyle wasn't killed by a heart attack. He was murdered, apparently after the bar closed. We need to know who you think might have been involved with Joe, and Lyle, these last few months."

She asked the dreaded question: "Should I have an attorney?"

Jenkins jumped in, trying to kill the question: "We know Joe didn't do it, because we talked to Joe, and he's down in Kansas somewhere. We think he's running for Mexico. Also, their father, Ike, was killed."

"Ike? They killed Ike? Oh my God, who *are* they?"

"We were hoping you could give us some help," Lucas said. "For one thing, it looks like they're eliminating people who knew about the hospital robbery. We think they'll try to get Joe, we think they'll try to get the witness at the hospital. We've got to stop this, right now."

A little chip of flint appeared in her eyes, as she looked up at him: "I don't know," she said. "I don't know if they were involved. I know they were scared of you. Listen, are you sure it was Lyle?"

"I was looking at him a half hour ago," Lucas said. "It was Lyle."

She stared into the middle distance for a moment, chewing on her lower lip, then said, "I don't know if they were involved with this hospital thing—it sounds crazy to me—but I heard them talking a couple times about a guy they called the doc. Like doctor. But I don't know if the doc was at the hospital, or was just a guy named Doc."

"Do you know anybody named Doc?" Jenkins asked.

"You know, there's about one in every bar. But there wasn't one at Cherries, as far as I know," she said. "How did they do it?"

"Do what?"

"Kill Lyle?"

"He was shot to death," Lucas said.

She clouded up again, but after a moment, said, "Well, at least he probably didn't feel anything. It was quick, huh?"

She was looking right at his eyes and Lucas flinched, and she looked at Jenkins, and she said, looking back to Lucas, "Oh, no." Then, "What did they do?"

LUCAS FUDGED, but she got the gist of it, and began sobbing again. They waited until she was rained out, and Jenkins brought up the coffee, still hot, and she warmed her hands around the cup.

Lucas asked, "Joe's running, in a car. Or a truck, or something—he's down I-35. You know where he would have gotten a car? We saw him selling his van, and we can't find another car registered under his name. We find a couple bikes, but they're both at his apartment . . ."

"Don't know," she said. "But he's a member of the Seed. So I suppose . . . he wouldn't have any trouble getting a ride, if he wanted to pay for it."

Lucas nodded: that made sense. "Okay. So we've got to get you out of here. Can you arrange for somebody to feed the horses?"

"I suppose . . . for a couple days. There's a handyman in town who does that, but I have to find him."

"Give him a ring."

"You really think it's necessary? I don't have a lot of money for hiring people."

"Look, these guys, the killers—if they even suspect that you might give them away, that Lyle might have told you something . . . they'll kill you. To them, they've already killed a bunch of people, one more won't make any difference."

"I don't have any place to go," she said.

"Holiday Inn," Lucas said. "State'll pick it up for however long it takes to break this. We should have it in a week or so . . . it's too crazy to keep going."

SHE GOT THE HANDYMAN, and he agreed to take care of the horses for thirty dollars a day. As she was packing up some clothes and personal-care stuff, Lucas asked, "Do you have a phone number for Joe?"

"No, I . . . You know who did? Lyle. He had a special phone. They both did."

"We've got that. Do you have a cell?"

"Well, sure."

"Okay—we may want you to call Joe on it," Lucas said. "We may need you to vouch for our story—that Lyle was killed. I'm not sure Joe believed us."

She stopped: "Why should I believe you? This could be like that moon-landing stuff. A big pack of lies." She looked at Jenkins. "You guys aren't lying to me, are you?"

"Honey Bee, Lyle's still at the bar. We can stop and look, if you want."

Pause. Then, "I'll think about it."

"The thing is," Lucas continued, "we know that Joe didn't kill the woman in the van. The Jill MacBride lady. Somebody else did. We got DNA from Joe, and from the killer, and Joe wasn't the killer."

"Really?"

"Really."

She nodded: "That makes sense. I don't think Joe's got it in him to kill anybody."

"We might need you to tell him that. The thing is, maybe he still kidnapped Jill MacBride, I don't know. But maybe not. If not, there's no reason to run. He'd be in a little trouble for running, but that's minor, compared, you know, to murder."

"He could come back and get the bar," she said.

"He might do a little time," Lucas said.

"But I could run the bar while he was in jail—I mostly run the place anyway."

"Works for us," Jenkins said. "But first, we got to get him back."

They exchanged cell-phone numbers, and she followed them in her truck, toward town, and halfway in, called and said, "I want to stop at the bar."

"You sure?"

"I want to look at his face," she said.

The place was overrun with cops and crime-scene people; Marcy and Shrake had gone. Lucas took her through the cops, to the body, which was still on the floor. He left her with a cop, stepped over to the crime-scene guy and asked, "Could we get a plastic bag or something, over his lower body? We got his girlfriend here to do the ID."

When the black plastic bag was in place, Lucas led her over, holding on to her arm. She looked down, nodded, pursed her lips as though she were going to spit, and turned and pulled him away from the body. Turned a bar stool around, sat down, and stared at the bar.

"You okay?" Lucas asked.

"No," she said.

"I want to get you out of here. Send you into town with one of my guys, get a statement, and get you settled at a motel."

She said, "Okay. Okay. Goddamnit, that hurts. If it's okay, I gotta go to the ladies'."

"Sure."

She wandered off toward the hallway that led to the ladies' room, and Lucas watched her until she went through the door, then moved over to Jenkins. "I want her to trust me, so I don't want to look like I'm watching her. I'm going down to the other end. But keep an eye on the ladies' can until she comes out. We don't want *her* running on us."

Inside the bathroom, Honey Bee paused for a moment, then dug in her purse and took out a key ring with two keys—one a Schlage and one a Yale. She stood at the sink for a moment, as though she'd been looking at herself, or washing her hands, but she wasn't: she was listening. After a few seconds, she moved quickly to a fire door set in the wall opposite two toilet stalls, opened it with the Schlage, listened again, then stepped forward to an electrical box labeled "High Voltage," and locked with a padlock. She opened it with the Yale. Inside were two small brown paper sacks, the kind that doughnuts might have come in. She took them, snapped the lock back in place, wiped it with a piece of tissue paper, pushed the door shut with an elbow, locked it, and scurried into a stall.

Inside, she dropped her jeans and underpants, sat down, and dug the bags out of her purse. Two solid stacks of currency—mostly twenties, she was disappointed to find. Still: eighteen thousand dollars in a quick count. Homeboy PayPal, for those hard-to-resist items that came in after midnight.

She put it in the bottom of her purse, stood up, flushed, washed her hands, looked at herself in the mirror, splashed some water on her face, wiped it with a paper towel, and went back into the main room. She saw Davenport down at the far end. He held up a hand and came to get her; brought her to Jenkins, who'd take her to BCA headquarters for a statement.

Lucas said, as they were leaving, "Hang on to her there, until I get back. Won't be long."

HE TOOK a call from Stephaniak, the Wisconsin sheriff. "Listen, I have what might be bad news for you, but I'm not sure."

"I could use some bad news, since all the other news has been so good," Lucas said.

"Yeah, well, you might want to get yourself some stainless-steel underwear," Stephaniak said. "You know, I told you about a bunch of guns and other stuff?"

"Yeah?"

"The crime-scene crew got down in there, in the tank, and they found this empty box. Military. There was one empty hand-grenade canister beside it, no grenade. It's just possible that these guys have a whole box of M67 HE frag grenades."

Lucas scratched his head. He didn't really know what to say.

"Hello? You there?" the sheriff asked.

15

LUCAS DROVE SOUTH on Highway 61, crossed the Mississippi into Hastings, took Highway 55 to the law enforcement center, checked in with the sheriff's office and was escorted to forensics. A tall, narrow, dark-haired woman met him at the door and stuck out a hand: "Lucas? Nancy Knott. Come on through. What's up?"

Lucas followed her to a cubbyhole office, took the visitor's chair as she settled behind her desk. Lucas asked, "You processed the scene at the Haines-Chapman murder, right?"

"Basically, Lonny Johnson did, but I was out there for a while," she said. "Lonny's off today. I did most of the in-house processing."

"So when I read your forensics report yesterday, it said that you found hay—wait, not hay, you said *straw*—stuck to the back of one of the victims. You thought that he might have died in an agricultural area. I understand the bodies were found in a ditch under a little bridge, in an ag area. So my question is, so what? Was there something about the straw?"

"There wasn't any straw there," Knott said. "It was one of those seasonal creeks, grown up with dead weeds. There was a bean field up the hill, so no straw there. And the bodies were in plastic bags, and the straw was stuck to the outside of their clothing, inside the bags."

Lucas dug in his pocket and pulled several pieces of straw from his pocket. "Hay like this?"

He dropped it on her desk and she leaned over and looked at it, then took a pencil out of a cup and pushed it around. "Straw. Yeah. Like that. Exactly. See this cut? Cut like that. Same color and texture."

"Is there any way to tell if it's the same straw? Or hay? Like genetically the same?"

She shook her head. "I don't know. Maybe the FBI could. Maybe one of the big ag schools could tell you what variety of straw it is, if that would help."

"I'm not exactly following—I'm a city kid. Hay, straw . . ."

Hay, she said, was essentially different from straw. Hay was a dried food crop, like alfalfa or clover, heavily fed to cattle, horses, goats, sheep, and sometimes other animals. Straw was the support stalk for cereal grains, like wheat, oats, and rye, didn't have much nutritive value, but was used for animal bedding.

"And what we had on Haines's back was several pieces of straw, not hay. It looked exactly like what you've brought in, and I suspect a lab could tell you that they were both, say, oat straw, or not. Or wheat straw, or not. About the genetics, I bet they could figure it out, but I'm not sure."

"Bedding material. For what kind of animals?" Lucas asked.

"Horses. You know, horses in a barn," she said.

"Huh."

"If you want to leave this, I can check around, see if we can find a place to compare it. If you have a scene where you think they might've been killed, well, just me eyeballing it, your samples look identical to what we took off Haines," she said. "And Haines and Chapman were living in the city, too—they wouldn't have just picked it up anywhere. So . . . I bet you found it. Uh, where was it?"

LUCAS CALLED JENKINS from the road: "You still got her there?"

"Yes. Having a nice chat."

"Hold her there."

GABRIEL MARET pulled the surgical team together outside the operating theater. "One more day. The cardiologists say there could be some benefit by holding off for another twelve to twenty-four hours, but not after that. So tomorrow morning, at seven o'clock, we're going, and we have to go the whole way, regardless of what happens."

Virgil had been leaning against the wall down the hall, and when Weather broke free of the group, asked, "Back home?"

She said, "I was thinking. About these latest killings. Lucas thinks that the hospital guy has to be involved somehow. He's one guy they don't have any ideas about, except for the accent."

Virgil nodded. "So?"

"So they killed this one man last night, and another one probably this morning. Who do we know who has a French accent, who didn't show up for work today?"

Virgil's eyebrows went up. "Not a bad thought. Who'd we ask about that?"

"Let's go down to admin."

LUCAS GOT BACK to the BCA office and found Jenkins and Honey Bee in a conference room finishing a pepperoni pizza. Lucas took a chair, pulled it close to her, and said, "Ms. Brown. Harriet. Honey Bee. When the bodies of Haines and Chapman were found, some pieces of straw were taken off their backs. I collected some straw from your driveway this morning. I've just been down to the Dakota County sheriff's office and we've done a comparison. We think we can prove that Haines and Chapman were killed at your farm."

Her mouth dropped open. *"What?"*

"We can use genetics techniques to prove the connection," Lucas said. "Very sophisticated, but they're better than fingerprints."

"I don't—"

Lucas beat her down with an angry snap: "Goddamnit, don't bullshit us. This is way out of control. Do you realize how many people are dead? Somebody's killed six people."

"Not *me* . . ."

"But you were involved, one way or another," Lucas said, leaning toward her, looming, tapping on the table with his index finger. "We've already got enough to convince a jury: you were intimate with Lyle Mack, you were friends with Joe and Ike, you were friends with the victims, Haines and Chapman, we've got the evidence of the straw, taken from your house. Have you helped us? No. You've stonewalled. You've given us exactly zip."

She looked at Jenkins. "I've been cooperating . . ."

"You've been talking to me," Jenkins said. "You've been nice, I gotta admit. But Honey Bee, you've given me exactly *no* useful information. Not even the simple stuff, like, who's the 'doc' guy?"

"I don't know who the doc guy *is*," she said. "I think he's a doper. Joe told me once that the worst doper he knew was a doctor, and I think it's the same guy. I think that's how they knew him. The guy was trying to buy dope."

"Did Joe sell dope?"

She looked away, and then said, "He might have, at one time. I don't know exactly."

"Oh, horseshit," Lucas said. "Did he sell dope?"

Long pause, then, "Yes. Not so much sell it, as trade it. You know, for stuff."

"What kind of stuff?" Jenkins asked.

"Office equipment."

"Office equipment." The two cops looked at each other.

"They used to sell a lot of office equipment on the Internet," she said. "And cameras and stuff," she said.

"In other words, hot stuff," Lucas said. "Stuff from burglaries, stolen stuff from offices."

"I guess," she said.

"Where'd they keep it?" Lucas asked. "There wasn't any at the bar, or their houses."

She started to cry, and the cops sat and watched. After a minute, she stopped, checking for effects, saw nothing but stone faces. *"What?"*

"Where'd they keep it?" Lucas asked again.

Another long wait, and then, "They have a storage place out in Lake Elmo."

"Do you know where it is?"

"Yes."

"Did they put the dope from the hospital robbery out there?"

"I don't know about the hospital robbery."

They pushed her around for a while, then Lucas said to Jenkins, "I think we better check her into Ramsey County."

"What does that mean?" she asked.

"Gonna hold you in jail for a while," Lucas said.

She thought about the money in her purse and said, "Oh, no. You said we were going to a hotel."

"Can't take a chance that you'd run," Lucas said. "You're in this up to your neck."

She said, "If you put me in jail, I'll get a lawyer and I won't say one more goddamn thing to you. If you need help, you can go fuck yourself. I'm trying to help, maybe I can help if you ask different questions, or maybe I can help some other way. If you put me in jail, I won't say one more goddamn word."

"I don't know if you can give us any more help," Lucas said. "You're looking at a murder one, and you're still stonewalling."

"I'll help you with Joe," she said. "Who else are you going to get to talk to him? That he'll trust? You can go fuck yourself on that one," she said.

Lucas looked at Jenkins. "What do you think?"

Before Jenkins could say anything, Honey Bee added, "I've got my truck. I've got my horses. I've got my farm. I *can't* run away. I'm forty-three years old and I got nothing else in my whole life."

Jenkins said, "I thought your driver's license said thirty-seven or thirty-nine. Like that."

"I might've cut a couple years off," she said.

LUCAS CALLED MARCY, told her about the straw from the driveway, about the storage unit, about Honey Bee's willingness to talk to Joe.

"He's not answering, but his phone is ringing, still in Kansas, and not moving," Marcy said. "I got a bad feeling about it. I think they ditched it. Threw it out the window."

LUCAS AND JENKINS drove Honey Bee out to Lake Elmo, to a self-storage place, and got the manager to open the unit. The floor was covered by wooden pallets, on which were stacked a couple of dozen TVs and computer monitors, computers, including a half-dozen Apple laptops, a gift box of Wüsthof knives, paper shredders, printers, speakers and audio receivers, Blu-ray and DVD players, a dozen GPS handhelds, fish-finders and marine tracking units, six new-looking Yamaha 25-horsepower outboard motors, and one snowmobile.

No drugs. Because, Lucas thought, the drugs had been at Ike's.

They called the Washington County sheriff, told them about the unit, knotted a piece of crime-scene tape on the lock, and told the manager not to touch anything.

"Nothing for us," Lucas said, as they pulled out. To Honey Bee: "We need Joe. We need a different phone, we need the doc, we need you to give us something we can use, or I'm slamming your ass in jail."

"I don't—"

"Think of something," Lucas said. "Or else. The doc: is he a French guy? Do you know anything about that?"

She touched her lips and said, "Oh."

"Oh, what?"

"The doc guy. Joe Mack once cracked some joke about a raghead. I think he was talking about the doc."

"The doc's an Arab?"

"Or one of those kinds of people who have, you know, turbans. I think so. But I'm not sure. That's all I can think of that might help."

"What's his last name?" Lucas asked.

"I don't know," she said. "I don't know anything else. I heard them talking about the doc."

"That's not a hell of a lot," Jenkins said.

VIRGIL AND WEATHER were put with the payroll people, who looked through a list of the French-accent workers. None had called in sick, but two of them had the day off. Virgil said, "I need to get you home, so the guys can cover you."

"You shouldn't look for them on your own," Weather said.

"So I'll take Jenkins or Shrake," Virgil said. "Gotta do it, though— this could be something."

They'd just finished when Lucas called for Virgil. Lucas told him what Honey Bee had said, and Virgil said, "If it's an Arab, that's gonna be a bigger problem. There're lots more Arabs around here than Frenchmen."

JENKINS AND LUCAS played good-cop bad-cop for a while, Jenkins suggesting that Honey Bee had helped some, and she might help more, and so deserved another chance. Lucas wanted to put her in jail. Eventually, Lucas backed away, and agreed to stick her in a Holiday Inn, in downtown St. Paul.

"You go out to eat, and that's it. You sit here and watch TV. If I call you on your cell, you better answer in one second," Lucas said.

"I will," she said.

*

Honey Bee sat in her room for a half hour, staring at her suitcase, watching the TV without seeing it. She was scared of the killer, scared of Davenport, scared of the future. She wondered if they were watching her: peeked out in the hall, saw nobody. Went back to her room, sat in the bathtub. Made a decision.

She'd make a practice run, she decided. She took the elevator down three floors, then the stairs the rest of the way, listening for doors closing above her . . .

On the street, head down, she walked to a sandwich place on West Seventh, a block from the X Center, sat in a booth in the back, and watched the door. Business was slow, no hockey on the schedule: a few people came through, but nobody who felt like a cop. She left by a back door, into a side street, got her guts together, crossed the streets to the X Center, took the Skyway first up and then down, to the tunnel, watched her tracks, got into the main system, moving fast now.

At the bank, she got directions to the safe-deposit area, took the elevator down, rented a safe-deposit box, showing her checks to confirm her status as a customer, and dropped seventeen thousand into it, kept a thousand as walking-around money.

Took the elevator back up, expecting to see Davenport waiting at the doors: nobody.

Walked back through the Skyways, looking for a pay phone . . . and found one, one of the last public phones in the world, she thought. She got quarters from a popcorn stand and dialed long distance.

Two rings, three. Then, "Hello?"

"Eddie? It's me, Honey Bee."

Silence. Then, "You with the cops?"

"Not now. They had me all day. I'm calling from a pay phone. I need to talk to Joe."

"One minute."

Joe came on and said, "Honey Bee. I was afraid to call you."

"I'm on a pay phone. Joe—everybody's dead. I saw Lyle dead. Somebody tortured him. *Tortured him.* They say your dad's dead, too. They say there was drugs up there, and they tortured Lyle to get them." She kept her voice down, watching people walking past her, but tears started, and she began to cry into the phone.

"We're coming back," Joe Mack said after a while.

"You know who it is?" Honey Bee asked.

"Maybe," Joe Mack said.

"Is it the doc?"

More silence, then Joe Mack said, "How'd you know about the doc?"

"They've been looking all over for a guy called the doc. One of the cops said that there might have been some kind of powder on Lyle, that came from doctor's gloves."

"Could be the doc. Could be another guy. I'm not sure. But if an Arab guy comes looking for you, or a skinhead guy, you stay the fuck away from them. You get behind your shotgun and you don't let them in the house."

"I'm not in my house; the cops hid me in a hotel."

"Good. Stay there. You got a phone?"

"Not a clean one."

"See if you can get one, call me back at this number."

"What are you going to do?"

"Find the doc and this other guy. Have a talk."

"They think the doc did it. They tortured Lyle something awful, and something they were talking about makes me think a doc did it. They cut him. I think they cut, you know, his balls . . . off."

"Ah, Honey Bee . . . Christ, his balls?"

Honey Bee started weeping into the phone, and Joe Mack said, "Listen to me. Listen to me. Do they still think I killed that lady?"

"No. They say somebody else did," she said. "They think it's the doc. I told them it might be. They were going to put me in jail unless I told them something."

"Okay. Be cool. Did you get the cash out of the circuit breaker?"

She nodded at the phone. "Yes. I put it in a safe-deposit box at US Bank. Seventeen thousand dollars. Don't go to the bar. The cops are tearing the place apart."

"Okay. Now listen. Sit tight. Cooperate, but don't tell them I'm coming back, and don't tell them about this phone. Eddie's got a lawyer pal in Wisconsin who's done a lot of work for the Seed. He's gonna sign one-third of the bar over to you, make it look like you owned it for a couple years, and he's going to make a will for Lyle that leaves half of his share to you, and half to me. So we'll be half owners, but you gotta run it, okay?"

She sniffed. "Okay."

"I'll be back late tonight or tomorrow. We're coming, Honey Bee."

BARAKAT TOOK the call from Joe Mack, who asked, "Have you seen Cappy?"

"I can get in touch," Barakat said.

"Tell him that the cops are looking for him. They might know about the van, too. He either better dump it, or dump the plates."

"Where are you?"

"On my way to Mexico. I ain't coming back, Al. Everybody's dead, and I don't know what's going on. I'm just heading out."

The dummy, being clever.

16

CAPPY AND BARAKAT nosed Barakat's car down the snow-covered track to the boat landing, talking about the van problem. Cappy said, "I'll take the California plates off my old van and put them on the new one. When I get to Florida, I'll sell the new van on the street, and buy a legit one."

"How will you sell it on the street? Do you know somebody . . ."

"I'll hook up with some bikers. They can take care of it. Everybody needs a van."

A few trucks had been down to the boat landing since the last snow, and there was a packed turnaround spot at the end. The water on the Wisconsin side was partly open, from the heat put in at the Prairie Island nuclear plant a mile or so upstream.

Nobody out there at dawn. They got out, looked across the rim of ice to the open water, and Cappy walked out until he was ten feet from the edge.

"What do you think?" Barakat called. He was afraid of ice.

"Looks okay to me."

"Is it deep?"

"It looks deep," Cappy said.

"You can try it," Barakat said, "but let me get the car turned around, so we can get out fast."

They got the car turned around, pointed back toward the highway a quarter-mile away, and then Cappy got one of the grenades out of the back.

"You're sure you know about this?" he asked Barakat.

"One hundred percent," Barakat said. "As long as you don't let the handle fly off, you're perfectly safe."

"Safe."

"Perfectly. When you throw it, throw it like one of your baseball players."

They walked to the ice together. Barakat stopped at the edge, and Cappy asked, "Won't the water put it out?"

"I don't think so. It's not like a match."

They both looked at the grenade, which Barakat said looked like a pomegranate, but Cappy didn't know what a pomegranate was, so they agreed on tomato, and Cappy said, "Pull the pin . . ."

"Throw the handle and everything," Barakat said. "Like a baseball."

"All right. Here goes." Cappy gripped the grenade around the handle and yanked the pin out. Stood there for a moment.

Barakat said, "Throw it. Throw it."

Cappy threw it, but it was heavier than he thought, hit the edge of the ice, skidded, and slipped over the edge into the water. Barakat started running away, and he called, "Run."

Cappy was running when the grenade blew. It wasn't too loud, but loud enough, and kicked up a twenty-foot plume of water. "Jesus," Cappy shouted. "Let's get the fuck outa here."

Laughing, they ran back to the car and drove away.

LATER, AT BARAKAT'S HOUSE, they were playing basketball, not because they wanted to, but because they couldn't help it. Too much cocaine: too cold to go out. Plus, a basketball game on TV, the volume on 84, and the Eagles on the iTunes, volume at 11. The ball was a wad of two sheets of typing paper, the basket was purely virtual—a blank spot above a door. The idea was to hit the blank spot with a shot, which was too easy unless they stayed right in each other's faces, and after a couple of points, it turned into war, a raucous fight to get the paper wad in the air, the two of them tumbling over chairs, tables, an ottoman, Cappy blowing a nosebleed, spraying blood around the room, Barakat driving down the lane between the couch and an easy chair . . .

When they quit, Cappy was leading 18 to 14, but he collapsed first, flat on the carpet, and groaned, and laughed, and said, "I'm fucked," and he also thought it might have been the best twenty minutes of his life, except for those nights roaring up the 15; the best night with *somebody*.

Barakat said, breathing hard, "I will tell you something, Cappy. This is serious. I know how I can get out from all this police business."

"Yeah?"

"Yes. I thought of it now, one minute ago. There is this man, from my town in Lebanon, his name is Shaheen."

"Shaheen."

"Shaheen. He is nothing, but he thinks he is a big man. He is another doctor, but he is not so much. But." His heart was pounding from the game, and the cocaine, and he stopped to take a half-dozen deep breaths.

"But," Cappy said, prompting him.

"Shaheen has an accent. More accent than I. And he is nothing. I am thinking, if Shaheen dies, and if in his room there are some drugs from the hospital, what do we think?"

"We think he is the man the cops are looking for, inside?"

"That's what we think," Barakat said.

They breathed together for a while, then Barakat asked, "You have a girlfriend?"

"No. Nope. Not so much."

"Are you a virgin?"

"Nope. 'Course not."

"Hah. I know a place in Minneapolis," Barakat said. "These girls."

Cappy rolled up on his side. "Hookers?"

"That's too bad," Barakat laughed. "One of them, she told me that she was a therapist."

"I don't know what that is, exactly," Cappy said.

"Like a doctor . . . like a psychiatrist. You know, to give you mental help."

"I could use some mental help."

"These girls, they like cocaine. They like amphetamine. They like marijuana, but we don't have marijuana. They like money."

"Don't have much money," Cappy said.

"There is this American song," Barakat said. "I don't know it, but one part says, 'The candy man don't pay for pussy.'"

"Yeah?"

"We got some candy," Barakat said. He staggered to his feet. "We got lots of candy."

"What about Shaheen?" Cappy asked.

"Girls first. Then Shaheen," Barakat said.

CAPRICE GARNER'S old man had beat him like a bass drum from the time he was a baby until he was fourteen, when he ran to California, thinking to become a beach bum or a movie star. He got as far as Bakersfield and a job as a roofer, a skinny kid with a thousand-yard stare and bad scars on his face, back, and soul, and then he fell drunk off a roof one spring morning and broke both of his legs.

With no medical insurance, he took what he could get, the legs fixed at a charity hospital, sweating out the summer in a concrete-block apartment with both legs in casts, no air-conditioning. The guy next door was a biker, took pity on him, brought him beer, crackers, cheddar cheese, and summer sausage. Back on the job, and still under the influence of the biker, Cap saved his money and bought a used Harley Softail and a window air conditioner.

Did the biker thing.

Let his hair grow down to his shoulders. Bought a high-end leather jacket and chaps at a Harley rally. Pierced an ear for a silver-skull earring, pierced a lip for a steel ring, bought himself a rich selection of do-rags. Got a tattoo on his back, ten inches across, a motorcycle wheel with the words *Razzle-Dazzle*.

Took some shit because of his youth. Had one guy who kept talking about taking Caprice into the desert and gang-fucking him, *to break him in*, the guy said. The guy laughed about it, but Caprice thought there might be something underlying it, so he killed him.

Went to his house with a street gun, and when the guy answered the doorbell, shot him in the heart and ran away in the night, the guy's girlfriend screaming from the kitchen.

Nobody figured that one out. But he was riding as an indie, and anybody might try to ride over an indie. He did the reasonable thing and got himself the Judge.

People who pissed him off tended to disappear, and bikers got careful when they were around him. Nobody knew, but they *knew*. He encountered Shooter Chapman, a fellow Minnesotan, in a friendship ride for cancer or heart health or kidneys or some shit like that, where the old guys all had flags on the backs of their trikes.

By the time he was old enough to be invited into a gang, he no longer wanted it: the brotherhood, the drinking, the ranking, the rules. He liked being alone. He could *trust* being alone. He dumped the Harley after he'd killed the man for his BMW, and the new long-distance ride, with the German name, set him further apart from the gangs.

Then one day he glanced at himself in a Burger King mirror, saw a piece of yellow cheese stuck to his lip ring.

He was a fuckin' joke, he thought, staring into the mirror. He needed to hone his act, he needed to get down to what he *was*.

He traded the high-end leathers for a fifties jacket that he found in Hollywood, black leather so old and sand-worn and sweat-soaked that it had turned brown. Got rid of the earring and the lip ring. Shaved his head. Threw away his do-rags. Bought a pair of Vietnam-era military goggles with round lenses and olive-drab canvas straps that made him look like a frog. Liked the look.

He got it so stripped down, so plain, so wicked, so weathered that when he walked into a biker place, everybody stopped talking to look at him. They knew he was *out there*, the place they talked about going, but never really did. He liked that, too.

Like the day a bunch of Angels rode into LA from San Bernardino, then hooked north up the PCH toward Santa Barbara, riding like a bunch of old women on their Harleys, graybeards with old fat chicks, Arrive Alive, Drive 55, and he'd blown their doors off, riding one-handed through the pack like a fuckin' guided missile at 110. He'd replayed that scene in his mind any number of hundreds of times . . .

When the roofing business went in the tank with the rest of the economy, and some bones turned up in the Mojave and got written about in the newspapers, Cappy moved back to Minnesota, looked up Shooter.

Shooter introduced him to the gang at Cherries, and got him a job throwing boxes at UPS. The good thing about UPS was, you worked all night, had a full twelve hours to drink and ride, catch four hours of sleep, and then, with a little help from your friend methamphetamine, the next shift.

With all that, Cappy . . .

Had never been laid.

HE KNEW how it was done; he'd even *seen* it done, live and in color, on a table in the Dome Bar in Bakersfield, among the bottles of Heinz catsup and 57 sauce and the clatter of silverware. It hadn't been pretty, but it held his attention.

BARAKAT TOOK HIM to a bar called Trouble on the west side of Minneapolis, out on Highway 55, Cappy filled with cocaine and trepidation. Barakat drifted through a crowd unnaturally large for the crappy kind of bar it was, black light and brass poles, and hooked them up with three women named Star, Michellay, and Jamilayah. There was talk of money, but Barakat flashed the Ziploc and they were out of there, across the street to the Shangri-La Motel, where the three women lived in adjoining rooms.

Star and Jamilayah, one white, one black, were all over Barakat, and Michellay, a thin blonde with a knife-edge nose and narrow lips, hung on Cappy's arm, which made him feel thick in the chest.

Like this was *it*.

And this was *it*, and it didn't take long, listening to Britney on the Wave CD, doing lines off the dresser top, playing grabass through the three rooms, and then they were on the beds, Barakat with his two, and Cappy with Michellay, who slipped him out of his pants like an eel out of its skin,

And heck,

Everything went Pretty Damn Well.

BARAKAT, WALKING through the rooms, waving his erection around, laughing, "Look at this, you bitches, look at this one," and Cappy drinking out of a tap, bent over the sink, and Jammy goosing him, and him almost going through the mirror, then chasing her down, the black woman screaming, Cappy rolling on top of her and bang.

It went Pretty Damn Well again.

LIKE RIDING out of Bakersfield, up into the hills and down the other side and out into the Mojave, screaming through the night with the wind in his face . . .

And they left at four o'clock in the morning, and Cappy leaned his head against the dashboard and said, "I think I just fucked a spook."

"About six times, my man," Barakat crowed, slapping him on the back. "You were wondrous."

"She was like . . . pink inside," Cappy said. They headed back into town, and Cappy felt a surge of gratitude toward Barakat. He hadn't known if it would ever happen, because women, generally, didn't care for him. He'd accepted that: there was something in him that cut them.

Now, he knew, you just had to find the right women.

SHAHEEN WAS a more intricate situation, and Barakat more sober about it: "I have known him for a long time. He is nothing, but still, I

214

have known him. I would like to do this quietly. No guns. We have to come and go, leave him behind . . ."

As an emergency room physician, Barakat had seen all kinds of trauma. After considering it, he decided that the best solution would be a blow to the head with something heavy. "When he is down, then we can finish him. The main thing, we attract no attention. With what the woman saw, Karkinnen, we don't want somebody describing me."

Shaheen lived in an anonymous tan-stucco apartment building in south Minneapolis. Barakat and Cappy left the van on the street and walked back to it, in the night, and Barakat said, "His light's on."

"He have a girlfriend?"

"Shaheen? No. There's a girl back home that he's supposed to marry, fixed by his father. But he's told me he doesn't care for her."

"Don't care about that—I just wondered if he had one, if she's up there."

"What are your ideas for this?" Barakat asked. "To be quiet about it."

"Got no ideas," Cappy said. "Just be simple and do it."

THE APARTMENT building had an interior door that was supposed to be locked, but Barakat pulled on it, hard, and the lock popped and they went through.

"How'd you know about that?" Cappy asked.

"Lock has been broken for two years," Barakat said. "Nobody uses their key anymore."

SHAHEEN PEEKED around the door to see who it was, then let them in. "Now what? Has something happened?"

"We came to tell you that nothing has happened, everything is okay," Barakat said. "The police have found the people who did it, and they were killed."

"The police killed them? I didn't hear . . ."

And they got into it, talking in circles about the people who'd robbed the hospital. Cappy had come lounging in the door behind Barakat. Shaheen glanced at him and then turned to his talk with

215

Barakat, glancing sideways at Cappy from time to time, but not asking who he was, or what he was doing with Barakat.

Shaheen's apartment was furnished in Poor Student, with ramshackle bookcases holding dozens of texts, piles of medical papers. A couch faced two old easy chairs, with a glass-topped coffee table between them, and, to one side, a wooden desk with a computer, printer, and more piles of paper. A bar separated a kitchenette from the living room. There were two interior doors, both open, one leading to a bathroom, the other to a bedroom. They could see the toilet stool in one and the end of a bed in the other.

Shaheen smoked. A large glass ashtray sat on the dining bar; as they talked, they moved past it, toward the circle of the couch and chairs. Cappy picked up the ashtray. Shaheen's back was to him and he lifted it in one hand, a question. Barakat gave him a tiny nod, and Cappy stepped toward Shaheen, who started to turn, and slammed it into his head, an inch behind his ear.

Shaheen went down as though shot. Barakat put his hands on his hips and said, "You know, I hate to see this."

"A little late to stop now," Cappy said.

"Oh, we can't stop." He knelt down and pushed a finger into Shaheen's neck. "Still alive," he said.

Cappy said, "Here," and he knelt beside the supine man, pinched his nose, put his hand over Shaheen's mouth, and pressed. Shaheen was profoundly unconscious, and never resisted. After a moment, he began to tremble and shake, and then he died.

Barakat checked again and said, "Well, that's that. Good-bye, Addie." Then he rolled him, fished his wallet out of his pocket, and took out a wad of cash. "He doesn't trust banks—there may be some more around, maybe in the refrigerator."

They found an envelope with $1,100 under an ice-cube tray; Cappy probed the bedroom, but found nothing more. Barakat had brought with him a dozen sample boxes of Viagra, distributed through hospitals and doctors' offices, two boxes of Tamiflu, and three bottles of stimulants.

They wiped them, then handled them with Shaheen's dead but still sweaty hands, and then put them in a shoe box under Shaheen's bed. The stimulants had the hospital's name on them.

"Now, we go away," Barakat said. They wiped the ashtray and touched the doorknob only with a paper towel, careful not to wipe it, and were gone.

"The thing about this is, this solves several long-term problems I have had," Barakat said, as they walked back down the sidewalk to the car. "I never liked Addie. He was always trying to climb out of his place. Also, he spied on me for my father."

"Hope he didn't tell your old man about the hospital."

"He didn't know about the hospital for sure. He thought I did it, but he wasn't sure. And now, it's not a problem," Barakat said. "You hungry?"

Cappy nodded. "I could use a bite . . . Man, like that spook was all pink down there, you know? I didn't know that about them."

He didn't think about Shaheen, because Shaheen was now irrelevant.

17

VIRGIL TOLD LUCAS, "I got tired of wandering around doing nothing, so finally I started asking everybody I met if they knew any Arabs with French accents, or accents that might be French, who've been acting flaky. Or Frenchmen who look like Arabs."

They were sitting at the dining table, with coffee. Weather was holding her head in her hands, and every once in a while said something like "Oh my God."

Lucas asked, "What happened?"

"Nothing yet," Virgil said. "The question hasn't had time to metastasize. I figure the politically correct wolverines will be onto it pretty quick. They'll blab it all over the hospital, and I should have about six formal complaints and three answers by noon tomorrow."

Weather said, "Oh my God."

Lucas patted her on the leg and said, "Don't worry. If it works, we're golden. If it doesn't work, and there are too many complaints, we'll reprimand him and tell everybody he'll be required to go to sensitivity training. He's going to the Bahamas in two weeks, anyway, so he'll be out of sight."

"Oh my God."

Lucas asked Virgil, "Run into any good-looking doctors over there?"

"A couple," Virgil said.

"I heard radiologists are hot. And dermatologists. They're more intellectual than, like, surgeons," Lucas said.

"I'll keep that in mind," Virgil said.

Weather said, "Sometimes, the two of you think you're being funny, but you're not that funny. I've got to work with a lot of . . . of . . ."

Lucas said to Virgil, "She's trying to find a softer word for 'Arab.' Like, 'Persons of Middle Eastern heritage.'"

"Fuck you," Weather said.

"See?" Lucas said. "A dermatologist never would have said that. They're more classy."

Lucas came to bed at one o'clock, moving quietly, and Weather said, "I'm awake."

"You should be asleep. Are you okay?"

"We're going to do it," she said.

"Yes. I hope that thing with Virgil isn't keeping you awake."

"No. I know how to prioritize," Weather said. "I even understand what he's doing, but you'll never get me to approve of it. You know, officially."

"Gods of correctness," Lucas said.

"Mmm."

"Thinking about the babies?" Lucas slipped under the blankets.

"They're just like us, but they don't understand," Weather said. "They're alive, they have emotions, they have intellectual processes, they are learning, they know some words . . . they're physically underdeveloped because they haven't been able to walk or crawl, but *they're like us*. They're lying there, maybe in some pain, wondering what's happening, and tomorrow, by this time, one or both of them might be dead, because of what we're doing."

"Weather—"

"I know. I wouldn't want to do anything else, or be anywhere else, but: it's a load."

"Did you take a pill?"

"No. I'll be fine. Maybe if we could just do a spoon for a few minutes," she said.

"Listen," Lucas said. "It's gonna work out. That's the karma here . . . it's going to work."

"You don't believe in karma."

"Snuggle up," he said. "Close your eyes. It's gonna work."

WEATHER LEFT at six, got to the hospital fifteen minutes later, bodyguards fore and aft. Maret was gathering the team together for a pep talk: "This time we must keep going. We are close, but still several hours away. Everybody must resolve to work quickly. If we can save five minutes here or there, it's worth doing. We're in a race. We are not sloppy, but we are quick."

Weather went down to the separation lounge and found the Rayneses talking to a stress counselor. "You okay?" she asked them.

"Gabriel says that one way or another, we'll finish today," Lucy Raynes said.

Weather nodded. "We will. The babies look better, but they can't take much more. We'll finish."

"God willing," Larry Raynes said.

She left them, went to the women's locker room, changed into scrubs; when she came out, the babies were being rolled into the operating room.

LUCAS STAYED UP just long enough to see her off with Virgil, Jenkins, and Shrake, then went back to bed, looking for another hour or two of sleep. It came hard: his mind wouldn't stop churning, looking for strings that might lead to the doctor. He finally rolled out of bed at eight, cleaned up and headed down to his office. He was just turning into the parking lot when he got a call from Virgil.

"Your pal Marcy's all over me," Virgil said.

"Because of the Arab thing?"

"That's ten percent of it," Virgil said. "The other ninety percent is, an Arab doctor from Lebanon was murdered down in south Minneapolis last night. He used to live in Paris. They're taking some unusual drugs out of his apartment, and some wrappers for more drugs they haven't found. Like, a lot of drugs."

"You're serious."

"She should be calling you in about two minutes," Virgil said. "I probably got in first because you're on my speed dial."

"Where's this at? The murder? You got an address?"

"No, but like I said, she'll be calling. Jenkins and Shrake are still here. I'm gonna run down there and take a look."

LUCAS'S CELL PHONE booped, and he said, "There she is. Talk to you later." He pressed the flash button, and Marcy came up. "You know what your guy Virgil did yesterday?"

Lucas asked, "So what's the address? You there yet? What kind of drugs . . . ?"

THE MINNEAPOLIS cops were all over the scene, Marcy standing in the hall talking to the lieutenant in charge of the homicide unit. She saw Lucas and walked down toward him and said, "That fuckin' Flowers. They were talking all over the hospital yesterday about how he was looking for an Arab, and see what happens?"

"The dead guy is an Arab?"

"Yes. Adnan Shaheen, from Lebanon," she said. "Decent rep, far as we can tell, but we've got some dope containers and other stuff, and it looks like it might have come out of the hospital pharmacy."

"This didn't happen because of Virgil," Lucas said. "He didn't kill anyone. We've got a stone killer who's cleaning up the mess left from the hospital holdup."

"Pretty goddamn far-out there, though . . ."

"Don't get on his case. He's coming by in a few minutes," Lucas said.

"Already been here and gone. And I *did* get on his case. He is the most uncooperative, insubordinate—"

"What'd you want him to do? Say he was looking for a *swarthy* doctor?" Lucas asked.

"Shut up," she said.

"So we got the doc . . ."

"And another problem," Marcy said.

Lucas nodded: "Who killed the doc?"

She said, "It's pretty clear to me that it's a gang thing. Somebody else in the Seed got wind of the robbery and hijacked it."

Lucas nodded and said, "Let me take a look."

NOT MUCH TO SEE—a dead man with a broken head and a small puddle of blood beneath it, lying on his back, arms beside his body, palms up, in what Yoga people called "the corpse pose," for good enough reason. Lucas watched the processing for a few minutes, then asked, "Who found him?"

"Neighbor. Another guy who works downtown, they carpool into work. He knocked a couple times, and Shaheen didn't answer, and Shaheen's car was still in the parking lot. He peeked in at a corner of the blinds, and he could see him on the floor. Like we did with Lyle Mack."

"Gives me an ice cream headache," Lucas said. "Listen, I'm gonna go put a damp cloth on my eyeballs."

"You do that," she said. "If you think of anything, let me know."

"I already thought of one thing. The doc was friendly enough with the killer that he let the guy hit him from behind."

LUCAS WENT OUT and sat in his truck for a while, then put it in gear and headed over to University Hospitals.

Virgil was lounging in the cafeteria, again, waiting. "Am I gonna get some shit?" he asked.

"Nah," Lucas said. "We were looking for an Arab. So what? Turned out we were right."

LUCAS GOT a doughnut and a Diet Coke and came back to Virgil's table and said, "When I think about a gang holding up the pharmacy, I think of a tight group of people: Joe Mack, who was seen by Weather, and

Chapman and Haines, with Haines confirmed through DNA. Lyle Mack was involved, probably as the brains behind the operation. Ike Mack was probably in charge of selling the drugs downstream. And the doc, who probably set up the robbery, including the theft of a key."

No one else would be needed for the job, he said, and there'd be no reason to tell anyone else about it. Telling somebody else would just be an unnecessary risk.

"First, I thought it was somebody in the group," Lucas said. "They'd committed a murder, inadvertently, and I thought the killer was probably wiping out anyone who could pin the murder on him. And I thought it had to be the doc. Everybody else we know about were friends, and knew each other forever, and now they're all dead. So the doc must be the killer.

"But then the doc was killed. And the doc . . . I don't see him as a longtime friend of this bunch. The Macks don't have medical friends."

"You're making a logical case for the existence of at least one more guy," Virgil said, "which we already know, unless the doc beat himself to death."

"But one more guy wouldn't have any function in the holdup. And that guy didn't know what happened to the drugs, because he had to torture Lyle Mack to get the information. So he's a total outsider. Then, the way Lyle Mack was tortured, I thought it had to be two guys, one guy sitting in the chair, pinning Mack to the floor, the other guy cutting on him. And that powder on him . . . I thought the other guy was the doc. The guy who did the cutting."

Virgil said, "Logically, if there could be one outsider, there could be ten outsiders. All the Macks had to do was tell one guy, and the outsider gets his gang together and hijacks the robbery. You don't need the doctor and . . ." Virgil paused, mid-screed, and then said, "No, that's not right, is it?"

"I don't think so," Lucas said. "Did the Macks tell everybody they knew what they were doing? Why would they do that? And why would the outsiders kill everybody in the gang, if they weren't involved in the pharmacy murder? If all they wanted was the drugs, if they were outsiders, they could have tortured Lyle Mack and killed Ike, and nobody would have known who they were. So why did they kill the doc? How'd they even know about the doc? Why did they make a run at Weather?"

"That could have been Joe Mack or Haines or Chapman, right?"

"No. Haines and Chapman were already dead. The autopsy suggests they were killed the day of the robbery. At least twenty-four hours before Weather was attacked. Weather says the biker was a small guy, and Joe Mack is notably large."

"So there's at least one other guy," Virgil said. "The guy who killed Jill MacBride. That's some outsider DNA, right?"

"If it doesn't belong to the doc." Lucas thought about it for a minute, then said, "But it won't belong to the doc, because the guy who killed Jill MacBride is the guy who tortured Lyle Mack. Same cold killer. Same . . ."

He stopped and turned away from Virgil and said, "Oh, Jesus."

"What?"

"How did the guy who killed Jill MacBride get to the airport? And how did Joe get out? MacBride's car was still there. . . . Somebody picked him up, and killed MacBride, right? The killer picked up Joe Mack. Joe either called him, or Lyle Mack called him and sent him over to pick up Joe. We know Joe Mack talked to Lyle, after he ran."

"They could have taken the train in and out," Virgil said. "But it's about nine hundred and ninety-nine to one that they drove."

Lucas stood up, suddenly excited: "You know what? You know what? The day Joe Mack ran, he was signing his van over to a skinhead. He signed the paper, but the guy never gave Joe any money. No check, nothing. Nothing we saw. I suppose the skinhead could have given Joe a wad of cash ahead of time, but that usually doesn't get done, you know, until the papers are signed. They were either friends, or Joe Mack owed him big. And this was a hard-looking guy."

Virgil's eyebrows went up. "The skinhead—what does he look like?"

"You know, a skinhead," Lucas said. "Probably twenty-five, wind-burned face, skinny, muscles in his face . . ."

Virgil leaned forward, intent. "Man, I've seen that guy, wandering around by the twins' team, doing nothing," Virgil said. "An orderly, or a whatever, a nurse. He's wearing a hospital uniform. I've seen him a couple times. I'm always catching his eyes—"

Lucas snapped his fingers: dug out his cell phone, called the duty officer: "I need the tag numbers of a van owned by a Joe Mack, M-A-C-K, sold in the last few days . . . I can wait."

They waited, no more than a minute, and the duty officer came back. "We've got a Joe Mack as the owner of a 2006 Dodge Grand Caravan cargo van, white in color, but there's no transfer come through."

"You got the tags?"

"Yeah. You want them?"

"No. Get onto the airport cops, find out if those tags came into the airport . . ."

Lucas gave him time and date and said he'd wait again. The duty officer came back after two minutes and said that it'd be another two minutes; and came back and said, "Well, you got it. The van came in at ten forty-two and was out at eleven-oh-eight."

"Thank you. Get all the numbers, tell the airport cops to be careful with the data, see if they've got a face in their van photo. Get back to me."

He clicked off and said to Virgil: "Got him. It's our skinhead. God-damnit, we should have scanned all the tags coming in and out around the time of the MacBride murder. It would have kicked out Joe Mack's van. I mean, I *saw* the guy."

"And if it's the same guy I saw . . ."

"Where's Weather right now?" Lucas asked.

"Either operating or up in the observation room." They both stood up and Virgil said, "This way," and as they hurried back toward the elevators, they both reached down and touched their weapons.

Lucas said, "He's maybe got hand grenades."

"I was just thinking that," Virgil said. "Shoot first, ask questions later."

WEATHER OPENED the operation as she did each day, moving fast now. Moving fast, she was in and out in ten minutes, laying bare the ring of bone that connected Ellen and Sara. Most of the bone had been taken out, and Hanson, at her elbow, was ready to take out all but about a centimeter of the rest of it.

"Anything I can do before I go?" Weather asked him.

"I could use a couple more sterile hands in close," he said.

She stayed, to help hold the babies' heads, six hands in close and tight. Maret asked, through the crowd, "Hearts?"

"Okay so far," somebody answered from the back.

The saw, in cutting through the bone, kicked up the stink of raw blood mixed with something else . . . almost a floral scent. Dead peonies, maybe.

Hanson was a half hour, against an estimate of forty minutes. His mask was dotted with sweat when he backed away. "We're good."

The neurosurgeons moved up.

Weather backed out, stripped off the operating gear, dumped it, washed, and walked down to talk to the Rayneses again.

Lucy, anxious, wide-eyed. "Is something wrong? You were gone so long . . ."

"I stayed to help with some bone removal. At this point, their hearts are stable, we've got everything but the last half-inch of bone out. Rick can take that out in one minute if he has to."

Larry: "So the neuro guys are working?"

"Yes. Still a way to go," Weather said.

They talked for a couple more minutes; the Rayneses said the overnight crew had reported that the twins had gotten their best sleep since the operation began.

A team nurse popped in, looked at Weather: "Gabe wants you in the OR."

"Something happened?" Larry Raynes asked.

"Looks like it's going okay to me," the nurse said. "I'm not a doctor, though."

WEATHER STEPPED inside the OR and said, "Gabriel?"

Maret looked up from the operating table and said, "Ah, Weather, come around here."

She walked carefully around the edge of the working crew, and Maret pointed at the babies' skulls. "The seven vein," he said, and she nodded.

The seven vein had been difficult to image, but they didn't know why, exactly. It rose close to the edge of the defect, up out of Sara's brain, before apparently edging over to a trough where it dumped the blood.

"It doesn't do that. It actually curled around the edge of the defect and dumps into Ellen's side. So, we can ligate it and forget it. But there's another vein we didn't see—we're calling it fourteen—that comes up beside it. If we could splice seven into fourteen . . ."

"How big are they?" Weather asked.

"Not big. But not so small as the ones you did on the toe operation . . ."

"I was using the scope for that. If we drop the scope on them, you guys would have to get out of the way."

"I think they might be large enough for you to do with your loupes . . . I'm hoping."

"I'll scrub up," she said.

SHE WAS BACK in ten minutes, robed in another five, operating glasses in place. Maret moved sideways, pushing one of the nurses away from the table, and Weather moved in close. The other neurosurgeon continued working on the other side of the babies' heads.

Maret said, "Here," and indicated the two veins with a tip of his scalpel.

Weather's operating glasses were equipped with an LED, and the light illuminated the patch of dura mater as though it were an illustration in a medical text. The veins were small, dark, wire-like—a bit smaller in diameter than the wire in a coat hanger.

Weather looked at them for a full fifteen seconds, until Maret asked, "What do you think?"

"How bad do you need it?"

"Well, it's impossible to know. But the babies are doing okay, so far, we are ahead of schedule, and better to do this now, if we can—we need to move as much blood as possible . . ."

"I can do it, but it'll take a while," she said finally. "Sandy might have to stop working every once in a while. I couldn't have the slightest bit of movement."

"How long?"

"Thirty, forty minutes. They're well exposed."

"Thirty minutes?"

"Thirty or forty."

"Thirty minutes. I believe you can do this."

THE VEINS were not especially delicate, but they couldn't be yanked around, either. Weather tied off the smaller fourteen, and began the process of splicing it into the seven. The process was slow: she would be placing four square knots, each smaller than a poppy seed, around the edge of the splice. Ten minutes in, she had one knot; in seventeen minutes, she had two.

An anesthesiologist said, "We've got a gradient showing up."

"I'll be out in ten or fifteen," Weather said. The gradient was the blood pressure in Sara's brain.

"Let's stay with it," Maret said.

Weather did the third knot and asked, "Where's the gradient?"

"Need to move along," the anesthesiologist said.

"We could bleed her for a minute," Weather said. "I think we're tight enough that we won't damage the established sutures."

Maret said, "How long to go ahead and finish?"

"Six or seven minutes, if there're no problems."

"Bleed her just a minute . . ."

Weather released a ligature on the fourteen, and blood began seeping out of the incomplete splice. They stood for a minute, then two, soaking up the blood, and the anesthesiologist said, "Better," and Weather closed the vein again.

Six minutes later she was out, removed the ligatures on seven and fourteen, and she and the other neurosurgeon, Sandy, watched the splice for ten seconds, fifteen, and then Sandy said, "Just like shooting free throws."

Weather said, "You should explain surgery to my husband."

Maret: "What does this mean, free throws?"

"Means we're good," Sandy said. "Get your ass back in here. We're coming to the stretch."

"Sometimes, I wish I understood English," Maret said. To Weather: "Thirty-two minutes."

"Best I could do," she said, a little stiff.

He said, "If you'd told me an hour, I would have asked for forty-five minutes. Thirty-two, I hardly believe."

That made it all better.

WEATHER WAS SITTING in the observation theater when Virgil and Lucas squeezed in, and Lucas reached down and tapped her on the shoulder and gave her the thumb. She followed them out into the hall.

"Have you seen a skinhead orderly around?" Lucas asked.

She shook her head. "Not close by. I haven't really noticed one. You mean a guy with a shaved head?"

"Not shaved, just a super-butch. Virgil's seen him around."

"You think?"

"We think. Gotta call Marcy, let her know, see if we can break out the guy's name. It bothers me that Virgil may have seen him here. So I'm sticking close. I'm going to get Jenkins and Shrake over here . . ."

"We'll be done this afternoon," Weather said. "We're moving fast now."

18

CAPPY SAID, "I don't see any other way to get her. Has to be inside the hospital, but the cowboy guy is all over her."

A car door slammed close by—the driveway?—and Barakat went to the window, peeked, turned and said, urgently, "They look like police. Man and a woman. Get in the bedroom, and keep quiet."

There were two open twists that'd held cocaine, sitting on the coffee table, and as Cappy disappeared into the back, Barakat snatched them up, looked frantically around the room for other problems, and stuffed the twists in his pants pocket.

Could they smell him? Cappy? He lit a Gauloise, blew some of the acrid smoke around the room, took another quick drag, blew it out, settled in at a desk, turned on the desk lamp, brought up his laptop, threw a couple of medical papers on the floor.

And the doorbell rang.

He took his time, checking the living room once more, and went to the door.

Man and a woman. They held up IDs, and the woman said, "Marilyn Crowe, Minneapolis police. This is Doug Jansen. Are you Dr. Barakat?"

"I am," he said, holding the storm door open. It was snowing behind the two cops. "What happened?"

"Do you know a Dr. Adnan Shaheen?"

"Yes, of course, very well. We were at school together . . ." Thinking: *If they found a note, if Adnan had a journal, if they found a letter to my father . . . we should have looked, we should have looked, stupid stupid stupid . . .*

"I'm sorry to tell you this, Dr. Barakat, but Dr. Shaheen was killed last night."

Barakat had seen this interview coming, had even talked about it with Cappy. He didn't react immediately. He simply froze. Then, "What? Addie . . . ?"

The cops waited for him to say something more, and the silence stretched, and then Barakat pushed the storm door fully open and said, "You better come in. Addie's dead? How did this happen? Are you sure, Adnan Shaheen? He has a Lebanese passport? He is a resident at University Hospitals?"

He let himself ramble, now putting himself in a place of shock and sadness, and said, "This . . . wasn't drugs?"

"He was hit on the head with a heavy object," Crowe said. "I'm sorry."

"Why did you think it might be drugs?" Jansen asked.

Barakat rubbed his forehead and turned away, wandered to his desk and sat down at the laptop. "He . . . I think . . . oh, no."

"Street drugs?" Jansen asked.

"I talked to him," Barakat said. "He sometimes used cocaine. I don't know where he got it, I don't know how he learned to get it. He said there was a man who was working his way through medical school by selling cocaine, but I don't know this man . . . but that's when he started, you know. Medical school was very hard for Addie, very hard. He had to study very hard. All the time, the cocaine made him . . . he thought it helped to concentrate."

"You never reported this to anyone?"

"He was my friend," Barakat said. "I tried to help him. He struggled for twelve years to get his degree. Now, so close . . . if I turned him in, it would be the end for him. So I did not. I turned my eyes away."

"All right," Jansen said. "If . . . when this is settled, could we call on you to take care of funeral details?"

"Of course. I will call his family—they are still in Beirut. I will call an uncle, who will tell his mother. Addie . . . he was the great hope of his family, you know."

"I'm sorry," Crowe said. "Had he ever done anything that, looking back, might make you think that he might have been involved with the pharmacy robbery at the hospital?"

"Addie? No! Not at all. He was . . . mmm . . . a timid man, really. This is one reason he liked cocaine, because then he was not so timid. He could go to parties and talk with the girls, you know? But a robbery, I can't believe this."

"How was he financially?"

"He had no money . . . "

THEY TALKED for ten minutes, and Barakat began developing an irrational fear that Cappy would do something insane, like flush a toilet, or appear with a gun, or even creak a floorboard. None of that happened, and the cops trailed off with a few incidental questions, and left, apparently satisfied.

When the car had gone, Barakat walked back to the bedroom, opened the door: nobody. Then Cappy asked, "They gone?" and sat up from a spot on the floor, behind the bed.

"They know nothing. Still, I am uneasy, you know? This woman . . . if she sees Addie's picture in the newspaper, or on the TV, she may remember another man in the elevator. I do not look like Addie, but there is a similarity."

"So, we take her out."

"If possible. Then, we have only Joe Mack. Joe Mack continues to worry me."

"He's gone, man," Cappy said. "I don't think even Joe is dumb enough to come back here, not after all this."

BARAKAT FOLLOWED Cappy to the hospital, up into the ramp, and then past him to the physicians' parking, and into the hospital through a different entrance. Cappy would scout the hallways in his civilian clothes, and then stop by the closet for the scrubs.

Cappy, Barakat thought, could become a problem. He would have to deal with that later, if the police didn't do it first. He doubted that Cappy, from the way he talked, would be taken alive; he was convincing about that, a young man rushing toward death.

AT THREE O'CLOCK in the afternoon, Sandy Groetch looked up from the operating table and said, "I'm done."

There was a rustle of talk both in the operating room and up above, in the observation room, as Rick Hanson moved in with his saws. Up above, Weather stood up and headed for the door, led by Virgil and trailed by Lucas.

In the hall outside, Weather said, "We're almost there."

"What was that talk about Ellen?"

"It's her heart again. The last time they dropped the blood pressure to try to reduce the stress on her heart, it got away from them and Ellen almost arrested. But now they've started treating them separately. Now we've got a chance."

"I thought we always had a chance," Virgil said.

"We liked to think so, but the chance was pretty small," Weather said. They got to the stairway and headed down, Virgil leading. "If both of them live, it'll be pretty much of a miracle."

They took her to the scrub room and waited there, in the hall.

*

ANOTHER PLASTIC SURGEON, named Tremaine Cooper, was scrubbing when she got there. She joined him, and he asked, "Got any ideas about the fit?"

"Can't tell, but Rick's stayed right on the nominal cut line, as close as I can tell. If he's a little outside it, we're okay. I just hope that he didn't get inside."

A maxio-facial surgeon at the hospital had prepared caps made from a composite material to fit inside the defects in the twins' skulls. Weather and Cooper would fit the caps into the defects, before stretching the expanded scalps over the holes.

Weather added, as they finished scrubbing, "I'll tell you what, Trey. They're gonna want one thing from us, and that won't be neatness. They're gonna want to get the last expanders out, the caps in, and the scalps stitched up, fast as we can do it. They want to get those kids out of here and into the ICU."

"Fast as we can," Tremaine agreed.

"So if you get done before me," Weather said, "don't hesitate to come over and help me out."

"I'll do that," he said.

Weather was faster than Cooper. By making the offer, she diplomatically cleared the way to help him finish, if that were needed.

Inside the OR, they waited while Hanson finished taking out the last bit of the ring of bone. He was sweating profusely, but five or six minutes after they stepped inside, he said, "That's it."

Not unlike drywall repair, Weather thought. Then: Well, yes, it *is* unlike drywall repair.

Maret: "Okay, everybody, we're doing good, now. Let's move the kids. First thing, check all the lines. We don't want to yank anything out, from clumsiness."

The checks were quick, but not perfunctory. The monitoring, anesthesia, and saline lines going into the children were now separate, but there were a lot of them, and included no-longer-functioning joint lines. The team traced them out, moved a few around, and then Maret said, "Let's make the move. Let's make the move."

Weather was standing in a sterile isolation area, where the non-sterile circulating nurses were not allowed, and had an end-on view of the tables. Hanson, Maret, and one of the anesthesiologists gripped the form-fitting foam cushion on which the twins lay, and carefully, slowly, pulled them apart.

As the cushions moved, the twins slowly, for the first time in their lives, drew apart, an inch at a time, then more quickly, until six feet separated them.

Maret turned to Weather and Cooper: "Quickly, now. Quickly."

WEATHER HAD SARA, Cooper had Ellen. She first took out the two expanders, silicone balloons filled with saline solution—a bloody process because the scalp had to be lifted away from the skull. Once the balloons were out, she worked around the edges of the loosened skin, where it was still attached to Sara's skull.

"Ah, shit," Cooper said. She glanced sideways and saw Cooper with blood spattered on his operating glasses. In cutting the scalp away from the skull, he'd cut through a tiny artery, which squirted blood up into his face and glasses. He cauterized it, and the smell of burning blood drifted through the room.

When she thought she was ready, with a little to spare, Weather said, "Cap," and a neurosurgeon moved in with a composite piece marked with tiny orientation grooves. He got it the right way around and placed it in the defect, and Weather saw it almost click into place. The cap would be held down by two tiny stainless-steel screws, and, finally, by the scalp, as it grew back.

The surgeon said, "You do good work, Rick," and, "Drill, please."

Weather stepped back from the table, holding her hands against her stomach to keep from bumping anything non-sterile, and glanced up at the watchers. Only a glance, and then she kept her head resolutely down, for she'd seen, in the glance, the skinhead. Virgil and Lucas had described him, and there was no doubt about it.

"First screw is in," the neurosurgeon said, and behind him, Cooper, working on Ellen, said, "Cap," and a moment later, another neurosurgeon said, "Just like the cap on a Ball jar."

Weather kept her eyes down, thinking. A surgical pen, last used by

Hanson, was sitting on an equipment tray. She reached out, picked it up, stepped behind the neurosurgeon, and wrote on the sleeve of her operating gown, "DO NOT LOOK UP. Go in the hallway and tell my husband that the skinhead is in the observation area. DO NOT HURRY."

She said to one of the circulating nurses, whom she'd known for a while, and who knew who Lucas was, "Kristy, could you get me one of the large gauze pads, please?"

The nurse stepped over to a supply cabinet, picked up a pad, slit the packaging without touching the sterile gauze, and brought it over to Weather. Weather held out the arm with the writing on it, still concealed behind the neurosurgeon's back, slowly pulled the gauze pad out of the packaging.

Kristy looked down at the writing on Weather's sleeve, and she almost looked up, but didn't. Her eyes came to Weather's, and she gave a tiny nod. No dummy.

Weather took the gauze pad and moved up beside the neurosurgeon, to watch him place the final screw.

"Second screw is in . . . as my girlfriend said to me last night," the neurosurgeon said. The women in the room booed him, and he said, cheerfully, "Just trying to speak truth to power."

Weather moved back up and stretched the loosened scalp over the cap.

Maret asked, "Is there enough?"

Weather said, "Of course. I'm even better at topology than Rick," and Hanson, the bone-cutter, who had been sweating the fit on the caps, made a rude noise. Out of the corner of her eye, Weather saw Kristy push out of the OR and into the scrub room.

Weather thought, *He might have a hand grenade. Oh my God, don't let him have a hand grenade*, then put it out of her mind and began suturing the scalp.

Maret asked, "Hearts?"

"Ellen is looking shaky. She's been worse," a cardiologist said.

"Sara's good," said another.

Weather was tying as she went along the suture line, adjusting the skin as she went. Some of the edges were drying, and since she had a bit extra, she snipped it off and sutured the more viable scalp.

She did a knot, couldn't help herself, and glanced up again: No Lucas, no Virgil, no skinhead. He'd gone.

19

CAPPY SCOUTED the halls from the back of the hospital down toward the operating rooms. He'd spent enough time cruising the various wards that he knew most of the ins and outs of the place, but still got lost from time to time.

The storage closet was the center of his explorations. If he hadn't been there to kill somebody, he might have thought about moving in. Nobody ever came to the closet, and he rarely saw anybody in the adjacent hallways. There were plenty of toilets and showers around. Hell, maybe he could have gotten a job. He'd spent quite a bit of time pushing patients around the hallways, was beginning to understand their ways.

But, he *was* there to kill somebody.

He didn't mention it to Barakat, but he'd put two grenades in his jacket pocket on this last day, along with the Judge in his belt.

Made him feel weird; like a suicide bomber.

On the other hand, he'd had a vision, the last time he'd been in his bed. The vision was simple enough: he'd been running through the halls of the hospital, trying to find a way to get out. He was being chased. He dropped a grenade and turned a corner, and the chasers were stopped. That was all: a long, long chase, with dropped grenades blowing behind him, keeping the chasers away.

Only trouble was, he always seemed to be running out of grenades, the chasers never quit, and the hallways were endless.

IN THE CLOSET, he changed into the uniform, picked up a piece of two-by-four that he'd found in the kitchen, and headed out, nodding at nurses here and there, the grenades in his leg pockets like medical instruments, or maybe a tool, bouncing against his thigh, the Judge stuck in his waistband, under the long untucked uniform shirt. He walked around the observation room in a big circle, looking down the hallways at the door. He saw people coming and going, but never saw the cowboy. Satisfied that he was okay, at least for the moment, he left the two-by-four tucked behind the stairs in the stairwell going down to the operating floor.

He'd hit Karkinnen as she came out of the operating room, from the doorway of the stairwell. Then he'd drop the two-by-four between the bottom step and the door, so it couldn't be opened. He'd go back up the stairs, down the halls, and be gone in one minute.

With the two-by-four in place, he went back to the observation room, squeezed through the door, quietly as possible, looked down, and saw the woman in the center of the OR, straight below him.

A man next to him, in a doctor's jacket, was watching so intensely that his mustache seemed to bristle. Cappy asked him, quietly, "Where are they?"

"Almost there. Five minutes," the man said.

Cappy checked the observation room: no cowboy. He could hear the people talking below, but it was so cryptic, so medical, that he understood very little of it. He took a seat.

Then the woman said, "Cap," and Cappy stiffened. Had she said his name? What? There was some shuffling around, and she looked up at him, and then away. The guy who moved in front of her was large, and all he could see was her head. He sat back, watching, tense. Nothing happened. Had he misheard?

She never looked back up. Still, he was uneasy. Then the other doc said it: "Cap." This time, he was sure of what was said, "Cap," but not what it meant. Nobody was looking at him.

What was happening? Maybe nothing. Still: maybe take a quick look in the halls, then come back and wait until she left the OR. Karkinnen started and ended the operations, so she'd be coming out soon. He stood up, backed through the door, and walked away.

KRISTY BURST into the hallway, looked both ways, saw Lucas leaning against the wall with the long-haired guy who'd been watching

Weather. She hurried down toward them. Lucas straightened as she came up, and she said, "Weather said to tell you, the skinhead is in the observation room. She's scared."

Lucas and the other man never spoke to her, but both sprinted to the stairwell, the long-haired man pulling a pistol from the back of his coat as he went through the door, and then they were gone. Kristy stood in the empty hall for a moment, wondering what had happened, and whether she should go back in the OR or . . . hide.

LUCAS STOPPED at the top of the stairwell and asked, "You set?"

"Go," Virgil said.

Lucas pushed the door and peeked. A man was walking away from them, a hundred feet down the hall, a skinhead, he thought. He was afraid to call out, because the actual skinhead might still be inside the observation room. Instead, he pulled back and said, quietly, "I think he's in the hall, but I'm not sure. I'm going after him. You check the observation area."

"Okay."

Lucas stepped out in the hallway and they both walked down toward the observation room. The man ahead of them looked back, as he turned a corner, a kind of double take, and Lucas said, "Fuck it, that's him," and shouted, "Hey!"

The skinhead disappeared around the corner, running, and Lucas and Virgil sprinted after him. At the corner, they stopped, did a quick peek—and saw the skinhead another hundred feet down the hall, running hard.

Lucas shouted, "Stop," feeling stupid, because the guy wasn't going to stop, and then they were after him again, a hundred feet, clearing the next corner in time to see the skinhead clear the next corner, going after him again.

At the next corner, the skinhead was in the open in a long hall of locked doors, and the skinhead turned and looked back at them and his arm came up with a pistol, and he fired once, a deafening *boom*, and they both jumped back behind the wall as buckshot broke plaster at the T of the intersection of the hallways.

"Holy shit," Virgil said, "that's a shotgun or something," and he cleared the hallway and fired a single shot after the skinhead, missing, and the slug popped into the brick wall thirty feet down the corridor.

"Ricochets," Lucas shouted, and the skinhead turned another corner, and then they were both half-jogging, weapons extended in front of them, and Lucas said, "Can't be much more of this," and Virgil said, "Easy, easy, he could ambush us at one of these corners, take it easy . . ."

They eased up to the next corridor, did a peek, and found the adjoining hall empty. "He's in a stairwell," Lucas said. He'd spotted the door, and they hurried up to it, pulled it open carefully, heard the clattering of feet on the stairs below them, and Lucas started down. Virgil held back, hanging over the rail looking down, his pistol dangling in front of him, and two floors below, the skinhead stopped to look up. Virgil could see his face, leg, and foot, and fired another shot.

The skinhead screamed, and Lucas was after him and then Virgil heard him yell, "No, no, get back," and Lucas was running up the stairs toward him, face white, legs churning, taking the stairs two at a time, and Virgil yelled, "What?" and then below them, a grenade went off like the end of the world, and a cloud of concrete dust rose up the stairwell.

Virgil: "Oh, Jesus."

Lucas: "You okay?"

"Yeah. You?"

"I almost ran right into it," Lucas said. He peered down the stairwell. "I think you hit him, weird as that sounds."

"He yelled something . . . what do you think?"

Lucas was already on the way down again, through the cloud, and when they crossed the landing at the bottom, Lucas said, "We got blood," and he did a peek at the door, and was through, Virgil a step behind. There were bloody spots on the tiles down the hall, and they went after them, around the corner, the blood still there, intermittently, and Lucas said, "I think you hit him in the foot."

Virgil said, "Another stairwell."

Lucas pulled the door open and all they could hear was the *rack-rack-rack* of something metallic bouncing down the stairs, and Lucas shouted, "Another grenade," and slammed the door and they both ran back down the hall, and a minute later, a second explosion rattled through the hallways.

"This is fuckin' nuts," Virgil said.

Lucas yanked the doorway open and looked through another cloud of concrete dust. Not a sound from the stairwell, and they started up, moving slowly now, scared.

A spot of blood. Came to the second floor, and Virgil saw another spot of blood, heading up to three. Virgil went that way, gun in front of him, while Lucas had his cell phone going, 911, "We got a police shooting going on at University Hospitals. This is Lucas Davenport of the BCA. We've had two grenade blasts, a man armed with a pistol and grenades, we're in pursuit, we need help . . ."

CAPPY TURNED in the hallway and saw them coming, the cowboy and the big guy he'd seen when he was buying Joe Mack's van. The way they were coming, the way they were fixed on him, there was no point in pretending. He was freaked, but not so freaked that it froze him. He took off, and they followed him down the tiled hallways, yelling at him. He yanked the Judge out of his waistband.

One long stretch, too long, and he turned and fired, and saw the cowboy's pistol coming up, and he ran, and the cowboy fired at him, and he banged through a stairway door and ran down and around the stairs, and he heard the door bang open above him. They were gaining, he thought. He reached the bottom and paused to look up, to assess, but they were in the stairwell; and there was a flash and muzzle blast, like a cherry bomb going off in his ear, and his foot was smashed and lead fragments spit around him. He pulled a grenade from his pocket, pulled the pin, and when he went through the door at the bottom of the stairwell, he dropped the grenade behind him and kept moving, limping now, pain arcing through his foot.

He was leaving a blood trail: didn't know what to do about that, then he was in another stairwell, going up this time, not far from the closet. He made the turn to the third floor, smeared some blood on a stair tread, then dropped the second grenade when he heard the door open below.

The grenade rattled down the concrete steps and he heard somebody scream again, then he was in the hall, and the second grenade went. He ran now with his bad foot tipped up, running only on his heel, toes off the ground, turned a corner, fumbled the keys, got in the closet, locked the door, turned on the light, listened.

Nobody in the hall—they may have bit on the blood trail, at least for the moment, but there'd be a million cops in the hospital in five minutes. He tore the uniform off, pulled on his street clothes, ripped the sleeve off the uniform, pulled his shoe off, jammed the sleeve into his shoe, and then his foot; he didn't take time to figure it out in detail, but it looked like he was missing most of his little toe and maybe part of the toe next to it.

Dressed again, he listened, then was out the door, down the corridor to the security door, and into the parking ramp.

Barakat had given him a key for his car, because of the problem with the van tags. He climbed inside, his left foot burning like fire, but got the car started and headed out. Sirens everywhere. Two blocks out of the hospital, a cop car passed him, running fast, and then he was on the ramp and down it and onto the interstate.

The foot hurt, but he'd been hurt worse; he focused on navigating the slippery streets up to the first exit, snow falling hard all around. He made it to Barakat's house in fifteen minutes, stopped, afraid to use his cell phone, and called Barakat on the land line.

"Things are fucked up, man," he said. "They know who I am."

"Are you calling—"

"I'm at your place. Calling on your phone," Cappy said. "I took your car."

"How did they know?"

"Maybe Joe Mack called them. I don't know. But I got to get the fuck out of here. And I'm hurt. One of them shot me in the foot, shot a toe off."

Barakat said, "Wait for me. In the bathroom cabinet there are three or four pill bottles. One of them is called oxycodone. If you have bad pain, take two of them. Lay on the bed, put your foot up on two pillows. If it's bleeding bad, get a kitchen towel and press on the wound. I'll be there as soon as I can."

"I never got close to the woman. She's still there . . ."

Barakat said, quietly, "Man, about fifty cops just ran in. I must go. But: they think you are here, I believe."

COPS SWARMED the hospital, sixty or seventy officers from all the jurisdictions in the area—campus cops, Minneapolis and St. Paul police, Ramsey and Hennepin County deputies. Media trucks were right behind.

Marcy got the cops in order, and they began sweeping through the hospital, working with janitors, opening every door, blocking every exit.

There had been a half-dozen media people waiting in the cafeteria for the end of the twins operation, and now they were walking through the hospital, completely out of control, questioning everyone. Marcy moved to get them out, and got filmed pushing a reporter.

When the reporter screamed at her, Marcy shouted back, "What is it you don't understand about hand grenades? You think this is a fuckin' talk show?"

Lucas, who'd been hiding, said with a grin, "That's prime time."

IN THE MIDDLE of the carnival, a bomb-squad cop told Lucas, "The thing is, a grenade's not all that powerful."

"What are you talking about?"

"Think about it. People are supposed to throw these things—and they weigh almost a pound. Most guys couldn't throw them a hundred feet, in an open field. They get maybe thirty, thirty-five yards, unless they're really strong. And lots of times, they're used pretty close-in. You can't have them killing your own people. So you get solid kills out to about five yards, solid wounding out to about fifteen. After that, not so much."

"What if somebody drops one on you, when you're in a stairwell?"

"Well, in that case, you're toast," the guy said. "But, you slam the door . . ."

"That's what we did."

"And you're good. If you'd done that in a movie, the grenade would have blown down the door and most of the wall. In real life, you probably won't even punch a hole in a fire door. You won't punch through a concrete block."

WEATHER HEARD only one far-off grenade, which sounded more like a door slamming hard; but not quite like that. She looked up, and then back down. Slowing a little bit, taking twenty seconds for neatness.

Then, "I'm out."

"I'm two minutes out, I think I'm okay," Cooper said. The people up above, in the observation area, were standing now, watching him finish, and Weather realized that everybody in the OR was doing the same.

When he finished, he held his hands up, like a referee signaling a touchdown, and said, "Out."

Up above, in the observation desk, people began to applaud.

SHRAKE SHOWED UP and said to Lucas, "I heard about it. You know what we need?"

"What?"

"We need for Cherries to be open," Shrake said. "If Cherries were open, we could block the place up, and squeeze them, and somebody would know the skinhead's name."

Lucas tapped him on the chest. "Call everybody in the files—the Seed guys. Call the guy down in Cottage Grove, and what's-his-name across the river, in Minneapolis."

"One more thing," Shrake said. "The guy might not have registered the van, but he might have insured it. Remember, Joe Mack told him that he was going to cancel his insurance. If he called it in to his insurance company, with a VIN . . ."

"Get somebody to start calling insurance companies. Get Sandy on it."

Shrake left.

VIRGIL CAME UP and said, "The twins are good. They're gonna make it, seventy-five percent. The Frenchman is happy, Weather is happy, they're all happy. They're putting the kids back in the ICU and turning them over to the overnight team, then they're gonna do a press conference, and then they're going to a place called Le Moue and eat frogs."

"Aw, for Christ sakes . . ."

"Weather's going with them. I told her you were fine. Should I go?"

"Absolutely . . . Tell you the truth, with the doc dead and the skinhead either running or locked up here, she's probably safer eating frogs than she would be here."

Virgil said, "Think what would have happened if that asshole had pitched one of the grenades through the observation window into the OR."

"I think the windows are Lucite," Lucas said. "The grenades probably would have bounced."

"And then would have blown ten thousand Lucite splinters into the OR," Virgil said.

"Maybe not," Lucas said. "Contrary to what most people believe, from looking at movies, grenades aren't all that powerful."

"What the hell are you talking about?"

"Think about it . . ."

WITH ALL the cops systematically working every hallway, every overhead, every closet, every bin, they found not a thing. A uniformed sergeant from Minneapolis told Lucas, "He might still be here. There are more holes in this place than you can believe. We could search for a hundred years and not find him."

Another sergeant said, "The TV people are calling it a terrorist attack, because of the grenades. Somebody ought to say something, if it's just some cracker shooting up the place."

Lucas called Marcy and told her about the terrorism reports, and she said, "Yeah, we know. I'm going out to talk to them in five minutes. I'll try to pour water on it. You remember his face well enough to do a sketch?"

"Not really—just generic skinhead."

"Yeah, I'm the same. I was looking at Mack, I hardly paid any attention to him. Check. Shrake and Virgil, maybe one of them could do it. I'd like something to throw out there."

"It's gonna be a screamer, isn't it?"

"Yeah. Biggest thing since the bridge fell down. Thing is, you're working for WCCO, and if it's a biker going crazy because of a robbery, it's a local story. If it's some kind of terror attack on a hospital in the middle of a twins separation, you'll go network. Now what are you going to do?"

"What an unhealthy way to look at life," Lucas said. "I'm shocked. *Shocked*."

"Think about this: Shaheen was a Muslim."

"Ah, man . . ."

BARAKAT HAD BEEN reading a magazine when the trouble started. He didn't hear any gunfire or grenades, because he was too far away, but then cops started pouring through the doors, and he figured something had happened.

Had Cappy hit Karkinnen? The cops acted like it. He checked out with the OR nurse and headed toward the operating suite; saw a nurse go by, whom he recognized from the separation team, stopped her and asked, "Is it done?"

"They're separate," she said, moving around. "What the heck are these policemen? Did something happen?"

So, whatever it was, it wasn't Karkinnen.

Then the rumors started, and finally, Cappy called.

After that, he sat out the end of the shift, a full hour, afraid to move early, praying that he wouldn't get a last-minute case. He didn't, briefed the night crew, and changed into street clothes. On his way out, he saw the separation crew, or many of them, heading for the door. Maret had been on television a half hour earlier, with the parents: the kids were doing well, and Sara was getting the full heart treatment she'd needed since she was born.

Maret and both of the Rayneses cried for the cameras, did a group hug, and then somebody asked, "Do you think this terrorist attack was because of the separation surgery?"

That had ended the press conference.

Now, most of the team went out the door, into the falling snow, Barakat tagging along, a half-block behind. They were all walking, going down the street as a group, Karkinnen with them, and the cowboy cop. Happy, laughing, expansive . . . Two blocks down to a French restaurant. Barakat stood outside, hands in his coat pockets, and watched them go up an interior stairs, to a private dining room.

Nothing to do. No way to get at her.

He walked away, heading home.

VIRGIL SAW WEATHER up to the private dining room, then walked back down and around the corner and got two bottles of Schell's Snowstorm beer, got the store guy to crack the caps, put them in his pockets and walked back to Le Moue, and up the stairs. Weather was working on a daiquiri when he slipped in next to her, and a woman said in a French accent, "Do you wish anything to drink?"

Virgil said, "Water would be fine."

Weather: "We got a bunch of finger food coming . . ."

Somebody else said, "When Rick was doing that last cut, I flashed on this thing, I mean, we were pulling them apart. Like, if there was some psychic connection between them, what would be going through their brains when we actually finally moved them . . . ?"

Virgil took one of the Snowstorms out of his coat pocket, flipped the top off, took a hit, leaned close to Weather and said, quietly, "You heard the doc was killed?"

She turned, said, "What?" a smile dying on her face.

He told her about the discovery of Shaheen. "So he was kind of like an Arab—he was Lebanese, a Muslim, and he did have an accent."

She frowned. "What'd he look like?"

Virgil said, "You know—dark-complected, dark hair, worn a little long, a black mustache."

"Oh my God," she said. "I saw him. The day of the robbery. He was in an elevator with me, when I was coming down from the parking ramp. I completely forgot about it."

"Huh. Then you got lucky. He didn't know that you'd seen the other guys," Virgil said.

"Oh my God," she said, hand to her chest. "He was so polite. And good-looking. Like Zorro."

Virgil said, "Good-looking. Like Zorro."

"Yeah, you know. Zorro."

"I went down to take a look at him. He didn't look like Zorro. He looked like Sancho Panza. He was about five-six and chubby."

She said, "Oh. Then he's not the man I saw. The man I saw was more than six feet. As tall as Lucas, but thin. Like you. But dark-complected, black hair, a mustache."

"A doc?"

She nodded. "He was wearing a physician's scrubs. But maybe . . . I'm misremembering. I didn't expect to see anybody there at that time in the morning, and we were alone in the elevator. Maybe it was this Shaheen man. Maybe he seemed larger to me."

"And thinner? And better-looking?"

"That doesn't seem likely, does it?"

Virgil stood up. "No, it doesn't. Don't let any of these French people take my beer. I gotta call Lucas."

LUCAS THOUGHT about it for a minute, then said, "Shaheen getting killed was pretty convenient, huh? An Arab-looking doc, who didn't keep any of the good stuff around his apartment, but did keep the cheap stuff and a bunch of packaging."

"That's what I'm thinking," Virgil said.

Lucas told Marcy about it, and she said, "I suppose it's possible. Not likely, though."

"Not likely, but Weather's got a good eye. And that part of the hospital is about empty—it's mostly equipment storage, mechanical systems, all that. Why would a doc be there, in scrubs, at that time in the morning?"

"I'll get some photos of Shaheen; she can check him out. Maybe when she sees a photograph, she'll recognize him."

Lucas sat alone and thought about it. And he thought:

If Weather could identify nobody but Joe Mack, and if Joe Mack was long gone in Kansas, and if they were going to get him for some involvement with the kidnapping and murder of Jill MacBride—and Lucas still thought they would, when the DNA came back from traces taken from the driver's seat of MacBride's van—then why was somebody still looking for Weather? Weather was no longer Joe Mack's big problem.

And the answer was, Weather had seen the doc.

The doc needed to kill Weather. And he would continue to need to kill her.

SHRAKE CALLED. "Guess what?"

"What?"

"I got something," he said.

"Did you hurt him bad?"

"Who?"

"Whoever you beat up," Lucas said.

"Hey—this was purely brain work. There's a skinhead who used to hang out with Chapman and Haines from time to time," Shrake said. "The guy I talked to said his name is Cappy. At least, that's what people call him. Rides a big BMW, might have come from California. That's all I got, but I think if I go around and hammer on people a little, I might be able to break out more. All we need is a license number, a last name . . ."

"Tell you what, I think you got him," Lucas said. "Push it. Something else: I think the doc is still running around loose."

"Whoa."

"Yeah. Take it easy out there."

LUCAS SAT SOME MORE, eyes closed, tried to visualize the moment he saw the skinhead in Joe Mack's office. Ran through the scene several times: he'd recognize Cappy if he saw him, Lucas thought, but really couldn't describe him for a sketch. The problem with a sketch was, it was the details that counted, not the generalities.

What had they talked about? Joe had said something about insurance? Back through the scene. Get insurance? The skinhead said his was good for thirty days. Then Joe said something about boxes? Could that be right?

Then he remembered something else. Honey Bee Brown had gone into the office ahead of them, to shout at Joe Mack about not telling her that Haines and Chapman had been killed. The skinhead had snapped something at her that shut her up. Would that work with somebody you didn't know?

He took out his cell phone and notebook and called Honey Bee Brown. She answered on the third ring.

"This is Davenport. Who is Cappy?"

"Cappy? Who is Cappy?"

"You've got this bad habit of trying to bullshit me, Harriet, and it makes me not like you," Davenport said. "Cappy is the skinhead who told you to shut up, after we told you that Haines and Chapman were murdered. He was in Joe Mack's office, buying Joe's van."

"Cappy. Okay, I got him," Honey Bee said. "He was a friend of Shooter's, from California. Uh, he didn't hang around that much, he mostly just rode."

"Big BMW, right?"

"Yeah. That's what everybody noticed. The other guys ride Harleys, but Cappy didn't care. He rode his Bimmer."

"You know where he lives?"

"No idea." She said it so quickly and solidly that Lucas believed her.

"How about where he works?" Lucas asked.

"That . . . I'm not sure about, but I know he always had to leave the bar early, before it closed. He worked nights. He doesn't have any skills—I heard that from somebody. Taking crappy jobs. Never graduated from high school . . . he's only about twenty."

"He looked older than that, to me," Lucas said.

"He does look older, but Lyle once told me that if the cops came in, get Cappy out of sight. He wasn't legal yet."

"You think he might kill somebody?" Lucas asked. She seemed to think about it for a long time, and he said, "Harriet?"

She said, "Yeah. I do. He is one scary little motherfucker. He's got eyes like a snake on *Animal Planet*."

So LUCAS SAT on the hospital couch, with troops of cops still moving through, and thought, *Boxes*.

A crappy job, no skills, after midnight. Boxes.

He thought, UPS. FedEx. Post office.

He took out his phone and called Sandy, a part-time researcher for the BCA. She was off, at her apartment, listening to what sounded like a Branford Marsalis disc, and she said she could have the relevant numbers in ten minutes.

Lucas put his phone back in his pocket.

What about the doc?

20

CAPPY LAY ON THE FLOOR in front of the television, tuned it to Channel Three, for the news, put his foot up on a couch pillow. He'd done what Barakat told him, and most of the bleeding had stopped. He hit the cocaine, once, but that seemed to make his mind focus on his toe: the pain grew worse. He stopped with the cocaine, tried to focus on the television: the cops were all over the hospital. A thrill here—he'd done this. He'd caused this chaos. People were paying attention. He was still lying, watching, there when Barakat got home.

"How bad?" Barakat asked.

"Not so bad, really. Mostly my little toe. But that's wrecked. I can't put any weight on it," Cappy said.

"Let me get some things," Barakat said. He went into his bedroom, did a twist, and another, and went back to Cappy with a brown leather bag that looked like a small briefcase. He popped it open, put it on the floor next to Cappy's foot, dragged a reading lamp over, and started unwrapping the foot. "Did you take the oxycodone?"

"Two of them," Cappy said. He told Barakat about running down the stairwell, and then getting shot. "I don't think the slug could have missed my head by more than an inch. I mean, it was like my foot being hit with a sledgehammer, but I almost thought I could *feel* the slug go by. Right in front of my eyes. Two inches back, and I'd be dead."

"Uh-huh." Barakat finished unwrapping the foot and said, "Okay. It's messy, but not so bad. I'm going to have to . . . uh . . ."

"What?"

"I'm going to have to give you a shot before I can work on it," Barakat said. "An anesthetic. It'll hurt too much, otherwise."

"Whatever you gotta do," Cappy said.

"Need a little hit first," Barakat said. He did another line of coke, came back.

Barakat had three single-use syringes in the kit. He took one out, unwrapped it, then said, "This is going to bite a little . . ." He slipped the needle in, and Cappy said, "Huh," and Barakat said, "There'll be three little sticks, here." He stuck him the three times, feeding the anesthetic around the base of Cappy's little toe.

When he was done, he put the empty syringe on a coffee table, stood up, and said, "I'm going to have to wash your feet. I need to get some alcohol."

He was back in a minute with the alcohol and some paper towels, and began washing the wounded flesh. "Can you feel that?" Barakat asked.

"Not too much," Cappy said. "Feels lots better."

"It'll hurt again later," Barakat said. He took out a forceps that looked like a big pair of tweezers, and began probing at the wound. The wound was still oozing, and after a minute, he said, "Hmm," and then, "You got lucky."

"Yeah?"

"Your small toe is mostly gone, but your fourth toe was only damaged by debris from the shoes. The bones and joints look like they're okay. I can clean it up and bandage it. The little toe . . . I have some work to do. You will have trouble with balance at first, because your little toe helps with that, but after you get used to it, you won't even notice that it's missing."

"It's mostly missing now, you said?" He tried to do a sit-up to look, but Barakat pushed him back.

"Lie still. Yes. I just have to clean it up, and bandage it. If you follow my prescriptions, it'll be okay."

Cappy lay on the floor and closed his eyes, and Barakat went to work, cutting off wounded muscle and skin, nipping off a piece of shattered toe bone, leaving a neat but tiny stump just above the joint closest to the foot. When he was done with that, he carefully wrapped it with gauze soaked in an antiseptic gel, covered that with more gauze, wrapped the fourth toe separately, and then wrapped the corner of Cappy's foot with medical tape.

"I'm done. Just lie there for a while," he said. "I'll clean up. You don't want to stand up in a hurry."

"I've got to stand up pretty soon, though," Cappy said. "They'll get a fix on me sooner or later. I need to get my ass out of here. Down to Florida, I'm thinking."

"Why not back to California?"

"I've never seen Florida."

"What you think best, but it's snowing like crazy out there," Barakat said, slapping him on the knee. He picked up the operating debris, got a plastic garbage bag from under the sink, and dumped it inside. He'd throw it in a public trash can somewhere, he thought.

He went to the bedroom for another hit.

When he came back, he gave Cappy a bottle of penicillin pills and told him to take the rest of the oxycodone. "If you drive all the way to Florida, your foot will hurt bad the whole way. Better if you got out of here, one day, maybe to Kentucky or somewhere, where there won't be all the cops looking for you, and then find a motel to stay in for a couple days. Watch TV and keep the foot up high."

They talked about the foot, and then about the chase at the hospital, and Cappy said, "I don't know if I dinged either of them, but I don't think so. I tricked them at the end, though . . ."

"Do you think they might know your name?" Barakat asked.

"I don't know what they know. They might know my name. The woman in the operating room . . . it sounded like she said, 'Cap,' like my name."

"Hmm. If they don't know your name, it would be best if you could stay overnight, leave in the morning, after this snow goes through. The highways will be impossible tonight. You don't need to get in an accident now."

"But I need to get back and load up my stuff," Cappy said. "I need to get my bike in the van."

"Do you need me to help?"

"Naw. I've got a ramp, I'll ride right up it. I don't have anything else heavy," Cappy said. And, "What are you going to do?"

Barakat said, "I am going to ask the hospital to give me time to fly home to Lebanon to see Shaheen's parents and talk to them about what a fine fellow their son was. I don't think they can say 'no,' so I will be out of sight. I will stay one hour there, and then go to Paris, maybe for a month. You should see Paris someday . . ."

"Don't think I'll see Paris," Cappy said.

"When I come back, I will think some more about this Karkinnen woman, and what she has done to us. If not for her, we would be done here."

"Good luck on that," Cappy said. "She reminds me of this dude out in California. He was the foreman at this company I worked for, and he used to give me shit all the time. I was going to kill him, but when I was ready to, he was always off somewhere. I couldn't find him. When I could find him, I wasn't ready. Just luck. Maybe this bitch is one of those."

"This is not a good thought," Barakat said.

AT NINE O'CLOCK, Cappy couldn't stand lying on his back anymore, managed to get to his feet without help. He couldn't walk on the front of his damaged foot, but could stump along on the heel. "Not as bad as I thought," he said.

Barakat was heavily stoned, flying: "You still have residual effect from the local anesthetic. It will get worse, believe what I say."

"That's great," Cappy said.

"One thing more," Barakat said. "We have not talked about Joe Mack. Joe Mack is the other threat. I believe that sometime he will call me again. If I find out where he is, it would perhaps be better if Joe Mack died."

"I think you're right. He is a dumb guy who'll get caught sooner or later," Cappy said.

"I will try to find out where he is, and will call you. Perhaps you could deal with him."

"If I can," Cappy said.

"And I will deal with Karkinnen. I will think of something."

THEY WERE STILL rather pleased with their friendship, and Barakat helped Cappy keep his balance as he stumped out to his van, where Barakat gave the younger man a quick Lebanese hug with a backslap. "I will call you. I will pack the drugs from the hospital, I will send them to you wherever you're at. You can make the connection, and sell them. I trust you for my share."

Cappy was embarrassed about the hug and the trust, but smiled and said, "Keep on truckin', dude."

As his van rolled into the night, Barakat turned back to his house and began to think about talking to the cops about Shaheen's funeral, and talking to the hospital about compassionate leave.

Cappy's taillights winked at the corner, and he thought, That might be the end of Cappy.

Now, he had to spend some time thinking about himself.

But first, he could use another twist. He had to think clearly.

21

LATE, DARK, SNOWING. Lucas kept the speed down, watching the nav screen, and Jenkins said from the backseat, "It should be right around here."

"Hope the guy hasn't left for work."

"He doesn't have to be there for three hours, so . . . might be out getting a drink," Shrake said from the passenger seat.

"Night like this?"

"Night like this tends to make me drink," Shrake said. "It's snowing so goddamn hard you can't see your own feet."

The car spoke up: *"You have reached your destination."*

The house was a dark tuck-under that Lucas thought might be red in daylight, when it wasn't snowing. He pulled into the driveway and said, "Wait," and hopped out, with a flashlight from the storage bin under the armrest. He walked up to the house and shined it on the house number: 1530. He walked back and said, "The car's right, this is it." He killed the engine, and they climbed two short sets of stairs to the front door; five inches of snow on the ground, Lucas thought, and coming down at two inches an hour.

There were lights in the front window, above the garage, but nothing on the left side of the house. Lucas rang the doorbell, and knocked, and somebody came to the front window and looked out at the porch, and a minute later, a man with a short, neat Afro looked out and asked, "What?"

"Are you Dave Johnston?"

"Yeah? What happened?"

Lucas held up his ID. "We need to talk to you about your employees. We're with the Bureau of Criminal Apprehension. The people at your office said you'd be the guy to talk to."

The guy looked at them for a few more seconds, then unlatched the door and pushed it open. "Come in . . . who is it?"

Lucas, Shrake, and Jenkins all stepped into an entry hall, and the guy's wife, a heavyset woman with skeptical eyes, came and looked at them, her arms crossed nervously under her breasts.

"A guy named Cappy—that's all we know," Lucas said.

"What'd he do?"

"We need to talk to him about several murders, and attempted murders. If you've seen the stories on television about the attack at the hospital this afternoon—"

"That was Cappy? Ho, shit," Johnston said. "I knew he was one crazy cracker."

"So—you know his last name, anything about him?"

"Caprice M. Garner," Johnston said. "He came in from California, rides a big expensive BMW. That's about it. He doesn't talk much to anybody. Comes in, does the job, goes away."

Shrake said, "Garner. G-A-R-N-E-R."

Johnston bobbed his head: "Yup. Caprice, like the car."

Shrake said, "I'll be in the truck," and left.

"Hard worker?" Lucas asked.

"Does the job. Doesn't bitch about it, doesn't seem happy about it. Just does it."

"What else?" Lucas asked. "You know where he lives? We're really kind of hurting here. The guy doesn't leave much of a trail."

"I think, but I'm not sure, that I heard that he had a room some-where, in a house," Johnston said. "Not like an apartment, but just in a house."

"You don't know where?"

"Got no idea. I don't know who'd know, either—he doesn't hang with anybody at work."

"You got a phone number for him?"

"You could check with the office, but I bet they don't. When he first took the job, he was living in a motel. No phone, and, you know, a motel address. He moved later, when he started getting paid, and I told him a couple times that he ought to update his file, but I don't think he did."

"And he's got no particular friends."

"Not that I know of," Johnston said.

They kicked it around for another minute, getting nowhere, then Shrake came back in and said, "The duty officer hooked up with Cali-fornia. They've got a current driver's license file for a Caprice M. Gar-ner. They've also got a note in the file that his whereabouts should be reported to Bakersfield PD intelligence."

"Wonder what that's about?" Lucas asked.

"Don't know. Duty officer is getting the ID photo. We'll have it in ten minutes."

"Hey," Johnston said, "that reminds me. I *do* know one more thing about Cappy. He's got a credit card."

Jenkins said, "Yeah?"

"Yeah. I saw him buying gas once, with a card. You reminded me when you said that thing about the ID, because the girl at the counter asked for an ID."

"You know what kind of card?" Lucas asked.

"Well, it was at a SuperAmerica, and he hadn't been here long, and I don't think they've got SuperAmericas in California, so . . . I guess it was a Visa. And it oughta have a billing address."

"That's good," Lucas said. "Can you give me one more thing? Anything?"

Johnston scratched his chin, then asked, "Can I make a call? I know a guy who might know more than me."

"He won't call Cappy, will he?"

"Not if I tell him not to—he's not one of Cappy's good friends, but he works around him a lot."

"Go ahead."

Johnston made the call, talked to a guy named Roger Denton, described the situation, and then said, "You don't, huh. Well, that's better than nothing. Anything else you can think of? . . . Call me back if you do."

He hung up and said, "He thinks Cappy's got a place somewhere, St. Paul Park, Cottage Grove area. But he wouldn't swear to it."

They thanked Johnston, Lucas gave him a card with his cell-phone number on it, told him to keep his mouth shut, and headed back to the truck. Lucas gave the keys to Shrake and said, "If you break it, you buy it."

Sitting in the passenger seat, he called the duty officer and got phone numbers for Bakersfield, and got the duty guy working on the Visa card. The Bakersfield desk officer referred him to a detective named J.J. Ball, and said Ball would call him back. Ball did, a couple of minutes later, and Lucas identified himself and said, "You've got a note on the driver's license file of a Caprice M. Garner, who calls himself Cappy."

"Not me," Ball said. "I never heard of the guy. Let me check with a couple other guys, see if anybody knows him."

BALL CLICKED OFF, and Lucas called Virgil. "Anything?"

"Your wife is tipsy. I'm thinking about taking advantage of her."

"You wouldn't survive," Lucas said. "She's a bear when she gets loaded."

"Yeah, well. I'd take care when you get home, then," Virgil said. "Because she is getting loose."

"That's okay," Lucas said. "It'll make the corn grow."

"What?"

"That's always what you say when the Weather is fucked up."

Silence. Then, "I'll pretend I didn't hear that. See you at your place, if I can get her loaded into my truck."

LUCAS SMILED and hung up, and Shrake asked, "Where're we going?"

"Let's head back to my place. We can wait awhile, see if anything develops. If not, we'll wait until morning."

"If the guy got out of the hospital, and he's running, and hurt, he won't get far tonight," Jenkins said. "This is awful . . ."

The whole world was white, and the streets were nearly empty. They found an entrance to I-35 North, took it, and plowed along the freeway at thirty miles an hour, through most of St. Paul, then west on I-94, following a snowplow.

They'd just turned back toward Lucas's place when he took a call from Bakersfield. "Al James. I work Intel with J.J. He said you're asking about a Caprice Garner."

"That's right. We think he may be involved in a number of homicides."

"That's why we want to keep an eye on him. We've had guys from the biker gangs here tell us that Garner might have killed some people," James said. "They've had some guys disappear after they had dealings with him. We don't have anything solid, except some people have definitely dropped off the radar."

Lucas filled him in on the trouble in the Twin Cities, and James said, "That'd fit with the rumors out here. I can make a couple calls, see if I can find somebody still in touch with him. Probably won't be able to get back to you until tomorrow."

"Okay. If he's running, he may be coming back your way," Lucas said. "Keep it in mind."

"I'd prefer to have you hang on to him," James said.

Lucas clicked off, told Jenkins and Shrake what James had said, and Jenkins said, "Building a file."

*

THEY WERE HEADING south on Cretin Avenue when the duty officer called. "I've got a mailing address for a Caprice Garner in St. Paul Park."

"That's good, that's what we've got," Lucas said.

The duty officer said, "I'm looking at the address on the Google Maps Satellite, and it's a house."

"We heard that he had a room in a house," Lucas said. "And how many Caprice Garners can there be? We gotta get some people together and take a look at it. Get the SWAT guys out of bed."

Shrake asked, "You gonna call Marcy?"

"Yeah," Lucas said. "Later."

THEY WERE SIX BLOCKS from Lucas's house, so they went on, found Virgil's truck in the driveway, and Virgil in the kitchen. "Weather's upstairs," he said. "She's tired, drunk, going to bed."

"We got a name and address," Lucas said.

"Terrific. I'm coming," Virgil said.

"Nope, bullshit. We need somebody here."

"I'm going," Shrake said. "I'm SWAT."

"So am I," said Jenkins. "No way I'm sitting on my ass for this one."

Virgil wanted to get some St. Paul cops to come sit, but Lucas shook his head: "I trust *you*. Also, what would happen if Weather or the kids woke up and there were a bunch of strangers in the place?"

"Goddamnit . . ."

They argued off and on for another ten minutes, with Lucas, Shrake, and Jenkins eating microwave pizza. Lucas snuck into the bedroom and got a set of long underwear; Weather was sound asleep and didn't stir.

He snuck back out, down to the basement, got hunting boots, slacks, a wool sweater, parka, and ski gloves. From his gun safe, a twelve-gauge semiauto Beretta shotgun, with two four-shot magazines loaded with four-O buckshot.

He changed, clumped up the stairs with the gun case in one hand and his work clothes in the other, and Shrake said, "Goin' huntin'."

Virgil said, "Goddamnit, Lucas . . ."

Lucas said, "Stay, boy."

22

THEY ALL RENDEZVOUSED at the BCA building; Shrake and Jenkins went to get armored up, and Lucas got his vest. The snow lightened up for a while, then got strong again: the radar showed crescent-shaped waves coming in from the southwest, and it didn't look like it would quit until morning.

A cop came in, crusted with snow: "Got the warrant," he said.

The duty officer, he said, had yanked a Ramsey County judge out of bed, found out that St. Paul Park was actually in Washington County, and so yanked a Washington County judge out of bed.

"That's what judges are for," Lucas said.

Lucas looked at his watch. One A.M. Marcy should be sound asleep. If he went without calling her, he would profoundly piss her off. He listened to the SWAT commander talking to the team, laying out maps of the house, pulled off the Internet, decided he'd waited long enough, and went to call her.

Her phone rang five times, then clicked to a message service. He hung up, let it ring another five times, and this time, he left a message. "We got a fix on the grenade guy. We can't wait, I'm putting the BCA SWAT guys on line. If you get this, call me—we're heading for the guy's house down in St. Paul Park. If you come, you need a four-wheeler and it would be better if you had two or three trucks: it's a blizzard out here."

He figured she'd call back in two minutes. It took a minute and a half: "What's his name and how did you find him?"

Lucas gave her the details and said, "We're ready to launch here. Are you coming?"

"Lucas, this is my case—"

"Marcy, bullshit. This guy could pull out of town, it could take us weeks to find him. He might already be gone. We're going. I'll be on my phone."

"Give me the address . . . Goddamnit, Lucas, you did this on purpose."

"You can talk to the TV people," Lucas said.

VIRGIL CALLED: "Listen, Weather woke up to go to the bathroom and saw what time it was, and came down, and I told her what happened. She said if I called a couple pals of mine from the St. Paul cops, they could come over . . ."

"No. Virgil. Stay there."

THEY LEFT in a convoy of six four-wheelers, vans, and SUVs and one truck, eight SWAT guys and four unarmored investigators. St. Paul Park was southeast of the Cities, along the Mississippi, right down Highway 61, the same highway famously revisited by Bob Dylan. They were good as long as the light poles lasted, but after that, it was a matter of staying inside each other's headlights.

Lucas rode down alone, Shrake and Jenkins riding with the rest of the SWAT team; the snow felt soft and slick under his tires: he turned on the radio, picked up Tanita Tikaram singing "Twist in My Sobriety," a good old golden oldie; he'd last heard it trickling out of an overhead speaker at a gas station, years earlier.

Twenty minutes after they left, moving slowly, they crawled past the Ashland refinery, the gas flares burning weirdly through the pounding waves of snow. Close now, he thought, watching the nav screen. They planned to hook up with St. Paul Park cops in the City Hall parking lot, and walk from there, four short blocks.

The first of the trucks took the off ramp, the rest followed, down through the quiet town. The local cops were waiting, and they all went inside, where the SWAT team commander, John Nelson, took the locals through the program.

"As we understand it, the house is owned by an old lady named Ann Wilson, and she probably sleeps in a bedroom in the back, and rents the bedroom upstairs. We're not going to rush the place because the noise will wake the guy up, and at this point, he's got no reason to give it up.

"So, we've got the snow and the dark going for us. We'll set up outside, around the house, and wait for him to come out. If Miz Wilson comes out first, we'll move her out. Then we'll just see—but we're putting the guy's name and ID photo on TV, so we figure he'll be moving early. He needs to get away from here.

"We're all going to go out and get set up, and then half of us will peel off and come back here and get warm and comfortable. We'll change over every hour so nobody gets too cold. The whole idea, now, is to stay out of sight . . ."

Then there were questions, and when the questions stopped, Nelson said, "Everybody be cool. You all know about the grenades, and the crime-scene guys dug some buckshot out of the hospital walls this evening, so the guy's got a shotgun going for himself. We think he's hurt, but we don't know how bad. The idea is to corner him, squeeze him. Nobody gets hurt. *Nobody gets hurt.*"

THEY WENT OUT in four squads, like an army patrol, circling the blocks to come in from all sides of the house, Lucas tramping along with Nelson. The St. Paul Park cops took them in, and they set up at the corners of the house, a lot away, behind whatever barriers or cover was available. A light burned in the second-floor window, behind translucent bathroom glass, but there was no sign of movement.

Nelson and Lucas set up behind a couple of large cottonwood trees across the street from the front door; they could see both the door and the front of the detached garage. Nothing happened for a half hour, when Nelson took a radio call, leaned over and said, "The Minneapolis guy is here. Sherrill."

"She's always wanted to be one of the guys," Lucas said, and, "I'm gonna sneak back there."

MARCY HAD BROUGHT two other investigators with her. She was wearing a ski jacket and had a pair of ski pants, rolled into a bundle, on the floor by her feet. She saw Lucas come in the door and walked over.

"Should have called," she said.

"It's more our jurisdiction than yours, but I don't want to fight about it. We figured out who he probably was—"

"I want to hear about that . . ."

And another cop, from St. Paul Park, called. "We got media. We're gonna hold them here."

"Ah, man," Lucas said. "Somebody's been on the phone."

"Not me," Marcy said. They stepped out in the darkened hallway and walked down to the front door, and saw a media truck from Channel Three, two guys standing outside talking to two cops.

"Well, here's your shot—you handle them," Lucas said. "Be nice."

SHE WAS BACK in five minutes: "They say it was a tip, but they know it's a SWAT thing, and they know it's the hospital grenade guy."

"So, what'd you tell them?"

"I told them what's going on, threatened them nicely, and they'll wait here until something happens."

"Any more coming?" Lucas asked.

"They don't know."

Three more stations rolled up in the next forty-five minutes. They let the reporters in the City Hall just to get them off the street. Then Ruffe Ignace, the cop reporter for the *Star-Tribune*, showed up: "Lucas Davenport and the prettiest little ol' detective lady west of the Mississippi," he said.

Marcy said, "Bite me."

"Anytime, anyplace—I mean, anyplace geographically. Or, come to think of it, anatomically. So you got this guy cornered like a rat. When are you going in?"

"Not till morning. There's an old lady sleeping in there and we'd like to get her out first," Marcy said.

"You running this, or the BCA?" Ignace asked her.

"It's a co-op deal," Lucas said, answering for her. "Minneapolis is handling the investigation, but since we're out of their jurisdiction down here, BCA is supplying the SWAT. St. Paul Park knows the territory, and they're setting up with us."

"How'd you get in on it?" Ignace asked. "You're not SWAT."

"I needed the overtime," Lucas said.

"And you're sure he's in there? Last time I went on a SWAT deal, they were outside the house and the guy was at a movie and he comes walking back with a six-pack of Mickey's wide-mouth—"

"We know about that," Marcy said. "No, we don't know that he's inside. We're hoping he's inside."

He was inside. Not sleeping well. His foot throbbed with his pulse, but he could live with it: the pain was dampened by the drugs. The drugs were doing nothing for his head. He thought, and thought, and couldn't see a way out.

If the cops knew enough about him to shout at him in a hallway, and chase him, they knew too much. They'd know his name sooner or later, and then they'd find out where he lived. He didn't know how they'd do that, but they would.

If not for the storm, he would have left already. Stop for gas in Iowa, stop for gas in Kentucky, and then those other states . . . He could be in Florida in twenty-four hours.

He tried to plan it out—pack his clothes, not much, put the bike in the van. But what about the van? If they knew his name, they'd find his van plates in California and put out a watch. So he needed new plates . . . Needed to sell the van, get cash, buy a new one under another name.

Lay in bed in the dark, sitting up every once in a while, to run his hands over his head, wishing for daylight.

He was sitting up when the yelling started. Sounded like a fight. He rolled out of bed, looked out the window across the street. Howard, he thought that was the name, was on his front porch, porch light on, yelling at somebody, and somebody ran up to him from behind a tree, not a kid screwing around, but a grown man, and said something to him, and after a second, Howard stepped back and turned off his porch light and the man followed him into his house.

Cops.

Cops outside the house. It could have been something else, but it wasn't. They'd figured out where he lived, and there they were. He laughed, a short snort: bound to happen sooner or later, and here it was.

He got dressed in the semi-dark: boots, jeans, sweatshirt, parka. Cigarettes, wallet, baggie of cocaine, gun. Stepped over to the bathroom, careful to stay away from the window, checked the cylinder: four shotgun, two .45 Colts. He stepped back to his dresser, dumped the box of .410 shells into his pocket, took the .45s out of the cylinder and reloaded with .410s. Took four grenades out from under the bed, thought about it, took two more.

"Nothing to do now, man. Run."

Had an image of himself busting out of the garage on the back of the BMW. Like a movie. Never happen in the snow. Thought about sliding down a roof, like a movie. Never happen: he'd slid off a roof before and broke his legs.

Peeked at the window, saw the ruts in the snow: no cars gone by for a while. Wouldn't have been many anyway, but the snow had killed whatever traffic there might have been.

But the ruts gave him an idea. He went back to the bed and pulled the sheet off.

THE ST. PAUL PARK chief said to Lucas and Marcy, "We had a problem."

They were sitting on a bench eating Twinkies and drinking coffee. Marcy: "What happened?"

"A guy across the street saw the SWAT guys trading places. He turned on his porch light and yelled at them. They shut him up, but . . . it happened."

"Anything happen upstairs?"

"No. But we don't know he's upstairs. We only think he is."

Marcy rubbed her face, then said to Lucas: "The snow muffles everything."

"Yeah. I don't know."

They talked about it.

CAPPY CUT a slit in the sheet and draped it over his head, so he was covered from head to toe in white, like a ghost. Said aloud, "Gonna feel like a fool if nobody's there."

But somebody was there, he thought.

He was down in the basement, having snuck down the stairs past Mrs. Wilson's bedroom door. Darker than the inside of a coal sack. There was a chair by the washing machine . . .

He lifted it over to the basement window, a low, eighteen-inch-high double-pane affair that hinged at the top. Probably, he thought, hadn't been opened in years. Didn't want to wake Mrs. Wilson, though she was hard of hearing, and so he didn't have to be absolutely quiet.

He stood on the chair, brushed his hand around the perimeter of the window, until he found the latch, worked it loose. Window didn't want to open. Got his knife out, pried around the edges, had to work at it, first one end, then the other, finally felt it give. A minute later, a rush of cold air and snow blew over him.

The snow was as high as the window. He stepped up on the dryer, put his gloves on, pushed the window up, and started to work through it. Not easy: he was wearing too much clothing and kept getting hung up. He struggled, pushing with his feet, and then with his hands, and finally dragged his feet through the window. He was lying flat on his stomach, covered with the sheet, in fourteen inches of snow.

He began low-crawling his way forward, like a worm, nearly invisible in the dark. He was headed straight out to the back of the lot.

LUCAS SAID, "If he's upstairs, and I don't know why an old lady would want to have her bedroom upstairs . . . if he's upstairs, you could come in from the side of the house where the roof comes down. You know what I mean? He can't see out that way."

Nelson, the SWAT commander, said, "Yeah, we could do that, but if he saw our guy . . . if he's moved downstairs, he could be looking out a window, our guy would be dead meat."

Nelson's radio burped and he put it to his face and said, "Yeah?" Listened, and said, "Can you get over there? Okay. Stay right where you are. I'm going to alert everybody. We'll be there with you in a minute . . . Sure it wasn't a dog? Okay."

He said to Lucas, Marcy, and the chief, "Billy Harris thinks some-body, or something, might have just hit the fence in Wilson's backyard. He didn't see it, but he heard it, and thought he might have seen some-thing."

"How could he get out?" Marcy asked.

"Don't know."

"Let's go look," Lucas said. "Let's get a couple guys to go with us."

THEY LEFT the building at a jog, five of them, running around the block, in the night, slowed by the snow. Nelson called up Harris at the end of the second block and said, "Careful, we're coming in."

They went in single-file, groping past hedges and garbage cans; the only light was from the streetlights, and there wasn't much, not in the close-packed older houses, with grown-up trees and bushes. Harris had been set up behind a neighbor's garage at the back of the house.

They came up and he said, in a whisper, "Right there, across the yard. Something big hit the fence."

They could see the back window of the upstairs room, a dark rect-angle in the barely visible house.

"I'm going out there," Lucas said. "Right around this house behind us, and then over to the fence. Johnny, tell your guys I'll be moving out there."

He slipped away to his left, groping in the dark, behind the neigh-boring house, sheltered by a hedge. Once across the yard, he forced a hole in the hedge, into Wilson's yard, next to the fence. Unlikely that he could be seen: he couldn't see the window anymore. But if Cappy was out there, with a shotgun, waiting . . .

He got his guts up and started crawling down the fence line. Fifteen yards down the line, he crossed Cappy's trail. Thought nothing. Turned to look at the fence: couldn't see anything. Listened. Nothing. Crawled down the trail to the house, and the basement window. "God-damnit." Never thought of the basement. He got to his feet, crouch-ing, and dashed across the yard to Harris's post, where the others were waiting.

"He's out," Lucas said. "But there's a trail. He's five minutes ahead of us."

Shrake volunteered to follow the track. He was wearing a helmet and full armor, and Lucas said, "Don't forget, he had grenades. If you see him, and go after him, he could drop one on you."

"I'm not forgetting that," Shrake said. "I think about it every two seconds."

"Five-meter kill zone. Four or five seconds from the time he throws it. The time is not precise," Lucas said.

"I can handle all that," Shrake said. "The question is, will we ever see it?"

"Don't push out front—stay way back. Keep your flashlight working."

They moved out in a V-shaped line two hundred yards across, fifty yards deep, with Shrake at the bottom of the funnel with a super-bright LED flashlight and a radio. The line was mostly invisible as they moved, with the exception of Shrake. As the trail went one way or another around houses, into the next street, Shrake adjusted the vector.

St. Paul Park put all their squads on the streets, moving, light racks flashing, on a perimeter, hoping to keep Cappy inside, but the snow was so heavy that he'd probably be able to cross the line. On the other hand, the flashing lights might make him cautious, and slow him down.

The search, Lucas thought, as he tramped up through the snow with his shotgun, had all the characteristics of a cluster-fuck, but he couldn't think of a better alternative. He was the first man up the funnel from Shrake, twenty yards to Shrake's left, fifteen yards in front of him.

Shrake said, "He's going around the left side of the house . . ."

They pushed through the first line of lots, into the next street, then through the next double line, the houses back-to-back. Lights were popping on here and there, people starting to check the flashing lights of the squads.

Through the second line of houses, and Shrake said, "Bearing left, bearing left."

THE THIN BLOND woman was lying on the kitchen floor, her ankles taped together, and Cappy stuck a grenade between her thighs and said, "Press hard, and don't move. Don't even think. The pin is out, and if the lever goes, it'll blow you in half. And if this fuckin' key doesn't start that fuckin' truck, I'll come back here and kill you myself."

"I won't move. I won't move, please don't do this . . ."

"Shut up. You just lay there."

Cappy took the key and slunk back to the front window and looked out. Nothing to see. A flashing light somewhere . . . he could see the whip of the light on the snow, like far-off lightning. Had the cops gotten onto him?

Had to go. He said, one more time, "Don't move, lady. Keep your shit together, and don't move."

HE WENT OUT to the driveway, fumbled the keys, found them again, got the door open, fired up the truck. Backed out of the driveway, and then, through the muffled air of the storm, heard a human sound, a shouting.

Had no idea where it was coming from. Left the lights off, backed into the street, and took off, and then the light-whips got brighter, fast, and a squad car pulled in front of him, another behind it, one blocking the street.

Cappy did a slide, cranked the wheel, backed around, went the other way. The second cop car came after him, and he fumbled a grenade out, pulled the pin, let the spoon fly, counted *one-and* and dropped it out the window.

The cop car was fifteen feet from the grenade when it went, Cappy another hundred feet down the street. The cop car went sideways and Cappy felt an exhilarating rush, a coke rush, and then saw a light to his left, coming through the snow, and then a man in front of him. Cappy hit the gas harder, holding down as far as he dared, without spinning, and aimed at the figure in the snow straight ahead . . .

LUCAS SAW the grenade go and the cop car spin out, the truck coming straight down the street at him. He could hear Shrake shouting something, but Lucas was focused on the truck. Then Shrake fired two or three shots with his M-16, and Lucas fired his shotgun into the driver's-side windshield, took four quick steps sideways to let the truck go past, bullfighter style, put the shotgun almost against the glass of the passenger-side window and pulled the trigger again.

CAPPY FELT a slug go through his thigh, the pain like being hit by a baseball bat; saw the lump out front pointing a shotgun, dropped down behind the wheel. Getting close to the end, now, Cappy: his face contorted in a rictus of a grin, teeth showing. The windshield got hit, but held; then the passenger-side window blew through the truck like the end of the world, shot smashing through his wheel hand, glass through his head and face. The truck went sideways. One hand almost gone, he pulled another grenade out of his pocket, pulled the pin. He was holding it when the truck hit a tree, and jolted to a sudden stop.

Somebody was screaming at him: "Out, out, out . . ."

Somebody else was yelling, "Careful, careful, careful . . ."

A voice close now, "Get out of there, motherfucker. Get out of there . . . Let me see your hands . . ."

Voice right there. Door was jerked open, and Cappy let go of the spoon. Cop was right there and Cappy grinned at him through bloody teeth and said, "Suck on this," but he wasn't sure he could be understood; he closed his eyes and counted, "Two-three . . ."

THE ST. PAUL PARK cop had a shotgun almost pointing in the window and Lucas, running up, screaming, "Careful," looked in the window and saw the quick flick and grabbed the cop by his collar and yanked him back from the truck and dragged him down by the front wheel and then the grenade went.

And everything stopped.

Nothing but the sound of snow, for ten seconds, fifteen, like the film had gotten stuck in the projector.

And started again, jerking unevenly to full speed. Shrake ran up and shouted, "You guys okay? You guys okay?"

Lucas stood up, and the cop stood up, and the cop turned white-faced to Lucas and said, "Boy, I almost fucked that up."

The grenade had gone off in Cappy's lap.

He was long gone.

ONE SECOND LATER, another grenade went off, most of a block away, and a woman began screaming.

23

WEATHER SLEPT LATE, for her, until six o'clock—three too many dai-quiris—and as she slowly surfaced, thought first of the Raynes twins, and then, quickly, of the fact that she was alone in bed. She rolled over and patted Lucas's side, saw that it hadn't been slept in.

She sat up, scratched and stretched, the worry pulling at the back of her brain—Virgil would have woken her if anything disastrous had happened, right? She threw the covers off, made a quick stop in the bathroom, got a robe and headed downstairs, still tasting the mixture of Bacardi rum and Crest toothpaste on the back of her tongue.

Virgil was curled on the couch, watching Channel Three's good-morning show. He sat up when she walked into the living room. "Where's Lucas?" she asked.

"Down in St. Paul Park. He's fine, but there was a big shoot-out with our skinhead. Caprice M. Garner. He's dead, he blew himself up with a grenade."

"No!" She stared at the television, as though the talking heads would refute what Virgil had just said; instead, the television told her about the joys of growing winter tomatoes in your basement, using equipment available in an ordinary hardware store. "Has he been on? Lucas?"

"Hovering in the background. Marcy's been up front."

"Good for her," Weather said. "Ambitious witch."

SHE RAN back up the stairs, cleaned up, got into jeans and a sweater, got her cell phone, and punched up Lucas's number. He came up and she said, "When are you coming home?"

"I'm just fine," he said.

"I knew that—Virgil saw you on TV. So it's done."

"There's a question about the doc. I would like to talk to the guy you saw in the elevator," Lucas said.

"Maybe I was off base—"

"You think so? The dead doc, Shaheen, was about an inch taller than you. You think you would have missed that, and thought he was taller?"

"Well. No."

"Then we've—"

"Let me make a phone call," she said. "So—when'll you be home?"

"There was a mess last night. I fired one of the shots, we're working through the reconstruction for everybody's reports. It'll be a while, yet."

"How do you feel? You okay?"

"You know. Coming down. Garner was hurt, but he would have made it—he pulled the pin himself."

WEATHER CALLED the MMRC and was told by the duty nurse that the Raynes kids were okay: Sara still struggling a bit, but coming on. Ellen was fine. "The parents are still here. They've been sleeping off and on."

"I'll be there in a bit," Weather said. "Has Gabe been around?"

"He's sleeping in the OR."

"Tell him I'll be in before ten. Don't wake him, though."

She spent the next couple of hours getting the kids off to school, talking with the housekeeper, watching television.

One piece of film they kept playing over and over was a freaked-out woman who'd been taken hostage by the killer, who had put a hand grenade between her thighs and pulled the pin. The reporter explained how a grenade worked, and how the woman lay on the floor for ten minutes before she got her hands free. She'd then cut the tape on her ankles, and had thrown the grenade through her kitchen window, right through the glass, and it had blown up in her side yard.

Nobody hurt, though Weather suspected the woman might need some serious counseling.

Virgil cleaned up, and when Jenkins showed up, took a nap. At nine o'clock, Weather was on the phone again to University of Minnesota Hospitals, a friend in administration.

A few minutes later, she stepped into the front room: "Virgil?"

Virgil's eyes popped open. "Yeah?"

"I didn't know if I should wake you. I talked to some friends over at University Hospitals, where the Shaheen man was doing his residency. You know when we were talking about checking people to see when they were working over at MMRC? I checked Shaheen. He was working the morning that the Macks were murdered. He started at six, and it's two hours up to Ike Mack's house."

"Huh." Virgil sat up, looking dazed. He had pillow hair, canted to the left side of his head. "That doesn't entirely mean he couldn't have done it. We know Mack was alive after one o'clock in the morning, when the bar closed. I mean, he could have been there, helped murder Mack, and then gone to work while Garner went up and killed Ike."

"Doesn't seem likely, though," she said. "If you're out murdering people, wouldn't you want to go together?"

Virgil yawned, rubbed the back of his neck. "I'm just thinking like a lawyer. If we accused somebody else, a defense lawyer could drive back and forth, starting at one A.M., get back and still have an hour to get Shaheen to work . . . assuming it only took one second to kill Ike," he said. "In other words, he could convict Shaheen, and get his client off."

"So, think like a cop."

"Well, shoot. That would mean we're not done. Still looking for an Arab, but a tall thin one with a mustache. Somebody who would know Shaheen. Who would know that Shaheen would look enough like himself to throw us off, especially . . . Hmm." His eyes flicked at her.

"Especially if I were gone," she said, brightly.

"Yeah. That would pretty much be the icing on the cake. For the doc, I mean." He looked around. "Where's Jenkins?"

"I got him blowing snow. I want to get down to look at the twins."

Virgil listened, heard the snowblower. "Okay. Soon as the driveway's clear, we'll head out. Full convoy again. Though, I think Garner was the designated hitter."

SHE LEFT THE HOUSE at nine-thirty in the convoy, headed to the hospital. Lucas said he was on the way back, and would take a nap.

At the hospital, Virgil left Weather at the ICU, with Jenkins leaning against the door, while he headed back to the cafeteria. Two Minneapolis cops were drinking coffee, and Virgil squatted next to their table. "Who's running things today?"

"Nobody much—I guess Lee Hall would be the senior guy," one of them said.

"Know where I could find him?"

"Let me buzz him," the cop said. He did, told the cop that Flowers was looking for him, hung up and said, "He'll be right down. He was up watching crime scene picking up blood."

Virgil took a table, and a call from Lucas. "I got a call from the ME," Lucas said. "Between the time Garner ran, and we got him, somebody operated on his toe. You hit him in the little toe. The ME says it's a professional job."

"And Shaheen was completely dead by that time."

"Totally."

"All right, we knew that," Virgil said. "The guy we want looks like a tall, skinny Shaheen."

Even with that information, it took Virgil almost four hours to find him.

"WE WERE SO blessed to have this team," Lucy Raynes said. "This whole thing has been so unbelievable."

"Not finished yet," Weather said.

"There's so much to do, I can't begin to cope," Lucy Raynes said. "I've got a notebook just to write it all down. There'll be educational therapy, physical therapy—they're physically so far behind where they should be, because they haven't been able to move on their own. We've got Sara's heart operation, and, if there are any adjustments to the caps, or any emergencies . . ."

Sara woke up, whimpered. She'd spent her short life sleeping on her back, always with torque from her twin, and now she seemed almost stuck that way, until she suddenly jerked her head to the right, and her face came around without resistance and Weather imagined she saw a flash of surprise on the baby's face.

"You know what the most amazing thing is? They always slept and woke up together, because . . . they were physically connected. Now, look—Sara wants to eat, and Ellen's sound asleep. That sounds so trivial, but . . ."

She started leaking tears.

"I'll see you two tomorrow," Weather said. Then, "How are things, financially?"

"They're fine," Larry Raynes said. "I took my vacation for the operation, and the insurance covered all but twenty percent, and the church raised money in town and about everybody gave something . . . Heck, if we could do this every couple years, we could start turning a pretty good profit."

His wife swatted him and he said, "Ow," and Weather walked away thinking that that had been the first sign of humor she'd seen from either of them.

THEY WENT BACK to the house by convoy, and Lucas got up, still tired, and they sat around and talked about it, and Virgil said, "I got the Minneapolis cops looking for another Arab, but a tall thin one, this time."

"Call me when you get him," Lucas said.

A LITTLE AFTER two o'clock a Minneapolis cop called and identified herself as Marilyn Crowe. "I heard you were looking for a tall, thin, Arab-type guy who sort of looks like Dr. Shaheen."

"Yup."

"Well, Shaheen's best friend, supposedly, is named Alain Barakat, and he works in the emergency room at MMRC," Crowe said. "My partner and I interviewed him about Shaheen. Barakat is probably six-two, one-eighty, got a black brush mustache."

Virgil smiled into the phone: "You know where he is?"

"He's in the emergency room until three o'clock," Crowe said.

Virgil said, "Thank you."

LUCAS SCOUTED the hallway outside the ER, found a spot, took Weather by the arm and parked her where they could see through the scuffed Plexiglas window into the main room. "Do not move."

A moment later, Marilyn Crowe walked into the ER, looked around, found a nurse, and Crowe asked, "Is Dr. Barakat here?"

Barakat appeared a minute later, spotted Crowe, and walked over. "I wanted to let you know," she said, "because of all the other stuff, it looks like it'll be at least a couple weeks before the ME can release the body. Did you call the uncle?"

Barakat nodded. "Yes. They were completely devastated. He was the golden boy of the family. You know this phrase? Golden boy?"

"I do . . ." she said. "If you go down to the medical examiner's office, they can tell you how to get the forms you need to fly the body back to Lebanon . . ."

OUT IN THE HALL, Weather whispered, "That's him. That's the guy."

"No doubt in your mind?"

"None. That's him."

BACK AT THE HOUSE, Marcy said, "Every time I come here, I wind up eating buns." Shrake wiggled his eyebrows at her, and she said, "Shut up," and took another bite.

Virgil said, "So to sum up, at this point, we have, on our friend Barakat, what is technically referred to as 'jack shit.'"

"That's where you'd be wrong, surfer boy. We've got that bandage on Garner's toe. If we find any DNA on it, and it's a good possibility, because Barakat was wrapping quite a bit of sticky tape, we got him. Or, if there's any up on those boxes up north, where they killed Ike . . ."

"Might sound like a good possibility to you, Deputy Chief, but it sounds thin to me," Virgil said.

"I'm with Virgil," Lucas said. "I suggest we try to find a judge who'll give us a search warrant on his house, based on Weather's identification. We hit his house tomorrow morning when he's at work."

"Tell you what," Marcy said. "Why don't we see if there's any hint of DNA . . ."

And so they wrangled on into the afternoon.

JOE MACK POKED OUT of the dimness next to the support pillar: "That you?"

"It's me," Honey Bee whispered. "Oh, God, Joe, I'm so sorry about everything."

"Yeah, me too," Joe said. "What about you and the cops?"

"I think they suspect everything, but they don't know anything, for sure. They're tearing up the world looking for you, though. They think you went to Mexico."

"I almost did," Joe Mack said. "Listen, did you bring the money?"

"Yeah. Right here . . ." She dug it out of her purse.

Joe Mack waved her off. "Put it back in the bank box," he said. "Everybody's dead. I'm turning myself in."

"Oh, Joe!"

"It's okay," he said. "You been a good friend, Honey Bee. I'll probably wind up doing some heavy time. Maybe you could give, like, ten K to the attorney . . . Keep the bar going, send me some spare change now and then."

"Is there anything I can do now?" she asked.

"Just keep the bar running."

"Well, I meant, you know . . . you need a little friendship, or any-thing?"

He hadn't thought of it, but looked quickly around the parking ramp. They could use Eddie's van, tell Eddie to take a walk. He looked at his watch. "I gotta be outa here before three o'clock," he said. "But we got fifteen minutes."

BARAKAT COULD no longer keep track of the world.

He was high most of the time, but still operating; but the whole business of planning, of figuring out the future, had gone away. He now lived thirty seconds at a time, one twist at a time. He'd had the pound of cocaine for less than a week, and already had the feeling that he was running dangerously low.

Had to find an outlet for the dope he had. Had to find a way to move it.

Couldn't plan.

Needed another twist.

Looked at the kid's sprained ankle, couldn't focus. Said, "I'll be right back. I don't think it's broken."

Needed the twist.

*

JOE MACK SAT in the snow, in the dark, actually inside the hedge. He was wearing insulated coveralls, his Carhartt coat draped over his shoulders, with his hands pulled inside. He was wearing gloves and boots and a black watch cap pulled down over his ears.

He'd been waiting since twenty after three, head down, not moving: a technique he'd perfected hunting deer, back when it snowed during Wisconsin deer season.

Three-thirty came and went, then four o'clock. Moved only twice, to stretch his legs out in front of him.

Cold and clear; the storm was done, the cold coming in behind it. At four-twenty, a car turned into the driveway, bucked up the hump. The drive hadn't been shoveled.

The car stopped, and Barakat stepped out. Joe Mack saw his face when the car's interior lights went on. The tall man got out and slammed the door, slipped a bit as he turned in the snow to head around the nose of the car. When he did, Joe Mack rose out of the dark behind him.

Joe Mack threw his right forearm around Barakat's neck, his hand catching the inside of his own left elbow, while his left hand went behind Barakat's neck. The other man struggled, tried to turn, but Joe Mack held him fast, bending Barakat's neck over his forearm.

He said, "You killed my family, you motherfucker."

Barakat tried to choke out some words, but failed. He actually heard his neck break; an instant later, he was gone.

24

AFTER THE DISCUSSION the night before, Lucas and Marcy decided they should watch Barakat for a couple days, until they knew what possibilities the DNA samples might hold. If he tried to move what might have been the drugs, if he visited a place where the drugs might be stashed, they'd have that.

And they'd figure something out.

*

AT ELEVEN O'CLOCK the next morning, Marilyn Crowe called Marcy for the third time and said, "Still no movement. I'm thinking I should knock on his door."

"Still a problem . . ."

"We know he was supposed to be at work. The phone is ringing in there. The car's here . . . I think I should go knock."

Marcy exhaled, then said, "All right, but take Dick with you. The excuse sounds pretty weak. He's gonna know we're watching him."

"But something's not right," Crowe said. "If he's skipped . . ."

"Okay. Knock on the door," Marcy said.

She was a little annoyed when Crowe called her back thirty seconds later and said, "He's here."

"I was afraid of that."

"He's on the ground in front of his car," Crowe said. "Dick says somebody snapped his neck."

THEY ALL RECONVENED at Lucas's place, which was only a mile from Barakat's and the crime scene, and Lucas ran through the logic. "Four guys rob the place. One of them is the doc, Barakat, who set it up, and we know he's the right guy, because we find that load of drugs in his house. The other three are Chapman, Haines, and Joe Mack. Haines gets scratched, and Joe Mack and Barakat are seen. The Macks and the doc decide that Chapman and Haines have to go. Probably because they know that Haines was scratched, and that we were going to identify him when we ran the DNA. Maybe they figure that they have to take out Chapman, too, because he and Haines were old buddies.

"So they do that. They bring in Garner to do the killing, because they know Garner's a killer. He kills Chapman and Haines. He takes a shot at Weather, because Weather has seen Joe Mack and Barakat, close up. He misses. Then Joe Mack freaks out when we jump him, and he runs. He kidnaps Jill MacBride, takes her to the airport. Garner comes to pick him up, and probably kills MacBride.

"Now they've got a bigger problem. Now we've *got* Joe Mack for a capital crime. Garner and Barakat start to worry about Joe dealing them, so they decide to cut the Macks out of the deal, and the idea is to kill them and keep the drugs. They get Lyle and Ike, but miss Joe.

"But they still want to get Weather, because she also saw Barakat, in the elevator. They get close in, but then Virgil and I jump him in the hospital, and Virgil shoots him in the toe."

"Nice shot, Flowers," Shrake said.

"I was shooting to wound," Virgil said.

"Shut up," Lucas said. "I'm talking here. So we track down Garner, and he's killed. There's no one left standing, now, except Joe Mack and

Barakat. Joe Mack knows who killed his family, so he ambushes Barakat and breaks his neck."

"That's the weakest point," Weather said. "You don't know that."

"In this whole episode, the only really tall guy was Joe Mack. He's taller than me, and stronger. The ME says the guy who killed Barakat was probably taller than Barakat, and had to be exceptionally strong to snap his neck like that. Joe Mack is the obvious candidate," Lucas said. "Killed him out of revenge. He knew that Barakat had killed Lyle and Ike."

"So Weather's okay," Virgil said.

"I'm a little better than that," Weather said. "I think I'm excellent."

Marcy: "You have the logic. If the DNA comes in on Garner, for killing MacBride, I'll buy the whole enchilada."

"I'll bet you a hundred dollars it does," Lucas said.

Virgil said, "I'm going home, soon as my shirts get out of the dryer."

HE STARTED packing up, Marcy headed for Minneapolis, Shrake and Jenkins were talking about an ice-fishing tournament on White Bear Lake.

LUCAS AND WEATHER were sitting in the kitchen, alone, and Weather went through the whole sequence of the final operation.

"So the kids are going to be okay," Lucas said.

"Well . . . they're going to have problems. With a good family, by the time they're in first grade, they should be, you know, more or less okay. There'll still be some issues."

"A happy ending," Lucas said.

"As for me, I'm going to get pregnant again," Weather said.

"You got the daddy picked out?"

"Yup."

"You're too old," Lucas said.

"No, I'm not."

"You're too busy."

"No, I'm not."

"Well. Okay, then."

VIRGIL CAME down the hall with his bag and shotgun case, and said, "Thanks for your hospitality. Let's not do it again."

"Drive carefully," Weather said. "The roads are terrible."

Lucas's phone rang, and he dug it out of his pocket. Caller unknown.

He pushed the answer button: "Hello?"

"Mr. Davenport?"

He couldn't quite place the voice, but it was familiar. State Farm? "Yes?"

"This is Joe Mack."

Virgil was turning away, but Lucas held up a finger, and he stopped. "Joe Mack? Joe—how you doing?"

Joe Mack laughed and said, "Well, not real fuckin' good, you know? After crackin' Al's neck last night, I went out and got seriously in the bag. Where I still am."

"In the bag?"

"In the bag. Anyway, I'm down at the bar, if you want to come get me."

"Give me fifteen minutes," Lucas said.

"HOW'D HE KNOW your phone number?" Virgil asked, as Lucas got his coat on.

"I gave my card to Honey Bee, wrote my home number on it. He's been talking to her."

They took Virgil's truck, with its flashers, and made it in ten, even with the snow, driving around the last block to come in from the back. With their guns drawn, they tried the back door, but found it padlocked from the outside, with crime-scene tape over the door. They eased around to the front door, where another lock had been broken off.

The window, broken by Jenkins, had been repaired with a piece of plywood, but they could hear the jukebox going inside: Robert Earl Keen, "The Road Goes on Forever."

And they could see Joe Mack sitting at the bar, a drink in front of him.

Lucas led the way in, Virgil a step behind, and then breaking away to the side. Joe Mack looked at them, with their guns, and said, "I don't got a gun."

Lucas and Virgil watched him for a minute, then Virgil put his gun away and said, "So, ready to go?"

"Give me a minute to finish my drink," Joe Mack said. "I got some stuff I want to say, too."

Lucas glanced at Virgil, who nodded, and Lucas said, "Any help you can give us, man."

Joe Mack snorted: "Help, my ass." He sipped at the glass of bourbon, then said, "Mostly, I want to say that Honey Bee didn't know nothin' about all of this. Nothin'. I'm not gonna tell you nothin' that will help you put me in jail, but I'll tell you that."

"You said something on the phone about crackin' Barakat's neck," Lucas said.

Joe Mack said, "Prove it."

Virgil walked up behind him and said, "I don't want to seem unfriendly, but would you mind standing up, so I can pat you down? I'd like to get myself a beer, but I worry about how you might have a gun. I hate guns."

Lucas had seen Virgil operate before, and though he was uncertain about the concept of a beer, he let him go.

Joe Mack slid off the stool and Virgil carefully patted him down, and then looked under the stool, where a gun might be stuck, and found nothing. "Got no gun," Joe Mack said, taking the stool back.

Lucas said, "I gotta say this. You have the right to an attorney. If you can't afford an attorney . . ."

When he was done, Virgil said, "Okay," and walked around behind the bar and pulled a beer for himself. "Lucas?"

"Maybe just a short one," Lucas said.

Virgil said to Joe, "Freshen that up?"

"Yeah." Joe pushed the glass across the bar.

Lucas took a stool two down from Joe Mack, and Virgil put the beers out.

"Why do you do all that rights stuff?" Joe Mack asked. "You could just lie about it, if anybody asked."

"Best not to lie any more than you have to," Lucas said.

Virgil: "Especially in court."

"I'll tell you what, Joe," Lucas said. He took a sip of beer and looked at Joe Mack over the rim of the glass. "Large parts of this case are really confusing for us. Did your dad know about the whole thing? Or was he just a victim? We know you put the drugs into the tank up there."

Joe Mack talked for a while, Virgil serving up a series of highballs—the broken front door started banging, letting in cold air, and Lucas went and wedged it shut with a chair—and when they were done, after an hour or so, they had the whole story.

Virgil said to Lucas, "You were mostly right."

"Bet I talked way too much, didn't I?" Joe Mack said.

"Well, hell, Joe, you know, this whole thing has been pretty awful," Virgil said. He shook his head. "That MacBride woman . . ."

"I get nightmares," Joe Mack said. "I blew my guts . . ."

"Doesn't help Jill MacBride or her daughters," Lucas said.

"Ah, fuck," Joe Mack said. He stared into his nearly empty glass. "The whole problem was, we're stupid people. That's what caused all this trouble. We weren't smart enough to run this bar, without buyin' and sellin' out the back door. We sure as shit weren't smart enough to pull off a big-time robbery. Mikey kickin' that guy? Just stupid. Cappy? Stupid. I only ran away from you guys because I'm stupid. I know that. Everybody knows that."

He finished his drink, the fourth since they'd arrived, and Lucas said, "Time to go."

"One more," Joe Mack said, pleading, his eyes watery. "You know, I'm an alcoholic. I always liked being an alcoholic. One of the only good things that ever happened to me. This could be my last drink, forever."

"One more?" Virgil looked at Lucas.

Lucas turned and looked out the windows, at the dirty cars hissing by on the snow-choked highway, the gray clouds piled up overhead, the barren trees like black lightning. The clouds were going out, and the cold was coming in: minus ten, that night, maybe fifteen below the next. He said, "Hell, why not? What better to do on a day like this?"